S0-ALA-182

TRINITY SIGHT

TRINITY SIGHT

a novel

JENNIFER GIVHAN

BLACK STONE
PUBLISHING

Copyright © 2019 by Jennifer Givhan
Published in 2019 by Blackstone Publishing
Cover and book design by Kathryn Galloway English

The characters and events in this book are fictitious.
Any similarity to real persons, living or dead, is coincidental
and not intended by the author.

Printed in the United States of America

First edition: 2019
ISBN 978-1-5385-5672-6
Fiction / Magical Realism

1 3 5 7 9 10 8 6 4 2   DEC 0 4 2019

CIP data for this book is available
from the Library of Congress

Blackstone Publishing
31 Mistletoe Rd.
Ashland, OR 97520

www.BlackstonePublishing.com

For my mama and my children
My every story begins with you

And for Andrew—
My heart's most hopeful Chance

"For perhaps we are like stones;
our own history and the history of the world embedded in us,
we hold a sorrow deep within and cannot weep
until that history is sung."

SUSAN GRIFFIN,
A CHORUS OF STONES

PART ONE
SHOCK OF LIGHT

"You don't have anything
if you don't have the stories."

LESLIE MARMON SILKO,
CEREMONY

O N E
SOMETHING STOLEN

A shock of light. Unbelievable light. Blood orange swallowing the Albuquerque evening. A pulling in, taking back, reclaiming something stolen. Halfway home from her Saturday-morning lecture, Calliope Santiago drove across the river toward West Mesa and the Sleeping Sisters, ancient cinder-cone volcanoes in the distance marking the stretch of desert where she lived. Only now she could see no farther than two feet ahead of her from the blinding light, the splotches in her eyes bursting like bulbs in an antique camera. She blinked, not sure what she was seeing. She meant to cover her eyes. Meant to shield her sight.

Instead, she clutched the steering wheel and keeled forward, belly contracting around her twins, less than two months from birth. For the second time, she'd become an incubator, something she was never more aware of than when she yanked against the seat belt squeezing into her gray tunic, sloshing the water balloon of her midsection that seethed with two fish.

The stereo played static, the music replaced with wiry scratches. She felt vaguely aware of an aura, as if morning sickness were on reprise. But this wasn't morning sickness.

She didn't know when she lost control of the car, only that it was spinning. Though she must have been screaming, she couldn't hear her own voice. She couldn't hear anything. Even the static had been replaced by a void louder than any sound she'd ever heard. She pumped the brakes as the car careened toward the guardrail. The brakes were useless. A canopy of autumn-yellowing cottonwoods in the bosque alongside the road lurched toward her, the initial burst of light staining everything—the leaves, the clouds, the reflection in the river below—deeply red.

Instinctively, she crouched low in her seat, curling herself into a caterpillar, her hands shielding her belly. Blood pulsed through her gut. Fetal hiccups. Bubbles popping. Just before impact, she recalled making peanut butter sandwiches with Phoenix, safe at home with Andres and her mother. Time, pliable as uterine strings when necessary, protracted wide enough for these thoughts: relief it was Saturday, relief for the empty booster seat behind her. Wide enough still for prayer. Rote memory took over and she began reciting scripture from childhood. Though she'd been estranged from her religion for years—since college, since she'd stopped bickering with her mother at the improbability of God, since she became an anthropology professor and found other ways of explaining human history, our shared stories, our deep-seated need for mythos—there in the car, under the palpable redness, in the moments before the crash, the only words that made any sense came streaming like rainwater: *Thou art with me. Thy rod and thy staff, they comfort me.* But after the prayer, a flickering. Cicadas buzzing and her bisabuela's voice in a dust storm. She was split between worlds, and the Ancient Ones grasped her tight.

* * * *

The rail held. The river didn't claim Calliope or her babies. She awoke to kicking inside her—the familiar prodding on her bladder. Her pants, wet and smelling of ammonia, clung to her sore thighs and groin, and her forehead throbbed. She pressed her hand to the sticky clumps that matted her wavy brown hair to her face and pulled the blood-caked strands out of her eyes. She wiggled her fingers and toes, reached for her cellphone on the passenger floor. No signal. Odd—she was still in the middle of Albuquerque, cellphone towers nearby. How long had she blacked out? Her class had ended around noon, and in mid-September the sun didn't set until after seven, but the sky had gone utterly dark. She couldn't have been stranded in the car for nearly eight hours, could she? Something was wrong. The streetlights past the bridge remained unlit. Her fingertips tingled; she felt nauseous.

Though it ached, she craned her neck to check behind her and figure out the logistics of her crash. The car must have circled completely so the passenger side hit the rail. But that also meant she was facing backward in the road. Why hadn't any other cars crashed into her? Or maybe they had. She couldn't hear anyone coming for her, couldn't see beyond her window. The usual glow above the forest surrounding Montaño Road had been replaced by a darkness, strangely narrow and stygian.

She pressed her palms to her ears in suction-cup motion, trying to unplug them, unsure why she heard nothing but a steady droning, the low buzzing of hummingbird wings fluttering against her ears. She stepped out of her car and placed ballet flats to concrete, squinting as her eyes adjusted to the darkness, following the wreckage. Had she been knocked out again? No, *she* was awake—*the city* had been knocked out. East and west, along the side of the road, in the sagebrush-covered median, wedged or gaping or beetling over the metal rails, piled atop each other in appalling angles: cars and trucks and minivans, all crashed.

She staggered forward, calling Andres under her breath. Tucking one hand beneath the twins for support, with her free hand she pried open the rutted trunk like a tuna-can lid, withdrew the first-aid kit and a small pen flashlight that Andres had cached there along with other emergency equipment she didn't think she'd ever need, and stumbled to the nearest car.

"Stay calm," she called as she approached the driver's side of an upside-down station wagon teetering backside-first over the edge of the bridge. "I'll get you out."

No one responded.

"Hello?" She wished she'd paid more attention to her paramedic husband's stories about the people he'd rescued. The gory details made her sick, so she never listened.

Groaning with effort, she knelt on all fours to face the driver she suspected unconscious. Bracing herself for blood and guts or worse, she peered into the open window, shining her light into the car.

There was nothing. No driver. No passengers. No blood. Only embankment gravel.

Disoriented, she heaved herself up and tried focusing on her surroundings; she must have missed something. Water lapped the cragged edges of river rock below. Cottonwoods rustled. She hadn't heard anything else on the bridge. No screaming. No calls for help. No sirens.

Supporting her belly with one hand, she lumbered toward another car across the street. This one, a sports car, lolled in the median with no immediate signs of damage. No broken windows. No dents. It too was empty. Car after car. Where was everyone? Where were the rescue workers? The ambulances? The other victims? She stifled the urge to shout. There had to be a logical explanation. Maybe she'd been unconscious longer than she'd thought. Whatever explosion had caused her crash was responsible for the others. When rescue workers came, they'd missed her somehow, and now, late at night, she was the only one not taken to a hospital.

Why weren't Andres and her mother looking for her? Surely they would've worried when she hadn't returned from the university. Where was the search crew? How *could* they have missed her? She hadn't been obscured by anything. Her car had crashed in plain sight with the others.

Her chest tight, she scrambled back to her car and turned the key in the ignition, willing the engine to start, then pulled away from the rail, slowly, thankful for the screech of metal scraping metal, breaking the uncanny silence.

Electricity across the city was out. She couldn't see beyond the hazy glow of her headlights, high beams sloping up the road toward Paradise Hills, where she and Andres lived with Phoenix and Calliope's mother. Calliope had moved back to New Mexico for a job, and, if she was honest with herself, guilt over Bisabuela, her great-grandmother.

Every stoplight was dark; every intersection, empty. She tried the radio again but got static. Checked her cellphone. Still nothing. The half-moon crept through grayish clouds, offering a spearhead of light. At the edge of town, she drove up Boca Negra, the black-mouthed road that wound through the painted rock wall and signaled entry to the volcanic caprock that formed the Petroglyph National Monument. Atop the hill came the familiar expanse of unlit desert that surrounded her house and stretched miles westward. At the corner of her street, she scanned the scattered clumps of beige and terracotta two-stories, sighing in relief: both Andres's and her mother's cars were in the driveway. Next door, a curtain swayed, a silhouette of a face she couldn't quite place peering out at her. It was too dark to see clearly. Even if there had been lights, she didn't know any of her neighbors. She'd never taken the time to meet them.

In the driveway, the garage door wouldn't open. She pressed the clicker several times, hard. It was battery-operated and should have opened. "Phoenix?" she called when she reached her front door, unlocking and opening it. "Andres? Mamá? Are you here?" No one answered. She was lightheaded. Her voice shriller, more urgent: "Phoenix, baby? Answer me."

She groped her way to the kitchen and fumbled through the drawer near the sliding glass door, where Andres stored flashlights and candles. Her pulse spidering at her neck, she fished out a flashlight and clicked it on, then slid open the back door. Why she expected to find Phoenix playing on his swing set or in his sandbox, she had no idea. But she headed there regardless. "Phoenix?" She shone the flashlight at the swing set below the slide. "Baby boy? You out here?" Beneath the picnic table, a hazy shadow, a slight twitch of movement. Could it be Phoenix playing a game, waiting for her to find him? Or huddled and frightened? She moved closer, her breath ragged. "Ay, there you are, mijito." She bent down and shone the light under the tablecloth, revealing two milky eyes, tawny fur. A rabbit. Her stomach clenched. "Dammit." She didn't shoo the vermin away as she would have normally done, to keep its potential ticks and diseases away from Phoenix. She stood up, dizzy from the exertion, and once more shone the light around the backyard and beyond the fence toward the stretch of desert surrounding her home. If there was life in the scrub, she couldn't see it.

Back in the house, Calliope flashed light on the dining room table, still laid out for Saturday brunch. Red, pottery-style ceramic dishes atop colorful place mats. In the center of the table, a pot of menudo, a platter of chilequiles, refried beans and cheese. The menudo was cold and gelatinous, the chilequiles wilted and spongy, the beans like playdough, hardened and cracked. Calliope began to shake violently. The babies cramped together in her belly, compressed her bladder with her ribcage, everything wiggling and softening, her innards poised to release if she didn't wrap her arms around herself and squeeze. She swallowed back bile and tried hard not to vomit.

It didn't work.

She staggered to the kitchen sink and, clutching the tile, let go.

Once she'd stopped heaving, she turned the faucet on, but it only spurted air. She shook her head and chuckled mirthlessly. Of course there wasn't water. She sighed and cleaned her mouth with a dish towel folded beside the sink instead, scrubbing at her tongue with the cloth. She hadn't checked upstairs. Her family could have been bunkered in a closet, unable to hear her while she'd been wandering around downstairs. She felt foolish for getting so upset, imagining Andres laughing as she told him she'd vomited in the kitchen sink. *You never can handle crisis*, he would say, *but I'm here now. It's all right.*

She climbed the stairs, panting from the effort and the high-desert altitude, crouching at the top to rest, her hands pressed against her leggings for support. After catching her breath, she called out again, "Mamí? Sunshine? Andres?" She checked her master bedroom first, resisting the urge to lie fetal on the little mattress on the floor where Phoenix slept most nights for fear of the dark. She imagined him lying there, his body curved into a horseshoe beside hers while she read to him about dinosaurs and woolly mammoths. He loved having an anthropologist for a mom; he'd ask if she'd ever uncovered any bones herself, ever dug an animal from the ground. She picked up the blanket Andres had knitted for Phoenix as a baby and held it to her chest. Where was her son?

The master bathroom. The shower. The walk-in closet. The laundry room. Phoenix's bathroom, decorated with playful monsters, for which they'd deemed it "the monster bathroom." His bedroom. Her mother's master bedroom. The balcony.

Desperate from losing some twisted game of hide-and-seek, sweat pearled around Calliope's neck and armpits, gluing her tunic to her body. Even in the muggy hothouse of the second floor sans air conditioner, she felt cold. Feverish. She shivered uncontrollably toward her mom's closet. This was the last place in the house they could possibly be hiding.

How many times had Phoenix asked her to play hide-and-seek with him? How many times had she told him she couldn't? She was too busy writing an article or grading papers. Now she ached for the rare moments she had put everything else aside and counted *one, two, three, four …* giving him the chance to find a good spot … *nine, ten … Ready or not, here I come!* He'd giggled from his hiding place. She'd played along. *Where's my boy? Where could he be? Fee-fi-fo-fum.* His delighted screeches as she swung open the door and "found" him.

She swung open her mom's closet and found clothes. Boxes. Shoes.

She crumpled onto a pile of laundry on the floor, atop her mother's dresses and suits, clasping Phoenix's blanket to her face and crying. Her stomach roiled, her mouth filled with paste, bile crusted her lips. She cried until she felt empty, the babies inside her quieted by the wracking of her shoulders, the rocking of her body.

Her eyes stung. She still tasted the vomit in her mouth. Once, when she was a child suffering a particularly bad bout of gastrointestinal upset and fever, her mother had become convinced Calliope was inflicted with mal de ojo from someone looking at her jealously before her father had abandoned them, before they had lost everything. Her mother had taken her to the curandera, who rolled a raw egg over Calliope's body then broke it into a glass of water. When her father left, her mother had blamed it on that case of evil eye. The curse hadn't been fully broken. Even Bisabuela said for Puebloans—one of the Acoma peoples—like her, it's not good to have too much, for others to envy you. It brings a witch's wrath.

Yet even now, even after she'd sworn off such twisted beliefs, Calliope felt the unmistakable tingling of *curse.* Where was her family? Who had been cursed? Them? Or her?

Minutes passed. Calliope sat silent, numb with exhaustion, unthinking, sweating. She might have sat there the rest of the night had she not heard the tap-tapping. Every few seconds. *Tap-tap.* Louder than raindrops. She scrambled to her feet and tottered downstairs, unsure if she should be scared, though her pulse quickened. The tap-tapping continued, a knocking at the front door.

"Who is it?" she asked, her voice barely a whisper.

Silence.

She cleared her throat, then bolder, louder, "Who *is* it?"

Still no response.

She looked through the peephole, saw nothing. If she hadn't known better, she'd have thought the neighborhood kids were ding-dong ditching. She shook her head and laughed bitterly. "Okay, it's no one." Hunger or fatigue. She was losing her grip. How long since she'd eaten or drunk anything? Her stomach rumbled despite her nausea. "I'm alone and crazy."

Tap-tap, again. Lightly. *Tap-tap*.

Calliope cracked the door ajar.

Standing in front of her, a wisp so slight she appeared to hover on the welcome mat, the Korean girl from next door. Calliope had heard her earlier that summer, splashing in a plastic pool in the backyard, singing loudly while Phoenix played in their own yard. She didn't know her name or her parents' names. But she wanted to hug the birdlike girl on the front porch. The city wasn't empty. There were people next door. Maybe they knew where Calliope's family had gone. Maybe they knew what was happening.

"I can't find my mommy and daddy," the girl whispered.

TWO
RIVERBED SPARKS

Mara's mother had tried to warn her about returning to New Mexico, the Land of Enchantment (as transplants like Mara's family called it), but Mara had been too young to take the warning seriously. Had it been just after Los Alamos? Just after Chaiwa and Lizard's Tail? Mara couldn't remember. But Chaiwa's words haunted her: *The earth will find a way to reclaim itself.* Though seventy-five years had passed, Mara Rothstein still heard her nanny's voice echoing from the grave, or what she imagined must have been a grave, a warning siren she mistook for a beckoning call.

Late that morning, nearly lunchtime, Chaiwa's voice shivered louder than usual through the cottonwoods. The corrugated metal of Mara's workshop contrasted sharply against the postcard-blue New Mexico sky. Barn doors wide open, she had an unobstructed view of the creek, watercress lining its slippery bed, evergreens and piñon foresting in the distance, the red-orange ocotillo and Mexican poppy, the muted jade and mauve rabbitbrush. The wildlife nearest the horses and grazing cattle were small and benign. In the distance, beyond the rolling sage hills, coyotes and mountain lions skulked after sunset, though they rarely bothered anything inside the fences.

Wearing her usual attire of sunflower-yellow coveralls that Trudy said made her happy and an indigo bandanna covering her faded-amber curls now streaked silver, Mara perched on the swivel stool at her metalwork bench, which had lately monopolized much of the studio. She hammered the delicate cactus wrens she was constructing from scrap copper to alight the spines of the barbed cane-cholla sculpture she'd been constructing in cast iron for weeks. Above each tap of her hammer, creek sounds and the warbling of sandhill cranes echoed through the chamber of her workshop, one of the reasons she'd chosen this location on the ranch. Working metal beside the water, she seemed to meld with the landscape.

A few minutes later, the distinct sound of children's laughter called her from her copper bird on the anvil block. The three boys who lived down the dirt road on the neighboring ranch were splashing in the creek again. They never paid attention to the no-trespassing sign, but she didn't mind them swimming. She just didn't want the responsibility if they drowned themselves.

After a lifetime of solitary traveling, Mara Rothstein had returned to the childhood home she'd lived in for only two years as a girl. But it had etched itself like graphite into her memory while she lived abroad in Europe and vagabonded through the United States. Nowhere had felt like home after the trauma of Los Alamos. Home was a cave dwelling inside her, dark and dank. But New Mexico had called her back six years before, and her trailer had become a permanent fixture on Trudy's ranch in an artist's town nestled in the hills below the Gila Mountains in the southwestern fold of the state's broomstick skirt. She'd chosen this life. Without kids. Without anyone. And it suited her just fine, living without obligations to anyone but herself. Until Trudy. Trudy had stay-cabled her to this place.

The copper wren Mara had sculpted from something elemental and shapeless, a coalescence of nature and machinery, was finished. Time to affix him to his new home, spiny cactus upon which he could sing.

She imagined life into all her artwork. That was the beauty. That was the joy.

Once she'd donned her welding goggles and torch, sparks began to fly in a brilliant conflagration of orange chasing white-hot blue, her favorite part in the process. Trudy often nagged Mara about safety. Their relationship was above tactfulness, and Trudy was not one for beating around the bush. "Aren't you getting too old for that torch? I swear, one of these days you'll burn your arm clean off." Still, Mara delighted in vexing her. In response, she'd quoted Edna St. Vincent Millay: "My candle burns at both ends. It will not last the night. But, ah my foes, and, oh my friends, it gives a lovely light." But now, fusing her little copper bird atop the spiraled metal cactus rung, Mara went fuzzy. An uncanny falling sensation overtook her. She released her hand from the torch's trigger, but the sparks did not cease. Outside the barn doors, crackling the once-blue sky, there appeared a horrifying blaze.

She'd seen it before, when her parents had helped create the world's first atomic bomb. Seventy-five years fell away and she was five years old again, watching the sky catch fire from a *safe* distance atop Sandia Mountain. Watching the world fall away.

Something deep within her, deep as Chaiwa's songs, told her this was not the bomb but what had happened after the mushroom cloud had faded …

A pain behind her temples grabbed her; she let the torch drop to the floor. Transfixed by the bloodred that streaked the sky, she stood immobile, as if still holding her mother's hand and crying. She didn't have a hand to hold now. Except Trudy's.

Mara needed to check on her.

Outside, birdsong had dissolved. The creek lay silent. The little boys' laughter had vanished. She scanned the water. Where had the neighbors run off to?

Wrapping her arms around her shoulders, she tramped across the dirt road, her vigorous gait belying her age. She called out, "Trudy? Trudy, you up there, hun? Did you see that? Trudy?" Though she knew she was still too far away to be heard, she shouted, recalling something she'd buried from childhood.

Something that made her fear Trudy would not reply.

THREE
SLEEPING SISTERS

Calliope lingered in Phoenix's Crayola-colored bedroom, clutching his Thomas the Tank engines. *Play with me, Mama*, Phoenix had begged. *Let's play.* She dropped the trains as if they'd stung her, then moved to his dresser and pulled out a pair of pajamas, which she folded and unfolded, searching the creases for some remnant, some clue. She wanted to pull his body out of hers again, to cesarean him back from wherever he'd gone. She wanted to lie on his bed, cover her chest and swollen belly with his knitted blanket, and wait. For his return. For God to fracture the sky again and bring him back. For an end to this nightmare. Her thoughts had gone fuzzy. Should she be getting on the road? What would Andres have been doing, if he were here?

Eunjoo Yeom was curled like a hedgehog on Phoenix's child-size sofa, steadying the flashlight and watching her. The girl didn't ask to play, didn't say anything even as Calliope had wandered from room to room in the suffocating heat of the dark house before settling in Phoenix's, unable to snap herself out of her languor. She stared into the girl's sad face, translucent in the gleam of flashlight, and sighed, at last, "Come on, we should pack."

In her bedroom, she changed out of her damp capris into a dry pair. Still Eunjoo quietly observed. Calliope could feel the girl's gaze boring into her as she grabbed toothbrushes, pairs of socks, clothes, books from nightstands, hair products, toys, and other trifles, cramming everything into duffel bags and backpacks, then tossing each hulking bundle down the stairs. She couldn't think straight. She hadn't eaten in hours, though she had no idea what time it was, and the gray murk emanating from the sky didn't help. It could have been midnight—it could have been five in the morning. The surrealism of their situation sent her head reeling. How long until sunrise? She didn't know if the sun still existed, though she knew its disappearance would have meant hers as well. Like the disappearance of all people besides her and Eunjoo in Albuquerque? In New Mexico? Farther than that? How many people were gone? She tried imagining an answer but couldn't think beyond the immediate. Hunger. The little girl whose hand she held. Calliope had tried the landline, thinking perhaps only her cellphone service was down. No dial tone. She'd tried the television despite electricity outage. It was dead. Same with her laptop. Even the battery was dead. She'd searched the closet for a radio, but couldn't find one. The car radio played static. In the street she'd screamed for anyone, Eunjoo looking on silently. She'd honked the car horn for a full minute. No one. Nothing. Nothing except her husband's words scuttling through her memory like wire scratches. *If anything happens, take Phoenix and go to your aunt's.*

The climate debate had soured. Superstorms had come like those that had launched millennia of prehistoric ice sheets, no matter what pseudoscientists and politicians had promoted about cyclical warming and cooling. The scientists had been silenced. Calliope's mother had chimed in: *It was fulfillment of prophecy.* It was too late to discuss how or why, Andres had said, and Calliope had, for once, agreed. It was time to prepare for the worst: the walls erected, the massacres already enacted, and more planned. The crisis would come to their front door as it had already come to so many others—fires swallowing forests, shootings punctuating every border, Gulf hurricanes demolishing her childhood home stretching inland as far as the Texas desert, floods destroying every coast, squashing shorelines, sweeping children from their mother's arms, officials invalidating US passports then, in riot gear, kicking in windows, burning down homes, first taking parents and grandparents while children attended school, then quickly, so quickly, murdering whole families in the too-bright light of day.

As a paramedic, Andres couldn't abandon his post. He'd said if something ever happened, she should take their son to Tía's hacienda in Silver City, three hundred miles south.

She'd reminded him they weren't activists or agitators. They were safe.

He'd held her shoulders and said she had to consider the possibility of being without him.

She couldn't do it. She'd squared her shoulders, shaken her head. There had to be another way. She'd be too frenzied, make a mistake, endanger Phoenix.

I have faith in you, he'd said.

Maybe she'd believed him then, but now that he was gone, she didn't know what she believed. She held Phoenix's baby blanket to her face.

Tía's hacienda. Were Andres, Phoenix, and her mom already on their way down? Had they mistaken Calliope as disappeared? Never mind their cars in the driveway. They could've hitched a ride with neighbors. They could've walked. She couldn't allow reason to kick in, couldn't handle the possibilities.

She stuffed the blanket along with pajamas into a bag, stoppering her tears with packing. In her own bag, her mother's rosary and a bottle of holy water. She'd allowed her mother to sprinkle the stuff on Phoenix's head whenever he was ill and to pray over him. Calliope's throat tightened. Was she praying over him now? Bisabuela had taught her the prayers of her people. Before Calliope had broken Bisabuela's heart.

Calliope crouched to face the girl she'd just met, who beneath the filtered gleam of the flashlight appeared as a tiny, pearlescent waif disappearing into a gloss of blue-black braids. "Let's find you something to take, chica."

Eunjoo didn't ask where they were going, only peeled herself from the couch as a shellfish dislocating from the seawall, bracing the flashlight in one hand and sliding her free hand into Calliope's. The soft skin of the little girl's palm reminded her of Phoenix, which both comforted and disturbed her. She resisted the urge to pull away.

Together the pair descended the stairs, a tug of war within Calliope, at once grateful for the child's presence and resentful she'd been spared while Phoenix had gone missing. She felt almost repelled by the quiet girl. It occurred to Calliope that she knew nothing about her.

"How old are you?"

Eunjoo unclutched Calliope's hand and held out her fingers. Six. Same as Phoenix.

Calliope stooped down to hoist the bags over her shoulder. Eunjoo reached for a bag, and Calliope grabbed Phoenix's Lightning McQueen backpack. Phoenix's rock collection lay on the tiled foyer floor. He must have been working on it before he left. She should take it to him. But it was so heavy. Instead, she grabbed one smooth turquoise stone and stuck it in her duffel bag. At the front door, she sensed a terrible heaviness. In the air, a strange metallic smell, and the sky, ashen as wind-blown forest fires. The lava rock xeriscape shadowed into animal shapes that seemed to bleed, reminding Calliope that the indigenous people of this land had buried their dead's bones dipped in ocher. At one ancient time, when the Sleeping Sisters were still wild beasts, the ancient lava had flowed all the way to her house, to her neighborhood and beyond. The lava had encased the desert floor for eons, had chiseled the earth, but the volcanoes had been silent for years.

She and Eunjoo shoved the bags into the trunk and turned toward Eunjoo's house. Eunjoo gripped Calliope tighter. Did she too sense danger? The relentless kicking in Calliope's belly reminded her of bones rattling. Two babies, fighting each other in the carved gypsum of her womb like cave flowers, dangling undone.

"I'm scared to go in," Eunjoo squeaked, her voice a small bird's. "They were fighting."

"Who was fighting, chica?"

"My mommy and daddy."

Calliope's pulse sped. "Did something happen when they were fighting?" What if there'd been a domestic dispute gone violent?

"I was playing with my dolls. There was an earthquake. I went downstairs, and they were gone."

Calliope couldn't leave the girl outside. She hesitated a moment, then reached out and set the girl above her protruding stomach. She seemed so light, almost feathery. A bird. How different from Calliope's own solid, heavy son, grown too large to hold.

Eunjoo wrapped her legs around Calliope, then lay her head down on the woman's shoulder as if relieved of a tremendous weight, a child's inclination to sink into a mother, even though they'd never met before. Calliope thought of the time she lost her son at the chile festival in Old Town. He'd gone looking for a carnival ride and lost sight of his mama for a split second. A split second on repeat. Calliope had that same sinking feeling now, unable to see or feel or hear anything except where are you, *where are you?* A seesaw-sick swishing, falling-and-falling kind of feeling. Only now, it wouldn't go away. Numbness did not take over. She was half-numb half-sick, and it lingered.

Calliope straightened and braced herself to enter the silent house. Steady breaths rose and fell against her shoulder. Eunjoo's body had gone limp with sleep, her small hands still clutching Calliope's tunic. Calliope knew the feeling; postpanic, the body tended to shut down. She opened the door. No disarray in the living room, no visible chaos. No signs of struggle or carnage. Two white candles in two red sconces had burned down to the bases at the bottom of each wick. How long ago had the candles been lit? How long did it take a candle to burn to the bottom? How much time could have elapsed if the candles were still burning?

She blew them out.

Her temples throbbed, a dull ache. She was thirsty. She thought of her amniotic fluid. Dehydration could cause premature labor, she'd been warned. She would search for bottled water, but first she'd gather Eunjoo's clothes. Upstairs, she found Eunjoo's bedroom, decorated with paper cranes that soared from strings tied to the ceiling. She placed Eunjoo on her bed and opened drawers, pulling out ruffled skirts and brightly patterned tank tops, stuffing them into a backpack. She was kidnapping her. What if this was a mistake? A misunderstanding? What would she tell the girl's parents if they came home and found Calliope, a stranger holding their daughter?

The room grew hotter. A deep rumbling shook the earth. Eunjoo awoke making a guttural sound and covering her ears, and above them, the cranes dipped from their strings, nose-diving in sharp angles. Calliope grabbed Eunjoo's hand and darted out of the room onto the balcony.

Across the scrubbed hills, from one Sister's sandstone habit, a cloud of ash and cinder skewered the sky. A screaming Sister howled back to life. Time swelled and contracted. Calliope coughed in dry wracking spurts, covering her mouth with the inside of her tunic. The air had been sucked away, replaced by a breath-stealing heat. They'd be turned to stone.

Eunjoo's coal-dark eyes fluttered. "What *is* that?" The girl's screech startled Calliope out of her stupor. A voice inside her commanded: *Run!*

She couldn't focus. Her stomach dropped as with labor pains. She needed to grasp something. She clenched Eunjoo tighter and cantered down the steps, ignoring the careening in her gut. She had to get the girl out. The divergent sensory perceptions flickered like camera flashes as Calliope ran: the water in her gut, the fire from the earth, the flapping birds and Sleeping Sisters, her aching muscles and bursting eardrums. The heat scalded. Glass shattered from shelves. Outside, the heat worsened. It was bladed glass sticking through her clothes. It pierced her skin, releasing bullets into her body. Jawed, thick black smoke. She had no breath. Eunjoo's mouth opened wide in a scream. She was silent.

In the distance, cones crackled and split like hornet nests. Calliope threw Eunjoo into the car and sped out of the driveway onto the main road up Paseo del Norte away from Boca Negra, where all the Sisters now spurted awake. She couldn't look in the rearview mirror. She gripped the steering wheel and pressed her foot hard on the gas pedal, ignoring stop signals, snaking through the broken-down cars on the road at full speed, jerking the wheel with no thought but *away, away.* The river. She had to get to the river.

The Río Grande in sight, she pressed the gas and lurched across the bridge.

Finally, on the other side, she stopped and allowed herself to look back. Lot's wife.

"Are you okay, chica?"

Eunjoo held a single turquoise crane, blue against the black smoke chuffing and whirring behind them. A blinking eye in a storm. The girl nodded.

Calliope quickly scanned the girl for signs of burns, then checked her own skin. It was hot to the touch, feverish, but not burned.

They'd made it out unscathed. She had no idea how. They shouldn't have been safe.

Through the charcoaled haze, the bright blaze of her neighborhood. The flames had gorged everything. Phoenix's swing set. Their home. Swathed in ash. A Pompeii destroyed and pumice-buried. The Sisters' skirts had spurred everything beyond the black mouth of the canyon.

Calliope opened the driver's door. Vomited on the bridge.

Under sheets of sediment, someday other archaeologists might find bits of animal bone, pottery shards, plants. What of the letters she'd written to her husband, photos of Phoenix on his first day of school, her mother's Bible, her bisabuela's rebozo, paper cranes? What details of everyday life might be preserved? New Mexico honey in jars? Plaster casts of victims in situ? Her home was a burial site. With no one to bury. Where was her family?

She looked away, salt water trickling down her fevered forehead. She wiped the sweat from her eyes.

What invisible damage had the heat inflicted, she wondered. She'd once read that a woman had cooked herself in a tanning bed, charbroiling her organs. Calliope pictured hard-boiled eggs, how she'd once cracked a rubbery egg open and found blood in the yolk. Now, pressing her hands to her belly, she waited for the familiar kicking in return. Knock, knock, anybody home?

FOUR
LIZARD'S TAIL

Trudy's truck wasn't in the driveway. She must've gone to town. Should Mara wait or go looking for her? She stared into the overcast sky, which bore an uncanny resemblance to Trinity Site. Her stomach churned a warning.

She collected pieces of scattered metal shorn to the ground like scrapped limbs of baby dolls. She'd had baby dolls once, and a nanny. Her father had worked on the military compound up on the hill, his mission secret. Even Mara had felt undercover. Her mother did not work, but she'd managed to convince the Los Alamos committee she needed domestic help anyway. There were rules about who could receive help and who couldn't, but pregnancy and illness moved a mother to the top of the list, so her mother often stayed in bed until noon while Chaiwa, a housekeeper from the San Ildefonso Pueblo, came to care for Mara, who'd listen each morning for the sound of moccasins shuffling against concrete. A wake-up song. The furnace in their small apartment over-heated, so they'd crack open the windows at night, even when it snowed. Chaiwa would turn off the furnace. Her mother and the other mothers on base called Chaiwa a girl, though she wasn't a teenager like the rest who came over from the Indian high school, but a much older woman, grand-motherly really, though she didn't have kids. She sang to Mara in Tewa.

Mother didn't like Chaiwa. But Mara loved her. She loved Chaiwa's long black hair, shining with singular strands of silver as dragonfly wings, whispering a melody Mara couldn't understand but couldn't shake. Chaiwa had taught her about Lizard's Tail—about the strength and cunning that a person needed to utilize its secret escape hatch, as Chaiwa had. Mara needed Lizard's Tail now, though she couldn't yet tell why. Chaiwa felt close. Like she'd never left.

Mara checked Trudy's house, a sprawling cabin with high-beamed ceilings. Nothing seemed amiss. The usual clutter—the disarray of clean laundry folded but left out, bills, flyers, and magazines strewn across couch cushions and coffee tables, chopped wood shrouding the entire mantle and floor around the brick, tools, gardening supplies, knickknacks and books. The house smelled of coffee beans and rich, nutty oak. The cast-iron fireplace, unused since winter, still released the scent of burning paper curled at the edges. Georgia O'Keeffe paintings colored the walls, bone desert and bright flowers. Why *was* Trudy's truck gone? She usually checked with Mara before she went into town to see if Mara needed anything or wanted to tag along. They didn't make the twenty-mile trip more than a couple times a week; it was nice to go together. Was Trudy checking on her son at the hospital? It was unlike Trudy not to tell Mara. She would wait for her at the ranch a few minutes before setting out to town. In the meantime, she'd check on Trudy's father, Loren, who lived in the smaller cabin up the hill, near the water tank.

Deerflies sank into Mara's skin like needle pricks as she tramped toward Loren's place. The air felt monsoon muggy. It was hot and swampy between the tall grasses behind Trudy's cabin. Mara peered around. Something felt off. No cows grazed in the fields. The past several months, she'd noticed the deer hadn't bedded down here as often. Maybe from drought? Deer were smart. They knew not to breed when conditions changed. They knew not to make babies when the earth could not sustain them.

Trudy should have been out taking pictures or tending her garden—picking tomatoes, broccoli, cauliflower, all blooming wild as weeds. Why had she left? An empty bird feeder swung from a splintered fencepost. A low vibrating hum twitched in her ears, a crick in the neck, sallow, like the machinery of crickets, beetles, burnt-orange dragonflies. Except these weren't bug sounds. She couldn't tell what made the noise, but it wasn't the bugs she'd grown accustomed to on the ranch.

A rustling in the sagebrush caught her attention. She turned.

"Trudy? That you, darling?"

A low growl rooted her to the ground. Her heart rapped, her mouth sandpapered. A mountain lion skulked in the brush. What was it doing here? They didn't wander this far downhill. Never onto the ranch. A hiker had been attacked in the hills last year. What had she done to survive? Fought back? Mara couldn't remember, and spry as she felt, she wasn't strong enough to fend off an attack. As she considered her odds of staying still and hoping the lion moved on without noticing her versus defying her age and sprinting back toward Trudy's cabin, she heard a loud grunting sound. The mountain lion was hunting a javelina, the skunk pig defeated before Mara had time to react. The lion gripped its prey as Mara circled back around to Trudy's cabin and toward her own trailer. She needed a truck.

Something inside her siren-wailed. She should leave, hitch up her trailer and drive, that familiar tugging away. Her father had swept her to Europe, and she'd grown up, away. She hadn't stopped running since. Until Trudy.

She'd almost made it to her truck when she noticed the moths, sheer-winged and flutterless on the hard-packed dirt. She stepped on them, but they were newly, softly dead. Nothing crunched beneath her boots. It was like stepping on wet leaves. Hundreds of them, moths dropped from the sky. She couldn't leave. She had to check on Loren and find Trudy.

Seat pushed all the way forward so she could reach the pedal, Mara plowed the landscape. Still wearing her yellow coveralls and indigo bandanna, her hiking boots covered in mud, she splashed through the creek at its shallowest point, cut through the field behind Trudy's house, smashing grass and weeds, across the gravel toward Loren's cabin.

She left the engine running, called out, "Loren, you okay in there?"

She knocked, but he didn't answer.

Behind the house, the creak of wood scraping wood and humming.

"Loren, that you?"

His voice came from the back porch. "You see that out there?" He rocked in the chair she'd made him a few years back, staring at the sky. "That light show?"

"I saw it." She glanced around. He wore a white cotton undershirt tucked into his jeans and a pair of walking shoes. His gray hair slicked as usual, his face shaved. Nothing seemed amiss. "Why are you out here in this heat instead of using your AC?" September in New Mexico still rose into the nineties. Loren didn't usually sit outside until after sunset. Too many bugs.

"Sun's going down early … just had lunch, and now it's supper-time. Look." He motioned with his chin toward the dusky orange sky, cloud-cover blurring sunlight. It was a strange sky. Strangest she'd seen in seventy-five years.

"Do you know where Trudy went?" she asked.

"Nah, ain't seen her since lunch. AC ain't working. Reckon you can fix it?"

Mara was the handyman around here, could fix electricals. "Is it plugged in?" She wouldn't put it past him not to have checked.

"Course. Coffee pot's not working either."

"Fine, I'll look. Loren, you seen anything else strange? Heard anything?" She thought of the mountain lion pouncing the javelina and shuddered.

"That light show sure was strange, wasn't it?"

Inside the cabin, framed black and white photographs of Loren from his service in the navy. He looked smart in his uniform. Another picture featured his wedding day. Trudy's mom had died in her recliner chair there a year ago, a few feet from where Mara stood. He hadn't been the same since. She switched on the AC. Nothing happened. Nothing in the house glowed. Blank screen where the microwave should've blinked the time. She tried the light switch. No electricity. At the circuit breaker on the side of the house, she flipped all the switches. Nothing.

Back on the porch, Mara stood arms akimbo, her fingers through the tool-belt loops of her coveralls, shaking her head. "It's strange, Loren. No power. I'll stop by the electric company when I get into town."

"Why are you going to town?"

"To find your daughter."

"Why would you need to find her?"

Mara stared toward the blank space of sky Loren was watching. Sunset orange, clouds dripping with rust. She shook her head. "I don't know, old man. Just have a funny feeling."

FIVE
MUD WOMAN, CORN WOMAN

Two other cars on the highway—or rather, two moving cars, both heading away from the Sisters. Calliope grabbed the flashlight, told Eunjoo to stay put, and scrambled out to flag the drivers down. The first didn't stop, didn't even acknowledge she was on the road but sped past her as though afraid the lava could reach all the way to the bridge. Calliope knew that those five volcanoes would burn her neighborhood to ashes, yes, but their slopes weren't tall enough to reach the Río Grande. Even if the lava could reach them, the river's wide depression was deep enough to staunch the molten flow.

The first car disappeared into the dark stretch of highway looming to the east.

When the other car pulled over, her heart cantered. Small flashlight in hand, she faltered toward the dark-tinted driver's-side window. It rolled down revealing the driver, a middle-aged white man with a gray spackling of stubble across his jawline, wearing a puffy orange camouflage vest and hunting cap. He nodded at Calliope like she was a police officer pulling him over. The gesture unsettled her.

"What's the trouble, miss?"

Calliope narrowed her eyes, searching his pasty face for clues. The trouble? Besides everyone disappearing and five dormant volcanoes erupting, likely killing anyone who'd managed to survive whatever had stolen everyone else? Was he serious? She cleared her throat. "I'm trying to find my family."

"You lost your family?" He took off his cap, scratched his matted gray hair. "That's very sad." His blue eyes went opaque. He stared past her toward the Sandia Mountains, glowing pink in the blaze.

Sad? That was it? "Yes, in the, um ..." she trailed off, unsure what to call it. "In the event. Didn't you see it? We both did, Eunjoo and I." She gestured toward her car.

"Miss, can't say I know what you're referring to. Myself, I'm trying to get up past Taos before sunrise."

"What's in Taos? Relief efforts?" Had he heard something on the radio? Could Andres have gone north toward Taos instead?

"I'm meeting a hunting buddy. Been planning this trip all year."

Calliope's lips peeled back reflexively, and she sucked in her breath. What was he talking about? The ungodly heat mingled with the cold rising from her chest; a rush of adrenaline pumped through her veins. She looked past him into his car, his hunting rifle on the seat beside him. Maybe she shouldn't have stopped this man. An ice chest jutted from the floor of the passenger side, secreting the smell of rotting meat. Her gut lurched.

"The flash? Didn't you see it?" she asked. "People are missing." She felt sick. She wanted to sit on the gravel and let the dizziness wash over her.

The hunter narrowed his eyes, scrunching his eyebrows, two white centipedes across his forehead. "Lady, I don't know what you're selling, but I ain't seen nothing wrong except you making me late for hunting." He fumbled for something beside him. The hairs on the back of Calliope's neck stood on edge. What was wrong with this man? She backed away, but he pulled out a cigarette and lit it. She looked back at Eunjoo, still in her booster seat. She'd never thought before that she might need a gun. Out in the country, her students told her, everyone carried guns. She should protect herself, though she wasn't sure from what.

"The volcanoes behind us," she said, with more force. "Look!" She wasn't crazy.

"Those volcanoes been dead thousands of years."

She searched his eyes, but he was unreadable. She felt nebulous, a dream in which one is floating and must awaken or disappear into the ether. "Your hunting buddy, have you been in contact with him tonight?"

He raised his eyebrows, centipedes outstretched. "No. These are long-standing plans. Why?"

"Can you try calling him? Just to check?"

"Now why would I want to do a thing like that?"

"Please." She kept her voice steady despite her trembling.

"I don't have a cellphone," he grumbled.

"A radio, then?" She nodded toward the CB radio on his dashboard. He turned the dial. Static.

"No signal."

"What does that mean?"

"Darned if I know."

"So maybe he won't be there."

"Look, miss, I don't know who you are, but I ain't got time for this."

She stepped back, hand on her belly. She wanted to ask how she could have been responsible for his lack of radio signal but let it go. Something was clearly wrong. Talking to him was useless. He flicked his cigarette out the window, inches from her ballet-slippered feet, and drove away. She slouched into her car, started the ignition. They needed food and water, that much she knew. The babies teemed inside her, pulling knots and rubber bands in her gut, heavier than usual. She had to get to the South Valley. She had a colleague there, Susana, who would know what to do. Susana was tough. She grew her own food, raised animals, used the acequias for farming. The smell of smoke grew stronger although she was heading farther away from the volcanoes. Still no lights. She felt like a cave creature, eyeless.

Eunjoo began crying.

"What's wrong?"

"I had an accident."

"We're going to my friend's house. I'll clean you up there." Calliope was thinking like the hunter. Assuming Susana would be there. Susana Díaz, PhD. A big-boned woman with skin the color of banana bread, deep-set eyes, high cheekbones, and the thick, straight black hair of her Chihuahua ancestors. Her partner, Reina, was a petite woman with short graying hair and skin the hue of gingerbread. Clean-cut in her pantsuits, Susana was an activist in the community and a poet. A few years earlier, Susana had welcomed Calliope to the Anthropology department at the university. Calliope specialized in archaeology, and Susana specialized in ethnology, which meant that while Calliope studied rocks, Susana studied people. On the surface, a coveted tenure-track position had called her back to New Mexico, but the truer reason she had returned to Bisabuela's homeland was to revise her dissertation, to find new research that would undo the harm she'd done. She owed her bisabuela that much. The Puebloans had an emergence myth, that this land was the center of the world—and she'd wanted to do right by Bisabuela. Make up for the mistakes she'd made. Their ancestors had renamed themselves The People. And this was The Place.

In the South Valley, panaderías clouded behind dirt streets and chile ristras strung from porches like red ropes around necks. She whispered into the blackness, *Give me back my boy.*

She pulled up to the casita. A woman sat cross-legged on the ground. Her friend was alive. Calliope unbuckled Eunjoo, holding her closely despite the girl's wetness. She pulled Phoenix's backpack from the trunk since she hadn't managed to grab Eunjoo's after the eruption. She trudged up the muddy walkway, past the cornfield, Eunjoo clinging to her, smelling of a sickly pungent straw bed. Why was Susana on the ground? Woman in the mud like petrified wood or a rock formation. Chickens squawked from their roosts, flinging feathers into Susana's dark hair. The petrified woman, Calliope's friend, drew scribbles in the dirt. Circles, tree rings.

"Susana? Estás bien, amiga?"

Her friend, the feminist scholar, barefoot and sundressed on the hard-packed driveway, buried her toes in mud. Her face, ashen and wrinkled, cellophane-papered. She didn't respond. Calliope set Eunjoo on the ground, knelt, and took Susana's hands in her own. "Susana? Qué ha pasado? Dónde está Reina?"

Susana hummed under her breath, began singing, childlike, an eerie pitch to her voice. "*Los pollitos dicen, pío pío pío, cuando tienen hambre, cuando tienen frío.*" Calliope knew this song from childhood. She'd always found it pitiful that the little chicks were so cold and hungry. But Susana sang it the way a ghost mother would. Like La Llorona searching for lost babies, swept away in floodwater. Or rather, like the babies, calling for their mama—their bodies washed onto embankments, bluish and waterlogged.

Calliope closed her eyes, inhaled deeply, then cupped Susana's face with her hands. "Amiga? Qué pasó? Are you hurt?" She searched her friend's copper-penny eyes, watching the ensconcing crow's-feet shrivel and shrink-wrap around them. When Susana didn't respond, Calliope tried again, "Voy a la casa, al baño. Ven conmigo?"

Susana's gaze dropped; she retraced circles in the mud. When she still didn't answer, Calliope told her she would be right back, and, holding Eunjoo, strode up the red porch steps that covered the length of the anterior. Tonight, in the eerie shadows, the steps cracked like teeth from the mouth of the house. Inside, she called for Reina, but the women's farmhouse, the house she and Andres loved, wore the same pattern as Calliope's and Eunjoo's. Untouched. A picture, static and unmoving. The women had bought the old farmhouse inexpensively ten years before and restored it. They'd spent their weekends tearing out floors and knocking down walls, refinishing the hardwood floors, rebuilding the kitchen.

Calliope led Eunjoo toward the bathroom, calling again, "Reina? Are you home, amiga?"

Wind through branches. Chicken scratches.

"What's wrong with your friend?" the girl asked. "Is she sick?"

"I think so."

"Did she lose her family, too?"

Calliope nodded, sucking in her breath. The smell of pee caught her throat again, churning her stomach. During her first trimester, both with Phoenix and with the twins, she'd held unlit candles to her nose in a constant vigil of nausea. Her mother's pots of garlicky pinto beans forever on the stove roiled her gut, and the small tin of eucalyptus-lavender wax protected her the way vinaigrette boxes that aristocratic women once filled with perfume-soaked sponges defended them from city odors, from waste and filth and death.

"Will you help her find them, like you're finding mine?" the girl asked.

Calliope didn't know how to answer. She cleaned Eunjoo with feminine wipes she'd found in the medicine cabinet, pulled Phoenix's dinosaur cho-nies from the backpack, and helped Eunjoo slip each skinny, knobbed leg in, then lifted them over her nalgas and hips. The girl said nothing about boys' chonies. Calliope figured that Eunjoo could do this on her own, but she helped the girl anyway, a pair of Phoenix's elastic-waist jeans and a T-shirt, rolling the cuffs and sleeves. She checked the faucet. No running water in the South Valley either. She couldn't wash Eunjoo's pee clothes, so she took them outside and hung them on the porch, then handed Phoenix's backpack to Eunjoo, who put it on her back. She was a miniature Phoenix, a beautiful, moon-faced impostor.

On the dirt driveway again, she implored, "Susana, can you talk to me now? Can you tell me what you know?" No response. Calliope won-dered if shaking Susana's shoulders would do any good. "Do you have any bottled water? Supplies? I need to get to my tía's hacienda. Andres might be there waiting. Susana? Come on, amiga. Talk to me. What happened to Reina? Why are you in the dirt?" She pulled Susana's arm, trying to lift her from the ground. Her uterine muscles ached with the strain, her back shrilled in pain. "We can't stay out here on the driveway. It's dark, it's not safe. I can't leave you."

Susana sang again, absently. Calliope walked back to the car and strapped Eunjoo into her booster seat so she could pull closer up the driveway to force Susana from the mud. But when she'd pulled up, the mud woman was gone. "Dammit, Susana. What are you doing?" She flipped on the headlights and told Eunjoo, "Stay here." Where would Susana have gone? Into the house to pack? Into the barn with the animals? This wasn't normal behavior by any stretch of the imagination, and Calliope was so confused and frustrated she wanted to cry. "Susana?" How many silent, dead houses would Calliope scour tonight? "Susana?" How many surreal and twisted games of hide-and-seek? "Susana." Her voice a command now, loud and urgent. "I don't know what's going on, but I'm trying to help." She'd thought *she* was the one who needed help. Chickens screeched and flapped. Corn rustled.

"I'm not going into the cornfields to find you," she yelled. "Where are you?"

An owl hooted in the distance. Then, a gunshot. Calliope jolted toward the barn, holding her stomach. No horses in their stalls, just those damn chickens. "Susana?"

Her friend lay on the ground in a pile of straw, soaked red.

"No. No-no-no-no. Oh god, please no. Susana?" She covered her mouth, everything inside her shattering. "Why? Why would you do this?"

She hunched over Susana's body, lifted her friend's head, cradling the dark mass of hair falling across her lap. Calliope pressed her fingers to Susana's neck and waited for a throbbing to press back, but nothing came. Calliope couldn't cry. Couldn't scream. Could do nothing but cradle her friend's lifeless body on the floor of the empty barn. The chickens were relentless in their squawking, feathers flying. In one lifeless hand, Susana's gun. In the other, a clump of mud and rock, pressed to her heart. The place that should have been beating.

Calliope imagined Susana as a queen bee of colony collapse.

She wanted to bury her, wrap her in one of Reina's sheepskin blankets beneath the cottonwoods. But she couldn't dig into the ground with a shovel. Couldn't lift her friend's body. Besides, she wanted to leave her friend where someone would find her. When this nightmare was over and the rescue workers came.

She took the gun out of Susana's hand and put it in the hip elastic of her own pants, the metal hot against her skin. She'd never held a gun. She took straw and pressed it into the wound. Susana seemed to be made of straw. She was sprouting.

Calliope thought of Shanidar Cave in Iraq, the first proof of deliberate burial of the dead, where Neanderthals left grave goods with their bodies— animal bones, boar jaw—beneath stone slabs. Johansen, discoverer of Lucy, saw it as a spiritual act. Calliope was never convinced. Art appeared in human evolutionary history only with *Homo sapiens*. She hypothesized the prehistoric burial was for hygienic purposes, to keep decaying bodies from contaminating campsites, perhaps even for respect. But love?

She opened Susana's mud-clenched hand. Susana held a rock, one smooth stone in the mess of dirt and blood and straw. Calliope polished it on her tunic and placed it back in Susana's hands, laying one atop the other across her chest. Now the rock was Susana's graveless grave good.

Calliope didn't know what prayer to say. Her mother's rosaries didn't seem like enough. Where was God anyway?

She sang Susana's song. "*Los pollitos dicen pío pío pío, cuando tienen hambre, cuando tienen frío.*" She felt cold. Who would discover her friend's body in the hay?

She walked back to the car, trembling. Eunjoo's door was open. Calliope had been such an idiot, leaving the girl alone. She whispered her name, unsure why she was whispering except that she was scared again, same as when she'd seen the hunter's rifle in his passenger seat.

Footprints in the mud. She followed them back to the house. From the kitchen, the faint sound of rustling leaves, the crumpling of paper, or was it the scuffing of boots?

"Eunjoo?" Calliope pulled the gun from her hip, unsure how to use it but figuring she could hold it for effect. "Chica?"

In the middle of the kitchen floor, holding a box of crackers and dipping them into peanut butter, the girl smiled, her mouth full with crumbles and paste. "I was hungry."

Calliope exhaled, relaxing, and replaced the gun in the elastic of her pants. All the digital clocks were blank, all the analog clocks stuck at twelve. Still, the darkness had taken on a hazy texture, as if light were nearby. If morning still existed, Calliope sensed it was approaching. "I'm sorry, chica." Her stomach growled, but she was too upset to eat. "It's probably breakfast time."

Eunjoo nodded, stuffing another peanut butter cracker in her mouth.

Calliope handed her a bottle of water from the pantry, so she wouldn't choke on the thick paste, and drank some herself. There wasn't much.

When they left Susana's house, Eunjoo still held her jar of peanut butter—and Calliope, a bag of food, a liter of water, and the gun her friend had used to shoot herself.

Outside, Calliope picked three ears of corn and added those to the bag.

"Look." Eunjoo called out, pointing toward the sky.

Beyond the Sandias, a trickle of pink irrigated the skyline. Morning. The sun was rising. Calliope *would* find their families. She still had hope, and a girl with peanut butter on her mouth.

SIX

AMY DENVER

Susana the corn woman shooting herself replayed through Calliope's mind, a film unreeling, as she drove toward the freeway. The stygian darkness around the car had blanched into an ashen dusk against the rising sun. How much of her beloved forests—Sandia, Gila, Taos—were ablaze? What was going on in the rest of the state, the country? Even before the flash of light and the disappearances, the news had become terrifying, the environmental agencies long-gutted, pipes everywhere exploding, not just on the reservations. Gunmetal gray emanated through the ash and smoke; she imagined Bisabuela watching this wreckage with her, whispering, *When they destroy the Earth, they do it in the dark.*

Calliope's grief, palpable, rode in the passenger seat beside her; it guarded the gun in the glove box. That gun was the culmination of humanity's toolkit, child borne of flint and core, borne of Clovis spearheads buried beneath riverbed. She merged onto the southbound 25, tangled with stalled, empty cars, piled into each other, some in pieces after catching fire. She wove through stopped traffic, twenty miles per hour to avoid crashing into the wreckage.

It would take forever to get to Tía's.

On the edge of the freeway beside the guardrail, a figure hunched beside a rundown scooter. Calliope slowed to a crawl. A white girl in hipster jeans, a sheer beige tank top with a faux leather jacket tied around her slight waist, and black army boots to her calves. She held a helmet at her hips, and bent over her bike on her haunches before standing and kicking the back tire. A petite young woman, jutting-wire skinny, ponytailed hair the color of summer squash, fawn skin with rose undertones. Her bare arms and shoulders were sleeved with colorful tattoos. Even from several feet away, Calliope could clearly discern Medusa, her snake-hair coiling the white girl's bicep like bracelets. The artwork didn't bother her; tattoo culture permeated Albuquerque. Years before, the fact that everyone and their grandma at church sported tattoos was a culture shock, but after a while she stopped paying attention.

Calliope hesitated. Talking to the last stranger on the side of the road had made her feel like a rag doll, toxic on the floor of a defective fallout shelter. She'd felt unstable. Or insane.

She didn't need insanity, she needed answers.

But as she approached the scooter, she caught the young woman's eyes, cerulean and lucid, the kind of natural response that implied *I'm normal and stranded. I'm so glad you came along.* Calliope stopped, shifted to park, and glanced back at Eunjoo, who was also staring at the woman. "Should we help her?" Calliope asked, aware she was ridiculous, asking advice of the six-year-old.

"Yep. We need her," Eunjoo answered, matter-of-factly, startling Calliope.

"Why do we need her?"

"She'll help us later."

Calliope smiled, bemused. Still, it would be useful to travel with another woman, an ally in this mess. Staring at the white girl, Calliope's hand on the locked car door, she imagined prehistoric people hunting and gathering across North America, what it might have been like when the last ice age hit, when those who survived did so by sharing resources and knowledge. No fossil record supported violence until resources became sparse, much later. Violence was taught. The natural instinct in crisis, evolved into the genes, was *help each other.*

Calliope opened the door. "Hey there," she called as she padded out of her car. "Need some help?"

"Oh my God, you're the first normal person I've seen all morning." She embraced Calliope in an awkward sideways hug, the skinny girl making Calliope feel even more massive, her belly bloating between them. "Look at you, momma," she said, laughing. "You're about to pop."

Calliope stiffened, defensive. "It's twins," she responded, pulling away from the white girl's embrace.

"Picked a hell of a time to be pregnant though, didn't you? In this nightmare."

Calliope breathed a sigh of relief, glad the white girl had acknowledged aloud that something horrible was happening. She extended her hand, introduced herself as Calliope Santiago, omitting the "Dr." title she usually prided herself in affirming.

"Amy Denver," the white girl said, shaking her hand.

Calliope was glad to have something to call her other than the white girl.

Amy said, "Seriously, momma. Do you know what's happening? Where everyone went?"

Calliope shook her head. "My family's gone, my friend is dead, and you're the first person I've met tonight who isn't insane. Where are you coming from?"

"Santa Fe. I'm a student at the art institute. I mean, I was. Now I'm a survivor on *Lost*, waiting for the polar bears. I'm just glad you're not a zombie."

"What happened up in Santa Fe? Same as here?"

"Same, yeah. Disaster scene from a zombie apocalypse. Except instead of zombies, it's just no one. Kind of freakier this way. It's a ghost town, only we're the ghosts ..."

"What were you doing when it happened? That light? Could you see it in Santa Fe?"

Amy shook her head.

Calliope shifted her weight from one sore foot to the other. "You didn't see what happened at all? I slammed my car into the bridge, blacked out, and woke to this wasteland."

"You think it was the government? A conspiracy, like the FEMA concentration camps?"

Calliope had heard this conspiracy theory before—that FEMA had built internment camps like those used for Japanese American citizens during the Second World War, which they would again use for citizens after a natural or self-made catastrophe, when they'd gained Constitutional control toward a new world order. Each time her students had written about this conspiracy or asked her opinion, Calliope had said it felt like a misuse of history, from which we could glean real truths and predictions. Misguided as the 2003 then 2012 Mayan calendar end-of-the-world forecasts. The massacres of the ancient peoples had occurred earlier than that.

She told Amy as much.

"Yeah, you're right. I don't see how they could disappear entire cities that quickly. I mean, without a ray gun or something." Amy laughed ironically, then said, "Hey, you think it was nuclear?"

Calliope *had* thought about it. Andres had once told her about a patient he'd picked up in his ambulance outside of Albuquerque. An older woman had called emergency services because her sixty-eight-year-old husband was behaving bizarrely—he hadn't returned from his walk along the bosque so she went looking for him. She found him near a dry arroyo, writhing on the sandy ground. He was nearly mad from pain and kept screaming, *The witches are burning me, the witches are burning me—make them stop!* When Andres got him to the hospital, believing he would be a psychiatric patient, the nurses had found red burn marks all over his body. Andres had felt such guilt for missing them. The burns matched those of radiation. Toxic waste. In the land.

She decided against telling Amy this. She didn't want to speculate about end-of-the-world theories. She wanted evidence. She wanted truth.

Besides, if it had been nuclear, that meant her family was …

"No. You and I wouldn't be here."

"Yeah, I guess you're right about that too."

Calliope sighed heavily and leaned against the broken fender.

Amy said, "You really smashed that thing. You get hurt?"

"Not much," Calliope answered, wondering why she wasn't more hurt from her crash on the bridge. "So, what's your story? What were you doing before … whatever happened?"

Amy's cheeks and neck blotched a deeper shade of rose. "I was indisposed."

"Meaning?"

Amy shuffled, stuck her hands in her back pockets. "I was, um, giving a private dance to this older guy. A client of mine."

Calliope blurted out before she could censor herself, "You're a prostitute?"

Amy rolled her eyes, sighed loudly. "No, an *exotic dancer*. There's a big difference."

Calliope's face heated with embarrassment. "I'm not judging. I have a friend who put herself through school dancing." This girl reminded her of one of her undergrad anthro students, and for a moment she wanted to believe they were discussing an assignment and not the end of the world.

"A lot of dancers go to college. It's no big deal." She pulled a cigarette from her bra, a lighter from her back pocket, lit, and took a deep drag. Calliope didn't mean to cough. Amy turned her face away to exhale. "Sorry, you're preggo. Should I put this out?"

"No, I don't mind."

Amy nodded, took another drag. "So I was at this guy's place, near campus, and everything was normal. I finished and was in his bathroom changing into my street clothes so I could walk back to the dorms, when there was this, I don't know, earthquake, I guess. I came out to see what was going on, but he'd left. I figured he was trying to stiff me 'cause he hadn't paid me yet. That wasn't like him, though. I've danced for him a few times, no problems. But you never know people for real, so I was pissed and tried calling my friend to come get me. I was too mad to walk. But my phone was dead. I tried using his landline, but that was dead too. No dial signal or anything. Outside the apartment building, it was like *this*." She nodded toward the chaos surrounding them, the accidents and grayness and ash. Calliope recalled what Eunjoo had described, her parents fighting, then an earthquake and they were gone.

"And the dorms?"

"Only one other person. Some girl screaming her head off, screaming bloody murder. I kept telling her to shut the hell up, but she wouldn't. Like she was catatonic, only screaming."

Calliope's chest hurt. "Wasn't there anyone else coherent like you and me?"

"I don't know. I didn't stick around to check. I grabbed my roommate's keys and took off with her scooter. It took me all night to get this far, fucking thing won't go faster than forty and keeps stalling out. Now it's outta gas too, but I'm not going back to a gas station alone, no fucking way."

"What happened at the gas station?"

"The pumps didn't work. And then some lunatic tried to grab me, so I took off."

Calliope shuddered involuntarily. A lunatic? Why were they abandoned to a world of the mentally unstable? She cleared her throat, tried focusing on the solvable issue at hand. "The pumps didn't work?"

"Nope. Fucking everything's a wreck."

"Where I just came from, the Westside, my neighborhood burned to a crisp."

"Jesus," Amy muttered sadly, shaking her head. "I'm sorry." She nodded beyond Calliope, toward the side of the car where Eunjoo was standing, so quietly Calliope hadn't even realized she'd gotten out of her booster seat. "Just you two get out? You and your daughter?"

"My neighbor. Her parents are missing." She motioned for Eunjoo to join them and introduced her to Amy.

Eunjoo stared Amy up and down, like she was sizing her up, then said, "You're coming with us, right? You're *supposed* to." Her bird's voice insistent, pragmatic.

Amy raised her eyebrows at Calliope, who shrugged.

"Where are you heading?" Calliope asked.

"My family's in Cruces. You?"

"My tía's hacienda in Silver City."

"That's on the way," Amy said, hopeful.

If the pumps were out of gas, could Calliope make it all the way to Tía's hacienda? Not if she detoured for Amy. Though Las Cruces was less than two hours out of the way, and she'd rather have another woman with her on the trip, she wasn't sure she should risk it. Maybe she could drop Amy off near Truth or Consequences, the closest town near the turnoff that would take Calliope into the Gila Mountains toward Silver City. Aloud, she said, "You can hitch a ride with us."

"You're a lifesaver. Last night was the scariest, loneliest of my life. And that's saying something." She flicked her cigarette to the ground, scuffed it out with her boot.

"Do you have anything with you? Backpack?"

"Nothing. I just jumped on the bike and took off."

Calliope wasn't the only one who hadn't been thinking properly. At least she'd managed to pack. "Come on," she said. "Hop in." The way they all piled in made Calliope think of a road trip.

"You have any water? I'm dying."

Calliope handed Amy the precious liter bottle she'd found at Susana's. "Only this."

She watched as Amy gulped the water, her mouth on the rim, drinking almost half the bottle before stopping for air.

"Slow down. I don't know where we'll get more." Calliope reached out and Amy handed the bottle over, but the way she stared after it, Calliope knew she needed much more. But so did she and Eunjoo.

Amy wiped her mouth with the back of her hand. "Listen, I didn't want to do this alone, after what happened at the gas station, but now that we're together, I think it'll be okay. We'll break into a store or something."

"I thought of that. I didn't want to leave Eunjoo alone, or take her in with me. Nothing feels safe."

"We need a plan. I'm starving. And I stopped needing to pee hours ago."

"So did I," Calliope admitted, driving away from Amy's dead bike.

"Shit. Doesn't dehydration cause labor or something? You're not about to give birth?"

"I don't think so."

"Good." She put her helmet on the passenger floor. "Is that blood on your clothes?" Amy stared at Calliope's tunic, her eyes wide, forehead creased.

"Yes," she said, her voice catching.

"Is it yours?"

Calliope shook her head. She didn't want to talk about Susana. Not in front of Eunjoo.

Amy didn't persist.

They passed a chain of fast-food restaurants.

"Do you think we should try any of those?" Amy asked.

"A convenience store would be better. Packaged food keeps longer. The power's been out a day, right? Fast food could be spoiled."

"I doubt it. That stuff's like cardboard. I saw this YouTube video about a McDonald's cheeseburger left out for *weeks* that didn't go moldy, not even a little. That stuff's not real food."

They passed the dim gold-and-red arches. Even the twenty-four-hour drive-throughs were dead. Calliope realized the ubiquity of chain restaurants and their neon night-lights across major cities and small towns alike had been a source of comfort. Strange what a person misses when it's gone. Had Andres brought food along on his journey, with their son? Was Phoenix hungry?

Daylight shone iridescent between smoke swirls, drifting in from the mountains to the east and the Sisters to the west; soft white ash sifted across the windshield like snowflakes. Calliope turned on her windshield wipers. This wasn't snow. It was the leftovers of her home.

"You okay back there?" she asked Eunjoo.

"Just thirsty." Although Eunjoo's small voice was not a whine, Calliope felt a tugging between maternal protection and irritation.

"We're gonna stop soon, chica." Her head throbbed despite the water she'd had back at Susana's. "That one," she said, pointing toward a gas station convenience store. "We'll break in there. We need gas anyway. We're below a quarter tank."

"You think these pumps will work?"

"I don't know. We have to try. Water first, then gas."

"What's the plan?"

"I've never robbed a store. I have no idea." She'd never been much of a wild child and sensed Amy was more suited for this kind of venture.

"We could throw something into the window, break it."

"If an alarm goes off, oh well. It'd be a miracle if the police appeared."

Calliope turned toward Eunjoo. "Chica, you stay in the car." She had no idea if Eunjoo would listen, but if there was a lunatic at this gas station, she figured the girl would be safer locked in the back seat. She thought of breastfeeding Phoenix during an electrical storm when the power had gone out. Calliope feared the dark storms and loud noises. She still slept with the bathroom light on most nights. But that night, nursing him, watching the way he suckled by candlelight, undisturbed, tucked between Calliope's breast and the pillow, she'd felt calmed by him. The baby boy, comforting his mama just by his being there. She mostly hated breastfeeding. It hurt, chafed her nipples, kept her awake at night. She'd developed mastitis three times, always with a high fever and rash. It was sheer bullheadedness that kept her at it. But that night during the storm, she loved it. Eunjoo's presence now comforted her too.

The parking lot was eerie with no lights or people, but no chains or closed signs either. Only empty buildings. Only whistling through the trees. Calliope stepped out, holding her belly below her abdomen. Amy watched her waddle around the front. "You're gonna pop any minute, huh?"

"Not for two months. It's just like this with twins."

"Yeah, my aunt had twins. She was huge too."

"I'm a cow."

"You're brave."

Calliope smiled briefly. She didn't feel brave, but she'd take it. She searched the ground. "Could *you* throw whatever it is we're going to throw through the window? I'm brave but not strong."

"Sure thing, momma," Amy replied, and Calliope cringed. That was the third time she'd called her that. Calliope hated when anyone said it. She thought of big momma, fat momma, old momma, and a whole stream of your-momma jokes she'd heard when she was a kid. But she couldn't afford to alienate Amy, so she held her tongue.

Nothing on the ground immediately stood out as throwable.

"We could try throwing the keys?" Amy suggested.

"I don't want to break them."

"Do you have one of those window-shattering tools?"

Andres might have stored one in the glove box, for emergencies. That sounded like him. But she didn't want Amy to know about the gun. "No, I don't have anything like that."

Amy shrugged, then chucked rocks from the median. They didn't make a dent. "Not heavy enough. We need something bigger."

"Trash can?" Calliope asked, nodding toward the metal can in its cement casement. "We could try pulling it out. It should be heavy enough."

Together they lifted and it slid right out of the concrete, a small box from a larger one, like a Russian nesting doll. Calliope helped Amy drag it toward the window, until they were standing less than ten feet away. And though she shouldn't have, she helped Amy raise it over her head, and at the count of three they heaved it toward the glass. Nothing happened. The metal scraped against the glass, then landed on the sidewalk with a thud, spilling garbage everywhere. Eunjoo squealed from the car in fear or delight, Calliope couldn't tell.

"It's bulletproof or something. Jeez. What the hell?" Amy was panting.

"I'll look in the trunk. My husband's a paramedic. He may keep a toolkit back there."

They pulled the bags and suitcases from the trunk.

"You don't pack light," Amy said.

A red flush speared Calliope's cheeks. She'd filled the car with things they wouldn't need and didn't bring anything useful. Except when she found Phoenix—he'd need his stuff.

Her mouth had grown stickier and dry. The girl had gotten out of the car and was staring blankly ahead, her eyes sunken. "Eunjoo? You feel sick, chica?" The girl nodded. All the ash and smoke didn't help; the water Eunjoo drank to wash down the peanut butter wasn't enough. Calliope had to let her drink more of their water, almost gone after Amy's gulping. She fetched the liter bottle from the car, handed it to the girl. "Here, chica. Sip this." When was the last time she'd felt the twins kicking?

Underneath the luggage in the trunk, they uncovered the first aid kit and a box of clothes, a flashlight, a blanket, but no water. Calliope pulled the boxes out, uncovered the spare tire. "We could use the lug wrench," she said, surprised at herself, as she lifted the fabric veneer from the trunk that covered the spare and its parts. She had never changed a tire in her life.

Amy took the L-shaped metal rod from her and pounded it on the convenience store's glass, cracking fissures with each strike. It didn't immediately shatter, the way Calliope had seen on movies, but after several hard hammers, it gave way, chinks of glass splitting. No alarms or sirens sounded. No one inside came to see what was happening. Nothing but glass on the ground. Even Eunjoo was silent. Amy stepped through the glass, her black boots crunching. Inside the store, she pushed on the front door, exclaiming "What the hell?" when it swung open. She pulled it shut again, calling to Calliope, "Try opening it from your side."

Calliope pulled on the door. It opened wide.

"It wasn't even locked," Amy said, exasperated. "All that work for nothing. We're brainless."

Calliope didn't care if they were brainless. She needed more fluids now, and so did Eunjoo. From the refrigerator, she pulled two 32 oz. bottles of Gatorade and took one to the girl beside the car before she began drinking the other bottle. "Don't gulp it or you'll get sick, chica. Just sip." She watched Eunjoo's small sips and tried following her own instructions. She felt vomity and dizzy despite the relief in her mouth and throat, so she sat down in the driver's seat, trying to regain her energy. She felt like she'd been running for hours.

Amy emerged from the broken window instead of the door holding a bag of white powdered minidoughnuts and a Pepsi. "I wanted chocolate milk, but it smelled gross."

"You should drink more water, Amy. That's all sugar. You're probably dehydrated, too."

"Nope, I go days without water. At school, I lived off junk food."

Calliope wondered how Amy stayed so thin then remembered she danced for a living. She chastised herself for comparing herself to another woman, here in the middle of an apocalypse (Amy's words, not hers). She glanced away from the white girl toward the glass shards littering the sidewalk, a crackling hole in the window. "We should gather supplies and keep moving," Calliope said, scanning the landscape that surrounded the gas station. They were near the Río Grande; cottonwoods and other trees of the bosque only grew near water. There was a Starbucks in this town where she'd stopped for a coffee and chocolate milk the last time she'd driven down to her tía's. Andres had teased her, *You and your Starbucks addiction.* She drank decaf mochas daily, all through both pregnancies, pointing out the safe caffeine levels and defending her right to drink coffee. *Give me this small comfort, at least. Humans might someday evolve like seahorses—and men will bear the children.* She reminded him that seahorse fathers went through childbirth and labor and were the ones physically distressed. She had asked, *Where, pray tell, does the biblical story of Eve figure into that?* Her mother hated when she disrespected God, but Andres never minded. Although he was devoutly Catholic, like her mother, and attended church every Sunday without Calliope—who preferred to spend her mornings sipping mochas and researching or hiding out at the planetarium—Andres always listened to her hypothesize without censure or judgment. Where could religion meet science? Answering that question had consumed her since Bisabuela's death. And not just religion but belief. Bisabuela's belief, for instance. At what cliff, what burial site, what meteor in the vaulted dome of sky did God, the Ancient Ones, and science coalesce? Could her family be there now? Andres, Phoenix, and her mother? They couldn't just be gone. It didn't make sense.

Her stomach twinged, the twins kicking. She choked back the taste of bile. She couldn't allow herself to linger on the possibility of their deaths. They had to be alive. There was no other way. She didn't have *faith.* She just knew. No bodies. No blood. No signs of struggle. The evidence said *keep searching.*

Though she wanted to ask Amy what she believed in, they'd wasted enough time already. Calliope still felt lightheaded, but they shouldn't stay in one place. They had to move. There weren't any volcanoes this far across the river, but whatever else the earth could conjure up to scare or break them, she didn't want to imagine. Storms atop storms had swept the country the past few years, hurricanes and tornadoes where they didn't belong, in states unaccustomed to such weather, leaving millions without power for weeks. If this was a global warming catastrophe too, where was the government relief? The helicopters? The Red Cross?

No one was coming. She must have known this already. But the realization wormed through her stomach, unsettling the fluid she'd just poured down. They were on their own.

She leaned against the car for support, dizzy again.

Amy cleared her throat. "You should make the kid pee now if you can," she said. "We'll be on the road a while. Might have to sleep in the car."

Calliope nodded, opened the door for Eunjoo. "You heard her, chica. Let's go."

Amy followed them into the store, filling her mouth with the two remaining doughnuts and leaving a trail of powdered sugar on her chin and tank top. "While you ladies relieve yourselves, I'll finish stocking up," she said. "This place gives me the creeps."

After Calliope and Eunjoo finished in the restroom (the toilets wouldn't flush), Calliope sent Eunjoo back to the car and grabbed a box of matches, canned vegetables and meat, a can opener, magazines which she figured she could use as kindling if necessary (how hard could it be to start a fire?), and packs of chewing gum to keep their mouths moist to help preserve water. She wasn't sure it was true but Andres had told her that a person could survive longer by sucking on a button to create saliva, and then drinking that. The thought of surviving on spit churned her stomach, but sugarless spearmint seemed all right. She carried her items to the checkout counter then laughed at herself. Habit. She didn't want to be a thief, but she didn't have her wallet anyway. It had burned with everything else.

She was dragging a five-gallon jug to the front door when she heard Eunjoo screeching. Calliope dropped the water and scuttled through the doorway. Outside, Eunjoo was cowering on the ground, Phoenix's back-pack still on her back like a tortoise shell, her arms covering her face. In front of the girl, just a few feet away, a pack of coyotes, their reddish-brown fur bristling against their rawboned bodies, their teeth bared, muscles tensed. With all the people gone, maybe they'd been out dumpster diving, a gluttony of garbage-eating, but there must've been plenty of food not yet rotten. Why attack a child?

"Scare them," Calliope hissed to herself or Amy or Eunjoo, she wasn't sure, momentarily frozen in panic. "They're afraid of humans." She looked over to check if Amy was seeing this, but she was still inside stockpiling junk food. "Amy," she shouted, snapping out of her immobility. "Help!" Calliope raised her hands above her head, waving them wildly.

Amy jerked her head toward the parking lot, and yelled, "What the shit!" Then she grabbed a rack of magazines and threw it out the glass hole toward the pack, but the coyotes didn't budge. "Shit-shit-shit!" Amy shouted, continuing to throw things.

Calliope dropped her load of groceries, ran in front of Eunjoo, blocking the coyote's path to the girl. Bile snaked through Calliope's throat and her chest pounded, but she kept yelling. The coyotes were growling but didn't move. Calliope scanned her mind for everything she knew about coyotes. They didn't hunt in packs. They only banded together if they were investigating, curious about something new. They didn't usually approach humans. They were afraid—unless they'd lost their fear because a human had fed them. Had Eunjoo fed them? She yelled louder, waving her arms frantically, Amy still throwing things—now six-packs of beer bottles. The coyotes howled, an eerie, otherworldly sound in the early morning light. One grizzled dog skulked forward from the pack, hackles raised, and Eunjoo began backing away. Amy finally hit one with a full quart-sized glass bottle, shattering against its flank, and the animal retreated, yelping. The distraction allowed Calliope time to edge backward, close enough to Eunjoo to snatch her up and scramble her into the car. As Eunjoo climbed over the front seat, Calliope turned the key, revving the engine. She threw the car into reverse and drove straight toward the pack, honking the horn. The dogs scattered, trotting toward a clearing of trees. Calliope drove to the front of the store, away from the glass. She got out to help Amy finish loading the car with groceries, but Eunjoo was crying, striking that hysterical pitch children reach when they've hit their emotional wall or are hurt badly.

"What is it?" Amy asked, coming up behind her. "Is she okay?"

"I don't know," Calliope said, checking whether the coyotes were still nearby. She didn't see any. She held the girl's shoulders. "The coyotes are gone, chica. You're safe."

Tears on her cheeks, snot at her nose, Eunjoo lifted her hand, which was bleeding.

Calliope instinctively pressed the bottom of her tunic to the girl's hand, to staunch the blood. "It bit you?" The girl nodded, wiping her nose. "Amy, get me some napkins." No answer. She looked around. "Amy?"

"Drive."

"What?"

"They're back." Amy threw her body into the passenger seat, slammed the door.

Calliope flung Eunjoo's door shut and moved as quickly as she could to the driver's seat. The coyotes formed a semicircle around the back of the car, growling, their reddish hair on end. Calliope pulled the gear into reverse, stepped on the gas, and drove.

SEVEN
PROJECT Y

Mara had to be hallucinating. People didn't just disappear. She'd put all of that out of her mind. Since Trinity and that mushroom cloud in the sky. Since the aftermath at San Ildefonso. And Chaiwa. As she drove into Silver City to find Trudy—the usual rolling green surrounding Trudy's ranch replaced with muted grays—Mara couldn't stop thinking of her first trip there. Seventy-five years earlier, on the train from Princeton, Mara had watched prairie give way to sage-speckled hills. The dunes grained with yellowing shrubs reminded her of the barnacle-covered sea rocks on Dover Beach. Her father had just taken a job with the Manhattan Project, and they were heading toward an undisclosed location in the mountains of northern New Mexico.

Mara, five years old, had breathed against the pane, tracing shapes in the foggy glass with her bare fingers. She refused to wear her white kid gloves or to let her mother style her red hair. She was born with a wild streak, her mother was fond of telling dinner guests and anyone who'd listen. She was like Esau, the twin whose birthright was stolen because of his foolhardiness.

Rose tried making Mara more ladylike, *befitting their family's position.* At every opportunity Mara batted away her mother's efforts. She was young. "Leave her be," her father would chasten her mother in his soft but rasping German voice. "She's just a little girl. Not a lady yet." He would kiss Mara atop her head. Even then, Mara could see that he expected decorum only from his wife. His daughter he let run as wild as the aboriginal people Rose expressed fear they would encounter in the strange new land to which they were destined.

It was 1943. They were traveling under assumed names, "Mr. Edward Lewis and family." Mara and her mother got to keep their first names. Mara had heard her mother complain she didn't want to move; she'd grown accustomed to their life in Princeton, those luncheons and teas. They were safe in New Jersey, in the prestigious American university; behind heavy oak desks, in ornate halls, under soaring campaniles and vaulted chapels, atop ivory towers, behind her husband's name, his status as a scientist, his degrees, his important civilian work, they were safe.

"Will it be safe for Mara?" she'd asked.

"Of course," Isaac had assured her, not looking up from his escritoire, where Mara was hiding. His dark hair combed to the side and disheveled from his fedora hat, his brown wool suit fitted to his angular frame, Mara thought him handsome. She wanted to be just like him.

"There'd better be indoor plumbing and no rattlesnakes," her mother had said.

The conductor called out, "Lamy Station." Mara couldn't wait to get off the stuffy train and into the wild. They stepped off into nothingness. No semblance of city. The small station stood alone on the side of the railroad tracks, a whitewashed adobe brick building with the metal block letters "L-A-M-Y" spelled across the side. To either side of the station, tumbleweeds and desert hills spanning as far as she could see. Mara thought it was perfect. She loved the muted hills, the terracotta bricks that made up the platform, and the reddish slats of the sloping station rooftop.

"It's like we've gone into Siberia," her mother breathed. "Wasteland."

Mara pulled out her sketchbook and hastily tried to capture the landscape with colored pencil, though her talent wouldn't catch up with the images she saw in her mind for many years to come. When she was much older, after completing art school, she would go through those old sketchbooks and remake all her early attempts at sustaining on the page the magical place that had arrested her since childhood. Though she was almost six years old, Mara didn't talk much. Her mother worried about her *unusual proclivity toward introversion*. Her mother didn't realize she was speaking all the time but through her art.

As her father strode toward the caboose to fetch their baggage, Rose took Mara's arm and shuffled her to the front of the station. Across the dirt road there squatted a derelict hotel, saloon in full swing. A lean man in denims, plaid flannel, a Stetson, and boots tumbled out of the bar, lit a cigarette, then climbed into a beat-up truck and scraped along the road into the hills, kicking up dust. Rose clasped Mara's arm tighter. Further down the road a bell chimed from a small Catholic church in the adobe style with a wooden cross atop, the arched doors painted bright blue.

A black limousine pulled up. A limousine, in the wilderness. Mara clinched her hands, grinning. "Is that for us, Mother?"

The man who appeared from the driver's side stood in stark contrast to the cowboy who had stumbled from the saloon. In a gray tailored suit and hat, he resembled more closely the kind of men Mara saw in the city, his russet hair cropped close to his head. He moved with purpose, strutting around the limousine toward Mara and her mother on the platform. He said he would be taking them up to the Hill.

"What's the Hill?" Mara asked offhandedly, not looking up from her sketchbook, where she was now furiously drawing the driver.

He flicked his cigarette to the ground, ignoring her.

No one spoke as the car pitched steadily higher, bumping over rocks and sinking into depressions in the dusty road. Terracotta-colored ranch houses mottled the rawhide landscape, along with black-and-white grazing cattle. Finally, a sign: Santa Fe. Her mother had read aloud from the WPA book: *a long-established artist's colony where the elite and wealthy afflicted with respiratory illness had been going for treatment for a decade.* The clear mountain air and artistic diversion offered at the sanitariums surrounding Santa Fe were highly touted, according to the book.

The GI cleared his throat, explained, "We need to stop briefly in Santa Fe to obtain your badges before we can proceed up to the Hill. No one is allowed entry without a security badge."

"Is the Hill much farther?" her father asked, his tone surprised.

"Another thirty-five miles or so," the driver answered.

Sprawling beyond the clusters of flat, rectangular adobe houses lining the unpaved streets, a kind of Bohemian culture emerged as they entered the Plaza. Among red strings of wrinkled chilies, elderly Native Americans with sunbaked faces hawked their pottery, turquoise jewelry, and other handcrafted wares on blanketed sidewalks in the storefronts of curio shops and cafés. Women wore velvet skirts and peasant blouses, clinking silver belts slung low around their waists, and crescent pendants. Mara found them beautiful. The men ambled through the streets, smoking cigarettes and stubbing them out on the dirt. They wore jeans, button-down flannels, and cowboy hats like the rancher outside the bar in Lamy. The car stopped in front of a hollyhock-entwined patio, adobe bricks showing through the plaster, a wrought-iron gateway, halfway concealing a small sign with red lettering:

US ENG-
RS

When they entered the building, a woman at a desk typed security passes on plain paper, and doled them out before they were whisked back into the limo and driven another two hours, first through a sparse village called Española and then up a cliff and onto a winding stretch of road, all the while plodding through dirt, the car bumping and jostling. Mara giggled. It felt like a roller coaster, the view breathtaking. Colossal red-cleft rocks jutting across the plateau from the switchbacks gave way to bright evergreen mountainous desert. They passed a Native American village the driver called San Ildefonso. On the side of the road, near a low, flat adobe home, a mangy dog lying in a patch of weeds watched them without moving or barking. Mara wanted to stop and look around, wanted to pet the dog. But the driver kept on.

Before they left the Indian village, Mara noticed a woman making a pot on her front porch. Mara smiled at the woman, who looked up, didn't smile back. Mara didn't know then she was seeing Chaiwa for the first time. The woman who would change her life.

They made a hairpin turn onto a one-lane suspension bridge crossing over a wide river.

"This is the Rio Grande, I assume," her father asked the driver.

"They call it Otowi," the driver said. "Place where the river makes a noise."

Watching the water as they drove slowly across the bridge, Mara felt drawn to its immensity. Did it have a secret to relay? She listened, hearing only the rumbling sound of the engine.

"Here we are," the driver said, nodding ahead. "Site Y. Your new home."

Across the river, the limo slowed outside a sprawling chain-link fence topped with barbed wire. Squat, gray barracks and hutments lined the dirt roads. Dust clouded around their car, pluming at the windows as they pitched slowly toward the gate. Army vehicles everywhere. Mara sketched furiously, creating a kind of shadowed, ink-blot version of the new world she was seeing—a shantytown, rickety trailers, overflowing garbage cans, laundry on the wire. She glanced at her mother, who'd gone pale. Mara sketched her face, a look of pure horror.

Now, as she pulled into the outskirts of Silver City, Mara imagined her face bore the same expression her mother's had years ago. Cars crashed. Fires. Trudy couldn't have been shopping at the Walmart. The Walmart was burning to the ground. Trudy had to be with her son. In the mental ward of the hospital where he lived.

* * * *

But inside was much worse. Beds empty. Thick white sheets, threadbare blankets, bars on the windows. Nursing station, papers strewn, notebooks open, computers dead. Med carts untended in the hallways. Chairs gathered in a semicircle around a blank TV screen. Blankets and pillows piled on the floor in heaps. Flies buzzing on trays stacked atop a food cart.

What grisly scene had she walked into? Where were the patients, the doctors and nurses? Her head hurt; the room spun. At the end of the hall, a Native American woman in scrubs. Was Mara seeing things?

She was five again. The whole Hill was buzzing with excitement. They'd dropped the bomb. People celebrated. She didn't understand then, but she'd replayed it in her mind many times over the next seventy-five years. A custodian from the San Ildefonso wearing beige coveralls grinned at a scientist in a pinstripe tie. "We did it, didn't we?"

"Yes, we did."

They'd held a country line dance at the San Ildefonso sweat lodge, brought glass bottles of Coca-Cola and the Native people had made fry bread.

Chaiwa had told Mara lizard meant close to the earth. Close to the dirt. The sand. *We all come from the sand*, she'd said. *Formed from the rocks.* Chaiwa wanted to teach her to be that low, that connected, again. *It's not something you should be able to teach*, she'd said. Like she was teaching her words in Tewa. *But I sense a lizard spirit in you.* The tail of the lizard meant breaking into a new reality, letting go of the old and making a miracle of the new—growing it right there, yourself.

Mara thought of this as she approached the lone woman in the hospital hall. The woman's voice reminded her of Chaiwa's, though Mara hadn't heard it in seventy-five years. "You shouldn't be here."

"Where is everyone?"

The woman in scrubs sighed, her long black hair in a braid down her side. She was tall, solidly built. "Gone."

"Where did they go? My friend's son, Julian Jimenez was a patient here. My friend would have come for him. After that flash. Did you see it?"

The woman nodded.

"You work here, right? You knew him?"

"You shouldn't be here," she repeated in a low voice, her insistence startling Mara.

"Please help me. I need to find my friend." Her boots scuffled against the linoleum. She walked closer to the woman. A nurse? A doctor? She couldn't tell. "Can you help me?"

EIGHT
BAD MOON RISING

Eunjoo was still crying although Calliope had assured her she was not badly hurt. She'd stopped driving long enough to examine the girl's hand, torn at the fleshy pad of skin connecting thumb to index finger. Calliope thought it wise to stitch it with Andres's suture kit. Phoenix had once sliced his thumb on his bicycle spoke while trying to fix a broken chain all by himself. Like Daddy, he'd said. They'd taken him to the ER when it wouldn't stop bleeding, and the paramedic at the triage said he would have done the same, would've taken his kid. *You don't fool around with hands.* Calliope had grimaced then, watching the ER nurses do their job. Now, each time she pressed the needle through Eunjoo's skin, she held her breath. The girl was so brave, hardly cried. Just like Phoenix. "It'll be fine, chica. No te preocupes, my bisabuela would say. It means don't worry, but everything sounds better in Spanish."

When Calliope drove again, her heart still pounded from the exertion of the coyote attack, her muscles ached from the pit of her stomach to her thighs, and pain radiated from her navel to her bowels. She breathed deeply and pressed onward, focusing on the headlights filtering dust in the road. The rundown cars growing sparser, Calliope accelerated through the rubble.

"That was close," Amy said when they were on the road out of Los Lunes. "I still don't understand why they attacked."

Calliope didn't answer for fear of scaring Eunjoo even more, but it must have been rabies. What else could have caused the coyotes' erratic behavior? She'd have to watch the girl for signs.

Desert coyotes didn't often hunt in packs; they usually ate mice and other small rodents, and if they ever came into town, it was solo, to eat garbage. Were they staking claim on the abandoned town? How had they known it was abandoned?

"What now?" Amy asked. "We didn't get gas. Should we try another station?"

If the coyotes had so quickly overrun the town, what else would lurk in the stretch of empty desert and farmland between here and Belen, the last town along this road before they reached Las Cruces, with no other towns save ghost in between? Calliope checked the tank. A little less than half. "We have enough to get to Cruces."

"If nothing else attacks us," Amy said, chuckling mischievously.

Calliope shot her a warning look, signaling her not to scare Eunjoo.

Amy sobered, said, "Hey, I'm only teasing. We'll be fine. Lead the way, momma."

Eunjoo said quietly, "I miss my mother."

"I know, chica. We'll get to my tía's and find our families, no te preocupes."

"They won't be at your tía's." The girl's voice was quiet but firm. Eerily firm.

Calliope checked the rearview mirror, surprised by the girl's pessimism. There was such heaviness in the girl's face, her eyes black and clear as night. Her expression crumpled like she'd received the wrong present on Christmas or spent a birthday alone and forgotten. "Don't lose heart, chica."

"I already know what happens, Phoenix's mama. They aren't there. None of them."

The hairs on Calliope's neck bristled at the way Eunjoo seemed so darkly sure. The little girl hadn't slept more than twenty minutes since she'd appeared at Calliope's house. She must have been exhausted. "Try to sleep. Things will seem better when you've rested."

The girl closed her eyes, and Calliope focused again on the road, still unsettled by Eunjoo's sudden Nostradamus direness.

When Eunjoo began to breathe steadily, Amy said, "Wow, she's a little bummer, isn't she?" She stretched upward like a cat and reached into the back of her tight jeans, pulling out a pack of gum she'd pocketed in the convenience store. She opened three mint-green sticks and shoved them all into her mouth at once, smacking as she chewed. She offered Calliope a piece.

"No, thanks."

Amy shrugged, put the gum back in her pocket then stared out the window, continuing her noisy chewing. "What do you think happened to her family? Do you think we'll find them?"

"Yes."

"How can you be so sure?"

Calliope sighed deeply. After a moment, she said, "Honestly? I'm not sure." Amy shrugged, though her face assumed the quality of a crumpled paper bag. Calliope didn't say what she felt in her gut: the fates of Eunjoo's family and hers, maybe even Amy's, were bound together. If they found one, they'd find the others. They had to. She sighed. "My mom's a devoted Catholic, right? Deeply pious. She wears a rosary and prays with it every day along with other novenas where she lights these santos candles and incense and leaves gifts at the altar for Mother Mary, the whole enchilada. Since I was a little girl I've struggled to believe. But her faith, her unwavering faith … Something keeps telling me she's safe. That my whole family is safe."

Amy smacked her gum, stretched her arms above her head. "I hear you, momma. Nothing like a mother who believes there's good out there. Sounds real refreshing to me." She looked out the window awhile, then turned toward Calliope again. "Hey, tell me something though. Calliope isn't a very Catholic-sounding name. If your mother's so devout, why didn't she name you Martha or something?"

Calliope laughed. This girl. "Well, my father named me, apparently. That's pretty much all I know about him. My mom says he named me after a circus instrument, and then ran off with one." Calliope smiled ruefully, recalling how she'd seen herself on an old circus advertisement in a museum when she was a child, which read, *Big Top Calliope, the wonderful operonicon of the muses.* She'd imagined her father riding off in a circus carriage, as if he'd gone black and white and disappeared into the past.

The past was safer, Calliope had thought. No one could hurt you there. No one could leave you. They were already gone. Later, she'd learned she was also the Greek muse of epic poetry, and although she couldn't write poetry to save her life, she'd felt better about being a strong woman rather than a mere instrument. "My middle name is Anne though, like St. Anne, mother of Mary. So my mom squeezed a little Catholic in there."

"Got ya." Amy yawned. "I'm glad she didn't name you Martha."

They traveled in silence after that, and Calliope wondered if Amy had fallen asleep same as Eunjoo, she'd become so quiet. Time passed by with the shrubs and tumbleweeds, in the muted grays of the landscape, usually shades of brown and ocher, now washed out in charcoals, as if they'd gone black and white too, like her father in his imaginary circus. The dashboard flashed. "Dammit," Calliope muttered under her breath. What had happened? They'd had half a tank just half an hour ago. Had the odometer been wrong? Had they ripped a fuel line? She stared at the dashboard light, afraid of what this meant in the middle of the desert with nowhere to stop.

Amy turned her head toward Calliope without opening her eyes, not lifting herself from the position she'd been sprawled in for the last thirty minutes, spindly legs stretched in front of her like vines growing from the front seat, dirty boots on the dashboard. "What's wrong?"

"We're out of gas."

Amy's eyes shot open. She sprang forward, dropping her legs and boots to the floorboard with a thud. "What the shit? I thought you said we had enough." She leaned over the center console. "Completely empty?"

Calliope nodded toward the light beneath the last rung of the fuel gauge. Her voice an apology, she said, "I don't know what happened." They should have stopped again when Amy had suggested it.

"Most cars can make it another thirty or forty miles. Did it just turn on?"

"I don't know," Calliope admitted, another thing she'd miscalculated, another thing she'd done wrong. "I wasn't paying attention."

"You want to turn around?"

Calliope shook her head. They couldn't go back to the station overrun with coyotes. Anyway, there might not have been enough gas left to get them there if they were brave or stupid enough to risk it.

"Me neither." Amy rolled down the window and spit her gum into the air. "Guess we'll have to hijack a car."

"It's not hijacking if there's no one in it."

"Steal then."

Calliope's stomach roiled. She felt dizzy. She'd heard a study on the radio, how even sober drivers tend to make the mistakes of drunk drivers when dehydrated. She needed water again. Though she didn't want to steal anything, what choice did they have? She nodded. The desert broiled beneath clouds of ash, concealing a storm. Past the shrubs and cactus spines in the distance, the charcoaled skyline touched the dirt; lightning crackled a warning. Where the highway in Albuquerque had been a burial ground of dead vehicles, on this thin strip of road nothing remained. They were miles from the fertile valley beside the Río Grande, no farms nearby, no trucks or tractors. Tumbleweed scattered in the wind, scuttling spiderlike across the dirt-blanketed road.

"There, you see it?" Amy pointed out the open window toward a mesquite tree in the distance. A thick dust storm was picking up a few feet ahead.

Calliope squinted through the haze. "All I see is a tree."

"It's a truck, I'm sure."

Calliope flipped on the high beams. Sure enough, adjacent to the tree, jutting into the thick trunk, a raised pickup, tires half the size of Calliope's whole car. Mesquite leaves draped the truck bed like a canopy. It reminded Calliope of an art exhibit, metal and bark. How had the tree sustained that crash and not split?

"It'll run." Amy peeled another piece of gum from her tight jeans pocket, stuck it in her mouth with a smacking sound, then pulled her blond hair into a ponytail with the rubber band on her wrist. Calliope's mouth curled into a smile at Amy's fighting stance.

"Do you know how to drive that thing?"

"Sure. My brothers and I'd go to the dunes outside Cruces all the time in White Sands."

Calliope nodded. She knew of the Trinity Site army base down there, though she'd never been. Andres had driven through on his way to Lincoln National Forest to help his crew fight a fire. He'd said it was beautiful, like hills of snow for sledding. Warm snow. He'd brought her a plastic bagful and they'd put it in a jar on the kitchen windowsill, promising Phoenix they'd take him closer to Halloween. Trinity Site was open to the public then, and Calliope had wanted a historical tour. She had a grim fascination for the atomic splitting, that nuclear explosion that had left cattle at a nearby ranch without hair, and when it had grown back, it was white and mottled, pocked with the evidence of the bomb—where lightning had burned sand into green glass and carbon bodies had clotted together. But Cruces in the summertime was scorching. 106 degrees some days. Warm snow Calliope could handle, but not hell snow. A pang of guilt sprang from her stomach to her chest like heartburn. Or were the twins kicking? She should've taken Phoenix anyway. She should've let him roll down the white hills like a desert snow angel. She should've done so many things. She berated herself thinking he were dead, that she might not find him and take him to White Sands. No. She wouldn't be able to move one swollen foot in front of the other if she didn't stop thinking that way.

"Let's hope whoever crashed it left the keys," Amy said. "Or I'll have to hot-wire it. Haven't done that in forever."

Amy was one piece of kismet in this nightmare. One shiny penny.

"You have a screwdriver in here?"

"I'm sure Andres left one in the trunk. He's got all sorts of tools back there."

Twenty yards from the mesquite truck sculpture, Calliope stopped the car. The accident made her uneasy. She checked on Eunjoo, still sleeping, still wearing Phoenix's backpack like a child's comfort blanket. A small red bloom seeped through the bandage on Eunjoo's hand.

Amy was already out of the car, tromping through dirt and brush in her high black combat boots, reminding Calliope of a tattooed soldier. She wanted to call out for her to wait, be careful, but instead she pushed open the glove compartment. There was Susana's gun. It startled Calliope, cold in her hand. She got out, looped her finger through the trigger, and pointed it toward the scrub on the ground. She should've worn thicker socks and boots, each step kicking up sand, filling her ballet flats with pebbles. Creosote scratched her calves. She squinted against the wind. "Amy?" Her voice came out a whisper. She didn't want to find dead bodies.

The truck's ignition roared to life, and Calliope aimed the gun at the driver's side.

"What the hell is *that*, and why are you aiming it at me?" Amy's voice was high-pitched. She jumped down, landing like a gymnast on both feet in the sand. She barreled toward Calliope, seeming much larger than she was. "You gonna shoot me?"

Calliope lowered the gun. "Chica, if I'd wanted to kill you, why in God's name would I have helped you escape those coyotes?" Truth was, she didn't know why she'd aimed at Amy or what she'd been scared of.

Amy stared at her like she'd just cursed in church. "*You* helped *me* escape?" She nodded toward the gun. "Where'd you get that thing?"

Calliope didn't want to explain Susana's suicide. It still didn't make sense. She shrugged, clicked the safety, then tried to tuck the gun into the waist of her leggings, but it was too heavy, and started slipping. She pushed the elastic down to her hip and tucked the excess material over the gun again, pouch-like, a makeshift holster.

"I checked the gas gauge. Three quarters of a tank should get us to Cruces."

Calliope looked away. She wasn't going to Las Cruces. They'd have to split up. Or she'd have to convince Amy to stay with her until they got to Tía's. Calliope needed Amy; it wasn't safe out here. But she couldn't rationalize the wasted time detouring to Cruces instead of finding her son.

They switched supplies from car to truck and woke Eunjoo. "Whose truck is that?" the girl asked in her bird's voice as she stumbled across the bramble toward the truck. Thunder roiled in the distance. "Has the man come yet?"

Calliope's pulse spidered. "What man?"

"The man with the black hair."

Calliope scanned the landscape. She saw no one. "Chica, you were dreaming. There's no man. Hop in the truck."

Calliope grabbed three Gatorades, handed them out. "Straight on till sunset?" Calliope asked Amy, who held a map across the steering wheel.

"Ain't no sun out here, momma." She folded the map, slammed her door, and backed the truck out of the tree.

In the tape deck, a cassette stuck out like a black tongue. Calliope pushed it in. Blaring from the speakers, Credence Clearwater Revival. *I hear hurricanes a blowing. I know the end is coming soon … Don't go around tonight. It's bound to take your life. There's a bad moon on the rise.*

"Tell me about it," Amy shouted over the music.

The sky so inky Calliope couldn't even see a moon, bad or not, she remembered a windstorm she'd driven through before she'd met Andres, before she'd become a mother and her life was bound to anyone other than her own mother, and that only tenuously so. She'd been freer then. Her stomach constricted at the realization: she'd missed that feeling, driving toward no one, home to no one. When she'd suspected morning sickness, the first time, she'd been too impatient to take the pregnancy test home, and found out she was pregnant in the Rite Aid customer's bathroom. She'd wept in the drugstore parking lot. Googled abortion clinics on her cellphone. The windstorm with Bisabuela, after Chaco Canyon. How those ruins had predicted her whole future, set her on this path. The first entry in the A–Z encyclopedia of the Chaco Canyon Handbook was *Abandonment*. She'd marked the page with a sticky note and highlighter yellowing the word for her dissertation. She'd wanted to prove what Bisabuela's people had known, before Catholicism and her mother's novenas. Abandonment. The Ancient Ancestors had erected these magnificent structures and then *departed*. They'd sometimes left potsherds, tools, and debris of living, which meant the moves had been hurried, unplanned, perhaps from lack of rainfall and not warring tribes, not external threat. The answer lay buried in the land itself. Bisabuela's people, wrought from the Chacoans a thousand years later, believed the ruins were anything but—not ruins but breathing still. When Calliope had explored Chaco Canyon as a graduate student she'd wondered why the ancestors would have chosen a place so remote, built a city center in the vast unbroken nothingness, save muted gray-green sagebrush cropping from the dirt. Bisabuela had warned her, *Don't pick up the broken pottery on the ground.* The potsherds were for honoring the Ancestors.

The windstorm that had taken Bisabuela had left Calliope with a PhD and a hole in her heart. In the parking lot, she'd held the number for a clinic in her hand and thought of shattered pottery, remnants on the ground. Abandonment. She'd wanted to swallow the shards. She'd gone back into the drugstore, bought a bottle of prenatal vitamins. She'd chosen family, then. Now, six years later, she'd still managed to abandon her family, or they'd abandoned her.

"Momma?"

Calliope bristled.

"Hey, momma? You all right over there?"

"Stop calling me momma."

Amy sucked air in through her teeth, whistling. Calliope heard Amy whisper "mood swings" sardonically under her breath, but she let it go, wiping her face with the back of her hand. They said nothing. Then, "I didn't mean any harm," Amy said. "I just meant 'cause of your belly."

Calliope couldn't explain to Amy why it bothered her. She stayed silent, observing through the window the alterations in her bisabuela's homeland, this place Calliope had returned to searching for answers. Clouding the sky, a brick red swirling that seemed to morph into a bird then split at the wings and separate into two distinct creatures. This wasn't a normal storm approaching, Calliope felt it, and they didn't have anywhere safe to hide. Anvil crawler lightning spread like limbs of a tree, branching purple across the birdlike clouds. But the sky remained illuminated much longer than normal, discharging in slow motion. How long until the strange lightning reached them?

When Eunjoo awoke, she had to go to the bathroom. Traveling with children was the same stop and go and stop again, no matter whose children they were.

They pulled over, Calliope instructing Eunjoo to squat beside the sagebrush in the arroyo wash. She'd let Andres take Phoenix to the roadside on day trips, show him how men can unzip and stand, relieving themselves beside any tree or bush. With girls it was an ordeal. Andres always teased Calliope for her squeamishness, her fear of outhouses and pit toilets. *It could grow tentacles and snatch me*, she'd tell him. *I could fall in and drown in a pit of shit.* It wasn't her mother's hellfire and damnation that scared her anymore but drowning in sewage.

From the truck, Calliope could hear Amy swearing and digging around. "Fuck. I'm all out of gum. Who doesn't keep gum in the glove compartment?" After a moment, "Camels? Camels? Dammit. Calliope, it okay with you if I smoke? I'll move away from the truck." Calliope called back that she didn't care. If she could handle volcanic ash, she could handle secondhand smoke.

Although Eunjoo was still a stranger she'd only known a day, Calliope felt almost comfortable showing the girl how it was done, if not motherly, then sisterly. Her protruding belly tipping her center of gravity, Calliope steadied herself and pulled down her own leggings and stuck her nalgas backward toward the sand, careful to keep her chonies, leggings, and Susana's gun that she'd pouched there for safety bundled together at her knees, away from the stream, toward a patch of reddish wildflowers wilting against a rock.

Amy's screams sounded like a barn owl screeching.

"Get the fuck off me, motherfucker!"

Calliope hustled into her leggings, quickly, whispered to Eunjoo, "Pull up your pants. Hide in the sage." She motioned with her chin five feet further from their squatting spot. "Don't move."

Eunjoo's black eyes filled with fear, but she nodded and followed Calliope's instructions.

Calliope unrolled Susana's gun from her makeshift pouch and disengaged the safety. She was sweating, although the storm clouds had made the hazy air cold, and the gun was slick in her palms. From the driver's side, she heard a scuffling against the blacktop, boots against asphalt. Calliope's stomach clutched. She steadied her quavering hand as she stepped around the back of the truck, and faced Amy, stomach to the ground, her blond hair loose around her face, a hand over her mouth, a man in an olive-green jumpsuit crouched atop her, his stubbled face pressed against hers, a knife at her neck. A pack of Camels beside her on the blacktop. The man's jumpsuit was open. He was whispering something in Amy's ear, and she was shaking her head, crying. He scratched the side of her face with the knife; Calliope saw the blood. She pointed the gun at his head. She braced herself. What if she accidentally hit Amy? She'd never fired a gun. She'd refused to go with Andres to the shooting range, refused to let Phoenix even practice with a BB gun and soda cans.

They didn't hear Calliope standing there. Amy was grasping the belt of her jeans at the hips, the man whispering furiously into her ear, his hand tightening at her mouth, the knife digging into her neck. What was Calliope waiting for? She needed to shoot before he hurt her friend. She meant to pull the trigger—

His olive-green body slumped forward, his head slamming onto the road, his hands slack. Blood pooled at his head, staining the ground around him. Amy screamed, pushed him off, and scrambled out of the blood. Calliope stared at her hands. She hadn't pulled the trigger. She hadn't killed him. She was poised to pull the trigger, but she hadn't. She'd hesitated. She hadn't saved her friend.

Then who had?

Still pointing the gun in front of her, Calliope whipped around to search the road behind them. A hundred feet away, a man holding a rifle.

NINE
CHANCE

The man walked toward them, rifle slung over his shoulder with a leather strap. Calliope called out to Eunjoo in the underbrush, "Stay hidden, chica. Don't move." To Amy, "Are you hurt?" Amy made a shrilling noise like a chipmunk, part sob, part inscrutable. "Pick up the knife. That man might have saved us, but he could be as insane as the rest of them." Three days ago, Calliope had been planning tenure and compiling notes for her dissertation. Her anthropology department was throwing a baby shower. Now she felt like she'd stepped into a horror show, and she knew what kinds of things happened to women in horror films after the cliffhanger.

As if the gun were glued to her hands, she held it steadily. The man didn't even halt, just walked calmly toward Calliope. He was tall and thick, muscular, wearing a button-down plaid flannel the color of hickory, only a shade or two darker than his skin, and brown cowboy boots. His glossy black hair swayed at his shoulders as he moved.

At twenty feet, Calliope called, "Stay back."

He didn't flinch or halt, but put his hands in the air, perhaps to show they were empty, which Calliope could already see.

"I'm serious. Stop moving," Calliope called again, her voice keeling sharply. "I'll shoot."

"No, you won't." His voice was deep, melodic, his accent familiar. "No soy como él, señorita."

"Hablas español?"

He smiled, his square jaw crackling into softer lines. "Sí."

"A donde eres?"

His smile widened. "The rez."

"You're not Hispanic?"

"Half." He wore a turquoise bracelet set in a wide, flat band of silver and a ring of turquoise and silver on his right hand.

"Why should I trust you?"

"I just shot that son of a bitch raping your friend, didn't I?"

"Unless you wanted her for yourself." The world since that red flash in the sky had no rules, or a set of rules Calliope didn't understand. This man could have wanted anything.

"Nunca, mujer. Créeme. I would never."

She did. Believe him. She wasn't sure why, but his voice was calming; it echoed of Andres. Calliope lowered the gun. "Cómo te llamas?" She spoke the language of home, as if she'd found a member of her family.

"Chance Guardian," he said, holding out his hand to shake hers.

She peeled one sweating palm off Susana's gun and offered it to Chance.

Amy sputtered behind them, a snort. "You're kidding, right?" Calliope turned around where her friend was leaning against the truck with the box of Camels in one hand, a lighter in the other. "That's your name for real? You're not messing with us? Chance Guardian?" Her voice was hard-edged, amused.

His grin intact, he motioned as if taking off an imaginary hat and bowed to the women. "Chance Guardian, mucho gusto."

Amy pushed herself away from the truck with her boot, stepped over the dead man, her composure apparently regained in the time it took Chance to walk toward them. She lit a cigarette, inhaled, and as she exhaled, "All right then, *Chance Guardian.* What are you? An angel or something?"

Calliope smirked at her friend's sass, relieved Amy wasn't hurt.

"An angel? Afraid not, though that would be something. I'm A'shiwi, or as you Anglos might call us, Zuni. I'm also a grad student at the University of Texas in Dallas, a theoretical physics nerd."

A scientist. And Zuni. One of the Puebloan peoples of New Mexico, like Bisabuela. Like Calliope. Then they were twice connected. A strange déjà vu, a vision of herself standing with Bisabuela at Chaco Canyon during a windstorm, but Chance Guardian was there. He was holding a figurine in his hand, a small wooden object.

Amy broke Calliope's trance. "You don't look like any nerd I've ever met … with that rifle. You hunting elk? Or just assholes with knives?"

Calliope stared at Chance. When she noticed she'd never let go of his handshake, her neck and cheeks flushed. She pulled her hand away, wiped it on her T-shirt. "I'm Calliope Santiago. This is Amy Denver." Calliope nearly laughed aloud at the absurdity of the introductions, greeting each other politely as if society hadn't collapsed, as if they weren't standing over a rapist's corpse. "I grew up in Texas."

He smiled. "Where in Tejas, mujer?"

"El Paso."

"I've passed through it."

The twins kicked inside her.

"Have you seen anyone else?" Amy asked. "Which road are you coming from? My family's in Cruces. Did you go through there?"

He adjusted the gun sling and stuck his hands in his jeans pockets. "Nah." Chance didn't seem scared or confused, but uncomfortable. "The main roads are blocked, empty cars everywhere. Fort Worth was a disaster." He drew in a deep breath, let out a low whistle and shook his head. "I took the back roads, Abilene into Roswell."

Calliope's gut lurched again, more than babies kicking. The disaster wasn't contained to New Mexico? "Was there no one?"

"I haven't seen more than two or three people since I left the university, all of them like this guy, crazy."

"Or in shock," Calliope added, her pulse quickening. She felt ill.

"Why aren't we in shock? We should be the ones shocked," Amy said. She told Chance about the man at the gas station, who'd tried the same thing. "My clients treated me with more respect."

"Clients?"

"I'm a dancer," Amy said. "*Exotic.*" Calliope watched Chance's face, noted no change in his expression, no bemusement or judgment. With a shrug, Amy added, "On the side. I'm in college too." If his opinion changed one way or the other, he didn't let on, his face set at a polite neutrality.

Calliope smiled at Amy's exerted toughness, although she had a point. Why was her group *normal*, in whatever capacity anyone can be deemed normal, while other people, her dear Susana, were not? What differentiated them? Why were others irrational and violent, but Calliope and her companions immune? So far. Andres and Phoenix, at Tía's hacienda, which camp did they fall into? She couldn't imagine them singing *pío, pío, pío* in the dirt, hurting themselves or anyone else. She needed answers, and maybe Chance had some. "We're searching for our families," Calliope said. "Mine weren't home … after that … red flash." She hated saying it aloud.

"That small girl in the bushes too?" Chance asked. "She with you?"

"Eunjoo." Calliope had forgotten in the chaos. "Come out, chica. He's a friend." Warning bells inside her. She didn't know Chance. No better than she knew any of her traveling companions. How did she know he was a friend? Why had she let her guard down so easily?

Eunjoo crawled from the sagebrush, wiped the sand off her knees, and walked toward them. Before the girl got to the truck, Calliope realized *all was not right.* She couldn't let Eunjoo see a dead man in a pool of blood. She rushed to the edge of the road and scooped Eunjoo into her arms, turning her toward the desert hills instead, the reddening sky.

"Do we leave the dead guy?" Amy asked.

"It's not like there are police we can call. I haven't seen the cops anywhere, have you?" Chance asked. No one answered. He continued, "Are you headed to El Paso then? You and your daughter?" He nodded to Eunjoo. "To your husband?"

"She's not mine," Calliope said quickly, then felt a pang like she'd betrayed the girl. Eunjoo was her responsibility—until she found her parents. "She's my neighbor. We're searching for her family too. Not in El Paso though."

Chance's eyes narrowed, hard-baked lines etched into his skin, questioning. She turned away, twirled one of Eunjoo's shining black braids in her fingers. Amy had lit another cigarette, released the catch on the tailgate, and let her legs dangle while she smoked.

"I'll go with you," Chance said. "To keep you safe."

"We've been doing fine without you," Calliope said, her heart pounding.

"Yeah, Amy looked real fine on the ground."

Calliope put a hand over Eunjoo's ear, pressed the girl's head against her shoulder, and made a hushing sound toward Chance.

"What?" he asked. "You think she didn't hear the gunshot? Kids are smart."

Calliope looked to Amy for support, but Amy shrugged. "I say let the cowboy nerd come. That asshole could've killed me. It wouldn't hurt to have a hunter with us."

Eunjoo leaned closer to Calliope, whispered, "That's him."

"Who?"

"The man from my dream."

Calliope's stomach flipped. She stared at Eunjoo's round face, so earnest and solemn. She turned to Chance, who winked. "Have you met him before?"

Eunjoo shook her head.

Calliope sighed. "It was just a dream, chica. Someone who looked like him." She tugged one of the girl's braids playfully, and asked Chance, "Did you lose anyone?"

"I don't know. Phones aren't working, I can't call home. I was on my way to the rez before I ran into you ladies. Yet, I have a feeling my people are unscathed. We're survivors."

She thought of the recent water crisis of the Sioux people, the snaking oil pipeline broken in the Heart River. *Our people are survivors,* Bisabuela had told her, at the graveyard outside Old Mesilla, where her sons were buried. They'd fought wars for a country that wanted a wall built around them, to keep them *othered* always.

His people were unscathed. Where were her people? The hills in the distance glowed orange. Why were they glowing? She squinted, set Eunjoo down.

She was holding her belly and running before she knew what she was doing, the others calling after her. A flashing, strobe-like pulsing, and she rushed toward it, a cicada vibrating in her ears.

Andres had given her a flashlight their first Christmas together and she'd laughed. It had a Taser setting and a strobe light. She'd laughed that he would give her such a gift, and she'd turned on the strobe, pointed it toward the ceiling, and danced, mimicking a beatbox and techno sounds (something she was low-level famous for at talent shows as an undergrad). Pajama'd and messy-haired, she'd jumped onto a couch and danced. When she'd calmed down enough to explain, she told him that she'd thought the strobe was for signaling her distress if she was lost—a not uncommon occurrence—while hiking or out on a dig. Andres had corrected her, in the way of overprotective husbands and mansplainers worldwide (a phenomenon she was well aware of, as a female professor in academia): the strobe was to render attackers dizzy, off-balance, and generally unable to assault. *I'll still use it if I'm ever lost, so you'll know where to find me.* She'd pulled him into her dance, kissing him. *It'll be my signal for you, our secret code. Scientist lost at dance party, come find me.* She had no idea where the flashlight went. She'd never used it. But it was their signal ahead, she knew it, knew it had to be Andres. The air was wet against her face, though it shouldn't have been humid. She felt the bile rising in her throat, her stomach ached from exertion. She should not have been sprinting.

Chance caught her easily, grabbed her arm. Panting, he turned her to face him. "What on earth? Mujer, have you lost your mind?"

She tried pulling away, couldn't. Turned her face toward the light instead, breathing hard, clutching her stomach. "The strobe, do you see it?" He raised his eyebrows skeptically. She groaned, said, "I'm not crazy, just look."

He made an expression like he would only turn around and look to pacify her, and she rolled her eyes, but, still holding her, he turned in the direction she indicated. "What the ..."

"I told you. Now let me go."

"Fine, but I should go check it out, not you."

"You can't tell me what to do. I barely know you."

"In case you haven't realized, you're insanely pregnant."

Her cheeks burnt. It was the first time he'd shown any awareness of her pregnant belly. When he talked to her, before, he hadn't looked down the way everyone else did. He'd kept his attention on her face, her eyes, like she was more than just a pregnant woman.

She cleared her throat. "I'm going."

Amy and Eunjoo caught up, Eunjoo on Amy's back. "Going where?"

"Toward that strobe light," Calliope said.

"Why don't we take the truck?" Amy asked. "It goes off road. I'm not lugging this kid piggyback all the way out there." She scrunched her face toward the hills. "What is it anyway? Looks creepy. Why would we want to follow some creepy lights?"

"Could be a distress signal. Someone needs help."

"We're a rescue crew now? Apocalyptic crime fighters?"

"This isn't an apocalypse," Calliope said. That word came from the Greek *apokálypsis*, which originally meant the lifting of a veil or revelation. Calliope didn't think Amy meant that version but the kind with brain-eating zombies. Calliope felt a slithering, like larva in her stomach. Baby feet. Snake feet. "You'll scare Eunjoo."

"What do you call most of the population disappearing?"

"You don't know it's most."

"Like hell. Anyway, you're the one scaring her. Running off like an escaped mental case."

"We'll take the truck," Calliope said, turning back.

"Do I have any say in this?" Chance asked, following.

Amy and Calliope, in unison, "No."

TEN
THE TRANSMITTER

The strobe grew brighter. Calliope dizzied as she watched. They veered into the brambles and sage, the truck jolting over ruts and furrows in the desert hills. A domed shape loomed above an overgrown field, a large building with a serrated aluminum roof, hay bales stacked against the sides, a dirt road leading toward the closed garage doors of a crop duster hangar. A communications tower jutted toward the sky. Static crackled the air. Calliope swallowed a metallic taste in her mouth. Something smelled of blood, the copper of wet pennies.

The sky reddened. She imagined the clouds had turned into wounds, festering as if they might drain blood. She squeezed Eunjoo's hand, a small bright bloom of blood flowering through the bandage on her thumb. The girl's face had gone pale. Whether from exhaustion or fear or the coyote bite, Calliope wasn't sure. She breathed out heavily. A voice inside like cicada song in the late-summer grasses, growing louder, beckoning her. As the truck approached the yellow light that pulsed into the hills and swirling clouds of ash, the cicadas' buzzing in Calliope's ears grew louder. "It looks abandoned. Except for that light." The strobe seemed to bore a hole in the sky above the aluminum roof.

"You think the radio tower works?" Amy asked.

"Depends what you mean by *works*," Chance answered.

Amy stopped the truck in front of the hangar. Calliope told Eunjoo to stay in the car, something the girl must have been tired of hearing, because Eunjoo gave a pained expression, opened her mouth to say something, closed it again. "I'm sorry, chica. I'll be right back."

"It's not that," she said. "I saw something."

"When? Where?" Calliope looked out the girl's window. Nothing but fields, wild with tall yellow grasses and rocky hills in the distance. "Outside?"

Eunjoo shook her head, pressed her bandaged hand to her mouth.

"You can tell me."

"In my sleep."

"You had a nightmare? My boy gets those too. They're not real, understand? Just pictures in our minds. When Phoenix has nightmares, I tell him to turn the page—like a book. You're reading a scary page, that's all. Turn it. The next one will be happier, I promise." She patted Eunjoo's hand, moving it away from the girl's mouth. The bandage was red but not soaked. She'd check on it soon.

As she stepped onto the dirt runway, her ballet flats, leggings, and T-shirt insufficient protection against the cold wind, the clicking vibrations in her ears grew louder, more insistent. Then the rattling sound gave way to a voice—someone she recognized but couldn't place, a human voice through the insect-like static. "Please tell me I'm not the only one hearing that."

Amy shrugged, untied the faux leather jacket from around her waist and slung it over her inked shoulders. "I don't hear anything, besides the wind."

Chance put his palms to his ears, cupped them a few times, released. "You mean the cicadas? Or the voice?"

Calliope stared hard at him. He smiled into her quizzical expression.

"I hear it too, mujer," he whispered to Calliope, putting his index finger to his mouth as if they shared a secret. Her limbs tingled. She crossed her arms around her chest, the air damp and cold.

On the closed hangar door, a rusted padlock. Chance slammed the butt of his rifle into the lock, and it busted open, debris of rust flaking to the ground like red snow. He and Amy pulled the massive hangar doors, each grabbing a handle at the center and walking away from each other. It screeched against the track, opening into darkness, a cave-like space inside, chill and dank. A loud flapping sound when the door stopped moving. Calliope looked up. An orange canvas windsock shook violently.

"I'm not going in there," Amy said. "You two be my guests."

Calliope had to know where the light was coming from. She imagined Phoenix huddled in the corner of the darkness, and her throat tightened. But he couldn't be in there; it was locked from the outside. If he were inside, who would've locked him in? She shivered.

"Looks like a dead end, mujer. Right?" Still, a catch in Chance's voice spurred her curiosity, like the cicadas; he wasn't signaling defeat but challenging her.

She turned toward Amy. "Did we bring the flashlight from the car?"

"In that box from your trunk."

Calliope retrieved the light then strode into the hangar as if fearless. The flashlight beam caught threads of ash floating through the air. If the hangar were sealed, the ash couldn't have gotten inside. There must've been an opening somewhere else, another way in. Her heart beat faster. She called out, "Phoenix? Andres?"

Heat at her neck, a hand on her shoulder. "They your people?" Chance had followed her.

"Yes."

"Why would they be in here? They know how to fly planes?"

The light illuminated several small airplanes lining the walls, crop dusters, the kind of small planes Calliope imagined flew circles, performing acrobatics in the sky.

"No."

He stood so close to her she could feel his breath on her skin. She moved aside.

"Mujer, I couldn't say in front of your friend, but I think there's a reason you're here. What did the voice say to you?"

Calliope's stomach clenched, pulse quickened. She shone the light into his face. He wasn't smiling. Lines creased his forehead. "It was my bisabuela's voice," she said, without meaning to. "But that's in my head, in my memory. I carry her voice with me everywhere."

He reached out and redirected the flashlight beam away from his face and toward a back corner of the hangar. "She led you here. Not just to this shed. To this land."

"I live here. My bisabuela's people are from here."

"Exactly." Something in his voice sent a chill through her.

She wanted to ask what he meant, and why he couldn't say that in front of Amy, but her light shone upon a rounded shape ahead, and she stopped, frozen in place. The lump appeared covered in tattered blankets, like a vagrant. "Is that a person?" she whispered, her voice shaking.

"You know who that is," Chance said. "Look closer."

The figure hunched on the ground, back curved into a hump, feet curled beneath a blanket, a rebozo draped over head and shoulders. A woman. She held a pot in her hands, no, a bowl. A red clay bowl. Calliope was shaking violently now. She whispered, "But how? Am I dreaming? Hallucinating?" Chance held Calliope's arm, led her toward the woman on the floor. Louder, Calliope said, "What is this, Chance? What are you doing?" She pushed against his hand, stuck her feet in place. The flashlight wobbled.

When the woman looked up, Calliope was staring into her bisabuela's face. Wrinkled in old age, gray hair wisped from beneath the dark rebozo covering her head, her honey-brown eyes the same as they'd always been, flickering firelight-gold as she spun stories for Calliope. The earliest stories Calliope could remember, her first memories, had come from Bisabuela.

Mija, mi vida. Her voice, sandpaper and moth wings, fluttered inside Calliope, prickling her senses like chile verde on the comal, roasting on the fire. *No tengas miedo. Y no te preocupes. Está bien. Soy yo.*

Calliope sealed her eyes tightly. Breathed in deeply, out again. Opened her eyes. Her bisabuela was still on the ground, the taupe lines of her face roping together into a soft smile, her eyes glimmering. The rebozo wrapped around her, colorful flowers woven into its hem. Calliope recognized it from childhood. Bisabuela had draped it around Calliope on cold nights, told her stories more than bedtime tales but truths, she had said. *Just because something isn't written down doesn't mean it's not true.* Calliope had shivered beneath the rebozo, and Bisabuela had lit a fire in the round adobe fireplace, made her Mexican hot chocolate, crushed the spicy granules with a mortar and pestle, stirred the grainy powder into a pot of milk and sugar. Calliope had loved her more than anyone.

"We're dead then? I'm dead?" She turned to Chance, the bile burning her throat, tears stinging her eyes.

Her bisabuela's voice—*No, mija, no estás muerta. Estás perdida.*

"Lost? Lost souls? We're in purgatory? Bisabuela, I'm so scared."

Ven aquí, mija.

Chance unclasped Calliope's arm, and she stepped cautiously toward the woman, still not believing what she was seeing. She wiped her tears on her arm then kneeled in front of her great-grandmother. "Tell me what to do, Bisabuela. I have to find my boy. Andres y Mamá también. Are they here too? Are they dead too?"

You're not dead, Calliope, I've told you. Estás perdida, pero hay otro camino. Una luz.

"A light? Like that flash? What *was* that, Bisabuela? Did it take them?"

Ay, mi vida. Por eso estás aquí. Entiendes?

"No, I don't understand one damn thing since I crashed. I'm in a coma, right? I'm in a hospital hooked up to monitors, and this is all a delusion? A figment of my broken brain?"

Her bisabuela laughed, wry and deep. She lifted her hands, rawhide and dappled with age spots, the way they'd looked when Calliope had kissed them last, folded them back into the coffin, buried her to the earth.

Bisabuela held out the clay bowl to Calliope's face, motioned her to take it. *Bébelo, mija.*

Calliope looked into the bowl, reddish water. Clay water. "You're dead, Bisabuela. How can I be here with you if I'm not dead too?"

Your journey is unfinished, mija. And Spirit is never gone.

Calliope winced. Spirit is never gone. The words recalled Kennewick Man, a nine-thousand-year-old nearly complete skeleton found along the Columbia River. And the source of Calliope's falling out with her great-grandmother. For twenty years, tribes of the Northwest claimed he was the Ancient One, their ancestor. Scientists like Calliope had stolen him. Bisabuela was so angry, they had *stolen* him—for research. He was too important to science to be buried in the ground, his body could yield too many answers. But his journey was interrupted, tribal leaders had argued. He belonged to his people, and his people needed to send him back to the earth, allow his journey to continue, allow his Spirit to continue.

Calliope had sided with the scientists, had presented a paper theorizing possible waves of migration to the Americas because of Kennewick Man, whose head shape and bone carbon signaled an oceanic diet of marine mammals like seals found along the kelp highway—not the Columbia Plateau, where his bones were discovered. A forensic archaeologist at the Smithsonian who had "won" the right to study Kennewick Man argued that he was likely of the Ainu people—from coastal Asia, a maritime hunter-gatherer more like the Ancient Polynesians. If that were true, then modern American Indians had no claim to him. The newspapers declared Kennewick Man was finally "freed to release his secrets"—but Native peoples felt differently. Some "secrets" are meant only for the ground. *You let those white coats disrespect us,* Bisabuela had said. *Human remains are sacred, mija. They are not science experiments.* Calliope had devalued her people's emergence story. Had sided with the white coats. With white people. With those who claimed the Americas were "the last continent to be conquered." And Calliope had broken her bisabuela's heart. Had she been forgiven at last?

"What will happen if I drink this, Bisabuela?"

Encontrarás tu camino. You'll find a path.

"To Phoenix? Andres? Y Mamá? I need to find them, Bisabuela. I need to find my family. My living family, pues."

Bisabuela gestured for her to take the bowl, for her to drink the reddish water. The copper penny smell, this was where it had come from. Calliope closed her eyes and drank. The liquid was cold, tasted like river. Bisabuela cupped Calliope's face in her hands. *Eres muy fuerte, mija, mi corazón. You're much stronger than you believe. And you're not alone.*

"You mean him? Chance? How does he know you?"

Es una guía—he'll guide you. Confía en él.

Calliope glanced back to see if he'd heard, if he'd understood Calliope's vision or delusion or whatever it was. His hands were folded in front of him, as if in prayer. His face, solemn. He nodded at Calliope, and she nodded back. Then she turned to Bisabuela.

But she was gone.

The bowl remained in Calliope's hands, and she handed it to Chance. "Will you hold this? Prove to me it's a concrete thing, not my imagination."

Chance took the bowl, knocked it lightly with his knuckles, pressed his fingers into the opening, wiped the bottom. Lifted his fingers back up to show Calliope they were covered in clay-colored silt. "As real as you and me."

"That's what I'm afraid of." She took the bowl, trying to catch her breath, trying not to hyperventilate. How could any of this be happening? "She said I'd find a path. I've been taking too long, following wrong turns. I need to get to my tía's right away."

"Did she *say* to find your tía?"

Calliope stared into this face, hesitant. What was he getting at? "It's what she meant."

He raised his eyebrows then sighed deeply. "Fine. Where is your tía?"

"Silver City."

He cleared his throat, seemed to debate the location in his mind. After a moment, he said, "Bueno. That's where we'll go."

She looked at him closely. Why would he detour with her rather than returning to his own family in Zuni as quickly as possible?

He must've seen the skeptical look on her face because he said, "I'm your guide, right? Your bisabuela said so. And we know better than to disobey Bisabuela." He cracked a grin, and Calliope noticed he had a dimple in his left cheek. A little button on his face.

She lifted her hand to his chest, looked him in the eyes. "Thank you."

His smile unraveled a bit, got crooked, and his jaw tensed. Just a moment. Then he was smiling wide again. "De nada."

* * * *

"Oh my God, I thought you guys had died in there." Amy rushed over and hugged Calliope. "That weird light's gone. Did you turn it off?"

Chance was glancing toward the hills. He said, "In a way. It was, um, a kind of transmitter. An old message. Nothing new." He put his hands on his hips, staring intently at something in the distance Calliope couldn't see, but his posture had gone rigid.

"Something wrong?" Calliope asked.

Chance squatted to the ground, balanced on his haunches, pressed his palm to the dirt. "Something's coming." He stood, his face alert, his eyes darting, searching. "Get into the hangar." He moved toward the truck. "Amy, you too. I'll get the girl." When Calliope didn't move, he said, insistent and loud, "Hurry."

His voice was so urgent, so full of alarm, she didn't argue. She clutched Bisabuela's bowl and scurried into the hangar, Amy close behind her. In the aluminum threshold, she turned toward the truck to make sure Eunjoo was following. The wind had intensified, the orange windsock fluttering maniacally, until it broke off completely and blew away. The swirling in the clouds made wings of the sky, an angry bird searching for prey. Calliope replayed the Sleeping Sisters' reemergence—howling awake.

Chance unhooked Eunjoo from her booster seat, and the girl ran toward Calliope, who bent down and opened her arms. "Hurry, chica." The dust eddied around her, a miniature whirlwind. The girl tripped, fell flat on her stomach. "Eunjoo!" Calliope lurched forward to grab her, but Chance reached her first, carried her inside.

"Shut the door, hurry." He was panting, set the girl down, helped the women lug the screeching metal door shut, closing the accordion from both sides, joining the handles in the center of the door. They were enveloped in darkness. The ground vibrated. Calliope gripped the wall. Another Sleeping Sister awakening?

Amy screamed, "Earthquake." She dropped flat to the ground, kneeling as if in prayer, except Calliope heard what she was muttering under her breath, not prayer but obscenities.

Calliope reached for Eunjoo, huddled on the floor covering her head as when Calliope had found her cowering before the coyotes. Although her own stomach lurched, she held the girl and hummed in her ear a Spanish song Bisabuela had sung to her.

Chance was looking around the hangar wildly, tossing things toward the door. The earth kept trembling; the air seemed to have frozen, a jolt of high-pitched sound vibrating through nothingness, as if the air had been sucked away and all that was left was noise—

A strange pause, a void in the atmosphere. Calliope cleaved in two, her skin too tight for her body, nitrate-cold splintering her skin. She tried to keep humming to Eunjoo, tears running down both of their faces, but she couldn't. Nothing would come from her mouth, as if she too were a void. She was dying. She was suffocating. She could not breathe.

The flashlight dropped to the ground, pieces of ash forming at the base like dust motes. They clouded Calliope's eyes, they sparkled. She shut her eyes.

Just when she believed she could stand the splitting no longer and her ribs would cave in the absence of air, the shaking stopped, and she gasped. She gasped as deeply as she could, coughing, letting go of Eunjoo's hand and rubbing at her throat as if to restart blood flow. Breathe in. Breathe out.

Once she had enough air to set her vision straight, she grabbed Eunjoo's shoulders, shook her. Was the girl breathing? "Chica? Chica, answer me." Her body hung limply, her lips were bluish, her face pale in the low light. Her eyes fluttered. "Chica, goddammit, wake up." Amy had crawled over, hovered beside Calliope, watching. Calliope tilted the girl's head back, her head a rag doll's, her neck stiff.

Amy was whispering again, but this time it sounded more like a prayer: "Don't-die don't-die don't-die don't-die …"

Calliope pressed her fingers to Eunjoo's neck—did she feel a pulse? She couldn't tell.

She laid the girl flat on the ground, found the space between her breast bones, clasped her hands together, pressed, afraid she would break the girl's ribs, pressed but not too deep, pressed and counted, pressed and counted, pressed—

At fifteen she stopped, closed the girl's nostrils, breathed two puffs into her mouth.

Wake this child up. She moved to press again and Eunjoo opened her eyes and sputtered, gurgling. Calliope lifted the girl, turning her face to the side as she vomited watery bile.

Calliope rubbed Eunjoo's back as she vomited. When she finished, she wiped her mouth with her hand. "I feel flat."

Calliope smiled. "Me too, baby. Me too." She hugged the girl, wanting to say, *Thank you for not dying*, but she refrained.

"What *was* that?" Amy asked. "I've never felt an earthquake like that—it literally squeezed my brain together, like, my head was smooshed, my chest, my ass cheeks, everything."

Chance was still grabbing miscellanea from the hangar shelves, throwing objects at the door, barricade-style. If he'd been squashed too, he didn't let on.

"Hello, earth to cowboy," Amy said. "What are you even doing?" To Calliope, she hissed, "He's nuts."

Without pausing from his work, he said, "That wasn't the worst of it, believe me. It's not over. Help me bar the doors. We need to find something to seal it." Under his breath: "I shouldn't have busted the lock."

"Seal it? Like a coffin? Nuh-uh. I want off this crazy train." Amy stood.

Calliope agreed—she didn't want to be trapped in a freezing hangar where she'd seen her great-grandmother's ghost then been nearly asphyxiated by some mysterious force. The only thing she knew that could so radically change the air pressure for that extended time was a fuel-air explosive, a vacuum bomb. She turned to Chance. "Are we being attacked?"

"Not yet." He was climbing a shelf, throwing down gear. "Help me."

"Not until you explain what's going on."

"There's no time. Please. Just trust me. Get the girl away from the door. Hide her." His voice was desperate. "*Please.*"

Hide Eunjoo? Hide her where? Calliope shone the flashlight across the vast expanse of the hangar until the beam reached the row of airplanes against the wall. "Let's go, baby." She scrambled up, clutching Eunjoo in one hand, the bowl Bisabuela had given her in the other, then pulled Eunjoo across the room toward the planes. Amy followed, muttering, "This is insane. Maybe I should just fly us away." She sighed, then said, "Well, go on, get the girl in the cabin," though she sounded unconvinced.

Calliope opened the small, hatched door of the plane at the end of the row, toward the wall where she'd just conversed with her dead great-grandmother. The hatch popped open. She motioned for Eunjoo to climb in behind the seats. The girl crouched in the back. Calliope asked if she could breathe back there, still not sure why she was asking her to hide or from what. Eunjoo squeaked her answer, a chirp Calliope was fairly certain was *yes*. This poor child. Was Phoenix safe, wherever he was? She stood back from the plane. It was a puddle jumper, yellow and white. The name on the back, in black sprawling cursive: *Vixen*.

A rumbling at the roof—strong wind? Thunder? Calliope expected Amy to get in and hide, but instead she was circling to the front of the plane, touching the propeller, the needle nose, the top, over to the left side, touching the wings.

"Amy, what on earth are you doing?"

"Preflight inspection." She said this like it was the commonest, most obvious thing. *Duh.*

"I see that. I mean, *why?*"

"To make sure this sky pig can get us out of here. Fuel, oil, tires, control surfaces, hull integrity, and electrics." She continued pulling and prodding at different parts of the plane. "Is there a cup in there? I need to check the fuel."

"Check it for what?"

"Water."

Calliope looked around, not seeing a cup. Eunjoo reached from her crawlspace in the back, handed Calliope a clear, hard plastic cup. Calliope passed it to Amy.

"Thanks. I'm assuming no radio or GPS. Not sure how we'll navigate."

"So, you … have your pilot's license?"

"You need to see my license and registration, officer?"

Calliope looked hard into Amy's face, gauging whether or not she was serious. Had she learned all that from a video game? YouTube?

A pounding on the doors, a scratching metal sound. Was that Chance? He might be more forthcoming away from Amy and Eunjoo, as when they'd been alone in the hangar before, with Bisabuela. Calliope left Amy to her game of checking the plane.

Chance lugged a metal propeller, then jammed it into the door handles, although a wrench lay on the floor. Apparently, it wasn't large enough for him.

"Look, I appreciate all you've done. Killing that psycho. Talking to my bisabuela with me. Agreeing to help me find my family." He didn't look toward her or acknowledge that she'd said anything, but kept ramming the propeller into the handles, grunting with the effort. His forehead and neck were sweaty, his face scrunched with exertion. She leaned in and touched his arm, lowered her voice, conspiratorial. "Pero dime. Qué pasa?"

He shoved the propeller again, and it lodged horizontally between the handles.

"That might hold it," he panted, wiping his sleeve across his forehead. He looked at Calliope as if just noticing her presence, the lines in his face furrowed. "Vamos. Ándale." He pulled her arm, leading her back toward the plane.

She dragged her weight, shoving his arm away. "No. Come on, Chance. What's this for?"

"You won't believe me."

"Like I wouldn't have believed you could conjure my dead bisabuela?"

His eyes darted toward hers, his eyebrows raised. "I didn't *conjure* anything." He looked hurt. "Is that what you think? That I'm some kind of pinche magician? A charlatan?"

She didn't know what she thought.

"Please, just trust me. That thermobaric explosion? It wasn't a bomb. The things attacking? Not people. We need to hide."

His eyes searched hers, probing, *will you trust me?*

The back of her neck prickled, her face flushed. She followed after him.

A rumbling from the back of the hangar, vibrating off the aluminum walls, then a cranking sound. Amy had turned the plane on. Ahead, propellers whirred, like huge blades of a fan, blowing a shock of air toward Calliope and Chance.

They hurried toward the plane.

"What are you doing?" They yelled as one, over the roar of the engine.

"I can fly us to Cruces. It'll be faster. Hop in!" Amy yelled back.

"Turn that off. It'll hear us!" Chance screamed.

"What?"

The propeller blew gusts of air toward Calliope. Ash. Swirling pieces of ash like black confetti. They eddied around her face. She coughed. Her whole body went cold, as if the temperature had dropped twenty degrees. Her skin prickled with gooseflesh. A pounding at the doors again. But this wasn't Chance shoving a propeller into the door handles. He was standing next to her. The pounding was violent, like crashes of thunder, over and over.

"Too late," Chance yelled. "Get in, mujer."

Behind her, a cold breath. There had to be another way into the hangar. She'd thought it when she'd first arrived. How else had the ash gotten in?

"Chance?" she said, her voice wavering. "I think there's someone behind us."

He turned. Exclaimed in a language she didn't understand. Pushed her toward the open cabin door. Jumped in. Slammed it down behind them and fastened the bolt.

He was hovering over Calliope, nearly sitting on her lap in the cramped space.

"Drive!" he yelled at Amy.

"Drive where? You bolted the hangar doors."

"Just drive!"

Gamboling toward them, rabid, with a twisted limping gait that made its speed impossible—a massive painted body, pitch black except for white dappled spots pocking its face and ethereal white hair flowing loose at its sides. A masked creature. No, it wasn't a mask. Horror pitted Calliope's stomach, lodged in her throat. The creature was not painted or masked. Its eyes bulged and its teeth were long, protuberant, tusklike. Its romping, hop-like movements as it sped through the hangar were a mixture of a terrifying ritual dance and an animal charging, its arms raised as if swimming through the air. Calliope recognized this monster. It should have been carved of wood or stone. She'd held it before in her palm at the Old Town marketplace. It was a Kachina, a monstrous doll meant to depict an indigenous god whose name she did not know. Only now it was a grotesque giant, close enough to smell, like rotting fruit, sprinting toward her. It was a Kachina, come alive.

ELEVEN
EUNJOO

I t wasn't a nightmare.

The dreams hadn't started when Eunjoo asked the neighbor lady to help her.

No. Long before that.

Because of the dreams, she had known exactly where to go, whom to ask for help. When her parents had disappeared.

She'd played lots of times with Phoenix, sometimes in the wading pool in his backyard.

His mama was never home, Phoenix had said. She was always at work.

My parents are always fighting, Eunjoo had replied.

Over what?

There must have been a reason.

Eunjoo had shrugged.

They'd splashed cold water from the green hose at each other's faces. Pretended it was a spitting snake. A water snake. They had laughed.

Eunjoo had dreamt of Phoenix's mama often.

Lounging in the backyard, a sun hat over her curly hair, dark sunglasses over her suntanned face, and with a book in her hands, always with a book in her hands.

That was before her stomach had bulged. But Eunjoo had dreamt her fat with babies too.

When Phoenix had told her his mama was pregnant with twins, Eunjoo had nodded politely, but she'd already known.

The dreams had shown her that too.

From her little hole behind the seats in the yellow-and-white airplane, she knew what was coming.

She'd awoken sweating in the middle of the night in her own bedroom with cranes dipping from the ceiling. She'd awoken after running from a black-and-white creature with blotches on its face, a creature that would sometimes catch her, sweep her into its basket, take her back to the peach orchard at the bottom of the mesa. Sometimes it had eaten her whole, like a peach. Down to her pit.

Sometimes she had crept out of its basket while it was sleeping. Run back to Calliope.

It was always Phoenix's mama in those dreams, never her own mother.

Her own mother with straight black hair, smaller than Phoenix's mama, and quieter.

She'd thought the coyotes had come from her dreams. She was touching one to see if it was real. Or if she'd awoken in her own room again. She'd dreamt this so often. Coyote calling her.

Once, she had thrown peaches.

The biggest piece of fruit, she'd picked from the tree. It was golden orange and squishy. She pulled her arm back, aimed for the blotchy creature, and threw as hard as she could. The peach stuck in its eye.

In the plane, curled into a ball on a stack of maps, the new grown-ups yelling over the roaring of the plane's belly, she hoped.

She hoped and hoped. That this would be the dream in which she defeated the creature before it could eat her. Or anyone else.

TWELVE
THE SUUKE

re the stories real, Bisabuela?

The rebozo slung around Calliope's head, a veil. Her eyes wide with ghosts.

Sí, por supuesto. We knew of the Red Sea, mija. Acoma song talks about it. How would we have known that otherwise? Our Ancestors were right.

Calliope had nodded in earnest at her bisabuela's wisdom. Then she had grown up. She'd realized perhaps their Elders meant something like the *red tide*, algal blooms, not blood.

Bisabuela had died before the DNA results came back on Kennewick Man, before Calliope could tell Bisabuela she'd been right all along—of course she'd been right—the Ancient One belonged to their people, his genome closer to modern Native Americans than any other living population. But Bisabuela was not there, not with Calliope, to celebrate when the Ancient One was released to his rightful ancestors and repatriated back into the ground so his journey could continue uninterrupted. If a renowned Smithsonian white coat had been wrong, if they were all wrong about separate waves of migration, and if Bisabuela's people were all linked, like she said, then maybe she'd been right about the other stories. Why couldn't Calliope believe Bisabuela was *right* about emergence? That there was no land bridge. There was no coastal migration. Bisabuela believed the Ancient Ones came from the earth. And returned to the earth. Calliope was determined to find answers. To prove her earlier research wrong. To find evidence that would support Bisabuela's belief instead. She knew that wasn't how science worked; you didn't go looking for evidence of a long-drawn conclusion but rather let the evidence guide you. Still. She was searching for evidence of a different explanation. She owed Bisabuela. She'd come back to New Mexico to *find the truth*, whatever that meant.

But Calliope had *not* intended to find the truth quite so literally. Not careening toward her, this monstrous beast. Eight feet tall, it hurled its muscular, athletic body toward the plane. Chance yelled at Amy to drive, and she turned the plane toward the creature. Calliope resisted the urge to shut her eyes. Her throat constricted, her breathing came in labored puffs. From the cabin, she watched the monster launch itself into the air, a panther onto a cliff. A forceful thud, and they careened backward, the nose of the plane tipping at an angle. It was on the rudder.

Amy screamed, "What *is* that?"

Still she held the wheel steady, taxied forward, gaining speed. They would hit the hangar doors. Except, the hangar doors were no longer there. Dim light through the ash, a hole through the aluminum, the propeller Chance had jammed into the handles cast aside, crumpled like a soda can on a sidewalk. In its place, another creature. Identical to the one hitching a ride on the back of their puddle jumper. The other creature must have ripped off the hangar doors and was waiting for them in the hangar's gaping metal mouth.

Amy was screaming expletives, Chance still yelling his one-word mantra. *Drive!*

Could they gain enough momentum to outrun the second creature?

The wings juddered precariously. Calliope shut her eyes, refusing to face the creature balanced atop the plane, afraid it would break into the cabin at any second.

Checking the airspeed indicator, Amy screamed, "Let's do this, motherfuckers!" before pulling back on the wheel. Calliope's gut was a sloshing sea of nausea. They were lifting off the ground. Calliope clutched the sides of the plane, as Chance dipped forward, against her.

The second creature lunged at them, but they were already in the sky.

Calliope looked back. Nothing on the rudder. Like it had been a bad dream. Except they were flying into a red, swirling sky, lightning piercing in the distance. One nightmare into another.

"Eunjoo? Can you breathe back there, chica?"

The girl, muffled by the propellers, asked, "Did we get away from the monster?"

"You bet your ass we did," Amy said, steadying the plane, cranking a small wheel and pulling levers on the control panel that made whining and clicking noises. To Chance, "What *were* those things?"

"Suukes," Chance said, clearing his throat, adjusting his crouching position over Calliope. His knee jabbed her in the hip and he apologized, smiling sheepishly. "Perdóname, señora. I would stay a more respectful distance, if I could." His wavy black hair brushed against her shoulder, his thighs pressed against hers. She was acutely aware of how close they had all just come to dying. How close they still were.

Amy asked, "Humans? Or animals?"

Before he could answer, Calliope said, "Amy, how are you flying this plane?" Amy launched into a list of technical terms, but Calliope interrupted. "Not *how* as in give me a lesson, but how do *you* know *how?*"

"Flying lessons." Amy turned back to Calliope, beaming. "Told you I'd fly us outta there. Didn't know I'd have to fly us away from Sooks though."

"Suuke," Chance said. "From Kothluwala'wa."

"Whata what now?"

"The sacred lake."

"Oh, much clearer." Amy's voice dripped sarcasm.

Calliope was as confused as Amy, though she'd read about the myth. But right then, she only wanted to be safe on the ground. She trusted Amy, to an extent. But she'd feel much better racing toward Silver City, toward Andres and Phoenix, in a land vehicle.

Silver City. Calliope's heart dropped as if they were taking off again. "Amy?"

"Yeah?"

"Where are we going?"

"Las Cruces. Isn't that the plan?"

No, it wasn't the plan. Tension balled in her chest. "Amy, I *need* to get to my son. Need to hold him. It's been two days since he disappeared. My aunt's is my last hope. You wouldn't understand. You don't have children."

"Wow. That's low, momma."

Calliope cringed. Said nothing. She hated that her best hope of getting to her son rested on this young woman.

Amy sighed. "So you're changing the plan."

Calliope's stomach twisted, her heart raced. "I never planned to go to Cruces."

"You lied to me?"

"Can you get me to my son or not? I'm not taking a detour. If you won't go to Silver City, then land this damn thing and I'll steal another truck."

Silver City was hours from her family on a normal day, without inclement weather—which used to mean snow or windstorms. Now it meant volcanic eruptions, earthquakes that python-squeezed the lungs of grown adults and nearly killed children, pieces of painted rock coming to life and attacking … She couldn't handle anything else. Tears stung her eyes. "Please take me to my aunt's."

Chance reached for her hand, squeezed it reassuringly. He whispered, "We'll find your family, mujer. No te preocupes."

Calliope's lips tightened reflexively; she resisted the urge to roll her eyes. He probably meant well, but she didn't need her bisabuela's words shoved at her. She never should've stopped at that hangar. A sticky sensation, a cracked jar of jelly, settled in her stomach. She couldn't have seen her dead great grandmother. It must've been a delusion. Some trick he'd conjured, whether he'd admit it or not. She pulled her hand away from his.

Amy sighed loudly, exaggeratedly. "Oh-Em-Gee, fine. I'll take the pregnant lady to her kid. I'm not a monster." She clicked on the radio. Static. "Problem is, how do we get there? No GPS, no radio. No communications tower. We're gonna have to old-school this. I've always wanted to go all Amelia Earhart. Fly rogue over the black triangle. Anyone have a paper map? They still have those, right? If we can find a map, we should be able to do this. As long as there are no clouds."

From the crawlspace, a shuffling of papers. A little hand appeared, holding a stack of aeronautical charts. Calliope took the maps from Eunjoo. One was brown and tan, with degrees in angles across the bumpy mountainous terrain. White crosses marked Rattlesnake, Minersville, Aztec, Indian Services, and so on. Calliope had never heard of these places. She looked closer, then held up the map for Amy to see. "What are the areas inside the fuzzy purple lines?"

"I remember now. Yeah, I *did* learn this." Amy mumbled something Calliope couldn't make out, like she was reciting a list. "I think those are FAA controlled airspace. Doesn't matter to us now, I mean, if no one's there anyway."

"The harder purple and blue lines?"

"Military. We could see if there's any military around."

His jaw gritted, his face hard, Chance said, "There isn't."

Calliope felt a tingling sensation of apprehension, but didn't ask questions. She just wanted Amy to get them safely on the ground of her tía's hacienda.

"The compass-looking things on the radio?" Calliope asked.

"Beacons for compass headings. They connect the paths between airports. But we're not going to an airport ..."

"So, what are we looking for?"

Amy was silent for a minute. "What else do you see?"

"What we see from the air. Yellow areas the approximate shapes of towns and cities, blue for water, hard black lines for roads, and black lines with crosses for railroads ..."

"That's it," Amy said, whooping. "We'll follow the railroads through the mountain passes."

"And we're safe up here?"

"We're fine. Engines use a self-contained high-voltage generator to create a spark for the spark plugs. Each engine has two in case one fails. Even if we were struck by lightning and lost all power, the engines would still keep running."

"Don't say we'll get struck by lightning." It was Murphy's Law. Calliope had heard Richard Dawkins speak about how this so-called law was nonsense since it required inanimate objects to have desires of their own or else to react to one's own desires. Calliope had agreed at the time. Science had held such a sway—her inner skeptic at its pinnacle.

But now … had she really seen inanimate objects come to life? Those Kachina figures Chance had called Suukes had almost ripped their airplane apart when they should've fit inside her palm. It didn't make sense. The second law of thermodynamics: we tend toward entropy, toward chaos. Everything in our universe when left alone tended toward greater and greater disorder. Toward ruin.

"It's coming from the north. We're going south. I'm not as worried about the lightning as I am the ash. It could clog the engine's air filter, choke it. I'll fly low to avoid it."

Chance said, "I only hope the Achiyalatopa doesn't come too."

"What's that?"

"Its feathers are made of flint knives, which it throws at objects. My people never said it throws the knives at planes, but I don't know why it wouldn't."

Entropy. Anything that could go wrong, would. Anything that could turn to ruin.

The clouds that had formed a red bird above them began to disperse into feathery pink stripes across the sky, the storm moving on, though ash still darkened the distance. Calliope read the map aloud to Amy, navigating where to fly, following the railroad tracks. She was proud of herself, keeping her composure in the air. They passed Truth or Consequences, a town whose name Calliope had always found amusing. They passed Lake Valley. Thirty minutes in the sky without incident.

Then, "Fucking ash," Amy whispered. "Loss of manifold pressure?"

The map shook in Calliope's hands.

"What?"

"We're going down."

"You're kidding, right?"

Loudly, "Do I look like I'm fucking kidding?" Under her breath, Amy muttered, "Dead foot, dead engine," as she pushed her foot against the pedal.

Calliope's gut was dropping.

Still muttering to herself, Amy was chanting, "Feather the engine.

It'll stop windmilling. Feather the engine. It'll stop windmilling. Fuck. Fuck." To Calliope, "Where can we land?"

Calliope wanted to answer *we're not landing until we get to Phoenix*. The chart in her hands went blurry, the black crosses marking railroads turning to sutures, like those sewn across Calliope's belly when Phoenix had cesareaned out of her. Nauseous, she narrowed her eyes at the map, trying to concentrate on finding a landing place, seeing nothing but wavy slashes.

"I just need a field, momma, come on. I can't see beneath the ash."

In answer, Calliope turned away from Chance, leaned toward the small cabin space beside her seat, and vomited a clear liquid across the floor.

"There's a clearing at the City of Rocks," Chance said. "It's a state park."

"I don't need a tour guide, I need directions."

Chance took the map from Calliope's hands, whispered to her, "We'll be alright, mujer." To Amy, "We should be right over it. There's a spur of road to the southeast of the rocks."

While Chance leaned closer to the pilot's seat giving Amy directions, Calliope unbuckled, turned around. Her stomach still ached and her body was shaking. But the girl should have been the one buckled, not her. "Eunjoo, crawl up here, chica. Hurry." Her little braided head appeared, from a crawlspace covered with maps. Calliope scooped the featherlight girl over the mess she had made on the floor. She buckled Eunjoo in her seat, haunching beside her the way Chance had been hovering the whole ride. She squeezed the girl's hand tightly, more for herself than Eunjoo, who didn't seem terrified at all. Whenever Calliope had flown, most children's composure had reassured her—happily chatting to their parents about the clouds, coloring or laughing above the turbulence. If children were calm, she should have been too. Or maybe they just didn't understand the danger they were in.

Eunjoo squeezed back, leaned toward Calliope's ear, whispered, "This isn't the end of the dream, Phoenix's mama. Don't worry. We haven't thrown the peach at the creature's eye, we haven't found the pit." Calliope feigned a smile, reassured in the way of childhood hope and imagination. But Eunjoo continued, solemnly, "We still have to find the path."

Calliope snapped her head toward Eunjoo's face, looked sternly at the girl. Had she heard what Bisabuela had told her? About a path, una camina? Bisabuela had said Calliope was lost, but there was a path, a light.

The plane jerked violently, Amy yelling expletives as they dipped. Calliope forced herself to keep her eyes open. They were descending but not falling. An open field of withered yellow grass swayed into view, alongside a long strip of empty dirt road. Amy chanted as she pulled the wheel, steadied it, turned it toward the road, "I got this."

Calliope wrapped her arms as far as she could around the seat, holding on for balance. Her legs and back ached from hunching, but she held tightly as they dipped again, bumping toward the dirt. Several skittering thuds as the wheels touched ground, knocking Calliope against the cabin wall, her head hitting thick glass. A loud screeching and backward force of momentum, and they stopped moving.

"Hell yes," Amy called out. "*That's* how you land a goddamn plane!"

THIRTEEN
INTRUDER

The Native American woman introduced herself as Dr. Yolanda Toya, then took Mara begrudgingly downstairs to the hospital basement where they kept the laundry to show her that, truly, believe her, there was no one hiding in the hospital, and she did not know where everyone had gone, least of all Trudy and her son.

Amidst the smell of bleach and starched white hospital-thick sheets, Mara felt empty.

"I'm going down to Acoma to check on my people," Dr. Toya said. "I've lost someone here too. I suggest you go find your people, make sure they're safe."

"I don't have anyone but Trudy."

Dr. Toya unlatched the beaded cross at her neck, removed her necklace. In the center was a stone pendant.

"Take this," she said briskly. "No one should be without their people."

"How will a necklace help?"

Dr. Toya sighed. "It's not the necklace but what it represents. The stone inside." She extended her hand, nudging Mara to take the necklace. When she did, Dr. Toya said, "If you can't find your people, come find me in Acoma. You know it?"

"Sky City."

"Yes."

Dr. Toya patted Mara's hand, and again Mara was reminded of Chaiwa. She knew it was stupid but she asked, "Do you know about Lizard's Tail?"

The doctor narrowed her obsidian-black eyes, squint lines creasing her sunbaked skin, examining Mara closely. "You're of the earth, aren't you?"

Mara thought about it a moment, nodded.

Dr. Toya pushed her long black hair back from her shoulders, turned to leave.

Before she walked away, leaving Mara with the beaded stone necklace amidst a hallway of clean sheets, she said, "Remember, if you can't find your people, come find mine."

Mara couldn't ponder long on Dr. Toya's cryptic message, though she put the necklace around her neck, tucked it into her flannel shirt.

When she returned to the ranch and pulled up to Loren's little house on the back lot, she gagged at what she saw, vomited on Loren's dirt driveway.

In his rocking chair facing the now dark sky where they'd watched the sunset hours before, Loren's mangled and bloodied body.

She ran back to her truck, seizing her rifle from the back seat.

FOURTEEN
MYTH VERSUS PARABLE

The City of Rocks State Park was a labyrinth of giants, families of tall rocks huddling together in formation, as if fending off an attack or staunching the rain or protecting some rock god within their circular bodies. Calliope marveled at the unusual group of rounded volcanic boulders, surrounded by flat, dying prairie. These rolling desert plains were not an obvious place to find unusual, eroded rock formations, but a half-mile expanse of large volcanic columns loomed ahead, some at least forty feet tall. One encampment of rocks, if she'd seen it isolated in a photograph, she would have sworn were human-constructed, human-placed—they so clearly resembled the wonder of Stonehenge, that most famous megalith among other ancient stone circles. Why hadn't she ever camped here before? It was stunning, these mossy-backed giants huddling around firepits, picnic benches, sharing the secrets of the land they guarded. She could almost hear them whispering against the fierce winds.

Calliope strode closer, spellbound, Eunjoo at her side, holding her hand. Sparse vegetation grew around the boulders, an occasional oak or emory between the rocks, bare, sandy chambers or narrow, slot-like passages. In one passage of the campsite, a blue canvas tent. Calliope looked inside. Sleeping bag, backpack, flashlight, boots. All the accoutrements of life. But no one living.

The rocks themselves were light brown to pink in color, many covered by lichen and eroded into surreal shapes remarkably like statues, intentional, like people. Calliope reached out with her free hand to feel the rock, half expecting it to be warm with breath, shuddering at what they'd witnessed in the hangar—those Kachina creatures. But these rocks were cold. Calliope could tell they were the result of wind and water erosion of compacted tuff, formed by the eruption of some nearby volcano millions of years ago. Not human-formed. There must have been a caldera nearby, a large cauldron-like depression in the earth, along with other volcanic residues. She glanced away from the stone encampment, into the distance. Dark mountain ranges past the valley—the Gilas. She'd cut through them at the end of last winter to see her tía. She'd thought the snow was over then, but the roads had been slippery with black ice.

They weren't far from Silver City. She looked toward the sky; though the red bird swirling from the ash was gone, the clouds behind the Gilas were dark with rainstorm. Thunder padded in the distance, heavy streaks connecting sky and mountaintops that meant it was raining there already. The lightning they'd avoided in the plane was drawing nearer. "We should get moving again," she called to Chance and Amy. "Chance, where's the map? I don't think we're far from my tía's hacienda."

He came toward her, the aviation chart folded in his hand. "Your head hurt, mujer? I saw you smack it against the window in our rough landing."

Calliope's face burned. He'd also seen her vomit and freeze when they'd needed her to be strong. He didn't seem to notice. Instead, he reached out, placed his hand above her forehead, smoothed her hair at her widow's peak.

"You have a bump?"

She resisted the urge to rest her check against his palm, to let him cradle her head in his hands. She pulled away, brushed her curls back over the place he'd just touched. "I'm fine."

He cleared his throat, stepped back, curtly. "Good." He handed her the map.

Calliope let go of Eunjoo's hand and unfolded the map as the girl followed Amy to the campsite. A minute later Amy called out, her voice cavernous, muffled, "Hey, I found a tent. One of those two-family, double-wides, the fancy kind they sell at REI and shit. I'll bet there's food." Calliope smiled in spite of herself. She was growing fond of Amy. She'd landed them safely. There was much more to her than a college kid who danced, Calliope could tell. She made her way toward the camp, where Amy emerged with a bottle of Pepsi.

Calliope asked, "Amy, how'd you know how to fly a plane?" Amy rolled her eyes, opened the bottle and drank a large gulp, and Calliope guessed Amy would answer with her usual snark, so she added, "*Why* did you take flying lessons, I mean."

Amy held the bottle against her chest, fingered the metal buttons on her faux leather jacket, and said, as if it pained her, "I'm a smart girl. Dirt poor, seen only for my body, but mostly, I'm smart. I got into this engineering charter high school, SAMS, you heard of it?"

Calliope shook her head.

"Southwest Aeronautics, Mathematics, and Science Academy. It's a flight school too. I earned my pilot's license when I graduated."

"Why didn't you go to an engineering college? MIT? Stanford?"

A flush of shame crossed Amy's face, briefly, then dissipated into defiance, a fiery streak in her eyes. "I followed a guy to art school."

Calliope understood regret well enough to recognize its mask. "A Renaissance woman."

Amy raised her eyebrows, in a show of toughness or apathy. Then she shrugged and said, "Are we done with the fifth degree? Am I dismissed?" before turning on her heels and marching toward the fancy REI double-wide.

As she disappeared inside the mesh flap, Calliope called after her, "Hey, grab me a soda too."

While Amy and Eunjoo dug through the tent, Calliope studied the map. Chance had climbed atop one of the boulders and was looking toward the Gilas.

As she'd thought, they were less than an hour from Silver City. They could take Highway 61 to the 180 and be there in forty minutes. She almost laughed aloud. She imagined the look on Phoenix's face when she stepped through the door of Tía's house, the same as when she'd come home from an out-of-town conference. He would be sitting in front of the fireplace, drinking hot cocoa, listening to Tía's stories, but he would jump when he saw her, spilling chocolate on the floor. Andres would be there. And her mother. They wouldn't believe what she'd been through—how she'd finally turned into the Indiana Jones she'd always wanted to be.

She called out, "Let's grab some food and go. We're almost there."

"How many miles?" Chance asked from his perch on the boulder above her.

She checked the map again, using the space of her finger and thumb in an open pinch to mark the miles of highway between her and Phoenix. "Only thirty-five if we take the 61 to the 180. It's a little farther south before it shoots northwest, but it's the quickest route."

He sighed loudly. "And if we walk there instead?"

She didn't laugh at his dumb joke. "Why would we walk?" She followed his gaze past the rock city. Yellow grass and shrubs as far as she could see. A small cabin-like structure in the distance, probably a visitor center. Dirt roads. A lake. Hills in the farther distance and the mountain range, inky black behind everything else. Her stomach dropped. What didn't she see?

Cars. There were *no* cars. How long did it take to walk thirty-five miles?

A drizzle of rain. She pulled her arms around her body, wiping the water from her skin. "We'll take the plane," she said, defiantly, her eyes stinging against the drizzle.

Amy called from the tent, "I'm not flying that air pig again, momma. In fact, no one is."

"I don't mean fly. We could drive it, right? It'll drive across the dirt, at least until we find a car."

Amy emerged from the tent's mesh doorway, holding an open bag of Chili Cheese Fritos, chomping away. "No, lady. It's a miracle we made it down. I'm talking Jesus Christ Superstar, full-on, put-us-in-the-Bible miracle. We were out of fuel. I didn't say anything 'cause of … you know … you were throwing up and stuff …" She shoved a few more chips in her mouth. "But yeah, I have no idea why we're not all dead." She paused a moment, then added, "Maybe we are dead. Do the dead like Fritos?" She tipped the open bag toward Calliope. The fake chili smelled chemically repugnant. Nausea uncoiled. Calliope turned away from the chips, face scrunched, shaking her head *no*, unable even to feign politeness.

Chance scaled back down the rock, jumped catlike onto the ground beside Calliope.

"Don't despair, mujer. I said I'd take you to your family, and I will."

She bristled. He and Amy kept belittling her, insulting her with their diminutives. He kept calling her *mujer*. She *wasn't* his woman. She wasn't *anyone's* woman—especially not his. She was her own. And she was going home. "Then let's go," she said. "Let's walk to the highway. We'll follow it until we find a car. The roads were stockpiled with cars up in Albuquerque, and you said the same of Texas. Why should it be different down here? Come on."

She turned northwest, began to walk.

No one else moved.

She turned back to face them.

"What's going on? Let's go." She yelled out for Eunjoo in the tent the way she would've called Phoenix running late for school. "Vámonos."

Eunjoo appeared in the mesh doorway holding a juice box and an apple. Rain pebbled the nylon tent. Amy moved back, stood beside Eunjoo in the mesh doorway, holding her chips. Calliope looked to Amy for help, but Amy shifted her gaze to her feet, swept dirt from the tent with her boots. Fine, let the white girl stay. Calliope was going home. "Let's *go*," she called again to Eunjoo, reaching her hand out for the girl's.

"I'm hungry," Eunjoo said.

"You can eat while we walk."

Chance sighed. "Mujer, you're not thinking rationally."

"Stop calling me *mujer*. And stop treating me like your damn wife. I'm a professor, I have a PhD. Don't tell me I'm not thinking *rationally*." Her face was sweltering, although the rest of her body was already numb in the cold.

His voice calm, unwavering, "I understand, I do. But we're not going anywhere tonight. It wouldn't be smart, or safe, to walk in this rain, in the dark. Not that far."

Tears were streaming down her cheeks, so she couldn't tell her tears from the rain on her chest. She turned away from them again, northwest. Before her family had been south of her—now she'd overreached, she'd passed them, she was on the wrong side, still lost, still alone.

She wasn't being fair. These people had agreed to follow her, postponing their own journeys. They were here, in the City of Rocks, for her. She choked back the lump in her throat, wiped her tears away, turned, and, without looking at anyone, hurried past Eunjoo and Amy into the warmth of the tent.

Amy was not lying about how fancy it was inside—and spacious, with three separate rooms divided by mesh and zippered doors, the first with folding chairs, the last with sleeping bags, and the middle like a kitchen with bags of dry food and an ice chest still cool with ice packs. How long had its owners been gone, and why hadn't they taken their expensive gear with them? Would they return? Calliope felt a bit like Goldilocks as she took an Arizona iced tea in a glass bottle from the ice chest, popped open the top, gulped it down. She hadn't realized how thirsty she'd been, how exhausted. She wanted to apologize to her friends, who were talking quietly in the lawn-chair room of the tent. Instead, she finished her iced tea in the makeshift kitchen and returned to the bedroom where she unrolled a sleeping bag and curled herself inside. She took Susana's gun from the pouch of her leggings, placed it on the ground beside a flashlight she presumed belonged to the camper whose tent they were occupying, and for the first time in two days, since she'd awoken from her blackout on the bridge, since her whole family had disappeared, she fell hard asleep.

* * * *

The rain pelted the tent in a continuous stream like static on a radio.

She dreamt of the Suuke. His body was spotted white, with two snakes painted on his chest. On his feet were blue-and-orange dance moccasins; on his right calf, tortoise shells and antelope hooves rattling. He carried a large knife, sweeping the hair from his mask with it. He also carried a bow and arrows and bloody eagle feathers.

An old woman in buckskin leggings and a dress made of rabbit skins, her arms and shoulders bare, carried Eunjoo away from the Suuke. In her hair was an eagle feather dyed red. On her back was a large woven basket, cornucopia-shaped and filled with twigs. She too carried eagle feathers and a crook. Calliope wanted to come closer, to see if Eunjoo was asleep. Or dead.

She awoke. It had been nagging at her, only she hadn't realized it until she'd dreamt it. How had the girl known there was a monster chasing them from her crouching place in the back of the airplane? She'd asked, *did we get away from the monster?* The only windows were the cabin and the front, but the Suuke was behind them. Was there a spy hole? Had she heard it somehow?

Calliope squinted in the dark. The rain had stopped, the static gone.

She groped around the tent floor for the flashlight, turned it on. Eunjoo's shiny black braids emerged from the top of the sleeping bag beside Calliope's. Amy snored rhythmically, a doleful percussion, from the bag opposite the girl, her black boots and clothes laid between her bag and the tent wall. For a brief moment Calliope wondered if Amy was sleeping nude. Then she noticed an open suitcase at Amy's feet. Clean clothes. Calliope must have smelled like a garbage compost. The whole sleeping compartment smelled of damp onions. She peeled herself from her bag and crept around the girl, quietly rustling through the contents, shining the light on the tags to check for sizes. Amy was much smaller than Calliope—what size were these campers? Child-sized clothes tucked to side of the suitcase, then a man's and a woman's. A family. The woman wore a medium, which would have fit under normal circumstances, but with her belly … She opted instead for the man's gray sweatpants, rolled over at her hips, and a white thermal undershirt, long enough to cover her protruding midsection. Deodorant. She applied it profligately under her arms, her breasts, and in between her thighs. If she couldn't wash, she could mask. She also found thick socks and a pair of women's hiking boots that should have been too large but fit her swollen feet in wool socks. She finally felt appropriately dressed to wander the chilling desert.

She went in search of water. And Chance. Where was he sleeping?

The next two compartments were empty, but the crackling of burning wood filtered through the tent's zippered flap. She unzipped charily and peeked out into the cold night air. From a lawn chair in the mud, Chance hunched toward the firepit, poking at embers with a stick.

"How'd you start a fire with rain-wet wood?" Calliope asked, only her face unzipped and visible, her nose already getting cold.

Wide grin lines dimpled Chance's face, though he didn't look up toward Calliope but stared ahead at the fire. "Mujer, arisen from the dead." He continued prodding the wood, a shadow replacing the smile across his face, his eyes glowing more serious than playful. "Perdóname, Calliope. I'm not supposed to call you that anymore." She nodded, swallowing back the metallic taste in her throat, and unzipped the flap the rest of the way, stepped her newly booted feet onto the mud. Chance stood, motioned for her to sit on the chair, but she continued standing. He said, "I would tell you the dry wood is magic, but you've already accused me of sorcery. I don't want you thinking I'm anything but a humble physicist. There was wood in the tent."

"Do you have any way of telling what time it is?"

He shrugged, but said, "Look up," motioning with his eyes.

She craned her neck toward the sky, breathing in sharply. She had never seen so many stars in her life. The clouds and ash that had menaced the sky since the flash had disappeared. It was impossible, she knew, but there it was. The Milky Way they were part of, luminous in purplish gold, banding a quilt of bright lights. She breathed out slowly, "No light pollution."

"The way we were meant to see the night. A'shiwi call it the Great Snowdrift of the Skies."

"It's beautiful." She gazed in silence a few moments before she was troubled again. "How could the ash clear so quickly? It should hover in the atmosphere for weeks, months even ... why else did it get so cold?"

"I'd say everything is breaking the laws of physics—but I sense that would be untrue. Everything is expanding. Showing its deepest self."

They stared quietly at the sky. She reclined in the lawn chair, kicked her feet to the firepit, scraping the mud from the soles of her boots. "Where did everyone *go?* I don't believe in Revelation, in rapture. People don't just disappear."

"The white man's bible is only one end-of-the-world myth."

She was silent for a moment, watching the fire as nearly all of humanity had watched before. "How have you done it? Reconciled your people's beliefs with your scientific knowledge?"

"There's not really a chasm, they're part of the same story."

"Max Planck said science can't solve nature's final mystery, since we're a part of that mystery, in the end."

"Our ancestors tracked these stars, all the celestial bodies, from these lands."

She thought back to her first astronomy lesson, atop the mesa. "Bisabuela took me to Chaco Canyon and showed me the sun dagger. Without meaning to, she got me started on the path toward anthropology, toward science and evolution. No one knew what made the ancestors leave. They built these elaborate buildings in the middle of nowhere and then abandoned them. I had to understand why."

"We don't believe they ever left. Their spirits still inhabit the places they created."

"Bisabuela said that."

"She's a wise woman."

"Chance, how could she be here? And the Suuke?"

"Do you want parable or myth?"

"I want the truth."

"Then parable."

Calliope laughed, exasperated. "How is that *truth*?"

"Listen … didn't your bisabuela tell you your origin story?"

She nodded, recited the story she'd learned as a child. "In Shipapu, the first two girls were born. The spirit Tsichtinako spoke to them, fed them, but wouldn't show itself to them. They lived in the dark a long time. Then they were given baskets of seeds, which they planted, and the fastest-growing tree broke into light. The sisters followed the light, climbed above, greeted the four directions and the sun." She sang, quietly, "*Already a long time ago from the underworld, southward they came with cloud, with fog, carrying useful things,*" then stopped singing, whispered, "and their eyes hurt in the new light."

She was shaking with cold. Cupped her hands toward the fire.

"Sounds familiar, doesn't it?"

"Are you saying we're *in* a myth? The myths are *real?*"

"No." He prodded the fire with his boot. Sparks rose. "I'm saying they're not myths."

A swilling in her gut. She scanned his face for a hint of a smile, the trickster she worried he might turn out to be. He was holding her gaze, stony and sober. She shivered. Her voice small, she asked, "Will we find them? My family …"

He sighed. "I don't think they're dead if that's what you're asking."

She nodded, for that was exactly what she was asking.

"I'll help you look for them. I promised you that already."

Because tears were stinging her eyes and she didn't want to cry in front of him again, she stood, wrapped her arms around her chest, took a deep breath. "I'm assuming we're not leaving until sunrise? Whenever that is."

"It's not safe otherwise."

"Then I'm going back to sleep. These babies sap my energy." She walked toward the tent, paused, turned to Chance, who had already settled back into the lawn chair, his rifle still slung over his shoulder. He was looking up at the stars. "Shouldn't you get some sleep?"

"Me? Nah. I'm fine. I slept in Tejas." He winked, and she laughed. "I'll keep watch."

She stepped into the tent, not asking what he'd keep watching *for.*

FIFTEEN
SILVER CITY

Bombs flying overhead. Cylinders popping. Propellers whirring. Calliope awoke to cacophony as alarm, Chance yelling in a language she didn't understand. Chance yelling anything wasn't a good sign. Eunjoo was sitting upright in bed, eyes wide with fear. Amy's bag was empty. Her boots and clothes were gone. Calliope knew better this time than to leave Eunjoo alone. She reached for Susana's gun that she'd left beside her sleeping bag on the ground, but it was gone. She pulled on the hiking boots then scooped up the girl and hurried to the zippered mouth of the tent. Chance was waving his arms in the air, calling out. In the sky toward the southeast, flying away from their destination, a yellow-and-white stripe moving away from them. Calliope couldn't see the writing, but she didn't need to; she knew it said *Vixen*. "Mentirosa!" Calliope yelled. "That lying snake. I knew it wasn't *out of gas!*"

"Where's she going?" Eunjoo asked.

"Cruces," Calliope spat, unable to take the bitterness from her voice. To Chance she demanded, "Did she say anything?"

His expression sheepish, he said, "I dozed, didn't realize she was splitting until takeoff."

If there was a deus ex machina in this apocalypse, it needed to come now.

Calliope felt betrayed. But why? She hadn't known Amy. They weren't friends. Naturally, she would've put her family above Calliope's. Why shouldn't she have? Every woman for herself.

Still. Calliope felt deflated—heavy with rocks.

After several minutes of cursing Amy in Spanish and pacing the campsite, wringing her cold hands, Calliope finally took a deep breath, turned to Chance and said, "What happened to the cars? The campers' cars. They wouldn't be in the middle of nowhere without some way of getting here."

Worry lines formed across his forehead. "I didn't want to scare you, but come over here. I have to show you something."

Holding Eunjoo's hand, Calliope followed him past the yellow grass, past the empty visitor center, past a dirt road, to a small lake.

It wasn't much of a lake. More of a pond, really. Sludged with blackish water. Protruding from the center like a bulging belly or makeshift island, the round red hood of a car.

"Are the campers inside?" she asked, horrified at the thought she'd brought Eunjoo to a slaughter scene, picturing a whole family submerged and pickling in the oily water.

He raised his eyebrows and took a deep breath but didn't answer her.

"How long have you known this was here?" she asked.

"Since yesterday, when I climbed that rock to assess our bearings."

"Why didn't you say anything?"

"I told you. Didn't want to scare you."

"What should we do?"

"Not like we can call the police."

"But shouldn't we check? See if anyone's inside?" Calliope resisted the urge to cover Eunjoo's ears with her palms. She'd already heard their conversation, witnessed the drowned car. The damage already done, Calliope couldn't keep shielding the girl from this nightmare. Eunjoo was as entangled as the rest of them.

Chance motioned Calliope and Eunjoo out of his way. He would wade into the oily mudpond. He took off his boots, then stripped down to his boxers.

Around Chance's neck, a turquoise stone on a silver chain. He must've worn it under his flannel; she hadn't noticed it before.

He slogged into the water, and Calliope debated telling him to forget it, the water was so disgustingly black. Nor was she prepared to see the camper family's corpses—she'd envisioned them off hiking, although she and Eunjoo were wearing their clothes.

But they needed to know. Had the campers driven into the pond trying to escape something? Like Suuke? It had rained, but enough to cover the car? There were no tracks in the dirt around the water. As usual, Calliope was at a loss for explanations, which would have exasperated her at the best of times. She had built her whole life around a need for answers.

Chance jimmied open the driver's-side door, took a deep breath, and ducked his head into the murkiness.

Calliope waited on edge for Chance to resurface with a corpse, but he arose alone, spitting and wiping his eyes. "Empty."

She sighed, unsure if she was relieved or frustrated. Either way, they were stranded.

Still, Chance kept his promise. He reclothed, drying off in the campers' tent and filling backpacks with food and liquids, and they left midmorning. There was no way to tell time but by the sun. Amy had flown away at daybreak. Eunjoo, Chance, and Calliope walked in the opposite direction, following the map Calliope had taken from the plane the night before, thankful for one small fortune amidst the crisis Amy had left them in. A map was a light in darkness.

Calliope expected to find cars beyond the curve of highway stretching away from the City of Rocks. She didn't expect to find the highway like this—

As she, Chance, and Eunjoo finally emerged from the scrub oak and brush and stepped onto the tarmac, the road unraveled onward, miles ahead, rutted with gnarled roots shooting through the broken slabs of asphalt and branching into the sky, pushing through cars, twisting through the metal. A forest had sprung up—when? Arizona ash, quaking aspen, bur oak piercing into the air, full-grown, covered in leaves. A highway sign slanted diagonally, away from a tree trunk growing from the place the sign had melded into black tar.

"What the hell?" Chance wrenched open a car door partway unhinged to begin with. A stout gray-brown trunk and broad crown of serpentine branches mangled through the floorboard.

The only scattered cars as far as Calliope could see were maimed by trees. Calliope asked the obvious. "How is there a *forest* growing out of this highway?" She looked at the map. "We're on the 180, right?"

Chance nodded.

"There should *not* be a forest, not according to this. The closest forest should be in Mimbres Park." She used her pinched finger and thumb as a ruler. "Fifty miles northeast."

Chance put his hands to his face, closed his eyes, breathed in, rubbing his hands as if clearing his eyes of what they were seeing, opened them and said, "I think we'd better keep walking. Find a usable car. Get you to your family." He pulled her close, Eunjoo with her. "Then I need to get back to the rez."

"What's on the rez?"

"Answers."

They veered around the smashed-car trees and continued walking.

For miles and miles, the road was a forest of accidents, the cars demolished from the sudden growth. She saw it. But she didn't believe it.

Chance kept looking toward the hills, the Gilas in the distance.

"What are you looking for?" Calliope asked. "More Kachinas?"

Chance laughed ironically, a note of bitterness. "Anglos call them Kachinas but that's not a Zuni word. We call them *ko'ko*. The ko'ko are our ancestors." He turned away from the hills, stopped for a moment and looked at Calliope. "But yes, I'm looking for more. I don't know how many ko'ko are out there, if there are others, in matter form, you know, instead of spirit."

"There are *two* Suuke," Eunjoo squeaked, walking steadily a few paces ahead.

Chance chuckled, quizzically. "That's right, little bird. How do you know the Zuni tale?"

Eunjoo shrugged, still not looking back.

To Calliope, Chance said, "It's a tale meant to scare children. Boys who don't help their fathers with the animals, or girls who don't help their mothers with the babies. They could get carried off by the Suuke to Kothluwala'wa—

the mesas where they were once exiled—and eaten. If they've come from the tale, there should be two Suuke, husband and wife."

Calliope's face scrunched, her lips puckered as if he'd said something sour. "*Come from the tale?* Chance, we're scientists. There has to be some logical explanation." She clung to skepticism, couldn't trust her experiential knowledge. Not when this experience didn't make any sense.

"Logical or no, I'll keep you safe."

She bristled at his paternal tone, gripped the straps of her backpack tighter. Since she had no rebuttal about the Suuke, she muttered, "This map is old. Forest could've grown in the last ten years."

"And the cars?"

"Abandoned. I don't know. Maybe they closed this road off and we missed a sign. There are lots of ghost towns across the state. Industry shut down, the whole place shut down."

"Those cars back there weren't that old."

She snapped, "You're an expert on cars?" She was acting ridiculous, yes, but she was frustrated.

Chance laughed easily this time, his eyes shining. "Nah," he said, lugging Eunjoo over his shoulders, piggyback, her matchstick legs dangling to Chance's chest, where the strap of his rifle slung across his flannel. He gripped her shoes. "I'm just an Indian interested in how things work. That's what took me to the white man's world, for academic training. But there's lots I don't know." Eunjoo rested her head and hands atop his head.

Calliope sighed. She was lashing out at the one person helping her. He wasn't the enemy. She didn't know who or what the enemy was, but she knew she needed to be kinder to Chance. *Es una guía*, the apparition of Bisabuela had said, a guide. Even if Bisabuela had been a figment of her exhausted mind, the message was germane. She should treat her guide with respect. "I'm sorry, I didn't mean it like that ... I just need a logical explanation, need this nightmare to make sense."

"Whatever answers I find from the Elders, mujer, I'll share them with you. One thing I do know—better to accept a mystery than an explanation with no logic."

This time she didn't bristle when he called her mujer. She knew he knew they were equals. She was beginning to like the apodo, the token of familiarity between them.

They kept walking. Despite the pain in her pelvis, the twins pressing into her bladder, Calliope's face inched into a smile when she saw that the little girl was twirling Chance's black hair around her bandaged finger, and he let her. He began a story, his voice a natural storyteller's, deep and laced with sorrow. His accent, somewhere between Spanish and Pueblo, reminded Calliope of a steady drumbeat. He spoke slowly, deliberately, as if attentive to the space the shape of his words made in the air.

"When my brother-in-law, Arlen, was a boy alone at his house one early fall night on the rez, his family had gone hunting and left him to guard the sheep. He was reheating stew and bread and heard, outside in the darkness, an eerie crying then rattling. He tried to ignore it and eat his supper, but the wailing then rattling grew louder until he could no longer take it. He grabbed his rifle and flashlight and went tramping through the brambles, past the sheep pens, past the alligator juniper, toward the arroyo, where he shone his light. Then he saw it: a bone sticking out of the muddy arroyo, about this long"—Chance let go Eunjoo's shoes and held out his hands six inches apart—"The bone was seeping with blood, the arroyo gurgling around it. And the wailing was unbearable. He waded into the water, snatched the bone, cursed it, screamed at it, took it to the embankment, and snapped it in half on the ground with the butt of his rifle." Chance indicated a stomping movement with his own cowboy boots on the cracked asphalt beneath them. "Then he went home and finished his supper. Next morning, his family returned and asked how he'd spent the night. He told them about the bone, how he broke it, destroyed it, and his father said it was a bad thing he'd done and he shouldn't have touched it. They returned to the arroyo, which had dried up. The water seeped to nothing, the ground a sludge of mud. But worse for Arlen and his family, the broken bone had become a broken animal half-buried in the mire. Now his family would pass away."

Calliope interrupted him. "Why? That doesn't make sense."

"Well, that's the Zuni way. I don't know what to tell you, mujer. It's how the story goes."

"You could change the story."

He murmured assent. "I suppose. But that's not how oral history works. At least not ours. We tell the story as it was told to us. We don't always know the entire story. For Zuni, there is knowledge only a few privileged leaders of the *kivas* can know. Though I'm an initiated member of a kiva, there are many things even I don't know. Entiendes?"

She nodded. It was how she felt about Bisabuela's stories. Although she didn't necessarily believe, she had a deep appreciation for the sacred.

Chance continued, "Anyway, three years later, his grandfather's people had all disappeared."

"Disappeared?" Eunjoo said. "Like my parents?"

"Well, I don't know, little bird. That's just how my brother Arlen tells it, but could be."

"You're always scaring her," Calliope said, reproachfully.

"It's scary times, mujer. Stories are for these times." He looked hard at Calliope, his expression tinged with something like guilt or regret, a haze she couldn't quite read. Then his face cleared, a kind of peace, and he said, "Mujer, you want another way of looking at the world than the beliefs you were taught. Well, I was fishing at Quemado Lake watching the sun skim the ripples in the water, nothing tugging on my pole, but I didn't care, I was thinking of an equation. The numbers and letters dancing in my head like they were part of a ceremony—they knew what their part was and they had to embody it fully to call their Spirit forth." He shook his hair back from his face where Eunjoo had scattered it, and Calliope imagined the equations dancing around the pair of them as he spoke, could almost see the shadows and shapes encircling the tall, two-headed statue they made against the slate of the mountains beyond, the impossible blue of the sky. His hair fell back in his face anyway. He spoke with the passion of a podium, his voice amplified by an invisible microphone. "There was a moment of light. The equation and the numbers became one and the same. They converged. The equation didn't just *represent* the concrete reality. The equation *was* the reality. As if a veil had been lifted."

Apocalypse. Lifting a veil. Calliope's heart beat faster, as on a dig, unburying fossilized fish scales from the sediment of a mountaintop and realizing it had all once been underwater.

"I never caught a fish that day. Not one tug. But I found something better. It's the same with the stories."

Her eyes stung from the cold wind, or his story.

They walked along the cracked asphalt forest giving way to yellow grasses again. Calliope checked the map every once in a while, to be sure they were making progress toward Silver City, though it might have been futile; if the map hadn't shown them the highway was actually abandoned and overtaken, how could she trust it at all? They were hamsters on a wheel. She'd never walked so relentlessly without breaking. Excursions for her dissertation she always had a vehicle and only trekked a few miles at a time.

Even with hiking boots and thick socks, her muscles alternated between warped as gummy plastic melting into a fire and tense as the brittle, contorted shape it twisted into once that plastic dried. Her pelvic floor ached, and she kept her hands under her belly for support. A sharp pain needled the small of her back. She clenched her jaw and kept walking, the forest yielding to scrub and rocks.

After several minutes of silence, Eunjoo asked, "What kind of animal was it?"

"Huh?"

"That your brother found, where the broken bone was."

"Oh that." Chance laughed. "You know, I never asked him. What kind of animal should it have been?"

"A coyote." She pressed her finger to his face, said, "A coyote bit me." She said this proudly. "It hurts."

"A coyote, oh yeah?"

He looked to Calliope, his expression asking *is that a tall tale?* and Calliope's gut twitched. She felt responsible, and explained as much, told him what had happened at the convenience store, how she'd found Eunjoo crouched in front of the pack.

He turned his head back, craning to look up at Eunjoo. When he couldn't twist that far, he pulled her easily from his shoulders, held her in front of him, face-to-face, and said solemnly, "Old Coyote is a trickster. He can't ever be trusted. Not fully." His lips curled into a sly smile, and he winked. "Coyote can also show you the deep mysticism of life and creation.

He reveals truth behind illusion and chaos. Do you know what chaos is?"

"No."

"I'm named after the theory, right? Chance." He smiled wide, the furrows of his brown skin like ruts in the earth. "Oh, my mother didn't mean to name me for an equation, but that's the beauty of chaos. Aristotle said the least initial deviation from the truth is multiplied later a thousandfold. If you don't know the exact initial conditions of a system, any uncertainty will be amplified and you'll lose predictive power. You follow me?"

Eunjoo shook her head no.

Calliope laughed. "She's a child, Chance. You have to break it down."

"Kids are smarter than grown-ups, mujer." To Eunjoo, "You've heard of the butterfly effect?"

Calliope again laughed. "I don't think they teach that in first grade."

"Hmm. Well they should. It's like this: the beating of a butterfly's wings can theoretically cause enough of an atmospheric disturbance," he paused, corrected, "*strong wind* to alter later weather outcomes. Tiny things. Big changes. So, imagine big things, the changes those could render. My mother told it to me like this: if the dung beetle moves, it's because someone has moved it. And when he moves, so too does the rabbit. And then the eagle. It never ends." He let go of her shoe, blew a breath into his hands, opened it again as if releasing a butterfly. "Listen, little bird. The wisdom of Coyote isn't straightforward. He's tricky." He reached for her hand, inspected her thumb. "This bite, he's telling you something." He lugged her back over his shoulders, and added, "If a small set of insect wings could change the world's world, imagine what Coyote's bite could do."

Calliope's chest prickled. Despite herself, she walked closer to Chance, periodically glancing into the Gilas and the scrub-covered hills that were now surrounding them, searching for coyotes or Suuke or worse. She said, "Those ko'ko, then. Even if I accept that they're no longer palm-sized dolls made of cottonwood and feathers, why were they after us? Aren't they gods? What would your gods have against us?"

"Back when the world was soft, the people climbed out of the underworld and crossed the rivers, joining the sacred lake Kothluwala'wa. But before we crossed the lake, mothers were warned their children would change, so hang on tightly no matter what. When we got to the middle and the children transformed into frogs, tortoises, snakes, dragonflies, they pinched and bit at the mothers, who, understandably, were terrified, and, despite the warning, let go. The children were lost to us. When we finally crossed to the other side, those children whose mothers held onto them became normal again, and the mothers who had lost their children in the water wept, but were told their children hadn't died. They'd become the ko'ko and danced underwater. It's like a dancehall down there. And when we die, we'll join them, as ko'ko. The twin gods told the mothers to take heart. When their time on Mother Earth was over, they would rejoin their children in Kothluwala'wa. There is no punishment after death like the Anglos believe. Only continued survival."

"Then where did the Suuke come from? If there's no punishment?"

"No punishment *after death.*"

He stopped walking, pulled Eunjoo from his shoulders, held her against his chest. Calliope turned and faced them, her stomach tightening from his abrupt halting, as when he'd crouched in the dirt outside the hangar and predicted the coming of the Suuke. Her throat tight, she asked, "What is it? Something coming?"

"I don't think so. Just, most ko'ko help the Zuni. Occasionally the Spirits come to us as clouds. That's why we dance, to ask for their intercession." He breathed out deeply. "But some ko'ko are like bogeymen. Well, bogeypeople really. Male and female, husband and wife."

"Where do they come from? I thought ko'ko came from the lost children?"

"No, the children joined the ko'ko. The ko'ko have always been. And I can't tell you how or why some are bogeys. Doesn't every culture have its own version of a disciplinarian? For Zuni, it's the Suuke couple, as ko'ko. Behave, or the Suuke will steal you away in their basket." He sighed. "My wife used to say that to our daughter."

Something sharp jabbed her. He was married? Why hadn't he said anything before? Why did that realization make Calliope feel sick? The ring on his right hand. Wrong hand.

"Used to?"

He began walking again, still holding Eunjoo at his chest. He cleared his throat, "She's underwater now, mujer. In that dancehall." He looked up toward the sky, where a storm was forming past the mountains. "Or maybe that cloud over there."

A lump in her throat. "I'm so sorry."

"It's not the end."

She nodded. Thought of Phoenix. Quickened her step, her whole body raw with exhaustion. She couldn't wait to hold her boy.

She also thought of Chance's wife. Back on the Zuni rez? Waiting for him? Then why was he detouring to help Calliope? Why not go straight home? She wanted to ask but couldn't form the words. They fell in step again, side by side as the road stretched ahead, vast and empty as grief.

* * * *

Hours later, they'd found a car not shot through with branches or wrecked. Calliope, quivering with cold, was relieved to climb in and blast the heater. They would have driven the rest of the journey but for entropy. "We are ruled by the laws of nature," Chance had said when the car had broken down and neither he nor Calliope could fix it. "Only, I'm afraid try as we might, we don't always know those laws, though in our human arrogance we think we do."

Calliope would have been glad to discuss physics and wrongheaded scientists except that her limbs were red with frostbite and she was hungry enough to gnaw on tree bark, all their snacks from the campers' tent already eaten. The distance between her pinched finger and thumb had grown teasingly thin—they were so close.

She found blankets in the trunk of the rundown car, wrapped them around herself and Eunjoo, and for what seemed like forever, walked on. Thin snowflakes were flurrying—melting before they hit the ground, beautiful granules of ice, nevertheless, landing sometimes on their dark hair and faces—by the time Tía's hacienda silhouetted into view. Sunset had turned the cloudswell on the horizon brightly purple, so the whole land glowed. Calliope was running even before she exclaimed *this is it* and Chance followed suit, calling, "Wait, mujer. Let's make sure it's safe."

"Safe?" Calliope called back, laughing with manic joy. She wiped the ice-rain from her cheeks like cold tears with her free hand, the other still under her belly, which screeched with labor-like pain she ignored. Panting, she said, "It's my *family*. Of course it's *safe*."

But she had to stop at the arroyo gushing across the dirt road. The log bridge Tía had built for crossing when the rains came and the waters rose had been knocked down, and though the wooden beams were partially damming it, the water still rushed swiftly.

Chance at her side, "Is there another crossing?"

"Hold Eunjoo," Calliope answered, and stepped into the icy water. A shock of cold seeped through her boots and sweats, instantly numbing her legs and sending veins of ice-pain up her thighs and into her pelvis. She trudged forward, pushing her body against the rushing force, conjuring Phoenix with everything inside of her. *I'm coming, baby. I'm almost there.*

"Ay, mujer," Chance murmured, hoisting Eunjoo upon his shoulders again, and following Calliope into the arroyo.

On the other side, her body was shuddering, her bottom half soaked and freezing in the ice-wind. She tried running, couldn't. Moved haltingly, and when Chance emerged from the water, he helped her forward.

As they approached the front porch Calliope's chest thudded along with their boots tramping wetly up the steps, littered with grayish white she thought at first was snowflakes then realized was dead moths. She turned the doorknob.

A gunshot pierced the air.

Two images flashed through her mind. Susana in the hay. And Chance's wailing bone.

PART TWO
FIRST PEOPLES

"A line of stories has followed us to this present moment …
All that is left is for us to record these images, these voices,
so that those who follow in our footsteps may meet …
the source from which we have all been birthed."

VANISHING VOICES

SIXTEEN
EMERGENCE

What was happening in the world hadn't come yet. Hadn't come to Calliope. The ceasefire fails, how the world didn't truly want freedom—at least it didn't seem that way to those in the rubble, amidst the water cannons and blizzards and roadblocks, amidst the genocide of the Ancients. It was always coming, she knew. The country had been scrubbed of science and common sense, so she'd planned with Andres: in the occasion of the roundup they'd threatened, the wall they were building, the explosion of another pipeline, the droughts-turned-floods devastating the states, he would stay behind and give medical attention, and she would flee with Phoenix to her tía's.

She hadn't shut out the horror. She'd sent supplies bought on Amazon: heat lamps and emergency Mylar thermal blankets, thick wool socks, waterproof parkas, milk of magnesia, buffalo jerky, water pouches. But she'd had fossils to sort in the lab, notes to jot, classes to teach. The world broke in segments, as a piece of bone at the joints. Her piece of world-bone had still been intact. How could she, pregnant, with a mortgage, seeking tenure, gallivant toward danger to hold the lines? Though she sympathized, though the news each night churned her gut and she saw Phoenix's face on every child's, she did not get involved.

Perhaps she was fooling herself, and it was simply easier to bury one's head in the past. *About suffering they were never wrong, / The old Masters,*

Auden had written in his famous poem about the fall of Icarus: *how well they understood / Its human position: how it takes place / While someone else is eating or opening a window or just walking dully along.* Calliope had argued back in an undergrad paper on postcolonialism how the "masters" had misinterpreted suffering—how those joined together in blood and pain and heartache understood the impossibility of turning a blind eye when that eye was shared.

But the years had turned her fire lukewarm, and she'd gotten comfortable in her cushy office chair, clacking insights at the keyboard, little ticks and tocks like notches in the flint; only her weapons had dulled, and she wasn't sure anymore what good they would do anyone.

What was happening in the world hadn't come yet. Until it had.

* * * *

The gunshot rang in her ears. She hunched in the doorway, the door swung partway into her tía's cabin. Chance pushed Calliope and Eunjoo toward the front wall, beside a moth-covered porch swing, shouldered his rifle, and called out, "Stop shooting! We aren't here to fight."

A woman's voice. "Who's there?"

Calliope's heart raced. She shouted, "Tía? It's Calliope," and rose from her crouching place.

Chance whispered, harshly, "Wait, mujer. We don't know it's her or if she's ..." He paused, grappling for words. He finally settled on, "Changed."

"She's not a zombie, she's my aunt," Calliope said, rising the rest of the way and standing beside Chance in the doorway.

"Tía, I made it!" A woman in bright yellow overalls, her silver hair draped across her shoulders, appeared in the doorway, holding a rifle. Her usually friendly expression pulled into a tight grimace, eyebrows raised. This wasn't Tía, but the artist who lived in the trailer down the creek. Tía's girlfriend. "Oh, it's you. Mara, you scared the shit out of us."

Mara's eyes darted past Calliope, toward the yard. "Come in," she said, her voice hushed, laced with panic. Calliope looked closely at Mara's overalls, red stains smeared across the bib and thighs, more bloodlike than paint. Blood handprints. And dried, caked mud. Her boots were stamped with mud as well. The hairs on the back of Calliope's neck prickled.

She stayed rooted to the porch. Her voice smaller, she asked, "Where's my aunt? And everyone else?"

The furrows at Mara's eyes deepened, her expression pained. The artist was a white woman, but her skin had always appeared sunbaked and leathery to Calliope. Mara had seemed tough, and Calliope liked that Tía had a partner and wasn't alone on this big hacienda. Now Mara seemed waxen, nearly opalescent, unstable. She gave off the aura of a radioactive isotope. Calliope thought of the crazy hunter, the rapist. Chance's words echoed through her mind, *what if she's changed?* Calliope wished that mentirosa Amy hadn't taken her gun. A sick swishing in her gut. She'd trusted Amy. She couldn't trust anyone—not even her tía's girlfriend.

Mara's voice on edge, she didn't answer Calliope's question but repeated, "Come in. It's not safe."

It didn't seem any safer inside with Mara. Calliope didn't move, the heat rising in her face. "Where's my family? Why were you shooting?" Ready to reach for Chance's gun herself, she asked, "Have you done something?" She shouted past Mara into the cabin, her voice shrill, "Tía? Phoenix? Are you here?" No one answered. She searched past Mara, her limbs tingling with cold and fear, imagining them cowering on the ground somewhere inside, their mouths duct taped. Or worse.

She glanced emphatically at Chance, asking him with her eyes to cover her, and he nodded, then he moved quicker than Calliope had ever seen any human move, pulled the gun from Mara, and held the older woman tightly in his grasp, her arms behind her back.

Calliope rushed past them into the cabin, screaming her family's names. Wood piled on the floor, dishes on the coffee table, blankets on the couch. It was messy but not unusual. No blood. The cast-iron fireplace was roaring, crackling with burning wood, but the house was otherwise quiet. No voices answered back. "Where are they?" she screamed at Mara, whose arctic-blue eyes brimmed with tears. She didn't wait for an answer, but tore through the living room into the kitchen, half fearing she'd find the source of blood staining Mara's clothes. There was an underground pantry past the kitchen. Calliope considered grabbing a knife from the carving board but decided Chance's gun was enough. She opened the pantry, her body shaking, and called her family again. It was the twisted hide-and-seek of three days ago, in the sweltering dark of her own empty house—except they *had* to be here. This was their sanctuary. Their escape plan. Their last resort.

She returned to the doorway where Chance still grasped Mara tightly, though the woman wasn't struggling. Calliope's voice trembled. "What have you done with them?" The tears were pouring freely down her face, her whole body wracked with sobs.

Mara was shaking her head, her eyes pleading. She whispered, hoarsely, "I don't know, sweetheart. I just don't know. They've all ... they've all ... disappeared."

Calliope let out a small trembling yelp like an injured animal, caught in brambles. "But they were here? You saw them?"

Mara shook her head again, her face crumpled. "No, I never saw them. Trudy's gone, that's all I know. And your cousin. Everyone at the hospital. In the town. But your husband and boy, they never came here."

Calliope had split apart when that light had flashed and she'd crashed into the bridge, then again in the hangar, when all the air had been sucked from the room and her lungs had smashed together. Now she was shriveling and shredding like a burnt piece of paper, ashes scattering into the wind. Everything hurt.

Her family wasn't at Tía's. She'd been wrong. They weren't here. They weren't anywhere.

"People don't *disappear*," she managed, her voice strangled. Her eyes stung, and she struggled to breathe. Where else could they have gone? She pictured the Ancient Ancestors roaming away from Chaco Canyon, from their elaborate stone buildings, their mysterious religious rites and astronomical pursuits—all of it, abandoned. Chance had said the myths were real. Were Calliope and her family caught in whatever ecological crisis had caused the ancestors to become refugees, to scatter and decline and all but disappear, their whole culture lost from archaeological record until they emerged again as much more modern Puebloans, hundreds of years later, the evidence for their sudden fall lost to the rocks, not yet uncovered? Was her family still out there? It was freezing. She had to keep looking. She had to find them before they froze to death.

A voice whispered, *What if they're already dead?*

Chance broke her thoughts, asking Mara in his lilting accent, "Whose blood you got all over you?"

Mara flinched. "Trudy's dad's."

His voice level, he said, "You murder him?"

She shook her head. "Found him dead."

"Where's his body? Show me."

Chance loosened his grip, although he still held Mara's arm in a cop-like vise. Calliope wasn't convinced the older woman was telling the truth, yet she was uncomfortable with a man steering a woman by the arm, especially an older woman whose fidgety, insecure demeanor could have been a sign of shock or exhaustion. Or she was hiding something. Calliope needed to see for herself whether Mara was being honest. She'd shielded Eunjoo once from seeing a dead man's body, but she couldn't leave the girl alone in the cabin. Calliope was still shaking, soaking from the waist down, but she grabbed Eunjoo's hand and followed the others outside where the snow was accumulating atop the dead grass and dirt, covering the white moth wings with crisp white flakes. Their boots crunched the snow as Mara led them past a water tower and an empty pasture, toward a smaller cabin beside an outcropping of trees.

"Any animals on this ranch?" Chance asked.

"Gone," Mara said.

"Run away?"

"Like everyone else," she said. "Just gone."

Chance murmured something indiscernible.

"There was a mountain lion on the property," Mara said. "I think that's what ... killed Loren. I don't know what else or who else could've done ... what it did ..."

Calliope shuddered, thinking of the coyotes. Eunjoo's bite. It could have been worse.

As they approached the front porch, a rocking chair came into view, and Mara warned, "This isn't going to be pretty. You may not want the little one to see."

Glistening from the oak of the porch and rocking chair in fat streaks and globs, dark rust-colored splotches of blood. Copious amounts of blood, splattered across the wood. Calliope braced herself for the body, saw nothing but red stains. "Where is he?"

Mara nodded toward a patch of juniper fifty feet away, where a dark trail of blood led from the porch toward the ground then stopped, buried by snow. "I couldn't just leave him carrion for the vultures, not Trudy's dad. She wouldn't have wanted that." Mara let out a coarse laugh that gave way to a look of utter dejection. "Trudy wouldn't have wanted any of this. I buried him over there. Not a proper burial, not deep enough. But better than nothing till I caught that son-a-bitch lion did this."

They followed her to the junipers, where a mound of earth was raised higher than the rest, camouflaged by snow—Calliope wouldn't have known it was a grave if she'd stumbled across it unaware. The thought made her shiver harder, imagining they were surrounded by graves, her family beneath the earth everywhere around them. She'd known Mara for years—eccentric, a free spirit, never vicious or violent. Calliope couldn't really believe Mara had killed her aunt, or anyone else. Could she? Still, the blood was harrowing.

Apparently, the burial mound wasn't evidence enough for Chance either. He asked, "Where's your shovel?"

"Back at Trudy's."

"Let's get it. Mujer, you two should get inside. It's freezing. I'll investigate, make sure her story checks out."

A stubborn refusal coursed through Calliope. She needed to see the body. Needed to confirm it wasn't anyone she loved. She felt callous hoping the dead man was Loren.

"We'll wait out here for you," Calliope said.

Chance shook his head, as if he'd already realized in the nearly forty-eight hours he'd spent with Calliope there was no reasoning with her once she'd made up her mind, and he led Mara back the way they'd come.

Alone with Eunjoo, the two stood facing the snowy mound, funereal.

Eunjoo said, "It's not Phoenix."

Calliope dropped the girl's hand as if it'd burned her. She turned and faced the girl, whose moon face gleamed bright against the snow, her cheeks pink with cold. "What makes you so sure?"

"I told you. I've seen things."

"Those are dreams, chica. Not real."

"If they *are* dreams, then we're *in* the dreams."

Calliope's legs spindly, paper-thin, she knelt beside the girl, the ice prickling into the knees of her sweatpants, stinging her skin. "If this were a dream, would my gut ache this way? Would I be so scared and hungry and feel like I'm dying? Aren't you cold, baby? You wouldn't realize how cold you were, if we were dreaming. You'd be able to fly, or build a fire in your hands. You know? Magic. There's magic in dreams, and we never realize how bad things are." Calliope wiped her eyes on the back of her palm; she hadn't meant to cry, to come across so harshly. But she was tired of thinking they were dead or dreaming. Her boy was missing. She should have found him by now, and she was failing him every second she was not looking. She didn't have time for dreams.

"Don't cry, Phoenix's mama. Phoenix isn't in the ground. You need the rock to find him. That's why you haven't found him yet. But you will."

Calliope's tears turned exasperated. She resisted the urge to shake the girl, tell her to wake up. "There are rocks everywhere, chica. Look around. We're in the desert. Rocks aren't going to help me find my son." Her voice rose hysterically. She put her face in her hands and breathed deeply. The girl patted Calliope's shoulder, as if she were the mother figure and not the other way around. Calliope felt ridiculous. She measured her tone. "Can you please drop this dream thing? I can't take it."

The girl nodded, her eyes bright with the unsaid. But Calliope didn't want to hear it.

From the distance, "Mujer? What's wrong?" Chance was jogging toward her, his cowboy boots kicking up snow. As he reached Calliope, he knelt beside her, worry lines furrowing his face. "Is it the babies?"

She shook her head, not admitting how much her uterus strained. "I'm fine. I was explaining to Eunjoo how this is real life, not a dream."

He breathed out, relief smoothing the creases at his eyes. He turned toward Eunjoo, then back to Calliope. Though he addressed Eunjoo, he kept his eyes on Calliope. "Oye, chica. In quantum physics there's a hypothesis of probability that asserts we could be dreaming at any given moment. The odds aren't as low as winning the lottery or getting struck by lightning, they're way higher. When we do the math, turns out the odds of us being in REM dreaming is one in ten. Some scientists think we're not conscious in dreams, but others, me included, believe consciousness just means thinking and being aware of a world. Dreamworld counts, yes? You might say *if this was a dreamworld, why would it be bound by the laws of causality?* Well, reality follows a strict set of rules, even if it gets a little blurry at the quantum level. Imagine if we were in someone else's dream, qué no? A simulation made by a higher-order reality. Maybe not a dream, but a computer simulation. Maybe not computers, but gods. There are scientists who imagine a time, perhaps centuries from now, when our descendants will have the power to model fully functional human brains in computers. These simulated minds could be placed in computer-simulated worlds, perhaps even re-creations of the past. They would never know they weren't real. Scientists say we could be living in a rerun where some weird event in the past had been changed just to see what kind of ramifications it had. Whether it's a simulation or dream doesn't matter. You can still plan your life, causes will have effects, and actions will have consequences. But the reality we perceive is just a small slice of what really is. As the philosopher-king Marcus Aurelius wrote, *The universe is change. Our life is what our thoughts make it.*"

Calliope couldn't decide whether she was more exasperated that he'd contradicted everything she'd told the girl, impressed that he'd conjoined Western philosophy with scientific quandaries and indigenous spirituality, or amused that he'd given a lecture at a snow-covered burial mound. She settled on amusement, but dialed her tone to chiding. "I was actually hoping you'd pinch yourself, Chance. Show her we're all really here. Instead, you tell her we *could* be in a dream."

"Children are too smart for anything but the truth, mujer."

"Yeah, but *whose* truth?"

"Exactly."

She'd been too engrossed in his speech to notice Mara digging the grave behind them. Sickness washed over Calliope as the wet dirt unclumped from the earth. She moved closer, Chance beside her. She realized Eunjoo was moving forward as well, and said, "Stay back, mija. Go stand behind that juniper bush."

"You're always telling me to stand in the bushes. I want to see the dead man."

Calliope bristled at the thought of a six-year-old wanting to see death and glared sternly at Eunjoo, the way she did whenever Phoenix disobeyed, as if silently counting before doling out the punishment.

Eunjoo raised her eyebrows skeptically and sighed but did as Calliope had instructed, slinking behind the juniper. The girl was emerging from her shell, it seemed. Not the shy baby Calliope had met four days ago, but a rebellious, opinionated tween. Grief ages us.

It's not my child in that hole, Calliope thought, forcing herself to peer down into the mud-gape at whatever Mara uncovered. Chalky and blood-stained, Loren's lifeless face shimmered sickeningly against the dirt. His body mangled, his flesh shorn off. Was Calliope relieved? Did this prove Mara hadn't killed anyone? Surely no amount of shock would derange her tía's partner to this beastly act. Calliope glanced at Mara, whose head was bowed, red eyes blotchy.

"The Suuke," Chance murmured.

"How do you know?" Calliope asked.

"This was no mountain lion."

Chance described their escape from the hangar, the two Suuke at their heels. This time though, he added a piece of information he hadn't shared with Calliope before: "We Zunis believe we only see the ko'ko, that they only show themselves to us, when we're about to die and join them." He looked at Calliope from the corners of his eyes. "I didn't want to scare you, mujer. But you might as well know the whole truth."

"But we didn't die."

He murmured assent, as if surprised about the fact himself, then took the shovel from Mara and reburied Loren.

They returned to Tía's, where an uneasy truce settled like ice-breath against windowpane, satisfied the threat was crouching in the shadows of the hills and not amidst the warmth and shelter of the cabin. Exhaustion replaced Calliope's lingering doubts, along with any hope of finding her family huddled in a corner or bathroom, hiding, safe. They weren't here.

Her clothes drying stiffly against her sore and frost-nipped skin, Eunjoo lying beside her on the couch in front of the potbellied iron fireplace, Calliope fell asleep. What else had people ever done when the night was long, the snow piling high?

SEVENTEEN
THE STRANGER

Phoenix chucked rocks at his mother. He picked them from the pocked ground, feverishly, his eyes malicious in a way no child's should be. Or maybe they were angry, Calliope couldn't tell past the painful thudding at her skin where the sharp rocks struck. She tried calling out, not *Stop* but *Come back.* For even as he was aiming for her, for blood, he was drifting further and further away, so the rocks had to travel vast distances, past a chasm in the rutted, red earth. He balanced atop one mesa like a vulture on a branch, and she another. Her tabletop mesa slipping, shaking, his rising toward the sky and away from hers. *Wait*—but no words came. She grappled, an animal on hands and knees, to keep from falling. The rocks pummeled her belly. Something rose in her throat and when she tried to speak, from her mouth she dislodged a rock. She was made of rocks. She couldn't move from the fossilized casing she'd once called her body.

Heat crackled nearby. A conversation wove through the fire. A child's sweaty body curled at her lap, chest rhythms of breathing, up and down, pressing against her.

"I didn't want to believe it was happening again ..." Mara's voice drifted somewhere between dreamworld and the terrifying space Calliope would find herself still trapped if she opened her eyes: her family's house without her family. "My dad was a scientist at Los Alamos during World War II. He helped make the A-bomb. Fucking scientists."

Chance laughed. "I'm a scientist."

"Oh yeah?" Mara joined the laughter, hers wry. "I had a nanny there, Chaiwa, who was of the San Ildefonso people." Mara paused, looked imploringly at Chance. "You ever heard of Lizard's Tail?"

"That it grows a new one?"

"Yeah, but it's more than that. Chaiwa was the wisest person I ever knew, and like I said I grew up around scientists. She told me the story of Coyote and Lizard, how Coyote heard Lizard singing and wanted to learn the song but couldn't remember it. When Lizard wouldn't sing it for Coyote, wouldn't let him steal it, Coyote swallowed Lizard. In his belly, Lizard began to sing. Coyote knew he would regret what he had done, and sure enough, Lizard cut Coyote's throat to his stomach from inside and Coyote fell dead. Lizard emerged singing."

Chance laughed anew, a deep belly laugh that made Calliope want to open her eyes to peek at him. She kept them tight.

"What about Lizard's Tail though?" Chance asked.

"Oh, well, Chaiwa talked about Lizard all the time. She taught me lizards are associated with dreamtime. When we dream, we imagine different futures and decide which we'll manifest. Lizard can break off her tail to escape predators, the tail left behind writhing, to take the predator's attention off Lizard so she can flee. Lizard can only perform this feat once in her life, since the new tail is made of cartilage and not vertebrae. So even though she's powerful and can rescue herself from danger by leaving part of herself behind, she has to be wise about her choice, her once-in-a-lifetime chance to flee."

Calliope couldn't stand it; she opened her eyes. "It's just a metaphor." Her voice cracked, her mouth still gluey with sleep paste. "It's stories people tell to make sense of their world, their perceived chaos. It's not *real*. It's *symbol*."

"Sweetheart," Mara said, "I don't think it is a metaphor. I didn't want to believe this had anything to do with what I saw when I was a child up at Los Alamos, but I can't deny it now. Not with what I've seen, what Chance tells me you've all been through."

"What happened when you were a child, then? What *do* you think is happening?" Calliope hadn't intended the boiling pitch in her voice, but she was angry. It wasn't fair to think of Mara as a stranger. Yet Calliope felt alone amongst strangers.

"They accused Chaiwa of witchcraft. Mother went crazy. Dad was discharged for her unhinged behavior, her erratic ramblings in public and failure to keep the place a secret. I chalked it up to being young and easily influenced. We moved to England, and Mother died shortly after. It ruined our lives."

"What did?" Calliope pressed.

Mara's face went ashen, her eyes distant, as if she couldn't believe she was going to say whatever it was … "People were disappearing."

Calliope sighed, exasperated. "Mara, I'm sorry about what happened to your family, but don't people often disappear in the military, during war, et cetera? Government is corrupt. Only now it's more bald-faced, but the populace is so gullible and forgetful, so wrapped up in cognitive dissonance and confirmation bias." She sighed again, adjusted her position beneath the heat of Eunjoo's sleeping body. "It's always been corrupt though."

"Not kidnapped or murdered, I don't mean that."

Chance reached out, touched Mara's arm. "What do you mean?"

"In front of our eyes. There one minute, gone the next. Vanished."

Calliope's stomach knotted. She wanted to say again, *People don't just disappear,* but the words felt as useless as a parrot's mocking singsong atop a shoulder. She thought of Bisabuela in the hangar. What was Mara saying, that her family had *vanished*? She'd never see them again? It was ludicrous. It was insane. She sat upright, peeled Eunjoo from her lap, and waddled off the couch, her legs pins and needles from sleeping under the girl on the couch all night.

In the bathroom, she turned on the faucet out of habit and startled when she realized water was streaming. For a brief moment, she took the water as sign that things had returned to normal in the outside world—but then she remembered Tía's land had its own water reserve, its own underground tunnels and pumps, that didn't rely on the town, one reason of the many she and Andres had chosen this place as refuge in the crisis they foresaw. But they never foresaw this.

She splashed cold water on her face several times, stared at her reflection, pink from yesterday's trek through the snow and the sunrise-pink light filtering through the undraped window. Her honey-colored eyes glowed in the new light, and she felt angry at her own hopeful visage. Her belly aching, she cupped water in her hands and drank it down in gulps; she was dehydrated, and couldn't risk inducing early labor, disaster atop ruin. She stared out the window at the rising sun. Today was a Monday. Today she should have gotten dressed and gone to her weekly ob-gyn appointment. She should have been listening to her babies' heartbeats. Twins were usually born early, at thirty-six weeks. She'd almost reached thirty-two. The doctor had wanted her to schedule a C-section, but healing after Phoenix's had been agonizing. She'd been bedbound, her stomach and uterus on fire for weeks. She wanted a vaginal birth. Today the doctor would have made sure that was still possible. The twins hadn't kicked all morning. She pressed against her rigid belly, whispered, *You both safe in there?* She had to keep them inside her if not the full month they still needed, at least until she had found—

In her dream, Phoenix was stoning her. The anger she felt, she'd seen that on his face. Was he scared, wherever he was? Were Andres and her mother with him?

Vanished. What did that even mean? Vanished *where?*

She turned off the faucet, slumped onto the bathroom tile, head in her hands. What proof was a batty old woman's story? Mara was an artist, what she described was a child's PTSD fever dream. Whatever she'd gone through during the war, she'd explained away or transformed through fantasy—that's what children *do,* what imagination is *for.* It was *not* for grown-up mothers who needed to find their child. Calliope couldn't give in to fantasy now. It hadn't worked for Bisabuela when she'd prayed for healing. The Ancients hadn't come to her when she'd refused Western medicine and died as a result. Why should they have come now? Myth was just that. Hell, Bisabuela and the Suuke were probably a result of Calliope's exhaustion, dehydration, and terror. She'd seen a woman almost raped in front of her, had almost *killed* the rapist. What she'd seen in the hangar—that was PTSD not reality.

Now that she'd gotten some sleep, in a warm and familiar place, she could sort out fact from fiction, could piece the puzzle together with critical intellect and not wishful thinking. Chance had been a bad influence, with his stories just like Bisabuela's. If she were inclined to believe in such things, she'd wonder if he was some kind of shaman or witch—if he'd slipped her something and brought on the delusions through a *hallucinogen*. When had she drunk that bowl of earth-tasting clay water "Bisabuela" had "given" her? She thought back to the strange encounter. The apparition in the rebozo had offered it to her right before she saw the "Suuke." Or maybe she'd never seen anything at all. Maybe she'd described a hallucination and the others had taken her word for it. Eunjoo was an impressionable child, susceptible to wild beliefs at adult suggestion. What about Amy? Had she *seen* the Suuke? Calliope couldn't remember now. Memory was blurring. She'd been so confused and scared in the hangar.

And yet, what motive could Chance have possibly had for drugging her? It didn't make sense. He'd protected her several times. He'd had ample opportunity to harm her and Eunjoo—if he'd wanted to.

She sighed, rubbing her hands vigorously across her temples and cheeks. Forget the supernatural. What were the *facts*? She'd been a terrible mother. She sighed again, leaning her head against the cabinet. She was allowing emotion to cloud her judgment, and she couldn't keep wallowing in guilt. Where had that ever gotten her with her Catholic upbringing, her own guilt-ridden mother always criticizing her for not believing hard enough, not being good enough. There was no room for her mother or her bisabuela. She'd tried things their way and ended up on a monster hunt, searching for a mystical path that didn't exist. She hadn't found her family. This wasn't about faith or guilt, which felt interchangeable to Calliope.

No, this was about bridging what she knew about the abandonment of the past with what she knew of the sinkhole she'd found herself in. That's what she lived for—connecting the pieces of prehistory to the present. The Ancient Ancestors left Chaco Canyon and Mesa Verde because of drought; severe hunger and thirst drove them from their elaborate structures, their society and way of life. Yet signs of an ancient horror lay buried beneath the rocks. Excavation uncovered a darker story, one Calliope was hesitant to believe and never would have shared with Bisabuela. Over a thousand bones and bone fragments, shoulder blades, skulls, vertebrae, ribs, arm bones, hand and foot bones, and teeth. Nearly all were broken and scattered in heaps in air shafts, irreverently. Like game bones after butchering.

Bisabuela had taught her that the Ancients had abandoned Chaco after supernatural intervention. The knowledge they'd gleaned, their ability to shape the natural forces of their environment, their closeness to the earth— they'd used their power in ways that caused things to change. *What changed?* Calliope had asked. Changes never meant to occur, Bisabuela had told her, and Calliope remembered because at that moment the clouds were swelling above the mesa and thunder grumbled, giving credence to Bisabuela's tale. She said these changes had set the migrations going again. Calliope thought of Room 33 in the great building at Chaco Canyon. The grave goods left there. Calliope had seen for herself in her fieldwork research that it was used for dark rituals. Room 33 had scared her, though she couldn't say for certain why. When the Ancient Ancestors abandoned their great architectural achievement at Chaco, the buildings and doorways were sealed, pottery broken, a ceremonial going away. Clans divided. Kivas burnt. The Ancestors had been so in tune with natural forces they could *control* those forces and abuse them. *Everything is meant to fall back to Mother Earth, mija. Some things in our migration history, we don't understand, but we don't need to understand. We no longer need to repeat that portion of the story. We've found our place, and that story no longer bears on our daily lives.*

Daily lives. *That* made sense to Calliope. Not the supernatural but the practical. The Ancients had starved, reduced to their basest instincts for survival.

Andres would have known how to survive. He would have gone where he was needed. Unless he needed help. Only the well could tend the sick. What if there'd been an altercation? A clash? She'd never known Andres to be a fighter, but in times of crisis people surprise us.

Where else could he have taken Phoenix and her mother? Once, when Calliope had explored a back road out of Albuquerque on her way to Chaco Canyon, she'd seen a sign that had caught her interest. Splitting the road into a fork, the sign had pointed two ways: one direction, shooting range. The other, winter shelter.

Ever led by curiosity, she'd followed the latter and come to a dead-end dirt road harboring a large, squat, metal building, encircled by a tall chain-link fenced topped with barbed wire, padlocked and bearing a sign made of red streamer-paper tied through the chains into a heart that read *Welcome*. The winter shelter had turned out to be a closed-down prison turned into a place to shelter homeless people each winter, bussed in from Albuquerque at sundown from the doorsteps of designated churches and train stations around the city. It was equipped with food rations, water, cots, generators. Why hadn't she remembered this before? She'd been so set on Tía's hacienda, it had never occurred to her they might have gone elsewhere.

She stretched her legs across the bathroom tile, wiggled them to get the blood flowing. She was still wearing the camper's hiking boots and thick socks. Her feet ached. At home, before all this, she'd complained of aching pregnancy feet almost daily to Andres, and he'd rubbed aloe vera on them. She unpeeled the boots and socks, pulled one swollen fish of a foot up to her thigh, and began rubbing it, tears stinging her eyes.

She'd come all this way for nothing.

Would journeying back north be another wild goose chase?—resting completely on the off chance that Andres had remembered her once telling him about the winter shelter in her rush of excitement at finding it. What *proof* did she have he would have gone? She'd described it to him, yes, but they'd never planned to meet there. She had to return to the beginning. What had set this off? What change? Bisabuela said it was a *change* that set the Ancestors migrating. Calliope's own research had corroborated Bisabuela's story. She rubbed her other foot, closing her eyes to think. What made the day she'd crashed her car different than any other? What made her group different than any other? What did they have in common? Why had *they* stayed behind while the others had disappeared?

If there was an explanation, it eluded her.

Morning light filtered through the window, warming her face. She opened her eyes toward the light—and was startled by a dark splotch against the windowpane, a sudden clang, a thud and blackness spreading, followed by a sticky red dripping.

She screamed.

Chance barged into the bathroom. "Mujer?"

She was on her feet, her hands over her mouth, staring at a smashed crow.

Chance's eyebrows furrowed, and he breathed out an exclamation in Zuni she didn't understand. "Did it *fly* into the window? Or …?"

Her stomached cinched. "Or *what*?"

"Stay here."

He flustered out the door as she resocked and booted, then scurried after him.

Eunjoo sat at the dining room table eating a granola bar while Mara stood in the kitchen, her rifle on the counter. She asked what was going on, but Calliope only rushed past.

At the front door, Chance saw Calliope following and chuckled, shaking his head like *Ay, mujer*—there was no commanding Calliope. The icy air nipped at her face and hands as she stepped outside. The sky wore a purplish-blue haze, although clear of clouds, the early morning sun shining bright. It was the clearest she'd seen the sky since before her crash on the Río Grande bridge. Easily three inches of snow enshrouded the yard in incandescent white, but the sun was already melting the ice on the porch rafters, drops of water trickling off the roof, down the beams, wetting the floorboards. Careful not to slip, Calliope caught up to Chance, her camper's sweatshirt brushing against his flannel. She stayed a step behind but close enough to smell his unshowered mustiness mixed with wood smoke from the fireplace.

He spoke softly in Zuni. "*Ulohnan uteya k'ohanna pottiye.*"

"What's that mean?"

"The world is filled with white flowers." He kept one hand on his rifle, still slung over his shoulder.

The bird's neck was broken in half, its body at a right angle to its head. Chance drew nearer to the scene than Calliope could tolerate; she turned away, leaned against the porch rail, searching for the dead crow's flock. She wrapped her arms around her chest. What would make a bird fly into a closed window? Especially a frosted pane?

"Chance?"

"Hmm?" He pulled a pair of work gloves from his back pocket. Had those always been there? She hadn't noticed. Her cheeks burned when she realized what she was staring at. She looked away.

"What did you mean it could have flown *or*? What are you insinuating?"

He pinched the bird corpse with a gloved hand, studying it. "It was used as a projectile."

"*Thrown?*"

"Right."

"By whom?"

"Exactly."

She squinted into the bright white yard.

"Who would throw a bird at a window? That's ridiculous."

"For a person, yes."

She sighed. "About that … Chance … Suuke? Really? I don't, I just can't … buy it."

He smiled, deeply, raised his eyebrows, still examining the corpse. "I didn't realize my people's beliefs were for sale."

She stammered, "I didn't …"

He cut her off. "You didn't realize my Spirit Ancestors needed your approval to exist?"

Her cheeks flushed.

He smiled mischievously.

She sighed and tried again, "If you thought a malevolent creature was skulking around the house, why would you have come outside?"

"I promised to help you find your family. I can't do that if you're dead. So that means I promised to protect *you*, yes? I told you to stay inside anyway. Do you ever listen to anyone?"

She shrugged, about to retort, when in the distance, beside the icy lake, branches began crackling, twigs snapping, snow thudding to the ground.

Chance dropped the bird, quickly peeled off the gloves, disengaged the safety on his rifle, and put his finger on the trigger. "Mujer," he whispered, "Por favor, escúchame ahora. Agáchate."

His imploring in Spanish, his palpable fear, Calliope listened this time and ducked down. Her heart pounding, she peered through the snow-covered bushes blocking the slats between porch rails. She wished she still had Susana's gun. Though that mentirosa Amy probably needed it more. For whatever reason, Calliope had Chance.

He aimed but didn't flinch otherwise, just stood, waiting.

Calliope couldn't see. She was tempted to ask, but stayed quiet and still as possible. A thought nagged at her. Had she remembered to close the front door? She should've locked it. Closed or not, she didn't want Eunjoo running outside. Whatever was out there, Suuke, mountain lion, anything else—she didn't want Eunjoo to find it. Calliope couldn't help herself. Curiosity won, and she elevated on her haunches high enough that her nose was touching the rail, her eyes peering above the top.

A loud upheaval from the branches, the empty hackberry and black walnut forest releasing a burden of snow to the ground followed closely by a black unfolding of crows into the sky. The screeching caws reverberated through the yard, the snow creating an echo chamber. Calliope covered her ears.

"Who's there?" Chance called. "Identify yourself."

Calliope couldn't see anyone. She was distracted by Mara bursting out the front door, shooting her rifle into the air. Calliope sucked her teeth. What was the trigger-happy nut doing?

"Mara, wait," Chance said. "I've got this."

"Like hell you do," she answered, firing again toward the commotion in the trees. "I'll shoot that son-a-bitch that killed Loren."

Hands emerged from behind a trunk. Human hands.

"Don't shoot," a man's voice called from the distance. "I'm a friend."

EIGHTEEN
NEWS FROM THE WEST

Was it Andres?

Calliope's pulse quickened, stomach dropped. She had to know.

"Stop shooting," she screamed, pulling herself up. "Stop shooting."

She skidded on the icy porch as she cantered toward the stairs, but Chance grabbed her arm, steadied her, held her back.

"Wait, mujer. We don't know ..."

"It's him," she said, desperately. "Let me go." She tugged her arm away, calling, "Andres? Where's Phoenix? Is he with you?" She glared at Mara, the woman's rifle still raised. "Don't you dare fucking shoot." She moved toward the stairs.

The man emerged from behind the tree, his arms upraised as if praising.

He wore thick snow gloves, a felt hunting cap, a jacket and jeans. His face contrasted against the snow, russet-brown and terrified. Calliope crumpled onto the icy steps.

It wasn't him.

Chance called again, "Mister, identify yourself. What business you have here?"

"I'm just looking for anybody," the man called. "Y'all a sight for sore eyes, lemme tell you."

"You got a weapon?" Chance asked.

"No, sir, I do not."

"Keep your hands up, I'll come to you."

Chance trekked through the snow toward the stranger.

How had the man gotten to her tía's in a snowstorm? Was he a neighbor from down the road? The nearest house was two or three miles away. Why hadn't he come sooner?

Mara muttered under her breath, "How'll we know we can trust him?"

Calliope was too upset to answer, though Mara's inhospitable tone meant he wasn't a neighbor.

A few minutes passed, Chance talking to the man in the snow. After Chance had searched him, the stranger finally lowered his arms and they trudged back toward the house.

Calliope didn't wait for them to reach the porch but went inside feeling heavy, and slumped in front of the fireplace, an iron-bellied soldier, a smoldering machine man. She would have pointed that out to Phoenix, who would have laughed his contagious little laugh.

The pile of firewood was running low. For no reason that made sense, she walked toward the back door, toward the unfenced backyard where Tía kept her ax beside the chopping block, passing Eunjoo playing at the dining table with salt and pepper shakers shaped as animal figurines, but she couldn't bring herself to say anything to the girl.

Outside, she brushed off the snow from the gloves beside the ax and slid them on her hands. She gripped the handle, positioned a thick chunk of wood on the flared stump, raised her hands above her head, fully cognizant that she should not exert herself, should not hold something so heavy above her head, should not swing, and brought the ax swiftly down. She did this several more times before Chance called from the back door, "Should you be doing that?"

Calliope ignored him, and the pain in her pelvis, and kept chopping.

"Mujer, I don't know much about pregnant ladies except what I went through with my lady and our daughter, but I don't think you're supposed to be chopping wood if you can help it. Here, let me."

She paused, rested the ax on the wood, caught her breath. "Who is that guy? Where'd he come from?"

"Vegas."

"His name is Vegas or he came from Vegas?"

Chance laughed. "You should come inside and meet him."

"Why?"

"He's got an interesting story."

"I'm tired of stories."

"I know." He sighed, reached for Calliope's hands, peeled off the gloves, put them on his own hands. He took the ax, and she stepped aside. "But that's why you need to keep listening."

"Who are you, Chance?"

"A guide, remember? Bisabuela said so."

She laughed uncomfortably. "About that, did you, I mean, when we were in the hangar ..." What would she ask? Whether he had drugged her, given her a hallucinogen?

"I'm just an Indian science nerd, mujer. Nothing special. But I made you a promise and I'm trying my damnedest to keep it. That means no swinging an ax or running toward gunfire. I'm no doctor, and I know nothing about childbirth. Don't go getting yourself into labor here, understand?"

He smiled, but her skin turned gooseflesh.

Labor. She hadn't even allowed for the thought of giving birth without Andres. A paramedic who'd grown up in a small town in northern New Mexico, he'd helped deliver plenty of babies. He'd been with Calliope for Phoenix's birth.

It had never occurred to her she'd have to find someone else to help her give birth.

In Spanish they said *dar a luz*—give light. She felt dark and cold.

* * * *

The stranger who'd called himself a friend had made himself comfortable in front of the fire. He'd taken off his hunting cap, revealing a thick mop of tightly coiled curls, and was eating chocolate chip cookies from a box Mara had given him from Tía's pantry. His voice was raspy though convivial with a Southern drawl. Calliope wondered how she ever could have mistaken him for Andres. She shouldn't have needed to see his rich, brown skin, the color of clay deep in the earth, two or three shades darker than her husband's, to know it wasn't him. He was taller and more broadly-built than Andres as well.

His name was Buick Janes and he was on his way home to New Orleans but had gotten lost.

"In the snow?" Calliope had asked.

"Nah, ma'am. Even before that."

He told her his story. He'd been on vacation in Las Vegas, triple cherries at the slot machines, enough to take his girlfriend out for steak *and* lobster, when the casino lights began flashing. As if in a dream—he couldn't find the city, couldn't find the lights.

"In the casino?"

"Or any casino. It was all desert as far as I could see."

He figured he was drunk—or someone had slipped him something. Maybe his girlfriend, though he couldn't see her stooping that low. But those were the facts. He'd won a jackpot, then he'd gone blurry and everything was gone. Someone must've drugged him and dragged him into the desert. He'd slept it off, then found a car with the keys still in the ignition.

Calliope listened through a vague aura of grief, the kind of numbing that comes when you've already processed the most horrifying information: your father has died, for instance. And now you're learning he'd had another family a few miles across the border, and you had half siblings in your city's sister, Ciudad Juarez. It's what you'd already figured, and though it might've ripped you apart when you were younger, more naive, or if he were still alive to defend himself, by the time police reports have been made and you're helping your mother choose wood for a coffin, cheap pine for an undeserving man, no other shock can really settle in.

Calliope had heard Amy's version of this story, and Chance's. She knew hers and Eunjoo's. And while she hadn't heard her friend say the words, her *pío pío pío* in the dirt before the bullet to her head haunted Calliope.

All she could do was listen as Buick Janes ate chocolate chip cookies on her tía's couch and explained how he'd misplaced an entire city. Then as he passed the Arizona-Nevada border on the road he always took to and from Vegas, something chilled his blood on the bridge over the Colorado River. "The Hoover Dam wasn't dammed."

"It broke?"

"I didn't see no concrete at all, you hear what I'm saying? Like it had never been dammed."

"Oh, we're damned alright," Mara said from the kitchen doorway.

"You know about Petrified Forest? You know what it is?" Buick asked Calliope.

She nodded. An archaeologist's dream, a fossilized forest. On Navajo and Apache counties in northeastern Arizona, log fragments scattered over badlands. She'd heard it disappointed tourists expecting the trees standing in thick rocky groves instead of lying flat in sections. But Calliope loved the felled trees that had lived in the Late Triassic, 225 million years ago. The sediments containing the fossil logs comprised the colorful Chinle Formation for which the Painted Desert was named. Ever since she was a child, Calliope had loved running her hands across the smooth, cold, stony surface of petrified wood.

Buick raised his eyebrows, sat forward conspiratorially, and said, "Well, it's not Petrified Forest anymore. Now, it's just forest."

Calliope felt a familiar paste in her mouth, the stirrings of nausea. "What?"

"I've passed through a hundred times. But now the cut-down petrified ruins are full-grown again and lush. Brand new. It's jacked up is what it is." He pulled a handful of cookies from the box, shoved them all in his mouth.

She didn't tell Buick and Mara about the forest that had sprung up on their way to Tía's from the City of Rocks. She didn't want to hear Mara's theories. She didn't want to hear anything.

But Buick's story wasn't finished.

"All the gas stations and ghost towns along the 40? They aren't ghost towns anymore. They're just ghosts. And Albuquerque? Disappeared. It's like I was lost, but there were the Sandias, just the rest of the land was covered in black lava rock."

The Sleeping Sisters had buried the city. Nausea hardened in her belly.

If her family had been hiding, she had to believe they'd gotten away, as she had …

She couldn't ignore the pain radiating from her pelvic floor down her thighs. She keeled over, pressing hands to knees, breathing in short spurts, instinctively.

"Ma'am? You gonna have your baby *now?*" Buick's pleasant Southern accent rang in her ears, the absurdity of the situation hitting her. Was she really going to give birth in front of this man she'd just met? That was surely more than he'd bargained for when he'd stumbled across her tía's hacienda. "Should I get the father?" He nodded toward the back door.

The cramping seized her tighter. She glared. He meant Chance. He thought they were together. If she weren't splitting apart, gripped with fear, she might've laughed.

By the time the contraction released her, tears wet her face. Eunjoo stood patting Calliope's hair, her little hand a cat's paw. Mara held a damp washcloth to her forehead, though Calliope wasn't sure what good the woman thought that was. A cloth to her head did nothing for the pain in her midsection. "He's not the father," she said, hoarsely, to a frozen-in-place Buick, cookies still in hand. "I don't know where the father is."

Buick nodded, his expression shifting from fearful to melancholy. "Ma'am, damn near the entire Southwest's gone missing … but I think that's the saddest missing-person case I've ever heard."

NINETEEN

LABOR PAINS

The contractions persisted into the evening, aftershocks to the initial quake, none quite as strong as that first and sporadic enough to mean false labor. But that didn't mitigate their effect. A message from Calliope's body, burning with fever, or her babies, squirming: calm down or brace yourself.

Mara had been right to bring the cool cloth. False labor commingled with exhaustion and sudden September winter. In Calliope's fevered state, she was barraged by crows, flailing themselves headfirst, breaking their necks against her body, turning her into a tree, rooted to the ground. She transformed into a crow, alighted from her own branches, wounded herself with black pinpricks, stabbed the ice-white sky. Fever. Dead crows. Suuke.

She sweated and cramped, sweated and cramped, for hours.

Chance had been holding her, she realized when she came through the haze. He'd been chanting in Zuni.

"Mujer, hesitant as I am to admit it, we've got to keep moving. I need to get you to the rez. My mother's people. They'll know what to do."

"Thanks, Chance. I appreciate you sitting here with me and everything. But I can't go to Zuni. I still haven't found my boy, my family. They won't know to look for me there."

He squeezed her hand. "I'm not telling you to give up. I wouldn't say that. Just hear me out. On the rez, many Zuni women have died in childbirth …"

Calliope pulled away, leaned forward, groaning. Chance put a hand on her shoulder, said, "Wait, mujer. I asked you to listen. Please."

She stared into the quartz of his eyes. Leaned back against the armrest.

"I'm not saying you're going to die. It's just that I don't know how to help you with childbirth. I'm out of my scope. A Suuke comes or a psycho with a knife, I've got you covered. You need to find food? You want to talk about bubble universes? I'm your guy. But little people crawling out of you? Look, I haven't told you what Zunis believe about giving birth 'cause you're not Zuni ... Bisabuela is of The People, but it's not exactly the same."

Calliope's head ached, the sweat of her fever had soaked her clothes. She needed to use the bathroom and change. "What's your point, Chance?"

"There are times we're more vulnerable to attacks than others. When we emerged from Ánosin téhuli, the lowermost womb or cave-world, we went to other worlds first. None of them was right. So we came to this world. But some of the creatures from the other worlds followed our ascent. That first world of sooty depth was growth generation, place of first formation, black as a chimney at nighttime, and foul as the internals of the belly. The second underworld was water moss, also dark. The third was a mud world. When we finally reached the fourth world, the one we're in now, there was light. We called it the wing world because the rays of the sun were like birds' wings. But we weren't the only beings to crawl through. Witches followed us, brought seeds with them. They bargained with our leaders, so we had to let them stay. They killed two of our children, and the rains came, and the seeds grew. After many years of wandering, when we finally found Halona Idiwan'a, Middle Place, the witches found it too. They've lived amongst us ever since, sometimes cursing us with illness, death. Whenever we're closest to the Spirit world, like during childbirth, the witches are never far away. We must follow ritual then, as our Ancestors instructed. It's the safest way."

She stared into his face. He bore the most sincere expression she'd ever seen on a grown man. He reminded her of Phoenix in some ways. She thought of the story Andres had told her, about the old man who'd thought the witches were burning him. It was radiation, not witches. There was always a scientific explanation. "My friend, I'm thankful you've helped me as much as you have. But I'm a scientist, not a mythmaker. I'm fascinated by our ancestors' stories. I love piecing together the puzzles they left us. But I don't believe them. You've asked me to believe I'm in danger of attack first by bogeymen called Suuke and now witches?"

His face fell, and she knew she had hurt him. He'd trusted her with his sacred stories, and she'd insulted him.

"I'm a scientist too, mujer. I don't understand why you're so dead set that science and belief are incompatible. Our stories are supported by evolutionary theory. Just because it's not written in a book doesn't make it false."

"I'm not saying that …"

"Look, believe whatever you want. I'm not asking you to believe. You've seen the Suuke. You've seen the landscape utterly changed. You've seen a forest burst from nowhere, overnight. You've seen volcanic ash disappear when your books tell you it should have lingered. Yet you don't believe anything you've seen. Science is about more than what the Western world tells you is true. It's about finding answers for what we *see around us*. Well, I'm saying let's find answers. My people have seen this kind of change before, mujer. This kind of shifting between worlds is the basis for *our stories*. We're an intelligent people, mujer. We're not a spectacle for your fascination …"

"I didn't mean—"

He cut her off. "You study the past. I study possibility. We emerged from the underworlds and theoretical physics says it's possible …" He moved away from the armrest, smoothed his wavy hair from his face.

"Chance, I—"

"Whether you believe or not, you're part of the story, mujer. You might as well start believing." He walked away, out the back door.

Through the window, the evening shone a reddish glow around him. He picked up a small piece of wood, propped one leg on the chopping board, pulled a pocketknife from his boot, and began whittling. His words buzzed in her mind like those cicadas she'd heard at the hangar, when her bisabuela had encouraged her to trust him.

Fine. She had no better plan. She might as well trust Chance.

TWENTY
THE COYOTE WHO KILLED

"**H**ave you seen Eunjoo?"

Mara and Buick were sitting at the table eating peanut butter and jelly sandwiches. Calliope's stomach growled. How long had it been since she'd eaten? Her last meal had been yesterday's snacks on the journey to Tía's. She was starving. Eunjoo would be hungry too.

Calliope had showered, thankful for Tía's water pump, and changed into clean clothes she'd found in the closet, a cable knit sweater and pair of black yoga pants—the only items Tía owned that would stretch over Calliope's belly. The contractions had subsided before the shower; afterward, they'd ceased altogether. She'd towel-dried her hair since she couldn't waste the generator on a blow dryer, and she entered the kitchen with a towel turban-wrapped around her head.

"I thought she was with you," Mara said. "She said she was tired and going to take a nap with you."

"I was in the shower … Eunjoo?" she called.

No answer.

Calliope opened the back door.

Chance was still in the yard whittling. "Peace offering?" He held up a figurine he'd carved.

"Have you seen Eunjoo?"

"She's with you?"

A stab of guilt. Eunjoo was her responsibility, not theirs. The girl *should've* been with her.

"Eunjoo, answer me." Calliope flung open the front door.

On the porch, Eunjoo's footprints.

Panic rose in Calliope's chest. Why would the girl have gone outside? She *knew* how dangerous it was. She'd seen the dead man's body.

Calliope called out again, grabbed a jacket from the coatrack beside the door, threw her hair towel to the floor, and rushed out into the snow.

Chance must've heard her calling because he came jogging from the side of the house. "She's out here? You saw her?"

Calliope nodded, pointing toward the small prints punctuating the snow. They followed the tracks toward the lake, which was covered with a crackling sheet of ice that couldn't have been thick enough to sustain a body, not even a child's. Through the ice, waterweed and coontail reeds wisped upward like downy child's hair. They moved quicker, calling out for the girl, scanning the ice for cracks or holes, any sign that she had fallen through. Inwardly Calliope chanted Don't-let-her-be-dead don't-let-her-be-dead. On the ground, a bright red bloom like a poppy growing from the snow: Eunjoo's blood-soaked thumb bandage. Calliope had been so consumed by her own grief, her own needs, she'd forgotten to check on the girl's wound. Now whispering her chant aloud, she picked up the bandage, tucked it in Tía's jacket pocket.

The footprints circled around the lake, leading toward an outcropping of piñon and ponderosa pine trees, joined by another set of tracks Calliope might have thought belonged to a dog except these were narrower, perpendicular to the girl's, as if she were following …

"Coyote," Chance said. "Why would she run after a coyote? She could get killed." He hollered, "Eunjoo?"

A few feet ahead, dappling the footprints like cherry syrup on a snow-cone, new drops of blood. Calliope's throat tightened. She ran, heedless of her former cramping. The cold air stung her face as she pounded into the small bosque screaming Eunjoo's name.

Mara's story of Lizard singing in Coyote's stomach flickered in Calliope's mind. An image of Eunjoo curled inside the animal like the twins inside of Calliope.

There she was. Cradled beneath a looming ponderosa pine Eunjoo hunched on hands and feet, her back arched high in the air like an animal on edge, face-to-face with the coyote, its tawny fur bristling, ears pointed, frozen in place.

Calliope sprang forward, but Chance held her back, signaling her to hush.

The déjà vu unnerved her. This had been the scene she'd come upon in the gas station parking lot, Eunjoo facing a coyote in what almost appeared as a confrontation for dominance. The first time, in the parking lot, the girl had cowered, terrified. This time though, she poised ready to pounce. Was she the one trying to intimidate the coyote? Calliope sucked in a gasp at how wild Eunjoo appeared, how menacing.

The girl turned sharply. Her eyes no longer soft coal but bright stones of citrine yellow. Highlighter yellow. Animal yellow.

TWENTY-ONE

WHAT COYOTE SAID

C alliope stepped back, unsure what she was seeing. Chance aimed at the coyote, but Calliope reached out, steered the rifle away; she'd been afraid to shoot Amy by accident, when she'd aimed for the rapist beside the truck. Chance was a hunter. He wouldn't miss. Still something told her the gun wasn't the answer.

"Chica? Are you hurt?"

Eunjoo didn't respond. The coyote and the girl continued staring at each other, unflinchingly, and Chance whispered, "We have to act, before she *is* hurt."

As if the coyote understood, it whipped its body in the opposite direction and sprinted away. Before Calliope could reach for her, Eunjoo raised herself onto her feet and was chasing after.

Calliope treaded heavy in the snow but Chance caught Eunjoo where the tree line met a wooden fence marking the edge of Tía's property, a mile from the house. The coyote was nowhere. Had it jumped the fence? Calliope wasn't even sure coyotes could leap that high.

Her breathing strained, her muscles aching, Calliope came upon Chance grasping a flailing and wild Eunjoo. This was not a mere child's tantrum. The girl's eyes still bright and glassy as citrine, she flung herself and clawed at Chance, scratching his arms and yowling, her usual bird's voice low and guttural. This wasn't rabies.

Warily, Calliope kneeled beside them and wrapped her arms around the girl, murmuring and hushing in soothing tones. "I'm here, chica. You're safe now. I've got you."

Eunjoo's thumb was bleeding, but not profusely. Calliope pulled the bandage from her pocket, wrapped it back around; although it wasn't sanitary, it was something. She would clean it as soon as they returned to the house.

Eunjoo grew rigid, her body stiff in Calliope's arms. Her yellow eyes fluttered back, as if in seizure, then her body relaxed again, eyes closed.

"Chica?" Calliope screamed. *Don't-be-dead don't-be-dead.* She pressed her ear to the girl's chest and breathed relief at the steady thumping. Why did this child keep nearly dying on her?

What strange god would have left her to Calliope's care?

Where was the girl's own mother?

Calliope thought of Phoenix. She hoped whoever was taking care of him was doing a better job than she was with Eunjoo.

"She's passed out," she told Chance.

"I'll carry her." He lifted her easily from Calliope, and together they walked back the way they'd come.

Mara and Buick were waiting in the cabin, anxiously, as Chance carried Eunjoo's limp body inside and laid her on the couch in front of the fireplace.

"She's not ..." Mara asked, without finishing her sentence.

"Passed out," Chance said.

A conversation about possible hypothermia ensued, Chance assuring them she only needed rest. Calliope ignored everyone and warmed the girl with water heated over the fire, rewrapping her bandage properly this time with supplies from the medicine cabinet.

Mara explained that she and Buick had stayed behind in case the girl returned. Calliope nodded absently, disinterested in their whereabouts or any other conversation. She bundled Eunjoo in blankets and watched the girl sleep fitfully.

* * * *

The sun was setting again. It felt like perpetual sunset since everything had fallen apart, crossing that bridge. Chance brought a plate with a peanut butter and jelly sandwich and goldfish crackers to the armchair where Calliope was curled, watching Eunjoo intently. Calliope shook her head, her hunger having turned into nausea and indigestion that made the thought of eating unbearable. "You have to eat, mujer. You can watch her and eat at the same time."

"Is it just me or are the days shorter?" She nodded toward the vaulted windows in Tía's living room, glass, ceiling to floor, overlooking the backyard and the desert hills beyond, swathed in the purplish haze of dusk.

"It's not just you." He pressed the plate toward her. "Come on, I made it special for you."

Though she wanted to cover herself with a blanket and fall into a sleep as deep as Eunjoo's, deeper maybe, Chance's smile was contagious. "Yeah, what's so special about it?"

"Extra peanut butter. It's magic."

She half smiled, rolling her eyes dramatically, and accepted the sandwich. The smell of the peanut butter washed away her nausea. Hunger overtook her, and she bit into the sandwich as if it were the first food she'd ever eaten, ate greedily, swallowing it down more quickly than she should have, the roof of her mouth sticky, her throat thick. "Water."

"I've got you covered there, mujer." From his flannel pocket, he pulled a juice box, handed it to her, and sat on the armrest as she slurped the entire contents of the box within seconds. He laughed. "Feel better?"

She nodded, picking at the goldfish piled on the plate. From his pocket, he pulled the figurine he'd been whittling. She asked, "What else you got in there?"

"My whole life, mujer. I carry it with me."

"You sound like my husband."

"He Indian?"

"No, New Mexican. From Española." She wanted to ask Chance about his wife. His daughter, in the dancehall of the dead. But she couldn't form the words.

He handed her the figurine, and she sucked in her breath when she realized what it was.

"How'd you know about the coyote? You made this before Eunjoo got lost …"

"Had a funny feeling Coyote needed to show himself."

"Would you have killed it?"

He shrugged, sighed. "Sometimes sacrifice is necessary. The Zuni don't kill anything, not even birds, without asking permission. I would never kill anything lightly, not even that trickster Coyote."

She handed him back the wooden coyote. "I've wondered if you were a trickster."

He gestured for her to keep the figurine. "I made it for you."

"Why?" Though it was an animal, Calliope couldn't help thinking it was similar to a Zuni doll carved from cottonwood roots and used to teach children about ko'ko spirits or as fertility charms for women. It could rightly be called a fetish.

"To show you I'm not a trickster."

"That doesn't make sense, Chance. I just told you that."

He shrugged again, smile lines creasing his face. "Want another sandwich?"

She shook her head.

"The girl will be fine, mujer. She just needs to process whatever Coyote told her."

Calliope sighed, stifling frustration, remembering her resolution to trust Chance.

"We still need to get to the rez. I'm planning how, so we should talk about it."

She nodded but said nothing.

When Chance took Calliope's plate to the kitchen, she touched Eunjoo's forehead. It was scalding. Calliope stood quickly, removed the blanket. The girl stirred then sat up. "Chica. You're awake." Calliope hugged the girl, whose body emanated almost as much heat as the fireplace. She motioned her to sit on the opposite side of the couch, away from the cast iron.

The others came from the kitchen, Mara with a mug of water she handed to Eunjoo, who sipped it gingerly. "Holy hell, girl, you scared us," Mara said. "Why'd you go coyote hunting all by yourself? You got a death wish?"

Eunjoo's eyes had returned to their former brushed granite, inky and human. Deep purple bags swelled beneath both eyes, and her skin was sallow. But her face had resumed the relaxed and curious demeanor Calliope had become so fond of—that had disappeared for those terrifying minutes in the snow when the girl was wild.

"Tell us what happened, little bird. Why'd you follow Coyote?" Chance asked, his tone more Socratic than confused. "He need to tell you a story?"

Eunjoo nodded. "But the story wasn't for me."

"Oh no? Who for then, little bird?"

Eunjoo pointed to Calliope. "Phoenix's mama."

Calliope's gut lurched. She nearly asked, *You talked to Phoenix?* as if that were possible. Her son was not a coyote. She remembered a bit of apocrypha about American physicist Richard Feynman, who'd worked on the bomb. He was called to his wife Arline's deathbed and hitchhiked from Los Alamos. It was 1945, weeks away from Hiroshima. The nurse recorded the time of death: 9:21 p.m. After mourning and making arrangements, leaving the room and returning, Feynman looked to the clock on the wall. 9:21. The hands frozen. Had the universe taken notice of his loss? Had time stopped for his grief? Could he believe for even a moment that his love had turned the world peculiar, that his wife had returned, a ghost he didn't believe in, come to haunt him from the skepticism of his science-hardened heart? Could he imbue this coincidence with deeper meaning?

He couldn't and he wouldn't. Instead, he remembered the clock had been fragile, that he'd fixed it several times. The nurse must have unsettled the inner workings when she'd picked it up. No miracle. Just an accidental jostle. An ordinary event. Eunjoo had followed a coyote into the cold. She'd become delirious with exertion. Those were the conclusions the evidence supported. No mysterious happening.

"Chica, you can tell me a story, that's fine," Calliope said. "But I don't necessarily believe the animal you followed wanted me to hear it. What you did was dangerous. I don't ever want you running outside by yourself again. That coyote was a wild animal. It could have killed you."

Her bird's voice guileless, she said, "Coyote told me you would say that."

"Oh, really?" Calliope raised her eyebrows, half amused. She sighed. The child had gotten lost on *her* watch. She owed it to her to listen. "Fine. Tell me Coyote's story."

Eunjoo's eyes, still black but flaked with citrine—she began in her birdlike rasp, yet clear and strong, as if she'd rehearsed this story many times before:

"In the days of the Ancients at the edge of Thunder Ridge where the gods of prey lived, there also lived the demon Suuke.

"The gods had made a village for themselves and tried to live and hunt in peace with their families, but whenever the children went hunting among the men or wandered to the outskirts of the village, the demon Suuke crushed and gobbled them up.

"The gods of prey asked who would kill the Suuke, for they needed a plan. Below the ridge in the gulch at the arroyo's mouth, Coyote made his furtive home, scattered with animal bones, a feast of sinew and gristle leftover from the village. He heard their pleas and dropped the bone he was gnawing.

"Next morning, he set to work digging a hollow in the ridge where Suuke lived, then rolled a heavy stone into it, then another, smaller stone. He gathered leg bones of antelope and placed those beside the stones. Finally, he brought a bowl of yellow medicine-water and sat on the large stone with the bones, breaking them with the smaller stone, pretending to bathe his lips in the medicine.

"The Suuke must have heard the pounding for he emerged from his cave and saw Coyote and asked what he was doing. Coyote replied that he was making himself a faster runner by breaking his bones and repairing them with the yellow medicine. *Is it possible?* the Suuke asked. *Will you show me?* Coyote set the antelope bone near his leg and pretended he'd crushed his bone, screaming in pain, then bathed it in yellow medicine.

"After he'd done this with both hind legs and both front paws, he arose and ran around the Suuke as fast as he could, kicking a fury of dust around the demon. Coyote said, *See. I'm faster than any deer or antelope.*

"The Suuke, eager to try, sat on the large stone as Coyote had. He picked up the smaller stone, held it high above his head, then brought it down with so much force it crushed his thigh to splinters. Screaming in pain, he applied the yellow medicine.

"When nothing happened, he asked, *When will the pain stop?* Coyote told him he had to crush all four bones, his legs and arms, before the medicine-water would work. So the Suuke proceeded to splinter his own bones.

"Once he had crushed both legs and one arm, he asked, *How will I crush the last? I cannot lift the stone with my broken arm.* Coyote offered to help him, and the Suuke laid his last arm across the stone.

"So ended the Suuke, but this is not the end of my story.

"Coyote returned to the gods of prey and told them what he'd done, but they did not receive him as the hero he thought they would. *That foul-smelling beast,* they said, *will always make a Coyote of himself.*

"Still, they allowed him to go hunting with them the next day, grateful at least their children were not snatched and eaten by the Suuke on their way.

"All day, Coyote tried and failed to catch a single antelope or deer, and all day the gods of prey laughed at him. Determined to show how capable he was, Coyote said he would go off on his own to hunt and would impress them with his catch.

"The gods of prey indicated much game could be caught along Wolf Canyon, if Coyote stayed to the east when the road forked, but it would go bad for him if he went west.

"When he came to the fork, Coyote could not remember which trail they'd said.

"And he trotted toward the west.

"He came upon a steep cliff and began to climb. No sooner had he reached the middle than chimney swallows began to swarm his head and peck at his eyes. He swerved and bobbed to dodge the swallows, lost his footing, and tumbled down the cliff until he struck a great pile of rocks below and was shattered to pieces.

"When the gods of prey finally found him, the only bone not broken was his head.

"They picked up a large stone and brought it down with as much force as they could muster.

"Now, whenever a coyote finds meat in a rock deadfall he is sure to stick his nose in and get his head mashed for his pains.

"So shortens my story."

As if the whole thing had been a rehearsed production, Chance briefly chanted a song in Zuni, then said, "You told that very well, little bird."

Eunjoo resumed sipping her mug of water.

Calliope looked at the pair of them like they were coconspirators. "Chance, did you teach her that story?"

"No, I did not. Did I, little bird?"

Eunjoo shook her head. "Coyote told me, in the snow."

"Coyotes don't talk. At least not language humans understand."

"I understood."

Calliope sighed. "Fine. What does it mean?"

"That's what you're supposed to figure out."

"Of course." She reached down, felt Eunjoo's head. The girl was cool, damp. The fever had broken. "Well, I'm too tired to figure anything out after being scared out of my mind that you were lost or bleeding to death or worse and then watching you fever-dream unconscious all evening. Let's get you something to eat, and then bed. You're sticking with me, chica. No more wandering out after wild animals. We have to get us both to a doctor, you for that infected bite, me for these raucous babies."

"The rez," Chance said.

"I saw a doctor," Mara said. "At the hospital in Silver City."

"You said there was no one," Calliope said, eyeing Mara suspiciously.

"No one except a doctor."

"That would've been useful information earlier, when I might've been in labor." Calliope couldn't keep the frustration from her voice.

"She's not in Silver City anymore or I would've said something. She went back to her pueblo."

"She Indian?" Chance asked.

Mara nodded.

"Buick, you see any other Indians on your way here? Through Gallup or anywhere?"

"Nah. As I said, I didn't see nobody."

Chance murmured inaudibly then said, "We should still get to the rez."

"I'm too tired to argue this tonight, Chance," Calliope said.

"Didn't you listen to my story?" Eunjoo asked, her cheeks bright pink.

"Yes, chica. It was fairly violent and depressing. You want us to crush our bones and fall off cliffs."

"You didn't listen."

"Come here," Calliope said. "Let me see your thumb." It had been bleeding steadily in the snow, dripping red into the ice. But now the white cloth wrapped around her skin was just that: white. Calliope unbandaged the thumb, gasped, "I don't understand." She turned the girl's hand over in her palm, examining it as if it were a specimen in the lab. "Where …?"

"What's wrong, mujer?"

"Her bite … the wound …" Calliope turned the pallid little hand over, back and forth as if she were making masa for a tortilla, searching for a slit, a scar, anything. "It's gone."

TWENTY-TWO
THE (QUANTUM) SUICIDE

People disappeared. Cities disappeared. Wounds disappeared. Even scars.

"None of this makes sense," Calliope lamented. Night had fallen and the wind rattled through the bare bones of the trees surrounding the cabin, branches scratching against rooftop, fraying Calliope to ragged, exposed nerves. She'd made Eunjoo a sandwich, the little girl happily eating at the table, playing once more with the salt and pepper shaker figurines as if she hadn't just nearly died in the snow, told Calliope a coyote had spoken to her, then miraculously healed right before Calliope's eyes. Mother would've loved this story, attributing it all to Jesus and making the sign of the cross. What would Bisabuela have said?

Chance said, "Mujer, at the fundamental particle level, reality is fuzzy. It's the uncertainty principle. We can never see simultaneously both the position of a particle and its momentum. Can never see, for instance, light as both wave and particle at once. We look away and when we look back can never know which it will be. We live in a world that wants to pin reality down. Quantum science tells us there is no pinning reality."

"Like I said, I've seen it before," Mara said, loading her rifle, pointing the muzzle away from the kitchen table, pulling back the bolt, and inserting the shells.

"Do you have to load that thing in here?" Calliope couldn't shake the bitterness from her voice. She'd put Eunjoo in harm's way enough times already. She couldn't let the girl get accidentally shot by this trigger-happy woman set on revenge. She wouldn't let guns in the house after the story of the rifle that went off through a window and shot and killed a girl across the street, most likely a malfunction from the cold weather that had set the trigger off even with the safety on.

"I know what I'm doing, honey. Been hunting with these rifles nearly fifty years."

Calliope sighed exaggeratedly, turned away. Outside, the sky was new. The stars shone impossibly bright. The cottonwoods closest to the cabin rustled in the wind, a wind-dance. She imagined them playing flutes of wind. An incantation. "Okay then, Mara. Tell me what happened when you were a little girl. Seems this is the night of stories."

"There's not much more to tell, sweetheart. Chaiwa, my nanny from San Ildefonso, was my everything. A better mother than my mother. But after Trinity Site, she disappeared."

Shadows bulged across the bosque outside Tía's window as the moon slipped in and out of clouds, snow hovering on the branches like white balloons floating in the darkness.

"What happened after Chaiwa disappeared?" Calliope asked.

Mara sighed. "Nothing. We never saw her again. My mother went crazy and my father was discharged and we left."

Calliope turned from the window toward Mara. "There has to be more to the story."

"It was Lizard's Tail, that's what I'm saying. I don't understand it, but I think she made herself disappear."

"Not witchcraft?" Chance asked.

Mara shook her head emphatically. "No."

"Lord, y'all plain crazy, that's what I think, that's just crazy talk," Buick said, his Southern geniality cracking, his voice rising an octave. He shook his head emphatically, dipped the butter knife into the jelly jar, and slathered it thickly onto the last piece of bread in the bag. "Guess I must be crazy too." He rolled his bread into a jelly doughnut and stuffed it into his mouth.

"Maybe we are crazy, honey," Mara said. "But if Trudy disappeared the way Chaiwa did, then I need to talk to your Elders, Chance. Find out if there's any way to bring her back."

"My people go to Kothluwala'wa when they die. Join with the Spirits. I've never heard of leaving for that place early. But it's worth a shot asking, I guess. There's lots I don't know. Believe me."

"Oh, I do believe you," Buick said, licking the jelly from the butter knife as if it were a spoon. "I believe none of y'all know what's going on, 'cause we're in the *Twilight Zone*, that's why."

Eunjoo said adamantly, "Coyote told us the answer. You're just not listening."

"This conversation has officially derailed somewhere in the rugged tundra of Siberia and is now skidding across the ice in concentric circles," Calliope said. She squeezed Eunjoo's shoulder. "Come on, chica. Bedtime."

"But I slept all evening."

"And whose fault is that?"

"Coyote's."

"Nice try. Let's go."

She glanced one last time out the window, unable to shake the feeling someone was watching. These stories were giving her the creeps, was all. Eunjoo's birds from the story killing Coyote and the dead crow flown into the bathroom window. Or maybe the coyote had come looking for Eunjoo—not to tell her stories, but to make her his meal.

She pulled the girl close, steered her toward Tía's room.

Before she reached the hallway, there was a knock at the front door.

She froze.

"Who's that?" Eunjoo asked.

"I have no idea," Calliope said, her heart racing. She couldn't dare think it was Andres and Phoenix, still exhausted from the disappointment turning to grief each time she hoped, as if she were losing them every time it wasn't them.

Calliope hadn't even moved toward the door, and Mara was already poised in the entryway with her rifle aimed. "Wait, Mara. You almost shot us and Buick. Please don't shoot whoever this is."

"Unless it's the son-uh-bitch killed Loren."

Chance and Buick right behind her, Mara walked to the door, peered through the peephole. She called, in the same hoarse voice she'd used with Calliope when they'd first arrived, "Who's there?"

Half expecting Eunjoo's demon Suuke or Coyote to come strutting through the door dragging their shattered limbs behind, Calliope breathed out when she heard the young woman's voice.

"It's Amy. Denver?"

As if they'd forgotten her.

Calliope smiled wide, let go of Eunjoo and rushed over, stepping in front of Mara and her gun, forgetting for a moment how angry she was, thinking only how good it was to hear that voice, the first voice of reason after the light on the bridge, and she unlatched and flung open the front door, to face the mentirosa who had flown away in their only vehicle by her damn self.

"Amy." Calliope embraced the white girl. She wore the same army boots, skinny jeans, white tank top, and leather jacket she'd worn before and smelled of rotten garbage, a sack of moldy onions. She was shivering, her thin body a freezer pop. But it felt good to hug her. "What the hell happened? After you left us? Why'd you *leave* us?" Calliope clutched Amy's shoulders, pulled away so they were face-to-face. Amy's was scratched and bruised, her lip cut and bleeding and swollen. "Oh my God, what *happened?* Come in, hurry."

Amy's eyes were red, brimming with tears. Calliope scooted her through the doorway, shut the door, and Amy turned around, wiping her eyes, a bittersweet smile quivering across her face. "You found your family," she said. "Calliope, I'm so happy for you."

Calliope's eyes darted from Amy's to the group gathered in the living room, confused a brief moment. Then she realized. "Oh, Amy. You didn't find yours?"

Amy's tears were streaming down her face now, plopping onto her tank top.

Calliope took her hand and squeezed it, hugged her again. "No, amiga. These are Mara and Buick. They're friends. I haven't found my family yet either."

Amy's tough bravado had vanished. Whatever had happened had changed her. She said, "I'm sorry I left you."

"I know."

Calliope introduced her properly, explaining how Amy had saved them, flown them away from the Suuke. She left out the part about the mentirosa stealing the plane and leaving them stranded.

"Another survivor," Buick said. "Safety in numbers." He had jelly on his chin.

"Wait, how'd you *find* us?"

"You told me you were going to Silver City. I figured you'd get here all right with Chance."

Calliope pursed her lips. She could've gotten to Tía's without Chance. Is that what everyone thought of her? That she was a helpless pregnant woman who needed a man to survive? She let it go, asked instead, "How'd you find my tía's?"

"Yellow pages and a map, in town."

"Smart girl."

"Yeah."

"There's running water here."

"How?"

"Tía's is a genuine sanctuary, Amy. You'll see. Go shower, eat something. I need to get Eunjoo to bed. Wait till I tell you what we've been through here, what this little girl has been up to. And I want to hear about your journey."

Amy laughed in her crumpled-bag kind of way, her smile lopsided. "Sounds good, momma."

Calliope didn't bristle this time. In fact, she was relieved to hear it.

* * * *

Calliope lifted Eunjoo's sweatshirt over the girl's head. "Get in the shower, chica. I'll get clothes." She dug through Phoenix's backpack: her son's clothes. She pressed them to her face, breathed in, hoping his scent might have lingered, though she knew it was impossible. These were clean—

they smelled of laundry detergent. Shower water jetting behind her like rainwater on pebbles, Calliope reached into the bottom of the bag for a clean pair of her son's chonies and felt instead a piece of paper.

A piece of eggshell-colored stationary, which she unfolded. It was Susana's letterhead, a letter, inked in Susana's hand.

Calliope was trembling.

When had she written it? It must've been old, right? A letter she'd written Calliope months before, that Phoenix had stuffed in there. She'd probably already read it.

Or Eunjoo had picked it up from the table at Susana's. A grocery list, a list of sites to explore. Directions. It couldn't have been anything else.

She was afraid to read it. The words swirled black ink across the page, hazy, unfocused.

Eunjoo was singing now, from the shower, her bird's voice rasping a tune Calliope vaguely recognized as a pop song from the radio.

She breathed deeply, read the first line:

Calliope, mija—

It was as if the paper had seared her hand, she dropped it to the bathroom tile. It couldn't have been a recent note. This had to be old. They had been comadres, colleagues. Susana must have written it and forgotten to give it to Calliope, before the world broke apart. It was a coincidence. Eunjoo had picked up a harmless piece of paper from the table. Coincidence Eunjoo had been carrying a letter from Susana to Calliope this whole time.

A clock picked up and jostled, hands frozen at the time of death, that was all.

She retrieved the letter from the tile, began again:

Calliope, mija—
She turned to stone.
I swear I'm not crazy, I'm not—
How will I return to her, ama? Dust. Ash.

Hold yours tight.
(She's in my hand, this rock. Entiendes?)
Ten cuidado. Me voy al otro lado,

Susana

Calliope sucked in the air around her. It wasn't enough air. She couldn't breathe. She pressed the letter to her chest, willed her lungs to expand.

"Eunjoo?"

The singing stopped.

"Eunjoo," her voice harsh, scolding.

The girl peeked her head from behind the shower curtain.

"Did you see where this letter came from? Did you see how it got into the backpack?"

Eunjoo's gaze darted to the letter, then briefly, fearfully at Calliope, then back to the tile. She said nothing.

"Did you put it there?"

Eunjoo stared at the floor.

"Did Susana say something to you? Did you talk to her?"

Eunjoo shook her head.

Calliope's voice caught in her throat, she whispered, "Please."

The water streamed behind the curtain. Eunjoo said, her voice small, "It was on the table."

When? How? She thought back.

There hadn't been time.

Susana had been scribbling into the dirt when Calliope pulled up to the house; she'd still been there, a statue on the ground, when she'd gone inside, changed Eunjoo, gone back to the car. Then she was gone.

But not to the house to write a note. How could Susana have written a note? She was catatonic. She was singing *pío pío pío.*

Then she was dead. In the barn. There'd been no time.

Unless she'd written the note before Calliope even arrived.

And Calliope had missed it. She'd missed it. How had she missed it?

She could've saved her friend. Susana, why?

"Why didn't you give it to me?"

The water running down Eunjoo's face, she looked scared.

"Why?" Calliope repeated, forcefully.

"I didn't want to make you sad."

Calliope sucked in her breath.

It didn't make sense. She looked at the letter.

She looked at the girl.

Eunjoo said nothing.

The shower poured.

"Turn the water off, chica."

Grasping the sink, she heaved herself up. Left the backpack on the floor.

Curled onto her tía's bed, clutching Susana's suicide letter. Numb.

And powerless to change one goddamned thing.

TWENTY-THREE
SHIFT

Calliope's mother had a dicho, a saying: *Ahogado el niño, tapando el pozo.* After the child drowns, close the well. Or, it's wisest to prevent tragedy before it happens.

Eunjoo was screaming from the bathroom. A heavy pounding against a wall, glass breaking from somewhere in the living room or kitchen. Sharp cracking booms of rifle fire. Firecracking of a pistol. The chaos too much to absorb, Calliope focused on only one thing. Eunjoo was screaming.

Calliope ran to the bathroom, stuffing the letter into her shirt as she ran. At the frosted glass of the window, where she'd witnessed a crow break its neck that morning, the leering black and white spotted face she'd wanted to believe a delusion, stared back at her with protruding, toad-like eyes. Its white hair long and jetting in the wind, as if wind-shoved into the window, flattening its ghastly face against the glass. Coiled around its neck, a moss-green snake. The Suuke's eyes darted toward Calliope frozen in the bathroom doorway, inches from a half-dressed Eunjoo squatting petrified on the bathroom rug beside the back-pack. The girl had stopped screaming and they both stared at the demon from Eunjoo's Coyote story, gripped, unmoving. The glint of a knife broke Calliope's trance. The Suuke scraped the curved machete blade against the window like an icepick, pounding into the thick, knobbed handle, and the glass began to crackle. She grabbed the girl, turned the lock on the handle with shaky hands, for the few seconds it might buy them, and slammed the door shut.

In the hallway, Calliope lifted the barefoot girl and propped her on her belly, then ran to Chance beside the fireplace, his rifle aimed at the shattered glass of the blown-out vaulted windows facing the backyard, a breach in the whole wall. Semicircle around him throughout the living room and kitchen, a grim mise-en-scène: Amy with Susana's gun, Mara with her rifle, and Buick with a butcher knife from Tía's drawer, all intent on the gaping aperture where the window had ruptured, and where, outside the frame on the snowscaped vegetable garden, the second Suuke knelt, hunched over, head bowed as if in prayer.

Was it hurt? There was no blood. Only white snow surrounding. What was it waiting for?

Chance steadied his gaze on the kneeling Suuke, whispered slantwise to Calliope, "Mujer, get back in the bedroom, lock the door."

Calliope whispered, "There's another Suuke back there."

He jerked his head to the side, looked at her, his eyes twitching nervously, belying his otherwise stoic composure. He flashed a covert gaze toward the front door, and she calculated silently with him how long it would take her to get there.

His lips sealed tight as a ventriloquist's, he whispered, "There's a truck where the old man was buried. Key's in the ignition."

She glanced back at the Suuke, its head bowed.

"Why isn't it moving?" she asked

"I don't know. Can you carry the girl?"

Calliope nodded, despite the painful weight compressing her lower back and belly; she struggled to keep from careening forward, her center of gravity askew.

She glanced at Amy, still in her tank top and leather jacket, caught her attention and nodded toward the front door, mouthed, *There are two,* held up two fingers, *One back there,* and extended her arm toward the bedroom. *We have to get out. The truck.*

Amy nodded.

There should have been pounding from the locked bedroom door. If the first Suuke was in there.

The second Suuke looked up, its bulging eyes casting a fire-bright target on Calliope. This one had no snake around its neck but black crow feathers darting from its neck like a choker of arrows. It carried a bow, pressed now against the ground in reprieve. A ceasefire. For how long? A basket strung over its shoulder like the old woman in Calliope's dream who had carried Eunjoo away. Calliope shuddered. Chance had called the Suuke a pair of bogeypeople, disciplinarians. What reason had anyone in this room given the creatures to *discipline*? What rules had been broken?

Eyes still glued on Calliope, the second Suuke sprang up, bounded through the broken window, and Chance yelled, "Now!"

Calliope didn't think. As he fired shot after shot, she held the girl wrapped around her as tightly as she could and threw her whole body shoulder-first toward the bedroom door, changing the plan. If the first Suuke had been there, it would have shown itself by now. She had a gut feeling the front door wasn't the way out.

Her muscles strained as she flung open Tía's bedroom and ran toward the opposite side of the room where Tía's side door was dead bolted.

She turned the lock, her hands steady with adrenaline, and the door opened to an icy blast of night air. She hoped Amy was following, along with Chance and the others. But she couldn't care about anything except the girl and the babies inside her. To Eunjoo she whispered, groaning with effort, "No te preocupes, chica. I have you."

The gunfire rang on. Did bullets inflict any harm on a Suuke? Or were they just noise to the demons?

She squinted into the blackness, willing her eyes to adjust to starlight, the bright strip of Milky Way that Chance had called the Great Snowdrift of the Skies, now clearly visible. Her boots crunched the ice-mud as she plowed through the scrub; she'd run this way countless times as a girl in hide-and-seek and knew the knotted landscape by heart. She darted over the rutted ground past the curandera's garden Tía had planted, now shocked with freeze, yerba mansa, arnica, pigweed, and datura, all used for healing by peoples of the past, now tangling in her path, crackling beneath her boots as she ran, Eunjoo's head pressed close to her chest. Yucca and black walnut branches scratched her face and neck.

Footsteps behind her.

She couldn't look to see if it was Amy or Chance or …

Her heart thrummed.

She couldn't feel bad for leaving Mara and Buick to fend for themselves. It wasn't them the Suuke was after. She wasn't sure why she believed that was true but felt it as surely as she felt the ice-wind tearing at her cheeks and neck, the cold light of the stars.

The mothers were warned not to let the children go, though they had transformed. Chance's words rang through her ears as she plunged forward through the brambles, her gut throbbing, lungs ripping as snow-heavy branches clawed at her and Eunjoo. She gasped for breath as she came to a clearing, the gravel driveway, across which lay the path to Loren's house and Mara's truck. She was scared to cross the clearing, stagnant and tar-black as night water.

Some mothers were frightened and let go.

The children were lost to us.

The Suuke would come and rip the babies out. Is that what it wanted of her? Her belly sinking, she clutched Eunjoo tighter through the frozen horehound marking the gravel's edge, the prickling globe mallow. The footsteps behind her grew louder.

She'd have to sprint across the driveway.

If she could have cried out in pain she would have. It took every ounce of strength to put one foot in front of the other and not collapse. *They did not die but joined the ko'ko in the sacred lake, gateway to Kothluwala'wa.*

Eunjoo's bird whisper, "It's coming, Phoenix's mama. Hurry."

The girl's face was buried in Calliope's sweater. How could she see the monster?

Calliope turned.

On the porch outside the front door a hundred feet away a massive figure towered; it was the first Suuke, the one with snakes around its neck, glinting knife in hand.

It turned.

It had spotted her.

Like its feathered partner, the Suuke locked its swollen eyes on her.

She gasped for breath, clamped her arms tighter still around Eunjoo, and kept running.

The Suuke leapt from the banister to the snow below.

Something grabbed Calliope. A knobby hand unrooted from the ground, grasping her tightly. Her ankle twisted and she fell forward, keeled her body to the side so she wouldn't land on Eunjoo or the babies. She kicked furiously at whatever had grabbed her, the Suuke's claw? She was throbbing in pain, scrambling as quickly as she could toward Eunjoo, barefoot and half dressed, sprawling on the gravel.

The girl pulled Calliope's hand, motioning her to stand.

The Suuke was gamboling toward them.

Calliope loosened her foot from her boot, caught in the grooved tree root that had tripped her. Freed and shoeless, she heaved herself up, and, Eunjoo's hand in hers, they clambered forward. She could see the truck parked in the gravel in front of Loren's cabin.

They wouldn't make it.

Chance sprinted out the front door, yelling, jumped onto the banister, and like the Suuke, leapt. Onto the Suuke's back.

He held it in a chokehold, struggling, shouting, "Go, mujer. Go without me."

Amy was at Calliope's heels, aiming her gun at the Suuke.

Calliope knocked her friend's hand down, panted through choked breath, "No, you'll hit Chance." She closed her eyes a moment to think. She should have been running to the truck, turning the ignition, driving Eunjoo and herself away.

Bullets had done nothing to the Suuke but slow it down, momentarily distracting it like wasps stinging a bear.

Its curved knife reflected starlight, inches from Chance's face, his neck. Chance swerved side to side, squeezing the monster's throat. The Suuke didn't flinch.

Calliope glanced at Eunjoo, who seemed impervious to the snow though she was nearly naked as a wild animal. Wild as a coyote.

Coyote's story.

Eunjoo had said Coyote told it to her for a reason.

Susana's letter—*turned to stone*. The Suuke, come alive *from stone*.

The stories were real.

"Chance!" she screamed. "It's like Coyote's story!"

Chance's gaze shifted momentarily away from the Suuke and toward Calliope, and in that split second the Suuke slashed his knife upward before Chance could dart away. The blade grazed his face, which bled down the Suuke's white hair, staining it red.

Calliope winced.

"With his *own* rock."

Chance nodded, let go of the Suuke and dropped to his feet on the snow, tensely circling the Suuke, his arms extended, his eyes on the Suuke's knife.

Calliope told Amy, "Get the girl to the truck, then come get me and Chance."

Amy's expression said *you trust me after I abandoned you?*

Calliope said, "And give me your gun."

"You got it, momma. You're crazy, but you got it."

Amy handed over the gun, scooped up the barefoot girl with her tortoise-shell backpack, and sprinted toward Loren's house.

Calliope breathed deeply, yelled, "Chance, *move*."

He darted sideways, toward the frozen hedgerow, as Calliope steadied her hand, aimed at the Suuke's hand, and shot. Over and over. Wasp stings.

The Suuke dropped the knife.

Chance sprang forward, grabbing it, and thrust it into the Suuke's neck.

The Suuke clutched at Chance, still holding the knife, by his neck, wrapping its large hands easily around Chance's throat, strangling him.

Chance pulled the knife out and thrust it in again and again despite his own choking, his own gasping for breath.

Blood poured from the Suuke's neck, but it didn't release its grasp.

Chance sawed back and forth several more times until one last thrust, he sliced clean through the Suuke's neck.

Its head lobbed to its shoulder, then fell, its white hair billowing across the now-bloodred snow. Its hands released, and Chance pulled away from the grotesque body as it too fell to the ground.

Chance knelt and began praying in Zuni over the Suuke's body.

Calliope came closer, in shock. A week ago, she couldn't even stand listening to Andres's stories of emergency response calls. Now, she'd just helped decapitate a monster.

Chance continued praying even as red welts sprang up around his neck like a noose, thick rope burns. "I don't know what happens to a person who kills a god," he said. He washed his hands in the snow.

"*That* was a god? I thought it was a monster … a demon."

"There's no difference in Zuni cosmology, mujer. It's represented as a ko'ko. No distinction. As I said before, there is knowledge not intended for us. I don't know what the punishment is."

"Seems to me we're already living in the punishment." She ignored the pain searing her pelvic floor and thighs. Braxton Hicks, she told herself, false labor. From the stress.

He nodded, continued chanting, brought the severed head back to the body, then stood.

Amy pulled the truck through the gravel beside them, tires kicking up icy sludge. She pushed open the passenger door, looked at the dead Suuke, said, "Holy fuck, you two are hardcore."

Calliope's stomach roiled; a strong premonition that the worst was yet to come. She realized what she'd missed, turned back to Chance, "Where's the other Suuke?"

"Tied up. The others are guarding it. I didn't know how to kill it until you showed me."

"The other one has a bow and arrow. Did you take it?"

"Mara's holding it."

"Maybe you should let someone else do it, Chance." She could see the psychic toll killing a ko'ko had taken on him. His eyes glazed over, his face furrowed with worry lines. The slash across his cheek clotted with dried blood.

"I've already gone this far," he said. "Get in the truck. I'll get the others."

"Keep the engine running," she called to Amy, then grabbed her boot from the tree root and followed Chance up the porch steps.

"You're too pregnant for this danger, mujer." He glanced at her belly, which she was supporting with her free hand. "You keep trying to hide it, but I know you're worried about those twins."

She ignored him, cocked Susana's gun.

The house was too quiet, fireplace lighting shadows on the walls. Broken glass crunched under Calliope's boots, the only sound. "Where are they?" she whispered.

Chance nodded toward Tía's bedroom.

The Suuke *had* come after her. And they'd stopped it.

Chance kicked open the door.

Right inside the room, Calliope saw where the Suuke should have been, from the coiled ropes knotted on the floorboards.

A few feet away, butcher knife dangling from his flaccid hand, his neck twisted at an unnatural angle, Buick lay on his stomach. Chance knelt down, checked his neck for a pulse then shook his head, murmuring words in Zuni over Buick's lifeless body.

Calliope felt sick. The stranger who'd called himself a friend. She wished she'd been kinder to him. Wished he'd never come to Tía's house. This wasn't a sanctuary but a snare; it was a fucking wasp's nest.

Beside Buick on the ground, Mara's rifle, split in two like a toy gun.

Mara slumped in the corner near the door Calliope had opened minutes before, her breath shallow and raspy, an arrow pitted into her left side, well below her heart. Her shirt was blood-soaked. She cupped her palms where the arrow protruded from her body. Her eyes fluttered. She opened her mouth to speak, no words formed, only a gurgling sound.

Calliope let out a sob, scanned the rest of the room.

Where was the Suuke?

Chance lifted Mara, motioned Calliope, "Let's go."

The arrow had punctured her lung, Calliope could tell by the rattling sounds of the old woman's breathing. If they pulled the arrow out, she'd bleed to death. They needed a doctor.

"The Suuke?" She imagined it crouched under the bed, a true bogeyman. Or woman. Chance had said they were both male and female. Which had they killed, husband or wife?

"Could be anywhere," Chance said, grunting, as he repositioned Mara so he could carry her through the bedroom doorway.

Why hadn't the other Suuke shown itself? Why hadn't it attacked in the front yard while they stood over its dead partner?

Chance crossed the threshold, turned back to Calliope as if reading her mind, said, "Hurry, mujer. I can't fight and take care of you."

She nodded, grabbed a blanket from the couch on the way out.

From the snow-covered gravel, Amy picked up the Suuke's machete-like knife. She wiped the blood in the snow. "This thing slayed a monster. It could come in handy." Amy dropped the knife into the back of Mara's truck, then climbed back into the driver's seat. "You coming, momma?"

Calliope nodded.

Before she climbed into the seat with Amy and Eunjoo, she turned toward the crow-covered piñon in the distance. In the starlight, she thought she could make out the silhouette of a coyote, howling up at the sky. But if anything was howling, the truck's engine drowned it out.

TWENTY-FOUR
DEADFALL

All the roads were dirt.

As Amy drove over the rutted road, Calliope dressed Eunjoo in Phoenix's clothes, though she didn't have shoes. They'd left those in Tía's bathroom. She put two pairs of socks on the girl's feet and cranked the heater up, then massaged her own belly from the painful jolting.

Chance whispered into Calliope's ear, "Why didn't you leave me? I told you to go."

"I couldn't leave my guide."

"You never listen to anything I say."

"You're my guide, not my husband."

"Do you listen to your husband?"

"No." She did not listen to Andres. She pictured his body lifeless as Buick's, that stranger-friend who'd said all the cities from Las Vegas to Silver City had disappeared, the world reverting to precivilization, the time of the Ancients. It wasn't possible, but there it was. She turned toward Mara in the back seat, who lay under a blanket Calliope had spread across her body, her head on Chance's lap. The arrow jutted from the woman's chest. Anything was possible in this world. *This* world. The thought hadn't crossed her mind until now.

Chance had torn a piece of his shirt and packed it around Mara's entry wound.

"Where are we taking her?" Calliope asked.

"Yeah, I was wondering the same thing. I'm driving *away*, but I'm gonna need actual directions," Amy said. "Just like old times, right? The family back together."

Calliope half smiled. Amy was right; Calliope couldn't have left them any more than she could have left her own family. Crisis brought people together that way.

"The rez," Chance said. "It's the only place."

"What do you mean, the *only* place?" Calliope asked. "The only place *left*?"

"The only place I know there will be healers." He paused, added, "For Mara *and* for you."

Calliope wanted to ask how he was so sure there'd be anyone on the Zuni reservation. But she didn't.

Amy said, "How do we get there?"

"Drive north. We can't take the 180 if the roads are gone like Buick warned, so we'll have to rely on the compass to get us there." He pulled a compass from his pocket.

Calliope said, "Your whole world in there."

He smiled. "Zuni's northeast of here. If we just continue north through the Gila Forest, through the pass at Mogollon Mountains, I can get us there ..." He paused, studying the compass then peering outside. Dawn was approaching through the pinkish gray haze staining the lower half of the sky to their right. They were on the right track. "I'll know how far east to go by the Zuni Salt Lake, Ma:k'yayanne." He lowered his voice, close to Calliope's ear, whispering, "Old Lady Salt lives there, mujer. It's a sacred lake."

"Can we make it there today? We didn't bring any food or supplies," Amy said.

"I should've planned better," Chance said. "I knew it wasn't safe there. We should never have stayed so long. I should've taken you to the rez in the first place."

Calliope was trembling. All the questions she'd been holding in came streaming out at once. "What aren't you saying? Why are the Suuke alive?

Why are they after us? Why are the stories real? Where is everyone? If you know, why aren't you telling us?"

He sighed, snapped the compass shut. "I told you, mujer. I have to talk to the Elders. Not everything is for us to know."

"I understand your beliefs are sacred, but we almost died. We *keep* almost dying. I found this in Phoenix's backpack. Eunjoo put it there, from the table at Susana's house." She pulled the letter out of her shirt, handed it to Chance. "It's a suicide note."

"Who's Susana?" Amy asked.

Calliope realized she hadn't ever told them about Susana. She told the whole story of finding Susana in the mud, how she'd shot herself in the barn.

Chance read the note aloud.

When he finished, Calliope repeated, "Turned to stone. What does she mean? Literally *turned to stone*? Did Reina become a *rock*? Is that a Zuni story too? Connected to the ko'ko?"

In the back seat, Mara's eyes fluttered and she moaned, "It's Lizard's Tail. Why won't you believe me? I need to get back to Trudy."

"I do believe you," Calliope said, filled with compassion for the woman, in much worse shape than any of them. "Save your energy. We're getting you help." To Chance, she said, "You didn't answer my questions."

"Mujer, I'm not an expert on Zuni cosmology by any stretch. But I'll tell you what I think. We've been shifting a long time. We came into this fourth world, and the white man calls it evolution, but we Zuni know that there's a metaphysical side to the story. Mother Earth, when she is fed up, will shake herself off. There are stories that Old Lady Salt did the same, and Moon Mother changed the tides after Neil Armstrong and the other astronauts tramped on her, and stuck American flags into her skin, and raided nearly fifty pounds of rock and dust from her body without so much as a cornmeal offering or prayer. I'm a physicist, yes. I believe in science. But what they did here in *our* Middle Place in 1945, that wasn't science. What the white man has been doing since …" He was silent a long while. "The genocide started again when the protests were growing and the energy was crackling like static electricity. Not just up north but in Zuni and everywhere, The People were trying to protect our land and our water. I watched an elder fall at my feet, his staff clattering to the pavement of the shut-down highway. Police barraged us with smoking tear-gas canisters from grenade launchers. They put us in cages, like animals. If we'd known what was coming next … We prayed and burnt sage and sweetgrass, we held dances, supporting our brothers and sisters in the North. When they threatened round-ups and destroyed Mother Earth, we knew it couldn't last long …"

"I felt something coming too," Calliope said. "Andres and I were planning for it. That's why I thought he'd be at my tía's."

They drove in silence until long after the sun rose, Eunjoo sleeping against Calliope, Mara against Chance.

Finally, Calliope said, "Chance, did you ever believe we would find my family?"

"I should've taken you to my people first. I still think we can find them. But we shouldn't have gone to Silver City. I realize that now."

Calliope squeezed her eyes shut as a fresh contraction wrung her into a dishrag, sodden with pain vibrating from her belly down her thighs.

"I'll get you there, fast as I can, momma. Don't have those babies in this truck."

"I'll try my best," Calliope said, between short, panting breaths, no longer deluding herself that they weren't due for two months. The babies were coming, she felt it. She only hoped they'd wait a little longer.

* * * *

As they rose through the winding pass of the Mogollon Mountains, the temperature dropped and the wind grew stronger. Snowflakes gathered on the windshield in six-fold symmetry. These ancient roads had borne the first peoples, then later, her bisabuela's people, the Chacoans; these roads had carried them northward into Chaco and southward into Mesoamerica to trade for cacao for frothy ritual drinks, Scarlet Macaws, copper bells, and colorful Mayan pottery. Calliope had long wanted to know what it felt like, being an ancient human—a cave dweller, one of the first in the Americas. Her research on the Clovis people in grad school had her trying out the atlatl, fastening a spear with a Clovis point affixed to the end, throwing it with the atlatl toward a target, a bullseye on a tree, where the only rules were these: nature and survival. Now, she'd experienced real hunting. She'd helped kill a beast. Unwittingly, she'd become a first person, and for better or worse, these people in the truck with her were her tribe. Until she found her family.

Mara awoke needing water, which they didn't have in the truck.

Amy pulled to the side of the steep, narrow road, where Calliope gathered snow in an empty mason jar she'd found in the glove box, and held it to the heater.

Eunjoo asked Mara, "Why do you keep a glass jar in here?"

"To collect samples." The woman's voice was garbled but understandable.

"Of what?"

"Don't bother her with questions, chica. She should save her strength."

"The earth," Mara answered anyway. "I collect Earth samples to paint and make colors. River water, mossy grass, cactus spines, white sands." She coughed, and Calliope handed her the jar of melted snow, hoping it didn't contain ash, though the ash had miraculously disappeared.

Miraculous, Calliope thought, wryly. She felt a pang of longing for her mother and family, who would have marveled at her use of the word, not in reference to any ancient belief but the present world. *Miracles happen every day*, her mother had said, *if you know where to look, if you know how to look. Not through the microscope, mija. Through the kaleidoscope of your heart.*

Calliope wished she would have told her mother what a beautiful thing that was to say, what a relevant piece of poetry, instead of bristling, arguing back in academic language she knew her mother couldn't understand. What a petty child she'd been, thinking herself so high and intellectual, a crab who'd escaped the bucket—only to find herself in the fisherman's mouth.

Her mother wasn't dead. Calliope had to believe a miracle was keeping them alive—and her searching for them.

Mogollon Road narrowed to a bottleneck, and Amy slowed the truck to steer a hairpin turn. A thick clump of snow from a crag of rock above plopped into the road forming a snow hill reaching up to the bumper.

Amy said, "Shit. We'll have to dig our way out."

"I'll do it," Chance said, lifting Mara's neck gingerly, placing her on the seat beside him as he slid out of the truck. "Got any tools in the back?"

"Yeah, a shovel," Mara answered, her voice ragged. Eunjoo had turned to watch the commotion, and Mara said to the girl, "To dig out Earth samples."

Eunjoo nodded, wisely.

"I'm gonna help the monster slayer," Amy said, sliding out of the driver's side. "Whoa." She skirted close to the side of the truck. "It's a long way down. Whoever dug this road forgot a shoulder."

"Or it wasn't built for trucks," Mara said.

Chance was already digging with a long metal shovel as Amy scooted along the edge of the truck, grabbed a small garden trowel, rounding the passenger side. "Look, I get the baby shovel," she muttered to Calliope as she passed her window.

Calliope felt useless, sitting inside, watching them work while she breathed deeply, counting cramps. Irregular, sporadic, nowhere near ready, nevertheless painful aggravations.

Eunjoo asked if she could drink snow too. Calliope reached to the back seat for the mason jar, stuck her hand out the open window, refilled the jar from a pile of clean snow heaped atop the rock wall, and handed it to the girl, who smiled wide and said, "Snowcone."

Eunjoo set to eating, as Calliope breathed and counted through a contraction, comfort in numbers, and watched Chance and Amy scooping snow and throwing it over the cliff's edge.

"You know Mara's right," Calliope told Eunjoo as the girl crunched the ice in her teeth. "These roads weren't built for us. The mountain we're on is called Mogollon, for the people who lived here thousands and thousands of years ago. They're part of the Ancient Ancestors."

"A'łashshina'we," Eunjoo said, a Zuni word Calliope didn't know.

"What does that mean?"

"Keepers of the path."

"Chance teach you that?"

Eunjoo shook her head, bit another mouthful of ice. "Coyote."

"You're a very intelligent child, to remember everything Coyote told you in that one brief encounter … you have an incredible memory."

Eunjoo shrugged. "I guess. Have you figured out Coyote's story yet, like he said you should?"

"I think so. Though it doesn't make sense, the stories are real? The stories are the reason we knew how to defeat the Suuke."

Eunjoo slurped thoughtfully for a moment, then said, "Yeah, that's good. But Coyote dies anyway. In the story."

"If Coyote died, how could he have told you the story?"

Mara said again, "It's Chaiwa's Lizard's Tail, I'm telling you. No one ever listens to the artist with the arrow sticking out of her chest."

Calliope laughed. Was Mara always this bizarre, this funny? Calliope could see what her tía liked about her. Could see why Tía loved her. Calliope felt ashamed of how angry she'd been at Mara when she'd first arrived at Tía's hacienda, how she'd accused Mara of killing her family when Mara was just as invested in finding her family as she was. When Mara had taken an arrow for her. Calliope owed her a debt of gratitude. "Okay, Lizard flees. Escapes. Maybe even *vanishes*, as you say. Can Lizard ever return? Can she *reappear*?"

"Now you're thinking, girl. Now you're *thinking*." Mara coughed a phlegmy cough. "Those scientists, and my father. They were there for a trigger, for a millionth of a second, for a violent chain reaction that treated us for what we are."

"What are we?" Eunjoo squeaked.

The old woman closed her eyes, and in her gargled voice replied, "We're matter."

Outside, Amy slapped the hood, yelled, "We're unstuck." She pressed her body against the side of the truck, shuffling gingerly back to the driver's-side door. Chance put the shovels away, then slid into the back seat, resuming his position as Mara's pillow.

"Careful," Calliope told Amy. "Eunjoo's afraid we're going to fall off the cliff, like Coyote in the story."

"That right? Don't worry, Eunjoo. I'm an expert driver. Remember I flew that plane?"

Calliope said, "Yeah, you might not want to bring that up. We all remember how you flew that plane *away from us* so we had to walk the desert for hours …"

Amy cleared her throat, her face red. "I'm really sorry about that guys. Heat of the moment, you know? No hard feelings?"

Eunjoo said, "At least you came back."

"There's the spirit," Amy said, grinning. "What's family for, right?"

Chance gave directions: the road would soon descend. Within an hour they should have been out in the clearing, then an hour to the salt lake (he didn't call it "sacred" when he instructed Amy on how to get there). After that, it was a straight shot to Zuni.

He checked Mara's bandage, a torn-off piece of his shirt.

"Hang in there," he said. "Our healers will fix you up."

"Oh, I'm hanging, honey," Mara gurgled. "You're a fine caregiver, you know that? You'd make a fine husband. You got yourself a wife in Zuni?"

Calliope's heart raced. She stared out the side window at the snow-covered hillside, counting her breaths in Spanish, focusing on her body.

"Yes, ma'am … she and my daughter passed on to the Spirit world a few years back. I stay in touch with her brother, Arlen. He lets me know how things are getting on with her family. I haven't had much other connection to the rez since they passed."

The air around Calliope went cold. Reflexively, she turned around to face Chance.

"I'm so sorry, honey," Mara said, reaching her hand painstakingly from beneath her blanket, patting his.

Chance held Calliope's gaze, their eyes locked on the sad thing huddled between them.

She hadn't realized they'd both died. How had she missed that? His whole family, gone.

She pictured his wife and daughter with his ancestors dancing in that underwater dancehall. Though Calliope wasn't Zuni, she imagined Bisabuela there too.

But not her family. Not her mother, not her husband, not her son.

The truck jolted, lurched forward, then stalled. The engine had died. Amy turned the ignition, a cranking sound. "Shit-shit-shit."

The silence between them broken, Chance said, "I'll see what's wrong," and got out. He lifted the hood, clanking metal.

"Can't trust a man," Amy said, and shimmied out too, sliding against the truck.

"We're cursed," Mara whispered.

"For what?" Eunjoo's eyes were wide.

"We're *not* cursed," Calliope said, staunchly. Though Chance's words reverberated through her mind, *I don't know what the punishment is for killing a god.*

They hadn't killed a god; they'd stopped a monster from killing them. It was self-defense.

A gust of wind. A pounding in the trees like a drumbeat. Crows shrieking in the sky.

"Mujer, lock the doors. Get down."

"Not again," Mara moaned. "I won't live through another attack."

"It's coming," Eunjoo said, her small body scampering mouselike below the dashboard.

"Amy," Calliope called through the window. "Come back inside."

"Like hell," Amy shouted. "I'm hardcore too, momma."

And the second Suuke was upon them.

TWENTY-FIVE
THE ARROW

Calliope locked the doors. Her contractions came stronger, burning her stomach, her groin, her thighs. She struggled to breathe deeply, struggled to breathe at all. She had felt brave earlier in the night, with the rush of adrenaline, the rush of triumph. Now, replaying the image of Buick's lifeless body twisted stiffly in death, she felt sick.

The Suuke in the light of day was even more terrifying, if that were possible. It cleared the cliff, jumping on the rocky crags, landing on its haunches. They'd killed its partner, and in its eyes glowed the fire of revenge. Whatever they'd done before to warrant the Suuke's ire was nothing compared to this.

"You don't even have a gun," Calliope called to Amy.

"Hand it to me, then." Amy's voice sounded exhilarated.

Calliope rolled down the window, handed Amy the gun. "You have to get its bow and arrow. That's the only way to kill it. Chance knows."

The Suuke watched from the cliff above as if planning its move.

Calliope scanned the rock face. She could do nothing, stuck in the truck in labor. She was worse than useless. What other weapons did they have? Shovels in the back. A glass jar in Eunjoo's hands.

"I threw a peach at it," Eunjoo said. "In my dreams."

"Not now, chica."

"In my dreams *before* my parents disappeared."

"What?"

"I knew this would all happen. I dreamt it before."

A rumbling outside.

"What do you want, beast?" Chance yelled. The Suuke snarled, revealing tusklike teeth. It raised its bow, steadied an arrow, released.

Chance dropped to his knees, tucked his chin to his chest, and the arrow struck the metal frame of the truck and wilted as a dead flower into the snow.

Rooted in the road, her lean body poised, a fury, an Artemis, Amy began shooting.

"Chance, the arrow," Calliope called, nodding toward where it had fallen in the snow, six feet away from where he knelt.

Eunjoo wriggled across the floorboard toward the driver's side and was opening the door. "Chica, no!" Calliope screamed, lunging forward.

The car door swung open and the little girl flew over the ravine, holding onto the car door. Calliope screamed for Amy—"Help her!"—then, holding the steering wheel, grabbed hold of the door. She pulled it, slowly, calling, "Don't let go" to Eunjoo. The girl's face was scrunched in fear and effort, her hands clasped around the doorjamb.

Calliope's spine knotted in pain.

Below the dangling girl, a drop at least a hundred feet, snow belying the craggy rocks and jagged skeletons of forest.

She couldn't fall.

Calliope couldn't let her fall.

"Don't let go," she repeated, her voice a whisper as she struggled to reach the girl without losing her grip on the steering wheel.

Mara sat up, groaning, leaned forward, and entwined her arms around Calliope's chest as Calliope leaned out of the car, pulled the door closer, straining as far as she could, lifting the girl back toward the snowy ledge.

Amy had stopped shooting, shuffled beside the driver's side, and grabbed Eunjoo. She pushed her back into the truck.

"What were you thinking?" Calliope yelled.

The girl's face streaked with tears, she breathed rapidly, a small, frightened bird.

Calliope repeated the question, gentler.

Eunjoo sniffled, wiped her nose on her sleeve. "I wanted to help."

Calliope hugged Eunjoo, hard. She understood the futile helplessness of hiding and waiting. She wanted to help too.

Amy still perched on the shoulderless ledge, leaning across the hood, aiming the gun.

She shot, and the gun clicked without firing, empty.

"Come back in, Amy. You're out of bullets." To Eunjoo, "Stay down this time, *please* chica." She understood now how Chance felt when Calliope had habitually ignored his instructions. She hunched low in the seat and Mara resumed her prone position in the back seat.

The arrow in the snow was gone—as was Chance.

Calliope scanned the rock face from her low vantage point of the passenger window.

He was nowhere.

The Suuke had jumped down to a lower rock, was stringing another arrow in its bow.

Chance emerged in Calliope's peripheral vision, crawling up the rock wall to the right of the Suuke, who didn't seem to notice, its gaze directed on the truck's passengers.

Amy nodded, abandoned the gun on the hood, and shuffled toward the road ahead, running twenty feet away from the truck. She waved her arms and screamed, "Bring it, monster."

The Suuke turned swiftly and shot.

Amy fell flat on her belly, the arrow whirring past her into the ravine.

She stood again, flailing her arms, mocking the monster.

The Suuke seemed unaware Amy was a ruse, and continued shooting at her, while Chance inched closer, hauling himself down from the precipice, onto a crag above the Suuke, its feathered arrow projecting from his back pocket.

Calliope's pulse jangling like keys in her throat, she watched the plan unfolding before her as though they were not cursed, as though they had luck on their side, for once, Amy playing well her part of distraction while Chance crept toward his target, pulling the arrow from his pocket and pointing its sharp tip toward the Suuke's neck as he readied to jump. Calliope could see the determination that furrowed Chance's face—demon or consequences be damned.

He lunged.

His flannel blended with the patterns made by the swirling feathers around the Suuke's neck, Chance's arrow and the Suuke arrows becoming one, fuzzy in the gray-black snow on rock. But the Suuke knew Chance was coming, or its reflexes were quicker than its partner's. It spun at Chance, knocked him to the ground before he could latch onto its back, before the arrow could break Suuke skin. Its foot stamped into Chance's torso, pinning him to the ground; the Suuke strung its arrow to its bow. Calliope unlatched her door, ignoring the jolts of pain shockwaving her own torso, and screamed "No!" It couldn't kill Chance. She couldn't let it.

Still lying across the back seat, Mara gurgled, "Under the passenger seat. There's another gun." There wasn't enough time. Why hadn't the woman said so before? Calliope grabbed the gun and the mason jar rolling beside it. Gun in one hand, glass in the other. She cocked the gun.

From her crouched position under the dashboard, Eunjoo said, "Throw it."

Amy was climbing the rock wall toward the Suuke, unarmed. What was she thinking?

Calliope aimed for the Suuke's face. But she couldn't get a clean shot. She had to hit it somewhere that would distract it more than a wasp sting to its rhinoceros-thick skin. She needed somewhere soft.

The Suuke shot its bow, straight ahead. The arrow struck Amy's neck, blood spilling down her body as she fell to the snow beyond the truck.

Calliope heaved the glass with all her strength. It hit the rock, shattered.

The Suuke turned, its face a snarl. Calliope shot it in the eye. It howled, stumbled back, blood seeping from the blackened socket. Chance wasted no time. He sprang, arrow still in hand, and jabbed it into the Suuke's throat. Like an oak felled, the monster tumbled from the ledge, landing beside Amy in the snow.

Amy.

While Chance climbed down the rock face, Calliope stumbled forward, unbelieving.

She dropped to her knees at Amy's side. Chance grabbed every arrow from the Suuke's clutch, pulled the bow from the monster's grasp, and shot one after the other in a row of arrows from his eyes to his groin. Then, not even bothering with a prayer, as if he'd gone too far this time for prayer, he kicked the corpse, rolling it through the snow, and shoved it off the ravine ledge.

Calliope grasped the arrow that had killed her young friend. And as a stinger burrowed deep in a child's skin, as any mother would, she yanked it out.

TWENTY-SIX
OLD LADY SALT

alliope, a small ponytailed girl standing in a windstorm on the mesa above Chaco Canyon with her bisabuela, shivered despite the autumn heat. They'd hiked the steep black basalt carrying a picnic basket filled with chile verde fry bread, sweet potato empanadas, and cold glass bottles of orange soda. They'd hiked the mesa even though Bisabuela was in her seventies, her silver hair covered with a knitted rebozo. She had to show her great-granddaughter the sun spirals. The mesa had been closed to hikers and tourists for many years, but back then it was still open. On the flat top behind three great slabs of sandstone, a spiral carving, just as a dagger of light pierced its center, a ray channeled by the rocks, capturing the sun's cycle. It could be no accident. *There's a language written in the architecture, mija. You have to find it.* The large spirals marked the solstices, and the small spirals, the equinoxes. These specific markings of the sun's cycle repeated on the mesa. In the center, a double spiral, like a pair of curved spectacles. Bisabuela had brought Calliope to the opening of the world not for a mere September lunchtime picnic but to show her this: at noon equinox the double spiral marked the middle of the day in the middle of the year.

She said it was the middle of time.

* * * *

Calliope thought of this as she knelt in the snow, a gush of hot amniotic fluid rushing between her thighs. She held Amy's limp body to her chest, rocking back and forth, blood smearing her own clothes. She was conscious of the middle place: between death and life. The young woman in her arms, the children in her body.

And that she had failed.

Chance peeled Amy's body away from Calliope, who clutched her tightly, still rocking back and forth, Chance pulling her away, saying, "We'll pray properly, mujer. Bury her. But we have to get you to the rez." He carried the dead woman's body to the truck. Then he came back for Calliope, still kneeling in shock, the snow beneath her melted with birthwater, tinged pink with blood.

Her vision blurred. Penumbras around every object. Sun splotches. Inkblots distorted with tears. She felt cold. Chance lifted her, carried her to the truck, as the thorned flowers in her belly swelled and shrank, needling her with each blossoming and dying.

Amy was dead.

Calliope sat shuddering on the front seat, as Eunjoo clutched her tightly, tears rolling freely down the girl's cheeks. Even if Calliope had been able to speak, she wouldn't have needed to sugarcoat anything for the little girl, who seemed to understand more than any of them. She rubbed Calliope's belly as she cried, and though the little hands offered no relief, felt like nothing more than cat's paws vaguely kneading at her skin, Calliope didn't brush her away.

Mara gurgled something about how sad it was. Calliope didn't answer.

Chance must've fixed the truck. Calliope didn't ask how, just leaned against the seat, her head tilted toward the window, and stared at the blurring rock wall as they careened down the mountain. Wet snow sloshed under the tires until they reached the mountain's eventual end, when the snow gave way to mud-wet roads, mossy-brown, edged with new growth.

No one said a word.

Eunjoo had worn herself out crying and was snoring against Calliope, who'd been clenching her teeth until her jaw ached and gripping the armrest until her knuckles went white. She felt as if she'd grown a tail, her spinal cord exposed and frayed and searing. Her ass ached. Her thighs throbbed. She squirmed uncomfortably, pressing her feet against the floorboard, bearing down in the seat. Resisting the urge to push. It wasn't time. She wasn't ready.

She steadied her breathing.

Blood streaming down her friend's neck, siphoning out of her onto the snow.

She felt the blood rushing between her thighs, a thick pulse in her pelvis.

Amy was dead. But she had to think about her babies.

She breathed in: *uno, dos, tres, cuatro, cinco.* Breathed out.

Chance said, "Sé fuerte, mujer. We're almost to Old Lady Salt." His voice, a pillar, but beneath the stone, slight fissures. "I'll ask her for a blessing for you and your babies."

Eunjoo woke, patted Calliope again. "Who's Old Lady Salt?"

"I thought you knew everything about Indian ways?" Chance said.

The girl shook her head.

"She is our mother. Ma'l Oyattsik'i, Salt Lady. She is sacred and we must treat her with respect. In the old days, she used to live near Black Rock, beside the rez, but people grew selfish, took her for granted, removed her sacred flesh without so much as a prayer stick or jeweled cornmeal offering, and she became angry and moved south so we would have to make a pilgrimage to see her and treat her better."

Calliope knew the controversy surrounding the sacred site, center of a decades-long battle over mineral and water rights. The nation's second largest electrical company, little brother to the one devastating the North, planned a coal strip mine twelve miles from the lake, along with a railroad line that would intersect with pilgrimage trails, documented graves, and other sacred sites nearby. The company would build wells to pump water eighty-five gallons per minute from underground aquifers near Zuni Salt Lake for use in settling coal dust. The aquifer and surrounding springs supplied the lake, and without this water source, the lake would dry up, the ecosystem irreparably damaged, obliterating Old Salt Woman and the ceremonies surrounding her.

The protests at Zuni hadn't turned as bloody as in the North, where the camps had burned and the Ancients with them. But Calliope had a feeling the battle wasn't over. Bisabuela's voice in her ear as she watched on the news, *When they live for greed, what will burn in the end is them.*

Now she felt ashen. Grief as bitter as salt in her mouth, swollen with it and feeling cursed with it, Calliope said, "What blessing could she give me?"

"That's what we'll find out, mujer. You know, Zuni women aren't allowed to visit Old Lady Salt. But you're a different tribe. It should be all right. I don't have cornmeal with me. I'll offer her my turquoise."

His jewelry. It was so beautiful. And he would give it up for a miracle.

He wouldn't call it a *miracle*. But it amounted to the same. She was about to give birth to two premature babies without a hospital or Western medicine. She needed a miracle.

She thought of the Upper Paleolithic shaman woman excavated from the Czech Republic, buried with mammoth tusks and a fox in her hand; it was such a remarkable discovery that spiritual healers even during the Ice Age had been women, where previous academic study had speculated it an all-male profession. Calliope had loved the idea of this woman and her ocher-painted bones, her hundreds of bake-oven, hard-clay figurines, talismans for ritual or healing. All over the world since humanity began, women were central to spirituality and medicine. Bisabuela would've loved the Ice Age shaman woman as Bisabuela would have loved Old Lady Salt.

Calliope wished miracles could exist alongside science.

"How about a blessing for the wounded lady back here," Mara quipped, her voice still garbled but spitfire. The silver halo of hair around her face glistened with the sweat of fever. "I could use some hope."

Luck already seemed on Mara's side. She hadn't bled out or stopped breathing yet. But she needed help as quickly as Calliope did. Maybe quicker. Calliope pictured Amy's dead body in the back of the truck.

"Old Lady Salt is gracious to those who respect her."

A pulling in her gut. Uterine strings twisting. Heat rushing between her thighs. She'd already released her amniotic waters. What was this?

Something was wrong.

"Pull over," Calliope said.

He slowed. "What's going on?"

She opened the door, vomited clear liquid onto the white earth and saltbush, the plant's papery four-winged leaves sparkling with it.

She could see the lake in the distance. She wouldn't make it.

She stumbled out of the truck, crawled on hands and knees across the alkaline soil, groaning. She had the urge to shit. Trailing behind her on the salted ground, bright red poppies.

Chance knelt beside her, his hands clutched around her waist, as if he couldn't decide whether to lift her or crawl with her, and so he held her, lamely, his voice trembling, "Mujer, you're bleeding. Is that normal? Is there supposed to be blood? If I could just get you to the lake, I could ask for help."

Eunjoo climbed from the truck, Bisabuela's bowl in her hand.

Calliope couldn't remember the last time she'd had it, thought she'd left it at Tía's.

Her vision was blurring.

She was hemorrhaging. Ruptured placenta? Stillbirth? She didn't know what was happening, but she was in too much pain even to cry out.

"Use this," the girl said.

She held the bowl to Calliope's face.

It was filled with water.

"How?" Chance asked.

"Old Lady Salt gave it to me," Eunjoo said. "It'll help."

He let go of Calliope's waist, dug into the white earth with his hands, opening a small pit, unlatched his bracelet, took off the ring from his finger, pulled the necklace over his head, and dropped them all in. Buried them. He murmured words in Zuni as he repacked the earth.

He nodded to the bowl in the girl's small hands. "Drink it, mujer. If it's from Old Lady Salt, then she is blessing you."

Calliope's head throbbed with dehydration. There was no way drinking salt water was a good idea. She didn't need an emetic.

If the water was *not* from Old Woman Salt, Calliope could die.

But where else would Eunjoo have gotten the water? The snowcone jar was gone, crashed against the rock wall. Calliope hadn't seen any other water in the truck and the lake was hundreds of feet away.

She took Bisabuela's bowl from the girl, remembering the clay water she'd drunk in the hangar, how she'd trusted Bisabuela, ghost or not. She could trust Bisabuela again, even if she didn't believe in Old Lady Salt.

Chance must have sensed her hesitation. He said, "She's capable of great things, great movement, mujer. She can get you to the rez unharmed. I know she can."

This time the bowl was warm. Its contents smelled of seawater, and for a moment as she held the water to her mouth, she recalled accidentally swallowing a gulpful of the Gulf of Mexico in Boca Chica the summer after Phoenix was born. They'd still lived in Texas and she'd carried him into the warm Gulf waters as a kind of secular baptism (she'd told her mother *no*, she would *not* have him baptized in the Catholic church), every experience a new introduction to the world. But a wave had knocked her forward and they'd both gone under. She'd sputtered and pulled him from the water, sure she'd drowned her child. His eyes red and wide against the sun, he wasn't coughing or crying. He was a sea turtle, resilient. She'd handed him back to Andres on the dry sand, watched him scoop handfuls into the air, into his hair, laughing his drool-mouthed, toddler laugh. She'd felt slogged with salt all afternoon, but he was fine.

She swigged the bitter saltwater now, swallowing the nausea swishing her gut. She wasn't sure what she was supposed to feel other than sick.

She was cold.

Eunjoo and Chance had been wrong. Or they'd tricked her. She would die on the salt beds in the fourwing brush, her babies drowning inside of her.

The bowl fell to the dirt.

She lay on her side, curled as a seashell. Cramping. Emptying. Drying. This was what dying felt like.

Chance was praying in Zuni again and Eunjoo was screaming Old Lady Salt's name as Calliope stared at the unclouded sky, New Mexico blue. Again, she thought of the middle of time, how she would soon rejoin Bisabuela, in afterlife or nothingness. She would join the lifeless matter of the universe. The sky so bright. What relief—giving in. Unloading the burden of this wasteland. This world without Phoenix. Or the rest of her family.

Salt grained against her palms. She scooped a handful and threw it above her like rice at her wedding, like sand on Boca Chica beach.

Then, whether Old Lady Salt was with her or not she couldn't say, only that the bleeding staunched, the nausea faded away, a hurricane passing the Gulf, and she was determined to stay alive. To give these babies light—then find her son.

Eunjoo was laughing, tears streaming down her face.

Chance hoisted Calliope unsteadily back to the truck and she heaved herself in, relieved she could once again lean back without searing pain in her abdomen or tailbone.

From the back seat Mara asked, less ironic than crestfallen, "None of that miracle water for me?"

Eunjoo handed her the bowl. But it was empty.

TWENTY-SEVEN
THE ONE WHO HAS ME

The rez was not what Calliope had expected. The bleeding had stopped, her contractions had eased, and her vision was less blurry, salt restoring electrolytes.

She stared out the window as Chance pulled into the village center.

When she was a senior in high school, Bisabuela had taken her to the lake—not really a lake but a dam, the ice cave only green sludge. A tarantula smashed on the doormat outside the gift shop of Clovis points and other disillusioned gimcracks. Zuni then was gas station corn dogs, cardboard pizza, and tinfoil nachos. Kivas, shacks, sheds, mattress beds, and tires in front yards, basketball hoops without nets. Empty mouthwash bottles splayed in the parking lot because the rez was dry and there was alcohol in mouthwash. The Bureau of Vital Records & Health statistics. Mangy dogs outside the rolled-up windows. She knew they were rez dogs, and she should have been kinder. She'd worn her mother's critical eye, tattered heart, the wind yelping with trickster coyote dogs that looked like they'd eat a stranger. She felt strange and out of place. That dry lake followed by the shock of the rez—not much different from where she lived. Poverty is poverty, anywhere.

She loved her people. But she was a teenager, spoiled by fantasies of escaping to a big-city university, wracked with false pride. She wanted to escape her own neighborhood and everything it represented: the maíz man selling cobbed corn from his cart, his yellow butter, powdered chile, and crumbled white cheese, her mother in El Paso, chasing after her father, before Calliope ever realized he'd grown another family. After the funeral, she never asked her mother if she'd known. She'd known enough. Calliope had known her mother's penury, her WIC counters and shame, suitcases sprawled on the front lawn like surgical bodies, peritoneal cavities, here a butterflied diaphragm, there a liver spitting bile, the heat-struck grass, mother stuffing grocery bags with clothes, shoes, and overdue library books into the clunker of a car her father had left. Bisabuela had taken her to see the Ancestors all over New Mexico, and Calliope had felt lost. Disappointed. It had taken years to turn that mal de ojo away from herself and her people—to see her false shame reframed as the destruction wrought against her people.

There was more than one way of seeing, yes, but back then, she had packed in her suitcase regret mistaken for ruin. Bisabuela had warned, *Don't pick up broken pottery*—shards meant for the spirits.

Calliope had left for college and, within a few short years, by the time Calliope was in grad school, Bisabuela for the Spirit world, and Calliope had been trying to get back to her ever since. It wasn't until Chance pulled into Zuni that Calliope even realized this. But it was truth, like the light on the Río Grande bridge, like the hallucination of Bisabuela in the hangar. It *wasn't* a hallucination. Somehow, she had conjured or joined the Spirit world. Or the mal de ojo had been lifted. And Zuni was her proof.

It was just as she'd studied in the books, in the black-and-white photographs from before the US had claimed it, before the Treaty of Guadalupe Hidalgo, when her people's lands had transferred hands and none of those hands were indigenous.

It was as if she'd traveled back in time, or as if the arrow of time had whirred forward for Zuni—only without the interference of the Anglo government. Tall, multileveled, apartment-like structures constructed of rust-red earth, logs, and stones rose toward the sky, an ancient city come back from the dead. Though she knew Zuni had never been dead. The people had carried it within them, and here it was. Restored. Gone were the 7-Eleven and cheap drywall. The signs boasting clean restrooms on the side of the road. No signs at all for tourists, no tourists, no turquoise booths, no hawking the people's art for their livelihood. The mud was tightly packed, the stone shining in sunlight. Rectangular flat-roofed terraces circled courtyards, connecting many-familied homes. It reminded her of the geometrical structure of honeycomb. From round kivas, rooms for religious ceremonies, gray-black smoke swirled and eddied through the air. Outdoor ladders connected each level of each building.

Though she didn't recognize most of the pueblo from her own childhood, she did know well the hornos: beehive ovens made of adobe-mud and used for baking bread and other foods outdoors, which most Puebloan peoples of the Southwest had still used, including Bisabuela. When Calliope was growing up, she would watch Bisabuela building a fire inside the horno and, when the proper amount of time had passed, scooping out with a shovel all the embers and ashes and placing the bread with a large wooden paddle into the blisteringly hot horno. In the case of corn, she doused the embers with water and then used a poker to insert the corn to be steam-cooked. For gauging the temperature, she'd sweep out the fire then toss in dried corn husks. If the corn husks burnt quickly, the horno was too hot. If the husks turned golden brown, it was just right. When cooking meats, she fired it white-hot, swept the coals to the back, shoved in the meats on a tray, and sealed the smoke-hole door with mud. Calliope had once helped her cook a turkey in the horno. It took three hours and came out more succulent than any turkey she'd tasted before or since. Calliope glanced around the beehive ovens, half expecting to see Bisabuela lurking nearby, preparing some meal.

The restored village on its own would have been enough to inspire Calliope's awe. But it wasn't the buildings alone that made her believe the Spirits could have been alive and dwelling here. What struck her most were the people themselves. Chance had called himself and his people A'shiwi. And Calliope imagined this was what he meant. The village was bustling. It was brimming with A'shiwi. She'd read that the population of Zuni had dipped dangerously low many times after interactions with Anglos, whether Spanish conquistadors or United States settlers, whether war, famine, or smallpox. Eventually it had stabilized again. Last she had heard, despite high unemployment, poverty, and alcoholism, and even though their land had been stripped and stripped again so that the reservation finally encompassed less than seven hundred square miles, the pueblo had boasted ten thousand tribal members, 90 percent of whom lived in Zuni.

But poverty was nowhere in *this* Zuni. The people, like the land, had been revived.

Many men wore colorful woven shirts and pants, and many women wore mantas—brightly patterned woven dresses made of linen-like material tied over one shoulder and belted at the waist. There were men and women in jeans and boots, but still others in moccasins.

Some people waved to Chance and called out greetings in Zuni; others went about their business, largely ignoring the truck driving the dirt roads through the village.

"Did you know it would be like this?" she asked Chance.

His face was wet with tears. He shook his head, wiped his face, then pointed toward a building twenty feet ahead, gardens on the ground and flat rooftops. "I shouldn't know this, since I've never been here before, not like this, but that's my mother's house."

"Your mother?" Calliope didn't see a woman or anyone outside who would differentiate the building he'd indicated from the others, but what stood out was the lush greenness and color emanating from the place. She recognized the ancient tradition of waffle gardens, sunken beds intended for water conservation in the desert: collect all the moisture you can and hold onto it for as long as you can. Each depression in the waffle would catch rainfall and hold water close to plant roots. How the crops could have grown into full shoots when the frost had ended only hours ago, Calliope added to her growing list of mysteries. Square beds teemed with corn, squash, broccoli, scallions, cilantro, and radishes.

"Her name is Malia Guardian."

Calliope's gaze shifted uncomfortably from the dazzling buildings to the back seat where Mara lay, her ragged breath, a low continuous wheezing. Why hadn't Old Lady Salt helped her back at the lake?

"And what about Mara?"

"I'll call on the *ak'waamossi*, medicine man, from Uhuhuukwe Medicine Society with knowledge of *iwenashnaawe*, which you could translate as the sucking cure." He paused, said quietly, "As a rule, Zuni don't treat anyone outside the tribe, not because we're selfish, but we've learned the hard way that outsiders do not respect our beliefs or our methods." He sighed. "But maybe these are extenuating circumstances. I'll risk asking." He bore the same troubled visage as when he'd slaughtered the first Suuke and queried the punishment for murdering a god, and Calliope sensed he was risking much more than he was willing to admit by bringing her and her friends here, allowing them into his sacred world.

Mara's raspy voice, "I heard a Fly buzz - when I died - / The Stillness in the Room / Was like the Stillness in the Air - / Between the Heaves of Storm -" As she coughed through the recitation, phlegm gathered at the folds of her mouth, peeling and chapped. "Dickinson."

"You haven't died," Calliope said.

"Want to bet?"

Calliope thought of Amy's lifeless body in the back of the truck. Whether or not this was the Spirit world, *they* were not dead, at least, not yet.

They climbed out of the truck, Eunjoo holding Calliope's hand, Chance carrying the old woman. At the wooden door atop the steps of the house, a woman with warm, rose-brown skin appeared. She wore a cobalt-blue dress and woven slippers, her hair dark save wisps of silver at her hairline, clipped back with turquoise barrettes. Crow's feet marked her laugh lines, and her square mahogany eyes were friendly. In her hands she held a bowl of soft corneal mush. She exclaimed, "Aktsek'i. You're home. I knew you would come."

"Tsitda. I'm home."

Calliope felt a pang at the exchange between mother and son, though she was glad for the warm welcome.

"Tsitda," he said, gesturing from his mother to Calliope, "This is my *hom:il'ona* … and her family."

Calliope shot him a questioning look, and he nodded reassuringly.

"Son, you got married again? And a baby on the way!"

He didn't answer but smiled broadly, his whole face aglow, while Calliope's stomach lurched and her eyes widened. She tried to mask the surprise on her face, but couldn't. She stared again at Chance, whose eyes narrowed at her, silently asking her to play along. She pasted a smile to her face as he introduced her to his mother, and as she reached out to shake the woman's hand, Malia embraced her, the bowl of cornmeal pressed against Calliope's back. His mother pulled away, still grasping Calliope's arms and looking into her eyes, then spoke softly and quickly in Zuni.

Chance said, "She doesn't speak Zuni. Only English and Spanish."

Mother/son spoke in Zuni, and Calliope understood from their glances toward Eunjoo they were discussing the girl. Finally, Malia nodded and invited them inside. The walls were whitewashed, the tall ceilings supported with hand-hewn beams. Chance carried Mara off to another part of the house, while Malia offered them a wooden bench at the large table where she'd been cooking. She brought them clay cups of water.

After gulping the water down completely and asking for a second cup, Calliope asked, "Do you know why or how this is happening? Did you see the flash here in Zuni?"

Whether Malia would have answered, Calliope couldn't know, for Chance had returned, his arms empty, and interjected, "Tsitda, the babies are coming. Old Lady Salt gave us her blessing, and Calliope is well now, but you should have seen before, at Ma:k'yayanne. She was bleeding in a bad way. I was terrified and asked Salt Lady for help. I knew it would be well once I brought *hom:il'ona* to you."

Malia nodded, but her expression darkened, worry lines creasing her forehead. "I'll get our Suski:kwe, the women are upstairs. We'll do this for you and your bride, and your babies. But tell me, Aktsek'i: have you encountered ko'ko on your journey here? Was anything bad for you coming home?".

He sighed deeply, ran his hands through his silky black hair. The muscles in his jaw clenched. He looked at his mother, his eyes darker and more troubled than hers. "You know, Tsitda. Don't you?"

She wrung her hands on a cloth, wiping the cornmeal from her fingers. "I hoped it wasn't so."

"Will the Elders speak with me?"

"You must, yes. But not yet."

He nodded, and she pulled her son toward her, held him against her, kissed his cheek. When she stepped back, she had tears in her eyes, but said briskly, "Come. There's much to be done. Hotda/Granddaughter, come with me."

Eunjoo followed Malia up the ladder, but turned back, whispering, "Don't leave me, Phoenix's mama."

Calliope smiled. "Never, chica."

Once they were alone, Calliope turned toward Chance. "Well?"

"Lo siento, mujer. I had to say something. I thought of the risk. It wasn't worth it. If my clan couldn't or wouldn't help you—what then? I had to tell her you were family."

"What did you call me, when you introduced me? Your *hom:il'ona.*" The word felt spongy as cornmeal in her mouth.

His face and ears reddened, and he looked at the ground. "It means *the one who has me.*"

She stared at him trying to decipher her reaction. It was part of his plan, to make sure she was cared for. Right? She felt the familiar pang in her pelvis and back, pain radiating down her thighs. She bent forward, breathing rapidly.

"We came just in time. You'll be safe now."

After the contraction passed, she asked, "What did you tell her about Eunjoo and Mara?"

"Your daughter from a previous marriage, and your aunt."

Calliope sighed. She was accustomed to ignoring his instructions. But this was his home, his people. She sensed his reasons were stronger than her impulse to argue. His mother thought they were married, that these twins were his. How would that affect her search for Andres? And Phoenix? For now at least, she had to pretend. Once she gave birth, she was free to leave.

"Está bien? You'll stay then and let my family take care of you?"

She nodded.

He leaned forward, kissed her forehead. "Thank you, mujer."

She clutched his hand, as if for balance, though she was the one sitting. She ached with confusion, or the salt miracle was fading.

"Chance … are you in trouble?"

He squeezed her hand. Kissed her again. "It'll be alright, mujer. I still have a promise to keep, recuerdas?" He let go, stood back. "Now, I'll go find the medicine man."

She had one more question before he left. "What's your clan's name? Your mother said it in Zuni, but I didn't understand."

He smiled, his eyes sparkling. "Check your pocket, mujer. I already told you."

She reached for the figurine he'd whittled for her.

By the time she held the wooden Coyote in her hand, he was already out the door.

TWENTY-EIGHT
GOOD LUCK MOTHER

alliope alternated lying and squatting on a mattress on Malia's floor, atop a pile of thick blankets, the women of the Coyote clan gathered around her, Eunjoo at the wooden table with several other children and women, eating corn cakes, fried-chicken parts, tamales, noodles, red-chile sauce, and ice-cold watermelon water. Normally it would have smelled delicious, and Calliope imagined she was famished, but her contractions had returned full force, churning her stomach. She sipped water and tried to breathe. They'd given her a dress to wear, lightweight and loose against her body, and it stuck to her skin with sweat.

In the hours she'd been in labor, Calliope had learned from the women that being around dying people or animals was unhealthy for mother and babies; she had to take care not to fall victim to witchcraft over the next several hours and days, when the veil to the Spirit world was thinnest, as was the case with childbirth. Wowo łashhi, Chance's great-grandmother, had made a hot tea of toasted juniper twigs and berries steeped in boiling water to relax the system and induce copious lochial discharge. Malia was a midwife, and she put a badger's claw on a string around Calliope's belly because the badger was good at digging his way out, and the badger was also good medicine for labor pains. Nala, one of Chance's sisters, told Calliope that Zuni women were expected not to cry or yell during childbirth but that since Calliope wasn't Zuni, she could cry if she needed to and they wouldn't think less of her. Malia told Nala not to be disrespectful to her sister-in-law, and Calliope felt like crying, but not with pain.

Chance had returned only to fetch Mara and take her to the Medicine Society. Calliope had asked after Amy's body. He said he would prepare her for burial, not to concern herself with death. It wasn't good in her condition. Since Zuni men rarely attended childbirth, he said, it wasn't his place. But he'd come once the twins arrived. Them, he wanted to meet.

The women comforted Calliope with stories, and once they knew she was delivering twins, they shared their sacred creation story with her, for it centered on their two most beloved twins. On two towering buttes called Kwilli-yallon (Twin Mountain) dwelt Áhaiyúta and Mátsailéma—twin children of Sun Father and Mother Waters of the World. Before the A'shiwi came from the belly of the earth, the underworld, Sun made love to Waters of the World, and two boys came from their union. They were called Uanam Achi Piah-koa, or the Beloved Two Who Fell. The time came when war and many strange beings arose to destroy the children of earth, and the hearts of the twins were changed to Sawanika, or the medicine of war. The twins guarded the Ancient Ancestors and guided them to the middle of the world, where Calliope was now lying.

Nala said, "With the gift of the medicine of war and wisdom of the Sun, the twins protected the Corn People of the Earth—that's us." She stretched her arms to indicate everyone in the room. "When they'd conquered the enemies, they taught a chosen few the songs, prayers, and orders." She wrinkled her nose, winking at Calliope. "They don't usually select girls, but every once in a while, a girl slips by and gets into a kiva."

Calliope liked Nala, she could tell. Or at least, if Calliope were not doubled over with the feeling that her ass was about to split open and the whole of the cosmos was going to come quivering out of her, she would have liked Nala. The young woman had a round, flat nose, and she kept her dark hair cropped short with a fringe of thick bangs, which made her face appear as a heart. Curved and shapely, but still babyish in the face, Calliope guessed she must have been seventeen or eighteen. She was lovely.

"The twins are the morning stars," Nala said. "In Zuni, all twins are good luck. So you must be a good luck mother."

This was not how Calliope would have described herself, but she tried embracing it, the warrior in a yogi's warrior pose. She squatted, her legs pressed against the mattress, rooting to the earth. She bore down. She leaned against Nala, who supported her weight while Malia stood behind and pressed her abdomen, kneading it with great vigor. Tears of pain flowing freely, Calliope breathed deeply as the urge to push asserted itself again and again, rocking her as when the labor had been false, but this time with a midwife, Chance's mother, and all the women of his Coyote clan surrounding her, she was ready. Then the splitting. Her body cleaved from within, so that even her ribs, her lungs, her throat, felt ripped apart, the children inside her cesarean-slicing her, shedding her like snake skin, as if she were the costume and they the real thing. They would kill her to be born. The dress the clan had given her, the color of creamed corn, clung to her sweaty skin. She was a summer sidewalk, a broken cactus, oozing. She pleaded, *Bisabuela hold me.* Nala whispered, "Good luck, mother, you can do this."

Calliope was exhausted.

Between her legs, the first baby slid, a slick eel.

Malia grasped the baby tightly, said, "A girl."

The first girl was screaming. A good sign. Healthy lungs.

Chance's great-grandmother cut the cord with a steel knife. An aunt brought a woven basket from the table of food to Malia, who dabbed the detached umbilical cord with raw fat and dough. Still breathing raggedly and sweating, Calliope asked what the dough was, and Malia answered, "Unbaked bread." Calliope smiled, though she didn't understand. She would ask Chance later.

The first girl was sprinkled with cornmeal.

Beneath the yellowish flakes, the downy fuzz on her head shone black as night. Calliope thought of Andres.

And how every woman in the room believed this girl belonged to Chance.

Still dizzy and dehydrated, Calliope meant to ask for water when the second pain cleaved her in two.

She wasn't ready; she needed a rest, needed time before pushing out the other child.

The world blurred.

Nala's face was no longer lovely but a fuzzy mass of shapes, and monstrous.

That *wrongness* she'd felt on the roadside at the salt lake. Before Old Lady Salt had intervened. It was back. As if Malia had taken the steel knife to Calliope and not the cord.

It shouldn't have felt like this.

She was screaming.

Her legs shuddered and gave out; she keeled to her side, curled into a seashell on the mattress. Her body went cold. She was dripping cold sweat. Had Old Lady Salt forsaken her after all? Had Bisabuela? She was dying this time. She was dying and there was no help.

Her first girl, covered in corn, wrapped in husks and a blanket.

Her corn girl.

Calliope rutted open, her body an earthquake-riveted landscape, a city fallen. She blacked out and came to, blacked out and came to, again and again, each time certain she had died. Nala, misshapen and fuzzy though she appeared through Calliope's milky-filmed eyes, was crying, and the other women were instructing her to calm down, to move out of the way if she was going to cry instead of help. Malia was speaking rapidly in Zuni, pressing strips of cloth against Calliope's pelvis and thighs, pulling them out blood-soaked, siren-bright red, then reapplying clean cloths and calling out orders. Someone was wrapping Calliope in large, damp towel-like cloths that smelled of patchouli, incense Bisabuela had burned in her home, what felt like a lifetime away. Malia reached inside of Calliope, her palms pressed together and cupped as forceps, and now her voice was calmer, quieter, rhythmic. She was praying. To whom Calliope didn't know. Her mind was swirling charcoal and blinding white, ribbons of curling smoke and strobing lights.

She couldn't push. Had no energy. Nothing left.

She felt Malia pulling.

A rigid, coldness from her birth canal.

Not a plum-packed head siphoning through Calliope.

Not a slippery fish.

Was her child dead?

There was no crying.

There were gasps.

The women's faces were alarm bells.

Was her child dead? She couldn't form the question into sounds. She blinked and blinked through the haze.

Malia was holding the silent weight.

She handed it to Wowo łashhi, who held it at a distance, chanting low and grief-stricken.

Malia reached back into Calliope.

Was there anything else?

She kneaded Calliope's abdomen.

An umbilical cord attached to nothing came sliding out like a snake. This was followed by two separate placentas, fat as steaks, the afterbirth.

Wowo łashhi, show her to me, show me my child. Is she dead?

Malia was packing Calliope with cloths. The women were sprinkling cornmeal on the silence in Wowo łashhi's hands. The age-furrowed grandmother turned toward Calliope.

The last image Calliope saw before her eyes tunneled and the world went dark—her child was not dead. Was not a child, was othered in stone, was petrified.

Her second girl was river-smooth, obsidian-shined. Basalt-heavy.

Her second daughter, black volcanic rock.

TWENTY-NINE
WATER JAR CHILD

Calliope dreamt she was bleeding out. She stood on a mound of desert shrub and wild grass covering a place she'd never been, a place the spirits called Hawikku Village.

Her ancient guides staunched her flow with corn husks woven into a blanket, which they wrapped around her, then led her down the red dirt path toward the stone shrines swept with cornmeal and turquoise and dedicated to the gods. The spirits surrounding her, their voices, a chorus. *This place Coronado once occupied believing it the seventh city of gold, we have reclaimed.*

Ice-wind battering her cheeks and face, she wrapped the corn blanket over her head as a rebozo. Beneath the mound, a pit house. Ancient ceremonial kiva. *So too the Earth will reclaim.* Broken pottery in colors of terracotta scattered the rock-lined trail encircling the mound.

In the place Calliope had bled, a trail of corn sprouted behind her. She picked the two tallest corn shoots then sat beside two large, smooth stone metates for grinding. From within her husk rebozo, she pulled a mano, shucked the corn, laid it on the altar, and with the mano in both hands, she began moving with the weight of her whole body, the strength of her shoulders and back pressing down through her arms, back and forth, shearing, until the corn became a fine yellow powder.

The Ancients sang her on as she worked. *When the Earth has had enough, she will shake her troubles off. She will shake her troublemakers off.*

She scooped this and mashed it into the butter of her hands. Rolled it into a ball, flattened it again. Shaped and shaped until the corn grew into a child, who sprang from the stone of her hands, laughing.

For she was finished, and sank into the earth, solid, hardened, at peace. And as her corn-made child ran from the mound to the grass below, the spirits intoned. *The Earth has all the power she needs.*

When she decides to use her power, you will know.

* * * *

She awoke groaning, guttural and mammalian, rooted to the bed.

The pain was primal.

It had not diminished but intensified.

The women had not left Malia's room; they surrounded Calliope's mattress on the floor. She'd been redressed and could feel the cloths, cool and fragrant with herbs, between her thighs. Still, the cloths stung against the knifelike pain of her perineum. In her palm, Malia crushed a plant Calliope did not recognize, poured it into warm water, held it to Calliope's mouth and helped her drink it. Like a child, the liquid spilled down her chin and landed on her chest, but she could feel relief almost immediately, a warming of her skin, a releasing of her leg and thigh muscles. Her uterus felt hard, like a pear. She reached down and touched her belly, the rigid mound softened, not flat but gelatinous, empty.

She searched the room. When she spoke, her voice was ragged, hoarse from screaming. "Where are my twins?"

Malia spoke in Zuni to another woman kneeling beside Calliope, and at Malia's bidding she arose to an adjacent room where Calliope could hear children's laughter. She listened for Eunjoo's voice, the girl no longer at the dining table as she was during the birth, but Calliope could not make out the girl's birdlike chirping amidst the other children's. How long had Calliope been unconscious? Time hadn't felt like itself since the light on the bridge, but it seemed even more pliable, more strange since she'd first gone into labor in earnest—pain had rendered time wobbly, set it wavering.

The woman (an aunt or cousin of Chance's) came back from the adjacent room, Nala beside her, carrying a large wooden object that reminded Calliope at first of a boat, like Noah's ark. Nala turned it around; she held Calliope's first twin, her corn girl, wrapped in an intricately woven blanket and strapped to a pinewood cradleboard with suede cords, a kind of face guard made of green cedar sticks protruding in a semicircle, half haloing her face, her neck cushioned by a smaller blanket. The infant lay faceup, her head flat against the board. Cornmeal flakes dusted her forehead, reminding Calliope of Lenten ashes. The corn girl cried softy, a cat's whining mewl. She was hungry. Calliope's pelvis clenched, her nipples hardened into berries and stung, as the milk swelled her breasts. She reached for her corn girl, searching for Andres and Phoenix in the baby's face, a shock of dark hair beneath the blanket enshrouding her head. Grief dropped as quickly as the milk, and the child latched. "Her twin?"

Nala's eyes flashed, briefly. Malia's eyes reproached her. Calliope's stomach lurched at the silent exchange between the women.

"We've buried her to protect her, E'lashdok'i. It's the Zuni way." Malia's voice was heavy, but soothing, steady. No hint of the quick anger she'd shown Nala. The silver around Malia's face gave her a holy aura. "If the baby is stillborn or dies before the fourth day of life, it is buried inside the threshold where all step on the earth grave. This allows the soul of the infant to rest while the mother can become pregnant again." She pressed a cloth against Calliope's face. "If we'd waited, you might have grown gravely worse or turned infertile. Or illness might have cursed this living one."

Calliope's salt tears washed down her chest to the corn girl. "And this cradleboard?"

"Belongs to our family. It was Chance's, now it's his daughter's."

Calliope swallowed the lump in her throat, closed her eyes, tears still flowing.

Perhaps Malia mistook her shame for confusion, for she continued, "We pass the cradleboards on as heirlooms. Unless a child dies in it; then it is burned to keep the child from evil spirits. The spirits are as free at birth time as at death time. When these occur at the same time, the spirits are even stronger. We have to remain watchful."

"Where's Eunjoo?"

"With the other children. We took them out once we realized what had happened."

What had happened? Calliope had given birth to a dead baby? She could have sworn it looked like ... but that was crazy. "I need to see my other child."

Malia stared at Calliope almost suspiciously. Like she was sizing her up.

Calliope pressed again, her voice cracking, "*Please.*"

Malia's forehead furrowed into a grimace, her lips pressed. "That would be unsafe, E'lashdok'i. Unwise."

The lump in Calliope's throat flowered, choking her. She wasn't Zuni. This wasn't her family. These were not her beliefs. How could she accept what she didn't understand? No. She had to see her baby. Even dead, it was still hers. She opened her mouth to dispute, the corn girl suckling at her breast. These women had saved her. Without them, both she and Calliope might have died, certainly would have died. These women were Chance's family. He'd risked their ire and punishment for Calliope and this corn girl. She closed her mouth. She'd wait for Chance, ask him what could be done. She had to see her other twin.

She steadied her breath. "Where's Chance?"

Malia's shoulders and arms tensed, her hands grasped together. The elongated disc of her face briefly scrunched, softer, in pain, then was stoic again. "The father is not part of the birth process, E'lashdok'i. He'll be here once your ceremony is resumed. We had to halt everything for your health. But you are restored, look. Your milk is flowing, your cheeks and face no longer sallow. You will survive."

"See, Good Luck Mother," Nala said, stroking Calliope's hair away from her face.

Calliope contained the rueful laughter she felt gurgling at her throat. She and her corn girl were a sham. Her second twin was ... what? Dead? What had she seen before she'd blacked out? Blackness. Basalt. Her other daughter was ... a rock. They'd buried. And wouldn't show her. She said nothing.

Malia continued. "Your own *e'lashdok'i* should not be on her cradleboard yet. We had to make do. She should be lying beside you on a bed of warm sand for the first four days. On the fourth day, her Wash Mother will wash her again with cornmeal, blessing and sealing her from the dark spirits, then give her names to her."

"Names?"

"Zuni and Spanish."

"Oh." Calliope wanted to keep calling her corn girl. It felt wrong to name her, let alone give her a Zuni name. "How long was I unconscious?"

"Night and morning."

The corn girl finished breastfeeding and Malia washed Calliope with water poured from a gourd while she stood, gingerly, the water falling to mats on the floor. She was still dressed. Nala placed a clean dress over the wet one, and Calliope slipped out of the wet dress, which Nala tossed into the stove. During this ceremony the other women removed the mattress she'd birthed on and prepared a new bed in its place. The new bed was a layer of hot stones covered by a layer of sand, then by warm blankets.

She lay down on the heat and her corn girl, free of her cradleboard, was given to her.

Malia still appeared troubled. As she spoke her hands fluttered to her neck, like birds searching for a perch. "Now we will call Chance."

* * * *

He stood in the doorway, haggard and weary. The corn girl was nursing again, but Calliope didn't bother to cover herself. No one instructed her to, even with all their modesty customs, and she worried it would break the illusion of intimacy. She was supposed to be his wife after all.

His face eased when he saw her and the corn girl, but then he glanced around the room, searching for the other twin. Her eyes stung with tears. He walked toward her, knelt down and began to kiss her forehead, his lips cool against her skin, warm from the rocks and sand. He didn't need to ask *What happened?* She wiped her eyes, whispered, "Necesito hablar contigo. *Solo.*" She couldn't ask the other women to leave; she didn't know her place in the unspoken hierarchy. But he could.

His mother's hands still clenched, her expression still pained, she nodded at her son and spoke authoritatively to the women what Calliope understood as *leave the parents and their e'lashdok'i* (which she had gathered meant daughter).

Before Nala left the room, she whispered to Chance. Calliope heard: *Brujería. Too late.*

Calliope didn't know which question to ask first.

They both asked at once, "What happened?"

She smiled at their mutual concern for the other. The ruts pressed into his leather skin, worry lines—something had gone wrong. With Mara? His talk with the Elders? His wavy black hair usually fallen across his shoulders was tied back in a tight ponytail, his shoulders and arms were tense, his jaw tight. He sighed.

"Mujer, the other twin didn't make it?"

"They won't tell me what happened to her."

"My family?"

She nodded. "Before I blacked out, I caught a glimpse. Malia had to pull her out of me. I couldn't push." Her heart raced, the pin prickling of sweat against her skin, the heat from the rocks and sand becoming unbearable. They'd made it too hot. She kicked the blanket off her legs, like a recalcitrant child. She wanted to tell him what she'd seen, the other twin, what Wowo łashhi had been holding. "It didn't make sense. I was delirious."

He pressed his hand against her shoulder; his palm was work-hard and damp with sweat. She resisted the urge to pull away from the heat. "Nala said witchcraft, but it could have been anything. No one knows what causes such things. It wasn't your fault."

Wasn't it? Wasn't everything that had happened since the bridge somehow her fault?

"I don't believe in witchcraft." Her voice was flat though her stomach roiled, her face feverish.

"Tell me what you saw."

She looked down at the corn girl still swaddled against her chest. On the ground beside them, the cradleboard. "They buried her."

He followed her gaze. "My mother gave you mine." His voice was soft, kind. Wistful. She couldn't stop the tears. He held her face, wiped it gently with the pads of his thumbs. "It was my daughter's. I'm glad it's gone to yours."

"You have to let me see my other girl. I have to see …"

"That she's gone?"

"They buried her."

The corn girl began to cry.

He reached for her. "May I?" His whole family had held her. They thought she was his. "What will you call her?"

She felt silly telling him what she'd been calling the corn girl. "Do you know where they buried her? They won't tell me. Malia said it's for my safety, and hers. Both girls."

"We believe that."

"Will you bring her to me?"

He sighed again, reached to sweep the hair from his face, but it was already pulled back in the ponytail. He touched the corn girl's baby-fine hair instead, cooed at her, whispered something in Zuni.

Calliope smiled. "What are you telling her?"

"How beautiful she is. Like her mama."

Calliope's cheeks and neck burned. The blood rushed to her breasts, milk dampening her dress. She reached for the blanket, covering herself. He handed the corn girl back to Calliope.

"I'll bring the other one to you, mujer. Only, I'm worried it'll upset you, seeing her."

"My baby died, Chance. I'm already beyond upset."

He stood, went out the front, returned with a small shovel, pried back the wood that planked the doorway threshold, and began digging. Calliope turned away, stared instead at the corn girl, imagining a lifeless version of her—same black hair, honey-raw skin, bluish veins butterflying her forehead and cheeks and eyelids. She was holding her breath. She released it. Chance kept digging. Calliope considered telling him to stop.

A scraping sound. Metallic.

He was chanting as he'd done in the snow at the body of the Suuke, then pulled a bundle from the ground he brought to her, wrapped in a blanket identical to the corn girl's. Calliope's stomach coiled into a thick rope, knotted in her throat. The same cinching of space and air as in the hangar, her lungs compressing. But not with any machine or mythical creature. She was staring at her other daughter. What she'd seen in the black hole of her memory was real.

Though she knew what she'd been expecting to see, she was trembling, her voice shaking. "Where's my *real* baby? What is *this*? What'd they do with her?"

Chance called out in Zuni and Malia rushed into the room. Had she been at the doorway listening the whole time? Had Calliope said anything to betray their lie? She wiped her eyes, turned from the volcanic rock in Chance's hands. This had to have been some kind of strange ritual. This couldn't be real. What had they done with her flesh-and-blood daughter? Why had they replaced her with a rock? It didn't make sense. While Chance and his mother held a spirited conversation in Zuni, Malia's hands flying to her face and in the air several times so it appeared as if she were signing or dancing, her hands little brown birds searching for a lost nest in the branches of a tree, Calliope stared at the corn girl. She wanted to go home.

But her home was buried under ash.

They'd stopped talking and were staring at her, their faces mirrors of each other's, in both appearance and gravity. "Mujer, I need to show you something else."

He handed Malia the rock baby, then stepped over the hole in the threshold and left the house again as when he'd gone for the shovel.

Calliope glanced at Malia and the rock baby, feeling not grief—but revulsion and anger. If Bisabuela or the Spirits had guided her to this place, what was the joke? What was she missing?

Chance returned with another volcanic rock, larger than the rock baby in Malia's hands, pocked with holes, more like pumice than basalt, and grayer, less black. It curved inward in the middle like a bean. Calliope sighed. Had he gotten it from the yard? A piece of landscaping? Was he showing her that the women of his clan had replaced Calliope's baby with a garden rock? That this was a sick joke? Where had they buried her real child? Outside in the yard like an animal?

He said nothing, so she took the bait. "What's this?"

"I found it in the back of Mara's truck, under the tarp, when I went for the trowel."

"Yeah, so?"

He sighed. "It was in the place I left your friend's body, where she should have been."

Calliope stared blankly, a numbness tingling her limbs and fingers. She stared from his inscrutable face to the rock in his hands, to the rock in Malia's hands. "You're telling me not only has my baby turned into a rock, but now Amy too?" She was shuddering with rage. She'd been right about him. He had been a trickster all along. His family was the Coyote clan, for good reason. "Has Mara turned into a rock too? Is that what you were going to say next? What about Eunjoo and I? Are we turning into rocks?" She shoved her hand into the air, mock inspecting it. "Just checking for signs of petrification. Does it look like frostbite? Or would I feel it coming on like flu?" She thought of Susana's suicide note, *turned to stone*. But it couldn't be. It didn't make sense. It was a metaphor. Reina was a flesh-and-blood human like Amy had been, like the corn girl's twin. Calliope had seen the sonogram. She'd felt two heartbeats. And rocks didn't have hearts. She pushed the thought of the suicide note out of her mind. Focused instead on her anger and confusion.

Chance turned toward Malia, who handed him the rock baby. He spoke softly in Zuni and she shook her head. He spoke again, more persistent. She turned toward Calliope, her expression pained. Then she left the room without another word. Calliope wished they'd quit speaking Zuni in front of her—what secrets were they keeping from her? Chance set both rocks on a small table in the corner, then sat beside Calliope, legs crossed. She glared at him, her anger palpable between them. He sighed.

"Mujer, I know you're in shock, and to say you've been through a lot in the past few days would be a gross understatement. I also know you're a fellow scientist and that you reason with your intellect what you read in books and only believe what experiential data you find in the world around you when it fits into the mold of that intellect, those books. When it conforms to the process of those who've taught you *how* to think. You're not of my people, and you don't know our ways. So I won't fault you for the disrespect you've shown, speaking to me that way in front of my mother, when she has just saved your life and your child's." He nodded toward the corn girl, and Calliope's throat filled with cotton, the anger dissipating, clouding instead into shame. She wanted to apologize for speaking so harshly in front of his mother. She'd risked their facade of marriage and family by treating him as someone she mistrusted and derided rather than someone she loved. But before she could say anything, he said, "I need to tell you a story." She closed her eyes and sighed. He wasn't deterred by her apparent disinterest, but continued in his lilting storyteller's voice:

"In Tewa, there once was a young woman who never wanted to marry and instead lived with her parents and helped her mother make water jars. One day while her mother was away fetching water and the young woman was mixing the clay with her foot, she put the clay onto a flat stone and stepped on it, hard, and some of the clay entered her. She became pregnant and gave birth. The mother's anger at her daughter's pregnancy ended when she saw what the daughter had birthed: not a regular child but a little water jar.

"The young woman cried and cried because he had no legs or arms, but after a time, the family grew fond of the little jar and found they could feed him through the jar mouth and soon he grew larger and could play with the other children, though he was a jar. When the snow came he asked his grandfather to take him hunting, and though the grandfather was reluctant, he gave in and took him down below the mesa where he could roll around to find jackrabbits. Soon Water Jar Child saw tracks and rolled after them, but when he found the jackrabbit, it began to chase him, and he rolled into a rock, breaking open.

"Out jumped a flesh child, glad his skin had broken. He had beads around his neck, earstrings of turquoise, a dance kilt and moccasins, and a buckskin shirt. He killed four jackrabbits before sunset.

"He came upon a spring where a man was fishing, and the man introduced himself as the boy's father. The boy didn't think he had a father because his mother had told him so. But the man took Water Jar Child to a village across the spring where many people ran to him and put their arms around him, glad he had come home. They were his family. He stayed there one night then returned to his mother's home and told her everything that had happened.

"Soon his mother grew sick and died. The child went to the spring to find his father. And there he found his mother among the people of the village. He discovered his father was Red Water Snake and told the boy he could not live in the realm of humans so he'd made the child's mother sick so she could come live with him. After that, they all lived together in the village across the spring."

The rhythmic music of Chance's story ended, and Calliope opened her eyes to the silence. She looked over at him to see whether he'd simply paused or was actually finished talking. When the silence grew unbearable she said, "That's it?"

He nodded.

"So it's the Tewa version of Jesus and Mary?" She could hear her Catholic mother's voice drilling her on her prayers, the stations of the cross, readying Calliope for her first communion and then her confirmation, the last rite of the church Calliope had participated in, to her mother's chagrin.

"If you believe there must be a Western counterpart."

"Okay, biblical or not, why tell me this story? Are you saying I'm like the young woman? I'm no Mary, believe me. This was no virgin birth, Chance. Your story explains nothing."

"Only if you believe story must *explain* anything, mujer."

Her voice rising to an exasperated whine, she said, "You're infuriating. Cut the Socratic bullshit. Why don't you tell me what you think is going on or explain how any of this could make sense instead of speaking in riddles?"

"They're only riddles if you don't believe in the stories, mujer." He wore an amused smile. "Haven't you been following your bisabuela's stories all along? Why say you trust something you're going to fight at every juncture? If you believe the Ancient Ones, believe them."

She had returned to New Mexico to prove Bisabuela right, that this was the Middle Place. That there was no land bridge. That the people had emerged from the earth. Right where they had said they'd emerged. Now she was at a Middle Place watching the earth perform incomprehensible acts of violence and recovery. The raw data was in front of her. Why couldn't she believe?

"Where is my child? That's all I want to know."

Chance pointed with his chin toward the corner table. "She's there. My mother pulled her out of you. Otherwise you would have hemorrhaged to death."

"She told you she pulled that rock from me?"

He nodded again, held her hands in his. They were cool against her overheated skin.

"Susana's note. It wasn't a metaphor?" She swallowed the cotton in her throat. What did it mean? How could she have birthed a rock baby? And why? "What does Malia say? And your Elders? Do they know what that light was? It started everything, I know it did. Whatever is happening, it's because of that light. A nuclear explosion? Radiation? That light did this to my baby. It made her a rock."

His face sagged, his smile disappeared. "I spoke to the Elders, yes. And I'll help you make this right, mujer. For your family. I don't know how much time I'll have. But I made you a promise."

"What happened with the Elders? Why is Malia so scared?"

"I killed two gods, mujer. There is no coming back from that."

"But those monsters would have killed us."

"Then I should have died with honor."

She didn't understand. He'd been saving their lives. Surely there was honor in that.

"What will they do? Punish you? How?"

"There's a ceremony for atonement. And a sacrifice."

His tone was so ominous her skin crawled. "Sacrifice? Like *human* sacrifice? I thought Zunis don't …"

"It's not like that, mujer. But I'm not a religious leader; I do not speak for my kiva. I'm sorry I can't say anything more."

"Not even to your *wife?*"

"In Zuni culture, women are not supposed to know the deeper ways of the religious ceremonies."

"But I'm not Zuni."

"Nor my wife."

She pulled her hands away from his as if she'd touched an oven.

"Mujer, it's not right, nor is it appropriate."

"Help me up, please. I can't stand this hot sand bed. I'm sweating like a pig."

"That's a misnomer. Pigs lie in the mud to cool down."

"I know that. Do you have any mud?"

"You shouldn't get up yet. The healing ceremony isn't over."

"I'm not Zuni nor your wife, remember."

He looked like she had punched him. "How can you be angry with me?"

She shrugged, scrunched her face. "It comes easily."

He took the baby from her arms as she propelled herself to her side, pushed herself up. He lifted her to face him. Sweat beaded her neck and breasts, her yucca-woven dress clinging to her body. She groaned with effort, her perineum and thighs still sore. The rags between her legs still damp with blood.

His voice thick, his breath hotter still against her skin, he said, "Aren't you going to ask me what I've done wrong? What's inappropriate?"

She wiped her forehead on her sleeve, his arm still holding her waist for support. "You've done something wrong? I thought you were lecturing *me* again."

"I never meant to lecture you. I've only ever wanted to help."

"Why? Why have you risked so much for me? You don't owe me anything. You don't …"

Her baby still in his arms, uncrying, he was kissing Calliope. Gently at first and then harder, pulling her body against his, firm. And she was letting him.

If she were honest with herself, she'd wanted this since he first began speaking, on the road to Silver City.

She was crying.

He pulled away, wiped her face. "I didn't mean to make you cry."

She sniffled. "Hormones."

"Mujer, I've loved you from the moment you aimed that gun at me, and I knew you would never shoot me."

"That's a little twisted, Chance."

"It meant you were brave. And strong. And kind." He kissed her cheeks, her nose, her forehead. She closed her eyes and he kissed her eyelids.

"I can't." Her voice barely a whisper.

He stepped back, but she pressed her face against his chest. This couldn't change anything. She couldn't give up the hope of finding her family. Of showing Andres his child. And holding Phoenix. How could she stay in Zuni with Chance? He was right. It was wrong.

He kissed her forehead again, this time with the curtness of friendship, and handed her back the corn girl. "I'll ask my mother to set up another bed for you, somewhere cooler."

She nodded. "Thank you."

"And we should rebury the child."

"It's not a child."

"Whatever it is. We can break some traditions, but my mother won't stand for an unburied stillborn. They bring curses, mujer. Whether you believe or not, she does. And this is her house."

She nodded again, and he began reburying the rock baby.

"What about the other rock?"

"I guess we could bury it too."

"Just put it back in Mara's truck."

He sighed heavily, his face creased with frustration. "Fine."

Once he'd finished patting the threshold dirt down and replacing the wooden slats, he said, "Finish healing. I don't know how long I have, but I'll make sure it's enough to find you your family."

She could not tell him how deeply she hurt, how she wanted to stay with him like the young woman in the story, who'd gone to the village with Water Jar Child and Red Water Snake; she couldn't. The young woman had died to get there.

And if Calliope was still alive, she had to keep searching. She wouldn't leave her family the way her father had left his. She was stronger than that.

PART THREE

QUANTUM UNCERTAINTY

"As you go forward in your life
You will come upon a great chasm.
Jump.
It is not as wide as you think."

—ZUNI PROVERB

THIRTY
BLOOD PUDDING

Calliope held the carved wooden spoon in the air and made airplane noises, whirring the bright orange heap toward the corn girl's mouth. "Here come your mashed sweet potatoes just like Bisabuela used to make. Eat up." She made yummy noises and pretended to eat the vegetables when the corn girl closed her mouth and refused. "Come on, stubborn girl. Eat. I'll give you more peaches if you eat the sweet potatoes." Malia's home-jarred peaches were the corn girl's favorite. Calliope took a real bite of the sweet potatoes. They weren't quite as good as Bisabuela's, but they were close. She scooped a spoonful of mashed sweet cornmeal, airplaned that toward the corn girl's mouth. "Corn, mmmmm …"

"Our corn girl still refusing her sweet potato?" Chance put his rifle in a locked case above the long wooden table, moved to the bench Calliope straddled, kissed her temple, then turned toward the corn girl and kissed the top of her head. "Are you trying to frustrate your mama, Miwe e'le?" He called her corn girl in Zuni, the only two names she'd ever received.

"She's eaten it for weeks but now she's acting like I'm trying to poison her. I don't know what I'm doing wrong. Even cornmeal she's refusing today. And she loves corn."

"Miwe e'le, you must eat your namesake. And stop stressing your mother out." He reached for the spoon. "Here, let me try."

"Oh, she'll eat for *you*, Chance. She does everything *perfectly* for you."

"She knows where her loyalties lie."

Calliope laughed and relinquished the spoon. "Always ganging up against me."

"Hey, I'm trying to help you." He didn't have to airplane at all, just swooped the spoon easily to the corn girl's mouth, and she opened wide.

"I told you she likes you better."

"She's just playing sides." He finished feeding her without further ado.

"Since you've got Miwe e'le under control, I'll check on Eunjoo." The little girl was supposed to be helping Wowo łashhi make blood pudding in the kitchen. At the counter, Wowo łashhi held a small pottery jar brimming with fresh blood and a large, half-moon shaped terracotta bowl, the rim partially concaved from wear and stained from prior use, filled with sheep's liver and stomach, along with ropes and ropes of mustard-yellow intestine. The old woman pushed the sheep's stomach toward Eunjoo, who didn't recoil as Calliope would have, but happily took the disturbing bowls in front of her to a wooden stool at the counter and rolled up her sleeves.

She asked, all smiles, "Want to help me empty the food from the sheep's stomach, Phoenix's mama?"

Calliope's gut lurched, not only from the revolting task but from the name Eunjoo still called her, a name that shattered her every time. "No thanks, chica. I'll leave the fun work to you."

Eunjoo turned the stomach inside out and washed it until the water turned cream-colored. Calliope did help mix the stuffing, pouring corn-meal and salt into the jar of blood, then adding diced potatoes, chiles, and fat. She excused herself as Wowo łashhi and the staunch little girl each clutched clumps of the mottled glop and crammed it into the long, limp intestine like filling an empty pantyhose with playdough. Eunjoo and Wowo łashhi reminded Calliope of herself as a young girl cooking with Bisabuela, minus the stinky bloody smell. Eunjoo had made this mess many times with Wowo łashhi, and each time Calliope had helped the girl wash the clotted blood from under her fingernails.

Wowo łashhi called to Chance in Zuni, and Calliope understood that she was asking him to fire up the grill outside; she wanted him to broil the sausages. Calliope's Zuni was very poor, but she understood more and more each day, often practicing with Chance in the evenings.

He came into the kitchen, Miwe e'le in his arms. Her face was stained orange and her clothes were covered in mashed sweet potato. Calliope laughed as he handed the corn girl over.

"Feeding the baby is serious business," he said, kissing her cheek, perhaps as ruse to whisper in her ear, "I need to talk to you, mujer. After the barbecue."

She nodded.

Aloud, to Eunjoo, he said, "Those smell delicious, little bird."

Calliope wrinkled her nose at the strong smell of iron.

He grabbed the plate and wafted it in front of her face, teasing her. "I'll save the biggest sausages for you, mujer."

"Please do," Calliope joked back, plastering an overzealous smile to her face. "You know how much I love them."

"You know how much I love you," he countered, his voice cracking where it should have been playful.

Eunjoo watched them, a curious expression on her face, as she'd done each day for the past several months. Calliope never asked if she understood. She was sure Eunjoo understood much more than even Calliope did. She must have, for she never brought up Andres, and when Malia had asked her who Phoenix was, she said her imaginary friend, which had nearly gutted Calliope, but she'd nodded along, agreeing what an imaginative child Eunjoo was, and that imaginary friends might well be Spirits nearby, protecting the young ones, answering the corn blessing and turquoise prayers.

"I'll be in our room cleaning this messy corn girl."

Eunjoo asked, "Can I go outside and play with Nastacio?" Chance's little nephew, a year older than Eunjoo, who had turned seven in January. It must have been almost Phoenix's seventh birthday. Calliope's heart pelted each time she thought about it—about missing it.

"Yes, but come in when it's time to set the table. You know how Malia hates when you're late for chores."

The first time Eunjoo had disregarded chores, Nala had warned her that the Suuke would snatch her away in its basket and take her to the peach orchards. Eunjoo had paled, but her reaction was nothing compared with Malia's, who had raised her voice louder than Calliope had ever heard her speak, the birds of her hands flying toward Nala's face this time instead of her own. Chance had calmed his mother, but no one ever mentioned the Suuke in Malia's house again. And Eunjoo never missed her chores.

After she cleaned the baby, Calliope wandered outside with the corn girl, free of her cradleboard, which she'd resisted using around five months old, fighting to release her arms from the constraints of swaddling. Malia had suggested strapping her in but allowing her the use of her arms to play with a rattling drum that Chance had made her, but even that less constrictive position the corn girl disliked. No, her daughter would not be strapped down, which was just as well. Her head was flat enough. Calliope had been frustrated at first that they'd flattened her daughter's head, but eventually laughed as she'd rubbed the flat spot beneath the shining black waves on the back of Chance's head like polishing a table. "It's a family trait," he'd said, before either of them had realized it couldn't have been true. Miwe e'le wasn't his.

The black pudding sausages when broiled were not any more appealing than raw, and the stench of the blood roasting on the grill nearly made Calliope gag. She waved at Chance as she walked quickly past, burying her nose in the milky folds of the corn girl's neck, the sweetly curdled smell of breastmilk still strong on her skin.

She wondered what Chance needed to talk about. Had there been another development? If their hypothesis was correct, then it was almost time. The bridge that had brought her across was opening again. She didn't know if she could believe it. But she had to hope. It was all she had left. Besides the family she'd built—here—beyond the waffle gardens surrounding the honeycomb structures of the clan-connected houses where Calliope had been living for almost six months, the pueblo stretching miles onward. Throughout the winter the land had remained warm; the brief freeze they'd encountered had cleared the earth for new growth, and the weather had remained temperate since. She'd known New Mexico to venture below freezing most nights and many days from November through March. But this winter she'd spent in Zuni had shown the land itself to be the real trickster, and the pueblo was overflowing.

The sheep and goats were grazing far beyond their previous limits, farther even than before the US government had usurped Zuni land in the 1870s, first for Anglo homesteaders then for the logging companies depleting Zuni forests of millions of board feet of timber for the railroads. They'd left Zuni land completely denuded.

But now the sheep had multiplied.

There hadn't been so many sheep since the 1930s, when the Bureau of Indian Affairs had built a fence around what was left of the reservation and prevented Zunis from both farming and herding outside their boundaries and instead implementing a sheep reduction program, rounding up thousands of animals, sold to Anglos in Gallup or slaughtered and dumped in pits, where they were left to rot.

Past the Coyote clan's outdoor grill, as she neared the pueblo center, far from the stench of blood iron, another, sweeter smell wafted through the warm evening air. Honeyed pork. Calliope wished she could join whatever clan was cooking that meal for supper instead. The Badger clan, perhaps? She'd met all the clans at the sacred time of fasting and prayer and ritual, masked dancing called Shalako at the winter solstice, following harvest.

She'd made it her business to investigate as much as possible, considering her stay with Chance's people a kind of anthropological study, but they kept the secrets of their religious ceremonies tightly sealed, and she could not probe much deeper than what Chance had divulged, what he said was too much information anyway—he was already in trouble, and did she want to get him even more punished? He still wouldn't tell her what atonement ceremony he'd had to withstand or what sacrifice was approaching. It loomed over the bedroom they shared, the nights he slept on the floor beside her bed, and she begged to know if he would be all right. She felt responsible for whatever was going to happen. She couldn't stand not knowing what or when. So many uncertainties beyond their main concern, her daily, no, hourly objective: *how do I find my family?* She hadn't surrendered hope. She'd only had to find a new way of looking at the problem. She was biding her time.

On the porch of a neighboring building, Mara sat with a woman of the Yellow Wood clan, who had been teaching her the past few months since she had healed how to sculpt traditional Zuni pottery. She was crafting a rounded pitcher that Calliope recognized as the Cíbola-style whiteware, Kiatuthlana Black-on-white, patterned with diamonds and triangular mazes centering on two fingerlike projections pointing toward each other, whose original she had seen in archaeological exhibits dating from around 850 AD, ascribed to the Anasazi, though Calliope had corrected the curator: *they are not the Ancient Enemy, a Navajo word, but The People or Ancestral Puebloans.* Bisabuela had taught her Anasazi was not the correct word for their ancestors, who were a lot of things and not all of them pleasant, but they were not the enemy. Calliope found it compelling that Mara would emulate this ancient pottery style characteristic of the four-corners region, more specifically, Chaco Canyon. Did she think it would help? Or was it a coincidence she was making this particular pitcher?

Mara noticed Calliope watching her and waved her over.

Calliope nearly asked how Mara was feeling, in a voice of sympathetic concern, as she'd done every day since Mara had recovered, but she stopped herself. At this point it only annoyed the older woman, who seemed as spry as ever. Instead, she said, "That pitcher is a beautiful recreation of the original whiteware."

Mara stopped painting but didn't smile. Her tone purposeful, as though she hadn't called Calliope over for chitchat, she said, "I'm taking it with us."

Calliope narrowed her eyes at the pottery, considering. "Will a replica do any good?"

"We don't know what will. Might as well try."

Calliope glanced at the Yellow Wood clanswoman. They shouldn't have been discussing this in front of her or anyone outside of the kiva Chance went to for help. His deceased wife's older brother, Arlen Cooeyate, member of the Eagle clan. No one else knew. And for all of their safety, they needed to keep it that way. Arlen was the voice of their religion, a role he'd inherited after his elder brother had died. He was not the Elder she had expected to meet.

Mara broke her trance, said, "Are you busy after dinner? I need to discuss something with you."

Had she and Chance been planning without her? "Chance needs to talk."

"Then I'll join you."

Calliope nodded, and the corn girl threw the rattle drum at Mara, hitting the pitcher. It bounced off and fell to the wooden porch. Mara didn't look amused. She handed the rattle back to Calliope.

Nala approached, a reddish-brown seed jar balanced atop her head. She was smiling widely, though walking cautiously.

Calliope asked the young woman, "Still practicing?"

"If we're to live as the Ancients lived, then I want to do it right."

"You're doing perfectly."

Nala was fresh air. Nala was the first bloom on a winter-bare branch. Calliope would miss Nala most.

"Thank you, *kyawu.*" She called her sister. "Come help me with the soap weed." Unlike the blood pudding, this work Calliope actually enjoyed. The seed pods of the yucca root were boiled and used for food, though she had helped Nala use the entire plant for various purposes. They'd made the leaves into brushes and given them to the kivas for ceremonial masks and altars. They'd also soaked the leaves in water to soften them and knotted them together for rope. They'd dried the leaves to split and braid for water-carrying head pads and mats. And pounded the peeled roots into suds for washing hair, wool garments, and blankets.

Calliope had learned to weave yucca into a linen-like fabric they used for clothing. The central leaves of the yucca plant were gathered and each leaf folded into a strip three inches long then placed in a pot of boiling water together with wood ash. They removed the skin from the leaves and the children chewed them. Eunjoo found this part of the process hilarious. After this, the fibers were separated and straightened, and once they dried, they were soaked in cold water and rubbed between the hands. The softened fibers were then pulled into a fluffy mass and spun and woven like cotton. Eunjoo's favorite game was mastering this new life, and she played it so well with Nala. Not everything here was ancient; a few modern accoutrements existed. But many Western ways were put aside for the old traditions. If Nala and the other young people missed electronics and those trappings of their modern life *before*, they never let on. Everyone here seemed content in the present, Nala especially. Her joy was so contagious Calliope wished she too could have built contentment here. And she might have. If she hadn't already built a life elsewhere.

How would blood sausage have tasted if she'd never known what it was made of? What would Zuni have felt like if it hadn't been the barrier between Calliope and her son?

THIRTY-ONE
POPPING BUBBLES

Dinner in Zuni was an affair every single night. The woman's role in the religion was preparing the food, for food wasn't meant just to be swallowed down like American fast-food culture had made it. Each meal was meant to be savored, slowly enjoyed.

Calliope found it painstakingly slow at first, struggled to adapt to the hours at the table piled high with vegetables from the garden: corn, squash, broccoli, scallions, cilantro, radishes. Clumps of pink salt crystal from Old Lady Salt, which Calliope remembered respectfully each time she sat for a meal at Malia's table. Jalapeño chiles, spicy carrots. Mutton, pinto bean stew, paperbread made from blue cornmeal. The blood pudding sausages Calliope refused more steadfastly than the corn girl her own mashed food. For dessert, thin wedges of honeydew and watermelon.

It bothered Calliope that the women didn't have a more active role in the Zuni religious and intellectual life, but she kept telling herself that though she was fond of these people, though their way of life spoke to her spirit, they were not her people. Because she did not fully understand, could never fully understand, she had no right to criticize or judge. So she took a bite of chile, swallowed. A bite of paperbread. A sip of melon juice. A spoonful of stew. A bite of radish. And so forth. Malia smiled approvingly, said aloud that Calliope was a wonderful daughter-in-law, who did wonderfully, the Indian way.

Calliope didn't tell Malia that her bisabuela was Puebloan, that Calliope had a part of the people coursing through her blood as well, the Ancients residing in her. She knew that Malia meant she was playing her part of an adopted Zuni wife well. She'd been practicing hard, to keep Chance from taking any other risks for her. She was trying to keep him safe. So she just smiled at Malia and took another bite of her spicy chile, the heat prickling at her eyes.

After dinner, Eunjoo ran off again with Nastacio to pick wildflowers. Calliope excused herself to change the baby, and Chance followed her. The rest of the family would wash dishes then gather on the porch as the sun set, gossiping and telling stories, some members smoking or rolling tobacco, a sacred item in Zuni.

None of their usual banter tonight though. Chance's neck and arms were tense. "We need to leave before sunrise."

She put the baby in the middle of their bed, on her stomach; the corn girl wasn't crawling yet. "Why tonight? I thought we had two more days."

"Arlen gave me a heads-up. Some of the men from my kiva suspect."

"How?"

Chance smoothed his hair out of his face, clasped his hands behind his head. "Nothing stays hidden on the rez."

"What will Malia say when she finds we're gone? And Nala? Wowo łashhi? Can't we at least say goodbye?"

"I don't want them to know where we've gone. Not for sure. I can't risk them accidentally telling anyone. It's bad enough Arlen knows."

"If it hadn't been for Arlen, we wouldn't have known where to go."

His brother-in-law and he were still close though Chance's wife had been dead eight years, most of which Chance had spent living in Texas. When the elders of his own kiva had shown their disapproval of Chance's actions, once he knew there would be retribution for his slaying of the Suuke, he knew he couldn't go to them for help. He'd confided all of this in Calliope; he had no one else to share it with. It would have been easy enough to let her stay on the rez, to continue pretending they were married, a family. She wouldn't be in as much danger then. But he was still at risk. And he couldn't ask her to stay. Not without him. He'd violated too many religious codes. He'd exposed too much. If she wouldn't stay as his wife, he couldn't ask her to stay as his widow. He had to get her out. He'd promised to get her back to her family.

Now that it was time, she didn't know if she was ready. Her stomach twisted. After all these months, she couldn't imagine what leaving would feel like. What leaving him would mean. She asked, "How far are you coming?"

His voice low, crumpled as dried corn husks, "As far as I can."

"Will you come all the way across … with me?"

"What are you asking, mujer?"

She didn't know. She had to get back to Phoenix.

The first night after her healing ceremony, she'd stopped bleeding and could leave the house. Chance had asked Malia to watch the corn girl, lying that he was taking his wife out for the evening. Malia had been so happy for her son she hadn't noticed or had chosen to ignore the fear in his eyes. He was taking her to Arlen, speaker of their religion, keeper of their way of life, interpreter of the gods, the Elder brother of Zuni, who was also his brother-in-law. Calliope had expected someone much older, with long white hair and a face rutted with wrinkles; a male counterpart to Bisabuela. Instead, Arlen was midforties, barrel-chested, walked with a slight limp, and had scars on his face that suggested he'd survived the streets outside of Zuni; he was leather-worn but handsome, though not compared to Chance, and only slightly shorter, with a rumpled crew cut. His physique was fit with the exception of his mild potbelly.

They'd met in the basement of his house; she wouldn't have been allowed in his kiva, and there was no other place they were safe from prying ears. On shelves lining the walls, hundreds of ko'ko, carefully carved and colorfully painted statues of their myriad gods. She looked for the Suuke pair that had almost killed her, that had killed Amy. She couldn't find them. A tabby cat had followed them down the basement steps and was rubbing itself against Calliope's legs, purring. She nudged it away but it wouldn't budge. She needed answers. How could her child have been transformed into a rock inside her belly? How could anyone else have been transformed? What was happening to the land? It made no scientific sense. Chance had told her to trust the stories. Fine. What were the stories?

Arlen had laughed wryly at her demands. He spoke to Chance in Zuni, and Calliope had the distinct impression he was making some joke at her expense. But then he said, "Though we don't normally share religious secrets with women, that is not our way, I will tell you what I know." She still didn't know what Chance said to convince Arlen.

When he first told her what was happening, she thought he was making fun of her again. How could it have been true? But then he had repeated the words from her dream, the words the Spirits had sung the night after she gave birth. He said, "Mother Earth is a protective mother; she shields her people. When her children, our ancestors, first left her four-chambered womb and came to the surface of her body, to this Sky World, she grieved. She wanted them back inside of her, where she could keep them safe. And these millions of years, what destruction people have wrought. What disrespect they've shown her sacred flesh. We Zuni have always known that when Mother Earth has had enough, she would shake her troubles off. She would shake her troublemakers off. Our great Mother has all the power she needs."

She sat on one of several wooden chairs, to keep from wobbling to the floor, and the cat jumped into her lap; it kneaded her dress with its claws, scratching her. She lifted it and set it on the floor. It jumped up again. She petted the damn cat to keep it from scratching her. The Spirits in her afterbirth fever dream had told her she would know when the Earth had used her power. She felt shaky, dizzy. Her voice hoarse, she asked, "But where is everyone else? When my family disappeared, where did they go?"

"Don't you see? When our Mother shook her troublemakers off, she took us with her."

Calliope glanced at Chance, who nodded reassuringly.

Arlen continued, "Your family aren't the ones who disappeared." He picked up a ko'ko known as a mudhead from a low shelf, its doughnut-shaped mouth and disfigured, knobby bucket head, harrowing. It held a knife. Calliope shivered. Arlen placed the mudhead on one of the wooden chairs beside Calliope. "*You* are."

They'd argued that night, nearly six months ago, after Arlen's terrifying words. Arlen and Chance agreed that the previous world still existed; only it had been split apart, and their world, which belonged to Mother Earth and her people, had been given back, restored to its proper balance. They speculated that those left behind in the previous world believed the splitting was a nuclear explosion, but it had come from Mother herself, so the scientists and politicians there would see it as the irrevocable consequence of stored nuclear waste in the land, which had been building since Trinity Site and had finally come to haunt them, causing volcanic eruptions and spurring a series of climate events and earthquakes. Mother splitting herself wouldn't appear Spiritual to them because they wouldn't know what they were looking for. It would be like the shadows left behind in Hiroshima and Nagasaki. They would believe the incredible but plausible idea that the few who had disappeared had been annihilated by the atomic bomb. Their shadows burned into the ground.

Calliope was a shadow burned into the ground.

But on the level of Spirit, what Mother's people understood, this was the unfolding of Mother's reclamation—which began millions of years before, when the first people started emerging from the fourfold underworld of her womb in their reptilian form. This was merely the next phase of evolution, of never-ending creation, what the Zunis had always known about levels of existence. They'd passed through several worlds before. Now they'd simply moved to the next.

The Zuni people, and all the Puebloans who were of the same Mother, would understand this. They wouldn't need it spelled out. Malia and Nala and Wowo łashhi, all of them. They'd understand what Mother had done for them. Protected them as she'd protected herself. As she'd promised them she would so long ago.

Arlen said, "They'll believe you dead, but you're not dead. No deader than any of us."

If she wasn't dead, then there was the possibility of return.

Calliope still didn't know if she could believe. Maybe Andres and Phoenix were alive, here, in this world. The only world she'd ever known. All the unexplainable phenomena could be explained—only she hadn't found the right equation, the underlying principle. Her family was somewhere else in New Mexico. The eastern part of the state, maybe, near Roswell or Carlsbad? Or anywhere at all in the US. They could have been anywhere. But another world?

She could cross a state line or a country. Those borders she understood.

But crossing worlds? It didn't make sense.

Yet Bisabuela's voice … the Ancient Voices she heard in the cicada song on the rocks …

Since girlhood she'd understood there was so much more than she understood.

The worlds had split. And she had disappeared.

Her pulse had fluttered at her neck and wrists, insects scuttling inside her, burrowing through her skin. She'd turned toward Chance. "You knew. You *knew* what had happened. Why didn't you tell me this before?" She wept, bitterness sludging her throat. "Why did you let me believe they were *here* … if you knew they weren't?" She'd slapped his face, so hard it hurt her own hand. "You lied to me. You *lied*."

He hadn't reacted to being slapped, even as Arlen spoke under his breath in Zuni, his tone repulsed, and Calliope wondered briefly how different she was from Chance's wife, as he was so different from her own husband. Chance had remained still, his expression not angry or guilty but searching. His voice level, his storyteller's lilt, he said, "Mujer, what you've crossed has been much more than worlds. What you've carried, heavier than doubt. You wouldn't have believed me. You wouldn't have listened to Bisabuela's words, allowed me to guide you, to keep you safe. I'm sorry that you're angry, but I've done what I've been tasked with. No more or less."

Phoenix was alive. He was alive but believed his mama was dead.

Had they held a funeral for her?

Their lives had gone on—as hers had gone on. Separately.

Arlen had seen through their facade. "Chance's clan, his kiva, the Medicine clan … none of them will look kindly at what's happened here. You can't let anyone know. Chance is in trouble enough as it is. How many taboos must you break, brother?"

Calliope bristled at Arlen's chastisement. In her mind, Chance had done nothing wrong. Nothing except keep the truth from her. But he'd protected her, he was right about that. The Suuke would have killed her otherwise, killed her corn girl. She asked Arlen, "Why were the Suuke after us? If they are gods, what reason had we given them to inflict harm? Is it such a taboo to help us?"

Arlen reached for a ko'ko on a far shelf, pulled out from behind rows of figures, the Suuke with the bow and arrow that had killed her friend. She remembered it lying dead in the snowy road beside Amy's body, a track of arrows from its neck to groin as Chance shot it again and again then kicked it off the precipice. It seemed so innocuous as a wooden statue in Arlen's hand, yet she knew its true form, its terrible power.

"Chance has told you of Zuni heaven?"

"The dancehall of the dead?"

Arlen nodded. "He's told you how it was created?"

"The children crossing the water in their mother's arms became amphibian, scaring their mothers, who let go, and the children drowned."

"But that's not how Zuni heaven was first created. The sacred lake, it already existed. They only fell into it, which is why they did not die but became ko'ko." He picked up the mudhead from the chair beside her. "As he was leading them on their search for the Middle Place, the speaker of the religion, Kā-wi-mō-saw, put in charge by the twin war gods told his two children to find a place to build a village. They ascended a peak and the girl was tired. She told her brother to go on and continue searching without her while she slept under the shade of the juniper. When he returned he watched her sleeping, her dress lifting above her thighs in the evening breeze, and he thus had relations with her. She awoke and realized what he had done and began screaming, distorting her face so that it became swollen and distended and puffy, turning her into a monster. Immediately she was pregnant and gave birth to dozens of hideous beasts for children. These are the mudheads you see, their bumpy helmet-shaped heads, doughnut-swollen lips, and protruding eyes. And their mother died, her Spirit releasing from the misshapen body and hurtling herself at her brother for thrusting himself on her and causing her such a fate. At that moment, their father Kā-wi-mō-saw climbed to the top of the ridge and realized what had happened and was most grieved. He yelled out for his daughter not to kill his son. And she could not. She went away, screaming and weeping. The brother in his shame descended the mountain and dragged his feet across the plains below where a river flowed and a lake appeared. In the depths were houses and a center, a great kiva with windows to view the dance within. Both brother and sister were transformed into ko'ko and their children with them. Thus, through sin and shame was Zuni heaven created. But even this darkness and evil were transformed into something good, saving the rest of Mother's people from a restless death and allowing them instead to live in peace after death. No matter what wrong one has committed in life, it is not too wrong to be forgiven and made right. But from that darkness, evil was released and gave rise to the demon ko'ko, like the Suuke. For though there is no punishment in death, there is always a price to pay for breaking taboo, as the brother broke taboo." He glanced at Chance, who stood straighter, shrugging back his shoulders, as if bracing himself. "Not one of us can escape the price."

Chance said, "I thought the Suuke was trying to root out anyone not of our people." He cleared his throat, his shoulders slumping now. "I couldn't let that happen."

"It wasn't up to you."

Chance's eyes were inexplicably sad, his voice low, nearly a whisper. "You don't know that."

"You skirt heresy, brother."

"I know."

* * * *

In the bedroom they shared in Malia's house, the wool blankets Chance had nightly spread onto the floor where he slept by himself each cool night were now folded inconspicuously on the bed so no one would know the difference. The baby they'd been raising together all these months lifted her head, stuck her fist in her mouth, drooling. Calliope hadn't known she was going to say it until the words were coming out. She reached for Chance's stiff arms, looked carefully into his eyes. "Come back with me."

He groaned softly with something like apprehension mixed with desire, mirroring her own, and slid his arms around her waist, now cinched and curvy, no longer swollen with baby weight, her body flat against his, clicking into place between his hips and thighs. She pressed her forehead against his chest, breathing rapidly at their nearness, after so many months of nearness. He smoothed back the hair curling around her neck, then kissed her neck, shoulders, collarbone, the warmth of his breath tightening her breasts into rose-shaped knots. He hardened against the folds of her dress, gathering at her thighs. He pulled her closer, though they were already locked together, as if he could shape them into one creature, connected like clay to each other.

Sundown filtering through their bedroom window, Chance's limbs tangled with Calliope's own, he kissed her mouth, kissed her with the thirst of a man in a desert and she, finally, no longer mirage but coconut water, she was breaking open for him. She slid the sleeves of her dress down her shoulders, slipped it along her waist and hips, shimmied it to the floor. From a string around her neck dangled the wooden coyote he had whittled for her. He met her eyes, smiled, then peeled off his shirt, revealing his muscular chest, a coyote tattoo across his left pectoral, over his heart; it howled at the moon. Calliope had seen him undress countless times over the past several months, had watched his sunbaked skin, the coyote skulking, by lamplight. She'd often been aroused by his rugged beauty, his gentleness. This evening, she dared put her mouth to his skin, roll her hands down the masa of his chest and stomach, unclasp his jeans, the same jeans she had washed for him again and again since she was his Zuni wife.

He spread a wool blanket on the floor beside the bed. The corn girl had rolled onto her back in the center of the mattress and was busily kicking toward the ceiling and sucking on her fists. She paid her mother and Chance no notice.

They knelt on the blanket facing each other, breathing heavily into each other's skin.

She didn't need to push aside thoughts of unfaithfulness or guilt, for in that moment she had given herself fully to story. The worlds had split. She could never understand how, though they had discussed bubble universes, their worlds like membranes floating trillionths of a trillionth of an inch apart from each other; dark matter separated them from the world they had come from, that Mother Earth had unfolded herself from, spiraling them here, across some hidden fourth dimension of space and across space into this parallel. They collided into each other, energy converting energy into hot matter and radiation, their impact no accident nor fate but part of the endless saga of creation and destruction and recreation. Two bodies pinned together with the force and mystery of a singularity.

She lay atop him, curled into him, as they finished, panting and slick against each other's bodies. He held her as if he were afraid she would again become mirage, turn figment and float away. She breathed out deeply, her laughter surprising her. "Why weren't we doing that the whole time?"

He laughed wryly, squeezing her, kissing her atop her head. "I didn't know it was an option, mujer, believe me."

She slid onto the wool blanket, and he turned sideways, facing her, their legs entwined, her head resting in the crook of his arm.

"You would leave your people for me? Though you're meant to be here? I sometimes feel like this is your myth, your people's story, and I've just fallen into it by mistake. I'm not meant to be here. I'm an intruder, not sure how I got pulled in …"

"You're my story, mujer. I made you a promise. I'll stay with you as long as I can. We'll figure out what to do next once we get there. First, we have to get you home."

Her pulse quickened at the word *home*. Here on the floor, lying with Chance, their whole lives seemed to stretch in front of them. It could stay this way. It didn't have to end.

She didn't have to rise from the dead.

He said, "It shouldn't take more than half a day to get up to Chaco." Arlen had suggested they try it and Calliope immediately agreed. It was a spiritual center for the people she'd been studying her whole life. Bisabuela had taken her to the sun dagger. And she'd been hearing her voice since the worlds branched apart, that light on the bridge, merging in her mind with Bisabuela's voice on the mesa. Arlen had confirmed her suspicion. Equinox, the middle of time. And Chaco Canyon had been the Middle Place for the Ancients. Calliope had found her path. The bridge seemed to have split open in the fall equinox. Best they could figure, the spring equinox was coming March 20—three days away, give or take. Time was strange here; it didn't work the way it worked in the previous world. It wasn't faster or slower, didn't evince any perceptible difference just *felt* different, thinner, maybe, stringier. Chance continued, "Even so we need to get moving. We can't account for weather or other ... events."

"You don't think there's anything else like the Suuke out there?"

"This is Zuni land now. Could be. You saw how many ko'ko there are."

"They aren't all demons though."

"No, they're almost all benevolent, in their own ways. But we still should be careful. It's not just ko'ko I'm worried about ..." He sighed deeply, buried his face into her neck. He stroked the indent of her waist, ran his hand along the curve of her hip and thigh. She coiled herself tighter against him, and he groaned into her ear. "We need to pack. Yet all I want is to get back inside you." He spread her legs with his knees, burrowed his hand in the wetness there, opened her mouth with his.

She was breathing shallowly, digging her fingers into his arms as she rocked against him, swaying against the rhythm he created for her body, on the brink of finishing, when a quick tapping on the door snapped her back, and standing in the open doorway was Mara, red-faced, wide-eyed. She stammered an apology and shut the door.

Calliope and Chance looked at each other and burst out laughing. After a few seconds Chance said, "She's right though. We should get a move on."

"Is that what she said?" Calliope was still laughing.

"I don't know, I couldn't understand her, she was so embarrassed."

"I'm not embarrassed."

"Me neither, Hom:il'ona." And it was true.

THIRTY-TWO
RIPPED AWAY

alliope had put on the black yoga pants and sweatshirt she'd brought from Tía's and the camper's trusty hiking boots, tired of wearing a dress in the night air. She found Mara out back, smoking homegrown tobacco. Chance was inside packing. The corn girl was asleep. Calliope stood beside Mara, breathing in the sweetly pungent smoke. "I didn't realize you smoked."

"Old habit. I quit, but tonight it smelled so good." She breathed out a puff of smoke. "I'm too old, really. Guess I'm nervous."

Again, Calliope resisted the urge to ask Mara how her chest felt. She'd nearly died. Calliope still didn't understand how the Medicine clan had saved her without the use of a hospital. She added it to the mile-long list of what she didn't understand but had come to accept.

Like the rock baby still buried in the threshold of Malia's house, which Calliope still stepped gingerly over or around, or avoided altogether by coming in through the back door. She could've sworn she could hear a faint heartbeat through the floorboards, as through a fetal heart monitor, a telltale heart. She was half tempted to dig it out each day and check for a rotting corpse. But she never did.

When Mara recovered, Calliope had told her what she'd learned from Arlen and what had become of her rock baby and Amy's body—or rather, what had unbecome of them. Mara had a less difficult time accepting the reality. "I knew my mother wasn't crazy. I knew Chaiwa had been right all along. Lizard's Tail was true. Only this time, I was Chaiwa. We all were." She said this through tears, her voice part amazed, part desolate. "I'm the one who left Trudy."

Calliope thought of Susana, the note she left: *turned to stone.* She'd watched her beloved Reina become a rock before her eyes. Only now that she'd given birth to a rock child did Calliope begin to comprehend the confusion and grief that had taken her friend's life. What had caused the few people they'd encountered to seem so insane, like the hunter. They were shell-shocked. In some ways, Calliope still felt shell-shocked, like she was wandering through a dream. She was still waiting to awaken.

At Mara's insistence, they'd buried the rock of Amy Denver behind the house, and that's where Mara was now smoking, beside Amy's grave.

"She should be going with us," Calliope said.

Mara nodded, stubbed her cigarette out in a small clay ashtray, set it on the back porch. Their silence filled with the chirping of night insects. It was summer come early, the buzzing of cicadas in the wild grasses. Mara finally spoke. "I'm sorry I barged in on you like that. I didn't realize you and Chance were ..."

"We weren't." Calliope's face and neck flushed, though she'd said she wasn't embarrassed. Talking about it felt trite, lessened it somehow. But she didn't have anyone else to confide in, so she continued. "I love him."

Mara smiled, said playfully, "I could tell."

"I also feel monstrous, a terrible person, like I've abandoned my child. My whole family. My husband ..." She sighed, unleashing the burden she'd held in for all these months. She probably should have been whispering, or not saying anything at all. But she couldn't stop herself, it felt so good to say aloud. "Maybe that was over a long time ago, and I was too scared to see it. How I relied on him to feel normal or capable. It's not really Andres I'm upset about. Though I miss him too." She hadn't said his name in months, hadn't allowed herself even to think it very often. Andres had been steadfast, had done everything for her. Maybe that was part of the problem. She relied on him too strongly. She sat down on the grass beside Amy's grave, pulled a long blade, split it into three strips and began to braid it. "I asked Chance to come back with me."

Mara raised her eyebrows, let out a low whistle. "Is that fair to him? We don't belong here, but doesn't he?"

"He says he belongs with me."

"What do you say?"

"I told you already. I love him."

Mara murmured something that didn't quite resemble assent, but perhaps curiosity. She took another rolled cigarette from the clay ashtray, struck a match, and lit up. Night insects formed a shrill choir again. Finally, Mara said, "You didn't leave by choice, honey. You were ripped away from everything you loved with that damn flash of light, just as I was ripped away from my beloved Trudy. So you fought hard to survive, and you have. And you've made do. You can't fault yourself for making your happiness where you are. That's what we do. All we can ever hope to do."

Mara crouched down beside Calliope in the grass, so spry and nimble for such an aged woman. She was likely Wowo łashhi's age and even perhaps Bisabuela's when she passed on to the Spirit world, yet Mara seemed much closer to Tía's age. They made such a sweet couple.

Though Calliope couldn't imagine their crossing at Chaco *not* working for what that would mean for herself—never holding her son again, a thought so terrifying she couldn't even fully form the possibility in her mind—she also hoped Mara would get back to Trudy.

What would it be like on the other side? If they could get through.

If universes had collided and created whatever tunnel they'd used to cross over, or branched apart creating a parallel copy they now inhabited, then what toll had it taken on her world? Over the past six months she had only thought about getting back to Phoenix. She hadn't considered what condition he might be in when she got home to him. She presumed he'd be fine. That Arlen and Chance were correct in their speculation that the people who'd stayed would assume she and the others who'd disappeared were dead. But what had that bloodred light done to the other world?

Or if the worlds splitting hadn't taken a physical toll on the earth, what had the people done to it and each other these past six months? How had the US government reacted to thousands if not millions of people disappearing? She assumed it was mainly the Puebloans who'd vanished, and she'd only gotten caught in the crosswinds.

But she couldn't know for sure. She hadn't ventured out of the Southwest and had no idea what the rest of the globe was going through. Had indigenous peoples all over the world had their lands rightfully restored? Were there others in this new world?

If she and Chance were not safe in Zuni, then perhaps there was another place, *here*, they could make their home?

Mara snuffed out her cigarette, sighed. "You've been awful quiet, sweetheart. You're considering it, aren't you?"

Calliope cleared her throat; she'd forgotten for a moment where she was, so lost in her disturbing thoughts. She'd braided three other blades of grass without noticing and woven them together in the shape of a ring. She slid it on her left index finger. "Considering what?"

"Staying."

Calliope turned toward Mara, who bore a mischievous smile.

She couldn't abandon her child. There was no way. She felt ashamed.

"No," she said, curtly, a little too resolute. "We're leaving before sunrise."

Mara murmured, again, not agreement or disapproval. She raised herself up to standing, groaning quietly, then said, "We should take the rocks with us. Bury them on the other side."

Calliope nodded. They dug Amy's rock out of the dirt, and for a moment Calliope feared she would reach into the ground and touch the rotting skin of her friend's corpse, the arrow still piercing her neck.

"How will I get the rock baby from Malia's doorway? She wouldn't stand for it."

"You'll do it when she's asleep."

Mara lugged the rock up the stairs, Calliope following.

Mara went into the house, but Calliope lingered on the porch, her hand on the open door; she hadn't seen Eunjoo since dinner. She should have come home already.

As if in answer to the warning that prickled Calliope's gut, from the grazing pastures in the distance, the girl screamed.

THIRTY-THREE
PROCESSION OF GODS

Eunjoo came running from the grasses of the sheep pastures, screaming. Calliope rushed down the steps, déjà vu sweeping over her. The Coyote girl that Eunjoo had once before become—had she returned? This time Calliope was strong enough to run, and she did, across the waffle gardens, past the honeycombed buildings, following Eunjoo's voice.

Half expecting animal-yellow eyes, she caught the girl in her arms, both of them gasping for air. "What's wrong?"

Her bird's voice almost inaudible for its high-pitched terror. "It's after me."

"What?"

"The Suuke."

That was impossible. They'd slain both Suuke, husband and wife. She'd watched them both die. Calliope glanced into the pasture. She couldn't see far in the dark. The spring moon was nearly full and bright but still low in the sky. She could make out the shapes of the squat shrubs she knew were juniper, rabbitbrush, saltbush, sage. All too low to hide behind. She saw no monster. Piñon trees made a small forest further back, but Eunjoo wouldn't have gone that far. She knew better.

"Where's Nastacio? I thought you were with him."

Eunjoo hung her head, bit her lip. "He left."

"Where'd he go?"

Eunjoo shrugged, obviously hiding something.

Calliope grabbed her hand. "Let's get back to the house. You can tell me there."

She hadn't felt truly scared since she'd come to Zuni. She was worried about the situation with Chance and his kiva elders, but she believed him strong and smart enough to work through it. She'd been confused and angry about the rock baby and the explanation in Arlen's basement but then somehow oddly at peace. Her family was alive, and there was a way back to them, a hypothesis, really, but still, it was a possibility, and that's all she needed—hope, and she clung to it.

But now she felt the ominous buzzing in her ears, the same as she'd heard outside the hangar, as she'd heard when she was a girl and the dust storm atop the mesa had made her and Bisabuela abandon their picnic. This was more than night insects chorusing. This was the Ancients, warning.

She tugged on the girl's hand, picking her pace up to a jog.

"Why are we running?" Eunjoo asked.

"It's dark," Calliope said, knowing that was an insufficient answer.

The lights in Malia's house were burning brightly through the windows. The back door was closed. She tried opening it, but it was bolted shut. They'd have to knock, something she'd never needed to do in Zuni before. Or go around the front. Step over rock baby's threshold.

Her heart fluttered in her chest, a caged bird flapping wildly at the wires.

Eunjoo pulled on Calliope's hand, hers slick with sweat. She whispered, "They're here."

"Who's here?"

"The ko'ko."

Three months before, the Shalako ceremony had shown Calliope the rigors of impersonating the gods, wearing the masks, and dancing. She had not been allowed to participate, as a woman and a non-Zuni, but she could see just wandering through the village watching those chosen how difficult it was physically and mentally for the boys and men who took on the role, the challenge, and the honor of becoming a god. She'd asked Chance if they really *became* gods. The answer was *no*, but their thoughts and actions were influenced by their role. In a way, their Spirits were given over to the gods they imitated. The masks were heavy and thick, smothering with heat, difficult to breathe in, headache-inducing. Those who wore them would practice the dances for hours and hours on end, perfecting each step.

Shalako meant messenger of the gods. And Calliope had seen the procession down the mountain and into the village square. She'd heard the steady beat of drums and wailing call of the flute signaling their arrival. In one of the Shalako houses built specifically for the occasion by all the Zuni, she'd watched the beaked and feathered, horned and striped, fierce-eyed and spotted gods dancing, rhythmically, forcefully, beside a row of altars, bristling with plumed prayer sticks. Her eyes had blurred with tobacco smoke and incense, her stomach knotted with apprehension. She hadn't been scared, not really, but she'd felt the power stirring from the dirt floors, the haze of dirt clouds scurrying through the stale air, the crowds of people knit closely together on chairs and benches, watching, praying. For moments at a time, she couldn't tell the difference between the masked dancers and the gods themselves—they were as real as the Suuke she and Chance had killed. The heat and a foreboding sense that she would be punished too had made her dizzy.

She'd left the Shalako house with the corn girl in her cradleboard strapped to her back and stood in the front doorway of Malia's empty house; everyone else was still attending Shalako. She hadn't realized Chance had followed her until he was beside her on the porch.

"Why rocks?" she had asked, staring at the threshold floor. "I don't understand."

He was quiet at first, took a deep breath, leaned against the doorway. The question lingered in the air before he finally said, "You're an anthropologist, mujer. You do understand."

She didn't bristle at his tone, which she might have deemed condescending at one time. She understood his mannerisms, his ways of drawing truth from truth. Her own question seemed to swirl above them in the Shalako night air. Why rocks. Beneath the dust and sandy loam—they were alive with the past. They were a connection to other times, other worlds. That's what she loved about uncovering meaning in the layers of earth, finding road maps back. He was right. She did understand.

Still it did not make it any less painful; still she could not step over the rock baby. She nodded in response, saying nothing aloud, turned, and walked around to the back door instead.

Now, fear prickling the hairs on her neck and arms, she led Eunjoo around the side of the tall, honeycombed building and up the front steps, the lights all burning on this side of the house as well. She put her hand to the latch, hesitated. Voices from inside, low and insistent, a kind of humming. She opened the door.

In the corner of the main room, feet from where Calliope had given birth, loomed several tall figures, some multicolored, others black and white, some with slits for eyes, others protruding and disfigured, beaked, horned, or feathered. All of them huddled together. Again, Calliope had the overwhelming sense of being unable to differentiate the masks from the real things. Impostors or not, why were they gathered here?

Across the room at the large wooden table, Chance stood unmoving, his arms outstretched slightly in a stance of negotiation. In the kitchen, Malia, Wowo łashhi, Nala, and Mara likewise stood motionless. As Calliope hovered in the doorway holding Eunjoo's hand, trying to figure out what scene she had walked in upon, one of the masked men grabbed her by the arm and pulled her close to him, still clutching Eunjoo, and the other masked figures circled around them. She yelped at the rope-burn pain of his grip on her arm, and Chance yelled, "No! Let her go. Leave them out of this."

She should have let Eunjoo go, but she clutched her tighter, the girl burrowing her face into Calliope's sweater. Where was the corn girl? Was she safe upstairs? Or were the masked men up there? Someone shoved a callused hand over Calliope's mouth, so close to her nostrils she had to gasp for air. Another masked figure or the same? She couldn't tell who held her. She wouldn't have thought any of them capable of creating this mob. She'd lived here six months without so much as a disgruntled look or whiff of violence. She'd thought Chance and Malia were overreacting to the punishment ahead for breaking taboo. She never imagined this. What would they do to her, to Chance? Her heart raced frantically. The hand on her mouth smelled of damp earth and she pictured them burying her like the rocks.

Again, Chance shouted, "Let them go. The women have nothing to do with it."

Calliope had shot the Suuke. She had everything to do with it.

One of the masked figures, in a low, menacing growl, "Then come with us."

Chance said flatly, "I can't. We agreed I'd come after the equinox, at the end of the full Worm Moon." The moon was nearly full now, the Worm Moon that marked the equinox, when the earth began to thaw and the earthworms reappeared from the mud. Chance had saved his punishment for after the bridge at Chaco had opened and they'd gone home—after he'd gone home with Calliope. Like Coyote, Chance was tricking the masked men.

The one holding her spoke again in his growling voice. "Your nephew told us you were planning to flee tonight, trying to escape your fate."

Calliope's eyes darted toward the little girl hiding in Calliope's sweater, stretching it out. Eunjoo looked up, as if she sensed the piercing questions Calliope was asking. *How did you know? And why did you tell Nastacio?* Calliope hadn't mentioned anything to Eunjoo. She hadn't seen her since dinner. Had she been listening at the door? Or was this another mystery of Coyote girl's strange knowledge? Either way, the harm was done. The men knew Chance's scheme. They were here for vengeance.

Chance said again, "Let the women go ..." He sighed deeply, pushed his hair back from his face. "Let them go, and I'll go with you tonight."

"Now," the masked man growled. "You'll come with us *now*."

His voice flat, defeated, Chance said, "Fine. Let her go."

Calliope searched Chance's face for a hint of a plan. He wouldn't really go with the mob, would he? He wouldn't break his promise to her.

His expression was unreadable, his eyes, stoic. No glimmer of light showing he knew what he was doing, and she should play along. He'd given up. He was accepting his punishment. She would have to go to Chaco without him.

She looked at the ground, at their feet, these masked men dressed as gods. Some wore moccasins and others, strapped and feathered sandals that revealed nearly bare feet. The growling man holding her was wearing sandals. She caught Eunjoo's attention, motioned with her eyes to follow her lead, raised her eyebrows to indicate *one, two, three* ...

She stomped her heavy hiker's boot on the arch of his foot with the force of her whole body and bit his hand hard enough she tasted the salt and iron of his blood, and as she attacked him with everything inside of her, as he growled again, this time in pain, falling backward and letting his grasp on Calliope loosen, she yanked Eunjoo's hand to follow her. She barreled into the backs of the masked figures encircling them and charged directly for Chance, the girl following.

She plunged herself and the girl under the wooden table, willing Chance to understand what she was asking him to do.

He did.

As she ducked, before the masked men fully realized what was happening, Chance had smashed into the glass case on the wall with his elbow and pulled out his rifle, which he aimed at the mob, comprised of his own brotherhood. She couldn't even imagine what taboo he was now breaking, threatening the members of his own kiva, in god costume, at gunpoint. What level of sacrilege.

He released the safety, put his finger on the trigger, steadied his breath. "Get out of my mother's house."

The growling man came forward from the huddle, his voice no longer a growl. Was it Calliope's imagination, or did he sound like Arlen? "Put the gun down, brother. You're already in enough trouble as it is."

His gun aimed directly at the man's chest, Chance said, "Calliope, go get Miwe e'le and my bag upstairs. Mara, pull around back. No one else move. You said it yourself, I'm already in trouble."

Calliope ran upstairs to their room, grabbed Chance's bag from the bed, and lugged it over her shoulder, stumbling backward from its heft. The corn girl sound asleep, Calliope picked her up, wrapped her in a long wool blanket she tied around her waist and chest, so she was weighed down with packs on both her front and back, like military rucksacks. At the doorway she hesitated. Turned back to the locked dresser, pulled a key from a clay pot, unlocked the first drawer. Susana's gun. She cocked it, then shuffled downstairs to Chance and Eunjoo behind the dinner table, keeping her back to the wall, pointing Susana's gun toward the men. She wouldn't let them grab her again. And she wouldn't let them hurt her family.

"You'd betray your own brethren, your oath, your gods, for that woman? She's not half the woman my sister was." Arlen's voice was unmistakable; it sliced through Calliope.

Chance said nothing in reply. He spoke in Zuni in a low voice to his mother, sister, and grandmother. Calliope could make out a few of the words and understood he was telling them he had to stay with his wife and make sure she got home safely.

Through the mask, Arlen spit. "She's not even your wife."

Malia asked, her voice crestfallen, "Aktsek'i, is this true?"

His voice was equally deflated, his whole demeanor a collapsed hot air balloon, falling. "Tsitda, I wouldn't lie to you. We're married in the Zuni way." In Zuni marriage, the couple is free to live together as husband and wife, to make sure they are compatible, before any vows are made. Either party can break the arrangement without consequence.

Malia pointed with her chin toward the corn girl. "And is that your child?"

Chance sighed. "Yes. Miwe e'le is mine."

"Filthy liar," Arlen said. "You disgrace us."

Chance said, "Do not follow us, brother. I do not want to hurt you."

Calliope lowered the gun in the kitchen. Malia was looking at her with suspicion. She hated to leave this way—to leave the Coyote clan women who'd shared their lives with her. She wanted to tell them she would return, that she would come home to them. She could bring her son—

She stopped herself. It would not work. The masked men would not have it. She didn't belong here. The way Malia was looking at her, she could not tell if she would ever be welcome again. Perhaps Malia blamed Calliope for what was happening with her son. For taking her son away.

Once they were in the truck, Eunjoo asked Chance, "They won't hurt your family, will they?"

His voice was sad, but he said, "No. They never would." And Calliope understood what he meant; they didn't see *her* as his family. She wouldn't have been safe there. She couldn't go back if she'd wanted to.

"Will they follow us?" Calliope asked.

"I hope not."

Mara sped through the dirt roads off the rez.

They neared Black Rock, the basalt bluff at the northern edge of Zuni where Old Lady Salt had lived before she'd uprooted herself forty-five miles south, because the people had disrespected her by urinating and spitting while swimming in her waters and wasting her sacred flesh; she had hoped that by moving farther away, they would appreciate her more. Their pilgrimage would mean something. She'd left a gaping hole in the center of the rock, the place she'd traveled through to find her new home.

"The rock baby," Calliope said. "I left her."

"You're carrying her, mujer."

Calliope's gut lurched, and she checked quickly on the corn girl in the wool sling across her chest, making sure the flesh-and-blood girl had not turned to stone.

"Not Miwe e'le. On your back. I exhumed the rock baby while you were in the back with Mara. I knew you'd need to bring her."

Calliope lumbered out of the heavy backpack straps and peered inside the bag. She pulled out the rock baby. Funny how she could have stoppered the hole in Black Rock, she matched so well, she could have staunched that gaping exit wound.

"Did you bring Amy too?" Eunjoo asked.

Mara patted the rock in the center console. "Got her right here."

"Good," Eunjoo said. "It would have been cruel to leave her. Since she isn't dead."

THIRTY-FOUR
QUEMADO LAKE

alliope still wasn't inured to Eunjoo's pronouncements or prophecies or whatever they were. She settled back with the corn girl still sleeping against her chest, tried to steady her breathing and clear her mind of the fear fomenting like stormwater in the bay of her thoughts. She couldn't help it. Even after Eunjoo had fallen asleep against her lap, Calliope kept glancing back every few minutes to make sure Arlen and the other masked figures were not following, reminding herself they were not gods but men; they would not bound atop the truck as the Suuke had thrown itself onto the airplane. Whatever Eunjoo had seen in the pasture, it wasn't a vengeful Suuke. They'd killed them both. Arlen's scalding anger could assure her of that.

They ran out of gas a few hours past Black Rock, hadn't traveled more than a hundred miles on the dirt washes and remnants of ancient dirt roads. The truck gears grinded to a halt beside a patch of rabbitbrush she could tell was bright yellow in the day, though it was covered in shadow now, the moon half hidden by clouds. They'd known they were leaving for months. Why hadn't they prepared? Were there even any gas stations left? She hated that they were stopping so near Zuni. What if Arlen and the others had followed them? They'd catch up any time.

Mara stated the obvious: "We really didn't plan this through."

Chance opened the cab door, jumped out, saying, "Maybe you didn't."

Calliope followed him to the truck bed, the corn girl stirring only slightly but then settling back to sleep as Calliope rubbed and shushed her. Chance shone a flashlight and lifted the tarp to reveal an assortment of tools, the Suuke knife that Amy had tossed back there at Tía's hacienda, and two steel barrels the size of beer kegs.

"You want us to drink our troubles away?" she joked, averting her eyes from the knife.

His mouth inched into a flaccid smile, lacking its usual buoyancy. He said nothing, just climbed the tailgate and lugged one barrel to a standing position on the edge of the bed nearest the gas cap. "Let me help," Calliope offered, filling the uncomfortable silence.

"You ever siphoned gas before?"

No. But she could learn.

He picked up a clear snake of plastic tubing, and she felt slightly ashamed that even with Chance, she was still relying on a man for help. If Amy had been here, Calliope bet she would've known what to do.

"Open the cap, insert this all the way down the filler neck."

She followed instructions.

"I'll do this part. Don't want you getting gas down your throat."

"Isn't it dangerous for you?"

Chance shrugged, his expression and demeanor since they left Zuni troubling Calliope. As if he were saying, *How much longer do I have, really?*

Once the gas was streaming through the plastic snake into the truck, she asked, "Are you afraid this won't work?"

He pointed his chin toward the flowing liquid, his hand pinching the tube. "It's working."

She tapped her foot in the sand. "Not the siphon."

"I know." He shifted his weight, leaned against the side panel, rubbed his temples and eyes with his free hand. "What other option do we have?" He sighed, took a deep breath. "It has to work."

"Chaco could be a dead end. Then what?" She would never see her son again? Never hold him? Never show Andres he had a daughter?

Mara called out from the driver's seat, "It's not a dead end. Keep the faith, honey. I'll be back to my Trudy this time tomorrow."

"It's not even equinox yet," Calliope muttered under her breath. "If there is a tunnel, it hasn't opened." They assumed, anyway. What did they actually know? What secrets they'd learned, they'd learned from Arlen. And Calliope wasn't even sure she could trust him. Nothing was written down. And if they were right, and Chaco opened a doorway home, what then? What would Calliope say when she took Chance through, to her house? Would she just open the door and bring him inside, the way he'd taken her to Malia's house and introduced her as his Zuni wife? How would this work? *Hey there, everyone, here's the man I crossed universes with. We fell in love and got pretend married and now we're home and want to get married for real, so I'll need a divorce, thank you.* She felt dirty. More than that, how could she do that to Andres? She'd loved him before all of this. Or at least she'd thought she'd loved him. Had he moved on? This whole time he and Phoenix must have thought she was dead, and now she was going to show up with another man instead. They wouldn't believe her story. They'd think she'd left them to live with Chance, maybe down in Texas. Or like her own father, that she had crossed the border. That she'd actually just abandoned them.

Chance pulled the tube from the barrel, then the truck. "Should be good." She stared at him while they closed and secured everything, covered the bed with the tarp. Was she searching for some sign from him that he knew what they were doing? That anything would be untangled once they got to Chaco, if Chaco really was a way back? He didn't look at her, and she felt cold in the night air, even with the corn girl wrapped in wool around her chest. Chance walked around to the driver's side and asked Mara if he could take the helm for a while.

Mara settled into the back seat with Eunjoo, now awake, looking out the dark window and whispering under her breath.

"Who are you talking to?" Calliope asked.

"Coyote."

Calliope had learned by now that the girl's imaginary conversations were anything but fantasy. She looked around. "Where is Coyote?"

"I'm calling him."

"What for?"

Eunjoo said nothing.

Mara said, "We're lucky to have this child with us. No one ever believes the children."

Calliope believed. But she couldn't see anything out of the ordinary.

In the passenger seat, the corn girl had awoken. She usually slept through the night, but this had been a strange night. Calliope unwrapped her, feeling for dampness. She wasn't wet. The corn girl brought her finger to her mouth, suckling on her skin, frustrated there was no milk, beginning to cry. Calliope put the girl to her breast, said, "You win, Miwe e'le. A midnight snack."

Still she was unsettled. As the girl nursed, Calliope imagined what might have just happened in Malia's house. Would they have killed Calliope? She was certain they weren't capable of that violence, but she knew their stories told of sometimes horrifying punishments for breaking taboos. In one account, the ko'ko Salamobia, personification of anger that needed exorcising, would come from the sacred lake and behead the offender. She thought of Arlen, spitting in rage, his voice twisted to a growl at the thought of Calliope and Chance together or killing the Suuke together. She couldn't tell which angered him more.

Her pulse quickened as a horrible thought took shape. "Chance," she whispered. "What if Arlen intended for us to go to Chaco tonight? What if that was his plan?"

"I've known Arlen since we were kids. What you saw tonight, that wasn't him. He wouldn't act like that. He hasn't been the same since ..."

Calliope filled the silence, whispering, "Since his sister died."

Mara asked, "What happened to her, if you don't mind this old busybody?"

He didn't say anything at first, and Calliope put a hand on his shoulder, her other hand still holding the corn girl to her breast. Chance didn't look away from the dirt ahead. They weren't going more than thirty or forty miles per hour in the dark without a visible road.

She didn't think he would answer, he was silent so long.

Then he said, "I couldn't save her," his voice immeasurably sad. "We were swimming in Quemado Lake." He'd told her about this lake, where he'd experienced a mathematical epiphany, and a veil had been lifted. "I'd gone fishing there countless times, I thought I knew that water so well." He paused, pulled his hair back, breathed deeply. "I should've been paying attention. I should've been holding our daughter. My wife hit her head on a rock. I was three hundred feet away. By the time I got there they were both at the bottom of the lake. I didn't know who to save. I tried saving them both." His voice cracked. "I was selfish. I tried saving them both, and I saved neither."

It was unbearable. His shame. His pain.

His story really was like the Zuni migration; he'd lost a mother and child to the water, to Zuni heaven.

Perhaps Arlen's words had brought it all back: *She's not half the woman my sister was.*

Arlen blamed Chance for his sister's death. Blamed Calliope for taking his sister's place.

Still Chance hadn't answered Calliope's question, and her suspicion lingered, palpable in the truck as his grief.

What if they were not driving toward a way home? What if they were driving into a trap?

THIRTY-FIVE
MIDDLE PLACE

Sometime during the night, Calliope had finally dozed off and now awoke to alpenglow. Sunrise over the San Juan Basin overlooked Chaco, the sky bright pink and purple above the canyon, illuminating the ancient stone buildings, the Great House spanning the height of four stories, rising against the canyon wall so it loomed even larger, its seven hundred rooms and round ceremonial kivas expanding to the size of the Roman Colosseum. She blinked, her eyes still hazy from sleep, and the sunrays casting a glaze over the buildings. These were not ruins. Calliope wondered how much power a great-grandmother wielded in the Spirit world, for what she was seeing was powerful indeed. The biggest of the Great Houses—Pueblo Bonito, which she'd been fascinated with since her bisabuela had brought her here as a child, this home of the Ancients' great unsolved mystery—had been restored. Had she expected anything less? Living six months with Chance and his family in the Zuni honeycombs of the Ancients should have prepared her.

It had not.

During her revisionist fieldwork, she'd knelt on the sandy loam of the posthole in Room 33, peeling sandstone and chinking rocks from the hundred-year-old excavation site (where the Hyde Exploring Expedition had trod the ancient, sacred grounds), searching for proof of her bisabue-la's stories, though she could never breathe that humiliating confession aloud to her colleagues. She was there to follow the research, not the other way around. She understood how unprofessional she would seem, what a zealot, a mystic. She'd have been laughed out of academia.

She'd pared away at the sandstone that aspired to be anything but rock, that tried hard to look like broken pottery, chipped stone, even shell. It was the most common stone in Chaco for groundstone artifacts, manos and metates, and yet most of the time sandstone was just sandstone, shaped for masonry or hearths and hatches. Figuring out which pieces of sandstone were actual artifacts and which were just rock took time and experience. She'd spent long, dirt-covered days and nights in Chaco, devoted to uncovering its mysteries in khakis and a hard hat, crouching under crumbling walls that took five scaffoldings to keep from falling in on her and the rest of the crew, scribbling her field notes but finding nothing truly tangible to support her bisabuela's emergence belief. Until now. If someone had told her then that she would reenter this place of her Ancestors, restored, made new, as if she had traveled back in time a thousand years, she would have laughed them off the ruins. She laughed now, tears streaming down her face. It was absurd. It was surreal. Yet here it was. Sometimes sandstone was just sandstone; other times it was a portal to another world.

Chance, his voice somber, said, "Everything has two forms, mujer. The outer layer, which is all many Anglos tend to see, and the inner, the sacred, the Spirit. Before you came here, you only saw the outer form. It's all you would allow yourself to see. Now, you see the inner."

Still laugh-crying, Calliope nodded, her tears landing on the corn girl's dark hair. "Except I think there must be three forms, or a person will never fully see at all. The outer, yes, and the inner. But there is another, inchoate in the imagination. I think I had to believe this impossibility possible to understand there was another way. Bisabuela's stories becoming real right in front of me ..."

Mara had awoken, said, "Honey, it's quite a sight."

Calliope finally understood why the Ancients had chosen this unforgivably desolate patch of high desert where food and water were scarce, where they had to lug by foot massive timber from distant mountains to build the center of their culture. She understood the purpose of their dark enclosed rooms that were not intended for living, with no ventilation for a fire and deliberately sealed when they left. This was the Middle Place, cut through the middle of time. It was the heart of their cosmology. The Ancients hadn't died out or migrated away or abandoned their sacred sites. They had used them to move through worlds. Somewhere the Ancients still existed. They had never ceased.

She searched the sandstone building for figures, human or ghostly, but saw neither.

Chance parked in the soft dirt, adjacent to the fortress wall surrounding the Great House.

"We should hike up the mesa, check the sun dagger," Calliope suggested. "Make sure it's the equinox." The others agreed, and she changed and fed the corn girl, drank plenty of water herself, and tied a scarf around her head and Eunjoo's to keep from burning in the sun. They were at such a high elevation, the sun's rays seemed magnified. Or perhaps space was stringier in this universe, enmeshed as it was in time and matter. She strapped the corn girl to her chest. Chance offered to carry Miwe e'le, but Calliope felt stronger with the corn girl, felt she needed to take her girl where Bisabuela had taken her.

"Look!" Eunjoo pointed toward the mesa's high flattop, the tabletop mountain itself glowing with sunrise, appearing as an ancient fortress, a stronghold. But that's not what the girl was pointing out. Swirls of blackish-gray smoke were rising into the morning-orange sky. Calliope's heart thudded at the sight of the campfire. Had Arlen passed them in the night? Was he waiting atop the mesa with his masked militia to take them back to the rez? She'd brought Susana's gun just in case, and as always, Chance had his rifle slung over his shoulder. Calliope couldn't turn back now, not when she was so close to finding her family. For all she knew, Phoenix was a heartbeat away. If they each resided on a membrane containing an entire universe, then Chaco was the umbilicus holding them together. Though she had no *proof*, she felt it. Like two maps of New Mexico, representing everywhere—unfolded, side by side, pinned together on the canyon wall. She remembered her early labor fever dream and shivered. Phoenix, in the dream, had pummeled her with stones. Because she couldn't reach him? No. She had to reach him. Bisabuela wouldn't have brought Calliope this far for nothing. She set her jaw, breathed in the thick scent of campfire, and began hiking. Whatever waited at the top of the mesa, she could handle.

They stopped for water at a flat crag two-thirds of the way up. Calliope watched Mara and Eunjoo passing the clay jar, the older woman and little girl reminding her of Bisabuela and her younger self; they must have been nearly identical ages as when she'd made the trek, a true parallel. Watching the pair, she wondered, *Why us?* Why had they been pulled through? Chance she understood, his Mother had brought him; this myth was his reality. But Mara, Eunjoo, and Calliope? Her stomach ached with shame at the thought of those she hadn't been able to keep safe here, in this world—Susana, Buick, and Amy. All of them together, those hiking beside her now and those she'd lost over the past six months, why *had* they come through? Was there an intention for them? Or had they all been an accident? A cosmic happenstance, flotsam and jetsam caught in the quantum stream? Could Bisabuela have orchestrated their journey? And for what purpose? Just to show Calliope that Bisabuela had been right? The lesson didn't seem worth the cost. Or was there still something Calliope was missing, some message she hadn't quite deciphered? Was it a fool's errand to search for purpose in a random world? Only, she wasn't in her world anymore, was she? Perhaps things weren't quite so random here.

They started up the mesa again, passing a clump of sage growing like tufts of hair from the rock faces. Atop the tabletop earth, a figure on a stone bench leaned toward the fire, back slumped toward them. Bisabuela? But before the figure at the fire could solidify into her great-grandmother, Mara called in a tone of childlike wonder, "Chaiwa?" and Calliope realized her mistake. A ghost to more than just Calliope, it seemed, the figure at the campfire was a woman, a flesh-and-blood woman, her long black hair braided to her waist, though she wore modern clothes, jeans and a T-shirt. She turned around, her sepia skin dewy and clear. This was not the older San Ildefonso nanny Mara had described disappearing from Los Alamos in the 1940s nor Calliope's own great-grandmother. In fact, Calliope didn't recognize the woman at all. She blinked the dust and disappointment from her eyes.

"Doctor?" Mara asked.

The woman's face warmed in recognition, as if she'd been expecting them. A thin smile formed across her mouth, and creases gathered around her dark eyes. "So you've made it," she said, her tone composed, almost welcoming.

"How do you know each other?" Calliope asked, the buzzing of cicadas loud in her ears. Could they trust this woman? Even Chance seemed suspicious, his arms folded across his chest.

"We met, briefly," the woman said. "In the hospital."

Mara introduced Dr. Toya and explained that she worked at the hospital where Trudy's son, Calliope's cousin Julian, was a patient. Right after the light, the splitting of worlds, Mara had met her in the abandoned hallway, and Dr. Toya had given Mara the stone necklace she now wore around her neck. She pulled it out for the others to see. A smooth piece of turquoise. Calliope had noticed it around Mara's neck before and thought nothing of it. "Dr. Toya is from Acoma."

Sky City. Bisabuela's people. Calliope and this doctor were connected somehow. She searched the doctor's face for familiarity, some resemblance to Bisabuela. Dr. Toya bore a turquoise stone similar to Mara's around her own neck. She smiled warmly, but guardedly, invited them to sit with her at the fire. Calliope accepted, though sweat pearled down her back and between her breasts, extra heat radiating from the corn girl's body pressed against her skin. Calliope drank from her water pot then poured the tiniest drops onto the corn girl's head and neck. "What are you doing here, Doctor?" she asked, searching the rock surface for the three stone slabs that would indicate the sun dagger's location. She couldn't quite remember from girlhood where it was. Had Dr. Toya already checked?

"Same as you. Trying to get back to the previous world."

Calliope's pulse quickened. If Dr. Toya believed they had come to the right place, then this added credence to Arlen's tale. Chaco wasn't a trap.

Chance raised his eyebrows. Calliope could still see the skepticism on his face and sensed that he had a reason to wonder—after all, why would one of Mother's people choose to go back to the other world, where their people and way of life had been so devalued? She wondered if Dr. Toya was silently asking the same of him. More troubling, Calliope wondered if

Chance was doubting his own plan. She knew there hadn't been time for sentiment but his demeanor had definitely changed since Arlen's mob had attacked them; something felt different between them.

Mara, never one to beat around the bush, asked, "Why are *you* going back, Doctor? Aren't your people here?"

"They are. But one of my patients was left behind. I don't know how or why." As the doctor spoke, she burnished the turquoise stone between her fingers. Calliope thought back to the day her family had disappeared—the day *she'd* disappeared. In the foyer of her house, Phoenix's rock collection had been scattered. She'd stuck a piece of his turquoise into a duffel bag, but on the journey, she'd lost it. "I need to make sure he's safe, bring him back …" Calliope raised her eyebrows, unable to hide her skepticism. Dr. Toya would risk leaving her people, getting stuck between worlds, or on the other side, for a patient? It hardly seemed worth the risk. Dr. Toya must've read the cynicism on their faces because she added, "My sister's son is schizophrenic. He needs me." The way she inflected *needs*, the way she rubbed the turquoise around her neck, Calliope felt the familiar tug. Did Phoenix still need her? He'd gone six months without his mama. She'd gone on, six months, without him. She couldn't waste another minute.

"Do you know how to get through?" Calliope asked. "Have you checked the sun dagger?"

Dr. Toya nodded, motioned for them to follow her as she stood and walked toward the northwest face of the mesa. At the edge, three slabs of slanted rocks. The sun was not yet overhead.

"I've been up here three days," Dr. Toya said, "watching the dagger move across the sun spirals. Today, at noon, it should cut through both the larger spiral and the smaller snake, which means equinox. The middle of time."

They should have been early. They should have had several more days. Time was stringier here. They had come just in time.

Dr. Toya nodded down toward Pueblo Bonito. In the center of the flat roofs, a hole, a skylight. It would be blindingly dark in those unventilated rooms. No windows, no lights. But in that center, there would be a pinhole cascading light, especially at noon when the sun would glare down from its highest point in the sky. Calliope knew without being told—Room 33.

Dr. Toya said, "The Ancients likely built this place to protect the portal. Or control it. But there's no controlling what's only theirs to *guard*." Calliope thought about the bodies buried in Room 33. It was an airless room, preserving the artifacts; the cotton shrouds encasing them had not decayed in a thousand years, which meant no air circulation at all. In the soil and yellow sand, beneath planks of wood, the Chacoans had buried bodies with their grave goods. Calliope remembered Susana buried in the straw inside the barn, the rock in her hand. The grave goods in Room 33—raw turquoise, jet, and gold, those bright and unrefined rocks—had they been more than offerings? *Turned to stone.* Had it happened to the Ancients? Had they meant it to happen? Were their grave goods never offerings but methods of communicating with the gods, of summoning them? Was the bridge through Chaco a portal of the gods? Based on the age rings of the pillars and wood in the walls, they had built Room 33 before any of the seven hundred others in Pueblo Bonito. They built the remaining rooms around it. Archaeologists had speculated it was an elaborate show, a theatrical exercise. But what if the Ancients had originally built Room 33 to protect the portal to the other world, the world Calliope was now a part of? And the bodies? Were those sacrifices to allow the Ancients safe passage? Or perhaps those who couldn't get through? Those who didn't survive the journey? She pictured Susana in the straw, her corpse rotting. Calliope should have brought her friend's body with them. And Buick, who'd said there was nothing left of Albuquerque, not even the South Valley—it was all covered in black rock. And Buick's body, rotting in Tía's cabin. This version of the world was beautiful, yes. But as any world, it was also a graveyard.

A wheeling sun circled bedrock. Broken potsherds scattered in the dirt. A crumbled band of red rock sandwiched between solid gray brows of sandstone. A branch of dead juniper ledged like a fence. The sun cut through the slabs, slitting through the shadows on both the snake and spiral. The doctor had been right. Their calculations had been off. The portal—if there was a portal, if Room 33 was more than a burial shroud or elaborate stage— should have been open *now*. Calliope glanced at Chance, and he nodded, though Calliope still couldn't quite read the look on his face. Apprehension? Doubt? Something else? She reached out for his arm. His muscles tensed.

They climbed down the mesa with Dr. Toya, Calliope's heart knotting, hemp and wick. Her skin bloomed with sweat. They were going down into the recesses of Pueblo Bonito. She knew from the viga rings, the rafters in the ceilings, that the ponderosa pine had been hewed and dragged from a forest hundreds of miles away to build the Great House. Tree rings in the charcoal from fires in the ceremonial kivas revealed how long it had been inhabited. From an aerial view the kivas would appear as crop circles. She knew the textbook material. Archaeologists had named it for a city since they believed that over a period of two hundred years, Pueblo Bonito had grown and expanded like a modern city, though always retaining a half-moon structure. But she couldn't believe it had ever been inhabited. Not in these cramped, cave-like rooms. Or not by the living.

She feared she wasn't going back to Phoenix but to her death.

A great sandstone wall, made of the same ocher sand bricks as the rest of the building, surrounded the entranceway to Pueblo Bonito. Calliope brushed her hand against stone. The group stooped into the low, dark interior of the Great House; they could have been any excavation party she'd been part of at the University of New Mexico: Dr. Toya and Chance as guides, Mara as photographer, Eunjoo as research assistant, and Dr. Santiago with her corn baby strapped to her chest as historian. Her stomach flipped with an almost manic apprehension. They were so close.

Room 33 stretched toward the northwest section of the Great House. They entered in the crest of the moon shape and headed toward the apex. They needed a flashlight, the low first rooms pitched black through an endless corridor of doorways save one pin of light in the direction of Room 33, approximately 350 feet away. She'd been right. There was a skylight.

Eunjoo began whispering as she had been in the truck. Calliope couldn't make out her words. She grasped the girl's hand and asked, "What are you saying, chica?"

In her bird's trill, "I'm calling Coyote."

"You want Coyote to come home with us?"

Eunjoo said nothing, but continued whispering under her breath, an incantation Calliope couldn't discern.

"Do you have your stones?" Dr. Toya asked, her voice an echo from somewhere nearby though Calliope couldn't make out more than faint shadows in the darkness.

The stones. Arlen had told Calliope and Chance that among the sacred bundles when the Zunis emerged was a stone, within which beats the heart of the world.

In Calliope's fever dreams, Phoenix had been showing the stones to his mama, hadn't he? He wasn't hurling rocks in anger. He'd been showing her the path back to him. It was as Bisabuela had predicted.

The rock baby and Amy. They were Calliope's stones, weren't they? Her keys through the portal.

She'd always meant to take them back to the other side, but she hadn't fully realized their power. She'd *need* to take them with her, if she hoped to make it through. When they'd hiked up the mesa, they'd been too heavy to carry. She thought they'd have more time before equinox. She'd meant to go back to the truck. But then, in her rush to get home to Phoenix, she'd left them behind. "They're still in the truck," she admitted, her cheeks burning, ashamed she'd almost left her rock baby and Amy.

"I'll get them," Chance said, his voice near enough behind her that she could feel his breath on her neck.

She wanted to grab his hand, tell him not to go, afraid he might not return to her in the tunnels winding toward Room 33. Instead, she said, "See if there's a flashlight."

"I'll be right back, mujer."

She could hear him walking away swiftly toward the entrance.

They stepped down further into the airtight rooms. The floors alternated dirt and wooden planks. She knew that in Room 33 the layers of floor varied; the initial layer was sand and then black soil atop, alternating back and forth, white sand, black soil. This was supposed to represent the layers of earth growing again. Now she wondered what else it could have meant. It was a record of something. How many times Mother had taken people through her belly? The hole in the floor, the sipapu, represented the emergence of their ancestors from the underworld—like climbing a tree, they'd exited the underbelly through a small hole in the earth. They were heading toward Mother's birth canal.

Calliope shivered.

Was it her imagination or had the air gotten colder? Eunjoo kept mumbling, squeezing Calliope's hand tighter. A rustling. Like leaves scuttling in a windstorm.

"What's that sound?" Mara asked, her voice tense. "One of you gals scratching the walls?"

Calliope turned toward the pinhole of light from where they'd just come; Chance's shadow emerged as he ducked back into the sunlight.

The rustling grew louder. It wasn't coming from the entryway but from deeper inside the rooms. She imagined the bodies buried in Room 33. Were the remains there now, as they'd been on the other side when archaeologists first exhumed them for study? She'd read the lists of findings many times, knew exactly what had been recovered: the first skeleton on its back, lower jaw detached. The second skeleton, bones scattered through the sand. The third, only a skull covered with fragments of cloth and turquoise. Several other skulls and pitchers and bowls. A skull with three strings of yucca cord hemmed through the left eye socket. The body on its back, head turned. Most of its bones in place, beside a black bowl with a lifeline design on the edge. More jaws strewn in the sand, and a fragment of corrugated jar. Another skull, crushed, the bones of the head broken, the jaws held together with something like mud. The victims allegedly the elites of Chacoan culture, buried in the recesses of the Great House for protection.

The rustling turned to footsteps, followed by the swooshing of— birds? Bats?

She clutched Eunjoo closer in one hand, untucked Susana's gun from the pouch around her waist. It was probably scavenging animals. Vultures, crows, maybe even coyotes. If Calliope's party stayed quiet, together, the animals would leave them alone.

Still her voice was shaky. "We should stop moving, wait for Chance to catch up."

She stepped back toward the stone-cragged wall, her foot crunching on something; it snapped onto the sand. A stick. She let go of Eunjoo's hand, picked up the stick. It was bent in half, as the crook of an elbow.

It wasn't a skeleton but a ceremonial stick. There were eight of them in Room 33, she knew. She scrolled through the catalog in her mind; all the grave goods they'd found.

Her gut lurched. A bow. There had been a bow. And eighty-one arrows.

The rustling was moving, swirling in the sand toward them. The footsteps familiar. Gamboling. As in the hangar.

She dropped the stick.

Her lungs constricted. She gasped, then screamed, "Run!"

THIRTY-SIX
GUARDIAN

The Suuke pummeled through the darkness. Calliope threw her body and Eunjoo's toward the doorway, sun striking a white dagger of light in the sand. Calliope glanced over her shoulder. Splintered arrows pinstriped the Suuke's gnarled body, great mounds of scar tissue securing the serrated edges in its skin.

The doorway loomed brightly ahead of them.

The Suuke was too close. They wouldn't make it out.

From beyond the Great House, someone was screaming. A man's voice, not a terrified scream. One of anger. "Come back and face your consequences. You need to make it right."

Beside the truck, a hundred feet away from the doorway separating them, Calliope made out Arlen's face, twisted in anger. He was not wearing a mask.

"No, brother. I *am* taking them to the other side."

Arlen plunged into Chance, pulling his gun off his shoulder, knocking him to the ground.

Her heart thrumming in her eardrums, her lungs burning, Calliope pushed Eunjoo against the wall. They wouldn't make it out in time, but Calliope could distract the Suuke so the others could get out. She turned her back to the demon/god, shielding Eunjoo and the corn girl, shimmying out of the woolen sling so it wouldn't take the corn girl too.

Mara caught up, yelled, "What are you doing?"

Calliope squeezed the gun in her hand. It wouldn't kill the Suuke, only anger it further. She dropped it to the sand, thrust the corn girl into Mara's arms. "When it gets to me, take the children to Chance. Take them through the portal."

Eunjoo yelled, "No!"

"Turn away, chica. No te preocupes, remember."

Tears in her eyes, Calliope stepped between the others and the doorway; in the Suuke's path, she braced herself. As its scraggly white hair swept against her skin like coarse grains of straw, she clenched her fists, set her jaw. Closed her eyes and thought of Phoenix.

The Suuke plowed past her, lunging at Chance and Arlen fighting in the dirt.

Calliope's body, still rigid from bracing for the attack, slackened. She let out the breath she'd been holding.

The demon hadn't been coming for her, but for Chance.

Chance was the one who had killed the Suuke's partner, not Calliope. It had been Chance holding the other Suuke's dagger. Chance who had sliced into the Suuke's skin.

"Stay here." She ran to the back of the truck, her mind racing. The sun barreled down from the center of the sky; sweat beaded her skin. She had no idea how she could do this.

She lifted the tarp, and from beside Amy's rock, she grabbed the long, machete-like knife that Amy had picked up from the snow and thrown there *just in case.*

The scarred Suuke clenched both men in the air from their necks like kittens by the scruff. He would choke them to death. Chance was kicking wildly, struggling to get free, his face reddening.

Calliope gripped the dagger in front of her body and barreled forward, running as hard as she could, pointing the blade straight for the Suuke's ribcage.

The Suuke threw Chance to the ground.

It grasped Arlen with both hands.

Chance's body lay on the dirt between her and the Suuke.

She cried out.

He couldn't be dead. He couldn't be.

Chance gasped for air, rolled onto his side, reaching for his gun.

He was safe.

She slowed. Arlen choked out, "Help me, brother."

Calliope called, "Chance, let's go." They should grab the rocks and run back to the portal. Leave Arlen to the Suuke. That's what he'd wanted, right? For them to leave the demon/god alone? Maybe the Suuke hadn't been after them. The bones in Room 33, the bones of the elite, the rulers of the people, religious leaders who'd held the knowledge of crossing worlds. Maybe the Suuke had been protecting that knowledge. Had been protecting the portal. Maybe the Suuke was the guardian.

Chance turned toward Calliope, briefly. Then jumped onto the Suuke's back.

What was he doing? Trying to save Arlen? Or the Suuke?

Calliope no longer had a clear path to the Suuke because Chance was in the way.

She grasped the dagger, searching the Suuke's massive black-and-white body for a vulnerable spot. How could she stab it without risking Chance?

She could throw him the dagger. Would he kill it again? This time for good.

From around the front of the truck, Coyote sprung at the Suuke's face, attacking.

Calliope stood dumbstruck for a split second. Eunjoo *had* been calling Coyote.

Its face bloody, the Suuke's hands went to Coyote.

Chance and Arlen fell to the ground.

The Suuke flailed, and batted Coyote away. The trickster animal fell to the ground on its side, emitting a grave howl.

This was her opportunity.

She lunged.

With all the force of her body, with the force of the Ancients and the Ancients holding her tight, she sliced into the Suuke's flesh, she sliced with one fell swoop and severed its head from its body. Like the bodies in Room 33, the skull fell away from the bones, head and body separated on the sand. Centuries from now, in this world or hers, would someone find this tusked jawbone buried under silt? Would they know what had happened? Who had left it thus? She was part of the story. Not only a historian, a pregnant woman, a mother. She was a warrior. A demon slayer. She dropped the dagger, keeled forward, her head between her thighs, heaving. She'd finished it.

She couldn't believe it.

She'd saved them.

She, not Chance, had killed the Suuke.

And Chance was free.

She looked up, where Chance was kneeling on the ground. He nodded at her, his expression still stoic though not quite as inscrutable. She'd done well.

Chance pulled himself up, reached to help Arlen, still lying on his stomach.

Arlen did not reach back. "Just go." He breathed quietly. "Brother."

They ran to the truck, grabbed the rocks. The sun was high in the sky, hovering directly above them. Was it noon? Had they missed it? Her heart pounding, they sprinted to the doorway of the Great House.

Mara handed back the corn girl. Calliope held the rock baby under one arm, the corn girl in the other.

Holding Amy's rock, Eunjoo nodded toward the doorway, said, "I told you he would come."

Calliope turned, and there was Coyote, haunching on the wall surrounding Pueblo Bonito, dignified, waiting.

"You told me, chica." She kissed the girl's forehead. "Let's hurry."

Dr. Toya led the way as they rushed through the dark corridors, stumbling through doorways, deeper and deeper into the heart, toward Room 33. The skylight from the apex of the moon was now glowing otherworldly, illuminating all the passageways.

They were so close. On the other side of that light—was Phoenix. And the rest of her family. She could feel it. She could feel *them*.

That shock of light. Unbelievable light.

She grasped the rock baby.

Room 33.

The cicadas buzzing in her ears. A windstorm. Bisabuela's voice.

The others in front of her, holding their grave goods.

Chance behind her.

She turned.

"Chance?" Her throat filled with cotton, tears prickled at her eyes.

There was no turquoise around his neck. No turquoise on his wrist. He held no stone.

He'd buried his precious ones at Old Lady Salt's sacred lake.

He'd buried them, for her.

He was so close she could touch him. His hand on the small of her back.

He nodded toward the light. "Go ahead, mujer. There is home. There is your family."

"Chance?" The tears were spilling down her face. "Where's your rock?"

He reached for her, pulled her close to him.

She leaned into his body.

His rocks were dancing at the bottom of a lake. They were in the dancehall of the dead, waiting for him.

She'd known that all along, hadn't she?

He kissed her forehead. "I'm right behind you, mujer. Tell Miwe e'le my story. *Our* story." He held her tight, then let her go.

She nodded, stepped back, into the doorway of Room 33. Into the light.

Into Phoenix and her family and grasping her corn girl and her rock baby with all her strength, she closed her eyes.

A pulling in, taking back, reclaiming something stolen.

THIRTY-SEVEN
THE ANCIENT CHORUS

She opened her eyes.

The sky gray and overcast, she stood upon the packed-dirt earth, crumbled with sandstone pieces, in the ruins of Chaco Canyon, the walls mostly eaten by time and elements.

A drizzle of rain blanketed her hair and face like a rebozo.

In her arms, the corn girl, sucking her fist—and her rock baby, now a flesh-and-blood girl, identical to her sister, save a pudgy fist curled up to her chin instead of in her mouth. Calliope kissed both girls.

Mara was laughing. "Holy hell! What a ride! We made it through. We did it, honey. We did it!"

She was hugging Calliope.

Eunjoo too was laughing.

And Dr. Toya.

Calliope looked back to Eunjoo.

She was hugging a woman, her colorful sleeve tattoos and white tank top, army boots, and a black leather jacket tied around her waist.

She had a scar at the center of her throat. Same as the Suuke.

"What the fuck just happened? I had the craziest dream that that goddamn monster got me."

Calliope, laugh-crying, threw herself, babies and all, at Amy. "You're alive."

"Bet your ass I'm alive, momma." She looked down. "Hey, where'd these little cabbage patches come from?"

* * * *

The others were gathering at the truck as the raindrops fell fatter and wetter. Calliope handed Mara the babies. "I'll be right there."

"You're getting soaked, honey."

"I just have to say goodbye."

Mara nodded.

Calliope walked back toward the mesa. The only rock standing in the canyon. The flat-topped mountain rock jutting up from the canyon. The mesa was not ruined.

Was Chance staring at the same? Their maps linked, side by side. Close enough to touch.

Bisabuela's voice shifted the wind.

If Calliope had known what would happen, would she have stayed?

She could have saved Susana. Could have brought her back to Reina.

And Buick. She'd left his body. She hadn't waited long enough to find out if either he or Susana had transformed. Were they waiting, in another world, for someone to carry them home?

Cicadas buzzing, Bisabuela's voice in her ear. *Don't ever worry the stories are not real, mija. You are the stories.* She was the motherwoman who gave birth to twins, one a rock, to travel through worlds—who carried the key between cosmos in her very belly. *Si no puedes creer, entonces recuerda.*

Remember. She'd helped create those cosmos. The stories were messages to other times, other worlds—the stories were messages home.

Calliope was a message home.

She grasped the Coyote around her neck, the cottonwood Chance had carved for her. It was smooth and cold. She looked down. It had turned to stone.

* * * *

As daylight dimmed and streetlights gleamed, the women pulled into Calliope's driveway. Amy had caught a bus down to Cruces. Dr. Toya had already made her way to Sky City.

"That was quite an adventure, wasn't it?" Mara said, setting the truck in park.

Calliope chuckled wryly. "Sure was."

"You know, hun, I saw the Lizard's Tail three times. First, with Chaiwa up in Los Alamos when I was a girl and that damned bomb in the sand set everything reeling. Then twice I've walked through worlds myself—with you."

Calliope smiled and hugged Mara, said, "Go find my Tía. Tell her I'll be down there soon."

Calliope met Eunjoo on the side of the truck. "I couldn't have done this without you, chica. You know that. You and Coyote."

She kissed the top of Eunjoo's head, her black braids shining under the streetlamp.

"You're a good mama, Phoenix's mama."

Calliope nodded, tears prickling again. "Go home now, Coyote girl."

At the neighbor's door, Eunjoo rang the bell. Calliope worried briefly the girl's parents would think she'd kidnapped her after all this time. Yet she had faith the Ancestors would work it out. She turned toward her corn girl and rock baby now flesh-and-blood girl as Eunjoo's mother answered, shrieking her shock and relief, hugging her daughter, risen from the dead.

Calliope's heart fluttering, a wild bird thrumming, she took her twins from the corn girl's booster seat, gave Mara one last hug, then headed away from the truck, up her own front walkway.

She took a deep breath.

She still had work to do. Her old life wasn't hers anymore. She had joined the stories, the ancient choir of rocks, and she must sing their history, the stories of the Ancestors.

But first, she had to open the door.

ACKNOWLEDGMENTS

I am indebted to Barbara Tedlock for her ethnographic memoir *The Beautiful and the Dangerous* (UNM Press, 2001), which recounts her experiences living with the Zuni people for over twenty years with her husband, Dennis Tedlock. Tedlock's memoir proved invaluable as I researched, and the Zuni phrase "Ulohnan uteya k'ohanna pottiye" and its English translation are taken from Tedlock's book, as are many of the Zuni words and phrasings.

I am likewise grateful for the Zuni people's own accounts, such as those found in Virgil Wyaco's *A Zuni Life: A Pueblo Indian in Two Worlds* (UNM Press, 1998), as well as conversations I've had the honor of participating in with tribal members on the reservation, at Zuni Pueblo Main Street, the Inn at Halona, the Ashiwi Awan Museum & Heritage Center, and elsewhere in Zuni and across New Mexico. I am so thankful for your insights.

The stories recorded in Frank Hamilton Cushing's *Zuñi Folk Tales* (G. P. Putnam's Sons, the Knickerbocker Press, 1901) proved vital to my quest for the Ancients, and many of the Coyote tales of my fictionalized novel are adapted from sacred tales that Cushing recorded, specifically: "The Coyote Who Killed the Demon Síuiuki: or Why Coyotes Run Their Noses into Deadfalls."

The Solstice Project's documentary "The Mystery of Chaco Canyon: Unveiling the Ancient Astronomy of the Southwestern Pueblo Indians"

(Bullfrog Films, 1999), directed by Anna Sofaer, likewise provided much original inspiration for my story.

Countless other anthropological accounts of Paleo-Indian and indigenous myths have gone into the creation of the worlds and characters this book imagines. I am indebted to archaeological and environmental field research conducted by Colorado College and the University of New Mexico, which is available online. And I'm thankful for my own hometown's wonderful library system, including the Taylor Ranch Library branch down the Boca Negra hill, which I frequent with my armfuls of books.

My love and gratitude always for my own bisabuela, Great-Grandma Veronica Martinez Lopez, for passing down the stories and taking care of me. My uncle, Dr. Ralph Casas, for researching the genealogy of our Laguna Pueblo roots, and my Auntie Laura for opening her hacienda to me. My whole Casas familia for taking us all to Las Cruces and the graveyard of our ancestors, and that lightning storm in White Sands, Grandma Linda rolling down the hills, all of us cousins learning that laughter and family are medicine. And always, my mom, Dr. Suzanne Casas Boese, for bringing me home to New Mexico, and for staying beside me every step of the way. Mi familia, you light my path. To the indigenous peoples of today and all our yesterdays, mil gracias.

This book has been a family endeavor from the very beginning. My mom for reading draft after draft, for nearly passing out with me at Starbucks from our twilight excursions and NaNoWriMo shenanigans, and for *gamboling* with the Suuke and me. Your laughter lights my path.

My Grandma Marge, fellow writer, lifetime mentor, whose courage, intelligence, grace, and generosity teach me again and again. I love you forever, Grandma. Thank you for keeping all my books on your shelf.

My partner, Andrew, for visiting every historic and archaeological site in New Mexico with me and our little wolf pack, howling at solstice moons, rolling down the White Sand hills, hunkering in a Los Alamos bomb shelter, watching and discussing every episode of *Through the Wormhole* multiple times, in all the bubble universes, and acting out action scenes with me so I could cross the arroyos and slay the beasts. I love you, my copilot on this endless adventure.

My daughter, Lina, for gladly climbing aboard my back or belly so I could run around the house feeling out just how a pregnant mama would have carried a girlchild through the desert. I'll carry you, always. And for lending Eunjoo your beautiful bird-squeak voice.

And my son, Jeremiah, for thinking through parallel worlds with me—your knowledge of deep story from superhero movies does my writer-mama heart good. And for lending Phoenix your backpack full of wonder. There are no worlds I wouldn't cross for you, my children.

Thank you all those loves and dear ones who read and offered insights. My mentor Lynn Hightower, who believed in the story from the onset. And who fell in love with Chance, as I did. For editor extraordinaire, Toni Kirkpatrick, for your inspiring, incisive feedback. For my Albuquerque bestie, sci-fi/magical real wonder, Jennifer Krohn Bourgeois, for our coffee dates, for introducing me to rumballs!, and for our smartypants everything-literary chats. You've been such a compass, such a lighthouse. Thank you. Dear UNM poeta, fellow California/New Mexico hybrid, Melisa Garcia, for your attention to Bisabuela's words, to making sure my acentos were on point! I am grateful for you. My dear poeta friend, Sherine Gilmour, who offered a heartful of edits and those fancy, flaming NY chocolates! My high school friend Nicole Ward, for believing in me all this time. Ann Sargent, who carried what Calliope carried and shared your story with me. My sister friend, Avra Elliott, for writing magic in the desert with me, for casting spells with me, for understanding me. My PFF, Alicia Elkort, for envisioning the strongest, most spitfire women and girls, and for being the sharpest editor I could hope for, the dearest friend— love you forever. My lovebug poeta, Stephanie Bryant Anderson, for the daily emotional support—I love you, woman. Fellow Wally poet Kerrin McCadden, for introducing me to your generous, know-how husband Cliff Coy, who schooled me on all things planes. Sci-fi poeta/novelist & Binder mama I adore, LaToya Jordan, for your always-helpful feedback. Dear poeta, Aurora Lewis, for encouraging exchanges. For all my friends and loves in Facebook Land who shared knowledge and joy with me—and taco memes. My dear magical poet, Stacey Balkun, for all the domestic fabulism and world-building and craft. You rock. Tarot-reader of light,

Eileen Murphy, for your friendship and support. Bordista sistas Lauren Marie Fleming and Jessenia Chena Lua, fellow Imperial Valley survivors, dear writer loves who believed in me even when I didn't believe in myself. My friend Leslie Contreras Schwartz for support, solidarity, and love.

All the gratitude for my dream agent, Laura Blake Peterson. Your staunch belief in Calliope's story, and all my stories to come, has made my dreams come true. I'm so thankful for your savvy support. My wonderfully supportive Blackstone Press editor, Vikki Warner. #TeamCalliope! I appreciate our shared vision of strong women doing badass things in the world. The whole Blackstone team has been amazing and I couldn't ask for a better crew on Calliope's journey! And Megan Tripp for pulling Calliope up from the slush pile. Thank you forever. For my dear editor, Peggy Hageman, whose patient incisions and astute sutures helped me see the story anew. And for Ember Hood, wonder editor, catcher of things great and small!

Finally, for my first writing teacher, true believer in love and light and following our dreams wherever they take us, even if they return us to the beginning—Irena Praitis. I carry your wisdom always.

It's been a long, arduous road to the fulfillment of my novelist dreams. My heart is full with the kindness of my many teachers, mentors, and friends along the way. Know that you have stayed with me, and I am thankful.